THE DRAGONS OF DURGA

◈ ◈

SIMONE L. SPEARMAN

This book is a work of fiction. Names, characters, places, and incidents either are the product of the author's imagination or are used fictitiously.
The question of Dragons' existence in the modern world remains open to the reader's interpretation and experience.

Copyright © 2017 Simone L. Spearman

All rights reserved. No part of this book may be sold or reproduced by any means in any form without the written permission of the publisher except in the case of brief quotations embodied in articles or reviews.

ISBN: 0-9992782-0-7
ISBN-13: 978-0-9992782-0-8

Library of Congress Control Number: 2017912213

For my daughter, Saja

CONTENTS

1	MIDSUMMER	1
2	LILY AND POHEVOL	11
3	ZUN	26
4	THE MIDSUMMER CELEBRATION	36
5	POHEVOL'S PLAN	58
6	SAJA'S CAVE	75
7	DRAGON HILL	93
8	STONES AND WATER	104
9	THE BURIAL WATERS	111
10	THE FINAL DECISION	129
11	LEAVING DURGA	149
12	FLYING NORTH	172
13	DRAGON'S LAIR	190
14	ICELOCH	200
15	DREAMING IN ICELOCH	213
16	THE UNDERWATER VALLEY	224
17	DRAGON CHESS	232
18	THE END GAME	245
19	RESCUE	263

20	Ice Feast	284
21	Journey South	295
22	The Siir	311
23	Jha'mah	323
24	Children of Jha'mah	333
25	The Cave of Hands	347
26	Dreaming in Jha'mah	359
27	Haemon and the Falls	371
28	Lake Whydah	385
29	Nightshade	396
30	The Pangolin and the Rift	407
31	The Absence of Nothing	428
32	The Sands of Ochre	442
33	The Dragon Palace	461
34	The Temple of Secrets	475
35	Egg Sisters	494
36	The Games	508
37	A Shift of Heart	522

⚜ I ⚜

MIDSUMMER

The Earth was alive. The Midsummer Sun hovered high in the pale blue sky, and one could taste honeysuckle in the air. All the animals were intoxicated with the sweet scent of wild flowers, and the scattered trees were lazy, rolling back and forth in the calm, occasional wind. Fields of clover buzzed with Honeybees and Butterflies. It was a time of plenty, a time of possibility. It was a time of Dragons.

Scaled Dragons and furry Dragons. Huge beasts and tiny, wispy creatures. Old Dragons and young Dragons. Dragons who sang beautiful songs in the first blush of morning and Dragons who grumbled in the darkest of night. Dragons who loved to laugh and Dragons who would rather crush a skull than hear a joke about the Moon, a Wolf, and some lost Opossum. Dragons who swam in the cold seas and Dragons who soared through the air. Dragons who slept in dark caves and Dragons who napped in the middle of broiling deserts. And Midsummer brought the biggest Dragon celebration of all.

The Earth was alive with Dragon activity, especially the Dragons of Durga. Zor, the cloak maker, was busy weaving magic capes for the baby Draglings. Labrys, the amulet diviner, fashioned rare jewelry for the Dragons coming of age and those tending the precious eggs. And Menet, an elder Dragon over 1,000 Suns, spent weeks preparing potions and heart-shaped tokens to give out at the ceremonies.

The resident Dragons weren't the only ones to welcome Midsummer. The Durgan Humans also prepared for the longest day of the Sun. Bright ribbons streamed from the trees, baked apples and candied nuts hung from branches and scented the air, pipe music floated in the wind, and soft voices sang out at random. The elders practiced and rehearsed their rituals while the adults perfected the spiral dance. The children busied themselves with paints.

Midsummer was a glorious cycle of day and night for the children. One could peek inside the huts and find candles glowing, incense burning, hushed voices, and pots of dye being passed reverently. For weeks the children practiced, painting on rock walls, trees, and the occasional naked baby. Fingertips dipped into luxurious reds, cobalt blues, and bright yellows. Bold streaks appeared across faces, chests, and legs. Fingers mixed greens, purples, and pinks. Huge Suns, crescent Moons, Ice Dragons, Sea Dragons, coiled Snakes, and wild Auroch horns found their way onto the children's bodies. As the paint touched the naked skin, giggles escaped. Anticipation filled everyone with excitement and a sense of the sacred.

The entire forest hummed. The Humans looked forward to this celebration for many reasons—eating and drinking, dancing and singing, as the sky stayed light for so long. The most important reason, though, the one that remained lodged in everyone's mind was this: Midsummer was the only time when all Humans and Dragons came together and communed as one.

Now this isn't to say that the Human children didn't commune with Dragons on a regular basis. Quite the contrary! The Dragons of Durga respected, as most Dragons did, the youth of all tribes. They knew that the young possessed a full memory of creation and the beyond, and thus deserved respect, friendship, and a place at the hearth of Dragons. For as long as anyone could remember, all Dragons had been able to speak with children without the aid of a translator. Yet when the children blossomed into adults, they lost the ability to communicate with their beloved friends and mentors. No Human understood why.

Midsummer, when the Earth's tilt was closest to the great Sun, was the only time during which the Dragons accepted the close proximity of adult Humans. Many of the Dragons looked forward to this day with great anticipation, as they deeply missed many of the children who had simply, through no fault of their own, grown up.

Sneaking through the trees, one could find full grown Dragons peering in mirrors, flattening wayward scales, pushing back graying flaps of skin, stitching up old wounds, and bathing. Bathing was quite a feat, as the huge Dragons, some as tall as oak trees, would wade into the various rivers and lakes bringing a slew of fragrant vegetable soaps. They would vigorously scrub and lather, humming and singing ancient Dragon songs. When they exited the waters, they would stretch under the warm Sun and apply fragrant oils over their freshly cleaned bodies. All this preparation was for the only festival shared with the entire Human clan.

The adult Humans were thrilled as well. Most of them had once shared a special relationship with one or two Dragons, and they eagerly awaited Midsummer as a chance to be young again. To eat baked almond crutes and sip sweet Dragon wine with an old friend. To place a worn hand on a wing or claw and remember the days of old. These were moments to cherish, for during the remainder of the Sun, the older Humans could only stare across the vast golden skies, watching the flying ones. They could only reminisce about the days when they napped under the protective wing of a special Dragon. The adults would often lower their voices whenever they heard a roar above their heads. When a Dragon meeting was called, the adult Humans would stare silently into the sky as the clouds echoed with the thunder of a hundred enormous wings.

Bittersweet pangs welled in their Human hearts, and the Midsummer celebration was the only consistent salve. Yes, the adults could live vicariously through the adventures of their children, but it was never the same. And although they could never quite pinpoint the exact reason, they knew they had forgotten something very important. And they knew that this was the reason they were no longer welcome into the exclusive circle of Dragons.

It lowered a deep heaviness upon their hearts.

But being understanding and appreciative Humans, ones who worked to accept what they had and not dwell upon what they lacked, they simply moved on. Full of determination, they looked forward to Midsummer. For as the Earth continues to spin round and round, Midsummer would come to Durga each Sun.

The festival was near. The children, painted and preened, ran to the forest clearing called Alder Ring. They laughed and shouted as they met with their friends. The adults and elders gathered cautiously, half-expecting the Dragons not to show up. The women stood radiant with silver and gold ribbons braided into their hair. They wore red and purple dresses with white sashes snug around their waists. The men stood proud and tall with freshly pressed tunics and pants. Their boots were scrubbed clean. Many had shaved and applied clean scents, and those with beards had them trimmed or braided. Most of the adults stood still, but a few wrung their hands nervously.

A hush fell over the forest. The Birds stopped talking, and the tree branches refused to let go of the weakest leaf. But then the air shifted, as a deafening gush of warm wind swept through the clearing.

The Dragons had arrived.

Some flew low over the treetops, brushing many leaves with the tips of their wings. Others could be seen making great spirals deep in the blue sky. The reflection of the bright Midsummer Sun bounced off their glimmering skins and filled the sky with a golden beauty. Some clutched huge baskets of freshly baked bread and just-picked fruit while others gripped in their claws wooden harps, sparkling flutes, and odd-shaped drums. The Humans watched in delight as the Dragons hovered above Alder Ring, looking down carefully and navigating their landings.

Zor was the first Dragon to arrive. A cluster of baby Draglings followed closely and mimicked his every turn and roll. Zor was as tall as a Giraffe and as long as two Elephants standing trunk to tail. His skin was a gorgeous burnt red, and he had pointed spikes in two straight rows along his back. He had immense wings—his span was twice the length of his body and as smooth as a Bat's. Atop Zor's head were two spiral horns that lay flat against the nape of his neck. His face was pointed and feathered like that of an Eagle, and he had a slight beard under a pronounced beak. His forearms bulged with well-used muscles and both had three tiny spikes jutting from the sides. He was a regal Tree Dragon, only 250 Suns old and full of magic and skill. He was known for his perceptive hearing and for his patience with the youth of all tribes. It was no wonder the little Draglings followed him everywhere.

Zor floated to the ground, extending his thick legs to grip the Earth while making sure there was enough room for his band of followers to land. The gaggle of Draglings landed roughly around him, setting up clouds of dirt and dust. They threw back their heads, screeching with quick, high yips. Zor looked at them and raised his horns. Immediately they became silent.

Anippe was next to descend. She was a long, thin River Dragon. She was half the size of Zor, but her wingspan was identical to his. Her golden brown wings were webbed and patterned like the leaves of a Maple, and her chest was covered with broad, smooth scales. She had a gentle, sloping head similar to that of a Horse, and next to her nostrils were two elegant, white horns, each with a slight curve. Her tail was long and flat, adept for swimming and flying fast, especially at low altitudes. She was known for her satisfying leek stews, and she loved to nap during rainy afternoons. She was intelligent, and as many Dragons had come to learn, very competitive.

Guldrun and Lin, two playful—and foolish—Mud Dragons, were next to descend. They landed near Lapis Lake at the edge of Alder Ring. They, unlike most Dragons, were egg brothers. Their mother had lain one egg, and after years of nurturing, the egg mysteriously split in two. The brothers were identical except in color. Both were round and stocky like a Rhinoceros or an Auroch. Both had bulging eyes, furry earflaps, and protruding teeth like river boulders. Their scales were as smooth as Snake skin, yet as thick as redwood bark. They had two sets of wings the same texture as their skin and thick tails that could be curled. Most noticeable were their legs and feet—veins protruded from underneath the thick skin and five gleaming claws like sharp, curved Elephant tusks extended from each foot as if they were separate entities. The only difference between the two brothers was their hue. Guldrun was pale orange while Lin was a deep purple.

Labrys, a pink and gold Sea Dragon nearly 500 Suns, followed the two Mud brothers. She was concerned that Guldrun and Lin would start basking in the lake's adjacent mud flats and then forget about the celebration. Weighed down with many sacks of jewels and sparkling gems, she flew over to the lake. She snorted, blew a large puff of steam from her pink nostrils, and landed on an oval boulder beside the water.

"No mud today!" she yelled.

"Just a little?" begged Lin.

"Just a smidgen?" added Guldrun.

"Mud brothers," Labrys ordered, "Midsummer means communing with Humans, not with mud." She raised her bags and shook them at the brothers. The wayward twin Dragons raised their pointy eyebrows at each other, flapped their wings twice, and pushed off the ground. They couldn't resist. With a loud spatter of sticky wetness, they both dove into muddy bliss. They wouldn't leave the lake for hours.

Labrys sighed and shook her head. She knew the attraction of wetness, so she harrumphed and made her way back to the clearing.

Labrys had a thick, round head with large eyes and curved teeth that protruded from her mouth. Her Dragon skin was pink with flecks of gold shimmering beneath. She was as long and thick as an Elephant, half the size of Zor. She had two sets of legs that she rarely used in the sea but were useful in the forest. She, too, had a double set of wings. One set was sturdy and strong like the fins of a Whale, while the other set was delicate and iridescent like the wings of a Fly. A long ridge of dull, triangular protrusions ran along her spine. Upon arrival at the clearing, she tucked in her wings and landed with ease. With a loud snort, she opened her sacks to display sparkling jewels and gems.

The Humans looked at each other cautiously before

approaching Labrys and her wares. Jewels were sacred to Dragons, and Humans treated even a glimpse of a Dragon jewel with respect. These precious stones provided strength to sleeping Dragon eggs and helped divine future paths. It was rare for a Dragon to offer a jewel to a Human.

One woman with long, white hair drawn back into a low braid came up to Labrys and bowed reverently. Without warning Labrys reared back and hissed steam. The Durgan Humans startled and stepped back, but then stopped when Labrys's wide smile and change of color became apparent. The Durgans had come to know that Dragons glowed bright and warm when happy, but became unusually pale and cold when angered. The crowd stopped to watch Labrys, now radiant and deeply pink, lower her head to peer closely at the woman. She looked inquisitively into the old woman's brown eyes, then sniffed the woman's hands and her perfumed hair.

The woman reached into her dress and pulled out a golden amulet with an amethyst dropped in an intricate oval setting. Labrys tapped one claw against the stone, and everyone watched as it changed color, turning gradually from the deepest purple to a bright red. The elderly woman gleamed and looked fondly up at Labrys, who opened her wings and tenderly hugged the woman. Labrys had been this woman's Dreamtime mentor over seventy Suns ago. Woman and Dragon, the two walked into the forest, hand in claw. Labrys swished her tail with pleasure, leaving a spiral trail in her wake.

More and more Dragons arrived, saluting the waiting Humans and calling out to one another in their foreign tongue. It was a grand affair with bright music and laughter. At times there were shy and somewhat awkward reunions. The Sun had scarcely moved before nearly every Dragon was present in Alder Ring.

~ 2 ~

LILY AND POHEVOL

Deep in the middle of Durga, two Humans remained. One was simply late. The other did not want to attend the Midsummer festivities. The reticent one knelt in a cave, painting on the cold walls with a stick of charcoal and a pot of red paint. His body was strong and rigid. His hair was a long and tangled mass. Small scars were noticeable on his arms and legs, the results of climbing over rocks and crossing craggy rivers. His name was Zun, and he was utterly alone. A boy of twelve Suns, he felt isolated and forlorn, haunted by his past.

Not far away from Zun's cave, on the other side of the Lazuli River in a field of wild grasses, stood the other. She was a tall girl, also twelve Suns, with dark brown hair and eyes. She stood confident, her bare feet planted in the soft grass. The scent of scattered rose bushes permeated the breeze, as she looked up at the burnishing Sun.

Lily was a strong girl for twelve, and she was gifted. She was about to become the first Human Shifter of

Durga. But she needed to master one final Shift.

Although she was late to the Midsummer celebration, she tried to ignore the gradual lowering rays of the Sun, the subtle shadows moving down the trees. Her pride led her to hope she could achieve the Shift before night came, and a part of her stubbornly expected it must come.

Lily needed to become a Raven. Her blood craved it. Her spirit desired it. She had practiced for weeks, concentrating on the low-pitch call, the black sleekness of a pointed feather, the lightweight floating of air and bone, the stillness of a piercing, all-knowing eye. She had Shifted into many animals including a Panther, Mouse, Rainbow Trout, and Brown Bear. But to master the creation of hollow bone and feather—that was pure skill amplified, of course, by Dragon mentoring.

Lily studied under the cantankerous Shifting Dragon, Caduceus. Caduceus was impatient and often cold-hearted. Unlike most Dragons, he preferred to sleep alone. He was fond of dusty books and steaming cups of chamomile tea. He loved arguing about the history of Shifting and the skills of the great masters who had preceded him. Even though he was a middle-aged Dragon, close to 800 Suns, he carried himself as an elder—though without the slightest bit of humor or humility.

Caduceus had burst from his egg covered in bright purple and green armor. The scales on his back were iridescent and the size of Dragon dinner plates. They shimmered and changed color in different lights. He had green eyes and a pointed nose that resembled an Alligator's. His legs were muscular, and he had five silver claws on the end of each foot. He also had three silver spikes on the very tip of his tail. One of the few Dragons hatched from mixed parentage, Caduceus's father was a purple Sea Dragon, his mother a Tree Snake.

Caduceus adored Snakes and rarely was seen without Serpents coiled around his neck, chest, and tail. His mother had been a Shifter, one of the largest Snakes Durga had ever seen. She could wrap her body around Mount Calyps, and when she shed her skin, Humans could make enough clothes and medicine from her offering to last many Moons.

But something dreadful had happened to her, something so horrible Caduceus would never speak of it. This lowered a sadness upon him that rarely lifted. He practiced Shifting in her honor, he slept, and he read. He was not carefree and appreciative like other Dragons. He went about his personal business and preferred to be alone.

But there was no denying his gift for Shifting. Eight Suns ago, the elder Dragons reminded him that it was his duty to share the gift, to pass it on to younger generations. When the group of old Dragons made the long trek to his cave, bringing gifts and sweet Dragon wine, Caduceus raised his scales, shuddered, and begrudgingly allowed them entry. The elder Dragons convinced him to take on Lily as his apprentice, as well as Simion the Black Bear.

He had submitted to the Dragon elders, but he was not pleased.

Lily had studied under Caduceus for over eight Suns now. He was often angry with her, always grumbled at her, and rarely offered encouraging words to her. Frustrated with his lack of support, Lily turned to Pohevol for encouragement and advice.

Pohevol was Lily's best friend. He was a Durgan Cat, as large as a Leopard, yet with a temperament closer to a Tabby. He was covered with black fur, boasting a white chest and chin, and he had enormous black-feathered wings. He was a majestic flying Cat. And he was the last Cat in Durga to possess this gift of flight.

Pohevol had saved Lily from death when she was a baby. Unbeknownst to others, she had crawled to the edge of an old, concealed well. Her parents had been busy gathering blackberries in thick, prickly bushes when they had heard the loud commotion. Pohevol let out a piercing Cat yowl, as he flew over the foliage. Swooping down upon the baby's pudgy body, he sunk his teeth into her neck, picked her up, and flew Lily back to her mother.

Everyone gathered around Lily's parents, shocked and speechless as they craned their necks to see the spectacle. Lily was lying limp in Pohevol's jaws. Her head dangled, and her limbs had lost all color. Lily's mother dropped to the ground, prostrate to the hovering Cat clutching her infant. Holding out her arms, she begged the Cat to release her child. Pohevol gently lowered Lily into her outstretched arms. The crowd was silent as they watched the large, flying Cat release Lily. As soon as he let go, the baby regained consciousness, opened her eyes, and smiled. Lily had not cried out in pain. She had not uttered a single sound of displeasure.

There were four puncture wounds from where his teeth had gripped her neck, yet Lily continued to smile and gurgle. Pohevol landed near the woman and child. He lowered his head to sniff the baby's neck. With his scratchy and persistent Cat's tongue, he licked the wounds that didn't appear to hurt. Lily reached out and touched his silky, black fur. She opened her mouth, let out a sigh, and babbled, "Pohevol." This was her first word.

Some said it was Cat magic, others said it was fate. After the incident at the well, Pohevol continued to protect Lily, and she flourished under his loving care. He taught her about respect and patience. He showed her how to walk through the woods without making sounds. She still wore his four prominent teeth marks on the back of her neck, and many believed these scars to be the origin of her Shifting ability.

Now it was Midsummer and her eighth Sun of Shifting apprenticeship. She had to become a Raven. Standing in the tall grass, Lily concentrated on Caduceus's monotonous words, "Focus, divine, create, become." His steady mantra filled her mind, flooded her thoughts, and she felt her slender arms extending, turning, spreading ever so slowly. She pictured the magnificent body of a black Raven—the silky feathers of black shimmering into blue. She imagined herself flying with the ebony stillness of love and patience surrounding her. She fell into the Silent Space—that moment when all concerns and distinct thoughts disappear, when the quiet enfolds a body and vibration and stillness are one—and then she willed the shape. She focused her ability and tempered her desire. Lily envisioned the immediate release, and it came to her. Her Human body grew light, as if transparent, and she collapsed in upon herself, and then in a new form and shape, she stepped out. She had become the Raven.

"Lily, the Raven," a soft voice entered her thoughts.

"Pohevol!" Lily flew to the ground and hop-stepped over to the black Cat. Her legs were as thin as twigs, and her body was draped with brilliant feathers the color of midnight. She blinked once and cocked her head to one side. She was a striking Raven.

"You have done it," Pohevol thought to Lily. "You have mastered the Raven."

"Yes, but it took me too long," she thought.

"It will get easier with time," Pohevol rubbed his mouth along the soft trunk of a tree. He walked around her body, sniffing and nudging. "Caduceus would be pleased," Pohevol raised one white eyebrow, "if he had the capacity."

"Caduceus is impatient with me," she thought. "He thinks every Human is a tremendous pain in the scales. I try to be silent, respectful, courteous, and attentive, but he still growls at me."

Pohevol thought, "He is middle-aged and full of a grief few understand. But he is also a master at Shifting. You must practice tolerance."

"I don't see why Saja can't teach us," Lily thought.

"Because Caduceus holds the proper wisdom at this moment in time, and Saja cannot Shift now, you know that."

It was true. Saja, a Spirit Dragon who could also Shift, had released an egg four Suns ago. Dragon eggs could take five Suns to hatch. The long gestation was crucial to their development, and during this time they were extremely vulnerable, open to influence. Saja could confuse her sleeping egg if she changed form now.

Pohevol looked to the West. The Sun was low, and the

trees were forming deep canopies of shade. He stretched out his front legs and then his back, "Are you staying here much longer? The celebration has already begun."

Lily opened her black beak and picked up a twig. She then tossed it in the air. "I need to find Zun before it gets too dark," she thought. "He doesn't want to go to the Midsummer celebration, but I think it will be good for him. He's still nervous about being close to . . . Dragons."

Pohevol nodded and unfolded his wings.

"Zun is full of conflict," Pohevol thought. "He is struggling through the pain of his childhood years without Dragon guidance, but let us hope he will always stay near the Dragon path of wisdom, even if he is on the periphery." Pohevol shook out his wings and groomed his feathers. He mouthed a clump of feathers and pulled them back against his teeth, taking care to unzip and then repair each feather.

"Now that you have mastered the Raven, would you like to fly with me?" Pohevol thought.

"It's what we've always Dreamed of doing," she smiled at him.

Pohevol stepped back and shook his freshly cleaned feathers. Although he was the last Cat born with wings, other Durgan tribes had individuals who possessed them. It was rare, but known to happen. Some Horses, Snakes, Rabbits, Goats, even Mice had wings. Some were thin and wispy like Bee wings. Others were soft as the skin of a newborn foal. Some were feathered and others were draped in fur.

Lily had heard tales about Humans who used to have wings. But something had happened, and the wings vanished. This was a sore subject with the Humans, and over time many started to believe that it was just a myth, a far-fetched story told to make children giggle. Something strange was happening though, as fewer and fewer individuals of various tribes were being born with wings. The Bird tribe was often consulted, and a few Dragons dedicated themselves to uncovering the reason behind this mysterious loss of flight.

Even without unfolding his wings, Pohevol was exquisite. His remarkable coat of thick, black fur had patches of snowy white on the paws and belly. He had a long tail with a slight curve at the tip, and he possessed a prominent belly pouch—a sign of wisdom and honor among the Cat tribe. But his most distinguishing characteristic was his white chin. With a striking black face, long Feline nose, and bright green eyes, his white chin stood out dramatically and had the hypnotic effect of drawing one deep into the brilliant white.

Pohevol had lived in Durga for many generations. In fact, no one knew his exact age. He never would reveal it, no matter how hard one pried. But despite all of his unique qualities and traits, Pohevol had one skill that made him the most rare individual of all. This skill made him as magical as all the Dragons in Durga. And because of it, he was trusted, revered, and honored by all the tribes of the Durgan forest.

Pohevol was the only animal who could move through and beyond time. He could travel to the past and the future. He could go back in time, and he could observe what was to come. He was a Visitor, and thus he was deemed most sacred.

He did not boast, and he did not use or abuse his ability randomly or casually—but his time traveling ability was something that all Durgan tribes knew about and respected. There were no queens or kings in Durga, as most decisions were made by the different tribes' various Councils of Elders, but Pohevol had a gift that all acknowledged. In times of need and uncertainty, he helped guide the way.

As Lily looked at Pohevol, she calmed herself and prepared her body for flight. They both pushed off simultaneously and extended their strong wings to the sky. The air shifted underneath their bodies, and Lily and Pohevol watched each other as they flapped through the trees, navigating left and right, ducking under low branches and thick clusters of leaves. They darted into a clear patch of sky and played with the wind. Lily would fly low, grab the tip of a tree with her talons, and then pump her wings to rise high again. Pohevol tucked in his wings, turned on his back and began a free fall, only to whip around, extend his wings, and soar back up to reach Lily's side.

As they circled above the trees, Lily saw Zun's cave and signaled to Pohevol. She thought, "I'll meet you at Alder Ring. I have to Shift back and meet Zun."

Pohevol flashed his green eyes at her, "See you at the celebration," and then flew off towards Lapis Lake.

Lily landed roughly near the banks of the Lazuli River. Keeping her wings extended in a stiff arch, she looked around nervously. With a visceral itchiness she felt the Raven's instinctual fear of predators. Sensing the absence of any nearby stealth, she shook her feathers loose and tucked them in close to her body. She scrunched up her shoulders and moved her head around in half circles. It was time to become Human again.

This Shift was easier. She need only think about her mother, a gentle woman named Calice. She would think of her mother's high cheekbones and black eyes encircled in a blanket of wavy black hair. She would focus on her mother's soft arms and her scented neck and chest where Lily had often snuggled as a little girl. Suddenly the Shifted body would melt away, and her own Human form would step out.

Calice often asked Lily to describe the Shifting process. She thought she might be able to learn the skill since her daughter had the gift. Lily would try to explain—she would describe the darkness and the blinding light of self-will and the return to darkness and the acceptance of nothing and everything circling in upon itself, one and whole. Her mother would get lost in the tumbling succession of words.

"I feel like I'm swimming in a muddy lake, trying to understand her description of Shifting," her mother would whisper to Lily's father late at night when discussing the maturation of their daughter.

"She's gifted," he would reply giving his wife a comforting embrace.

"It's miraculous," she would add.

"I hope she's careful," his voice would trail off.

Now back in her Human form, deep in the forest, Lily touched her arms and legs and inhaled a deep breath. Every time she Shifted back into her natural body, she silently thanked Caduceus for his wisdom and skill. She looked around the forest and saw the Sun was barely visible now, as its last light crept through the tree branches and rested along the dark hills. She knew the celebration was in full motion now, and the spiral dance would soon begin.

Lily was silent as she listened to the sounds of the forest. She could hear the evening calls of Jays and Crows echoing in the distance. She felt the soft wind moving through the trees. She knew Zun would be in his cave, drawing his same visions on the walls, and that it would take great creativity and persuasion on her part to drag him to Alder Ring.

∽ ∾

As Pohevol flew over Durga, he smelled the wafting smoke from the celebratory fires. Dragons swooped around the trees, some even flying upside down. They were basking in the longest day and shortest night of the year. His body tingled with anticipation, and he felt a warm purr begin to form in his chest. The sky deepened to an orange and purple hue, and the pale clouds spread out like gentle ripples across a pond.

He flew near the base of Mount Calyps and saw Sophia, an immense brown and green Dragon with seven heads, stretching her massive body. Sophia was as tall as a young redwood and just as strong. She was Durga's most experienced translator, thus the Midsummer festival was her busiest time. Pohevol watched Sophia elongate her seven necks, each like a smooth and sloping tree trunk, twisting and turning, reaching to the sky and dropping to the ground over and over again. He heard her speaking in her multiple tongues, each head passing the same phrase to the next. He heard the languages of Humans, Dogs, Hawks, Wolves, and Squirrels in one pass. Raven, Lion, and Lizard in another. She was a Tree Dragon with extending patience. Throughout the many Suns, Pohevol had learned much from Sophia's wealth of knowledge and benevolent temperament.

Sophia adored wild flowers. When she wasn't translating, she would spend hours lying on the ground, each head sniffing and sighing. She would roll around and stare at the sky, content in a sea of fragrance. Even when she was busy practicing for the Midsummer communal, Sophia would take a quick moment to dip her head and inhale a sweet tulip or daffodil, sometimes frightening a feasting Honey Bee or Hummingbird.

As Pohevol flew around the West face of Mount Calyps, he felt the slightest tug on his wings. He looked below and saw the Great Tree. Her specific type was unknown to the Durgan tribes, and even the Dragons did not know her true name. The elder Dragons meditated near her often, waiting for her name to be revealed, but each Dragon came away even more perplexed. Some swore she said, "Alanse," while others were certain she whispered, "Fortuna." Many names emanated from her leaves. Unable to agree, the tribes settled on "Great Tree," and that she was.

She was as tall as a Cedar, as wide as a Cypress. She had wide, flat leaves, yet she never shed them in the fall. The autumnal Equinox would arrive, and her leaves would turn golden yellow and then crimson red. Come winter, instead of dropping to the ground, the leaves would turn deep purple and hold fast to their branches.

When spring arrived, the leaves would turn lavender, and then as if new growth, light green. A dazzling deep green would show itself in summer, and thus the tree would continue her annual dance. Some of her branches were thin and willowy while others were thick and knotted. Most unique was her textured bark. It would turn bright pink in summer and peel off in long strips. The children would take her offerings and make hair-bands, belts, and sashes with the beautiful bark.

She was delightful to look at, and she always smelled like summer roses with a hint of lilac. Although she did not produce a flower, her leaves would often change shape, thus resembling different types of flowers. Her scent drew many animals. Birds lived in her branches, and Squirrels lived in her trunk. Rabbits, Moles, Groundhogs, and other small animals lived at her base near the large underground roots.

As Pohevol soared above the Great Tree, her branches and leaves seemed to beckon him. The wind shifted, and he felt his body turning her direction.

And so it begins, he thought to himself.

He closed his eyes and allowed the breeze to lower his body. He focused on the Great Tree's desire and question. He felt her life force drawing him in, and so he opened his heart to her will. He surrendered. The wind shifted his balance, ruffling his feathers. Slowly, the wind lowered him to the base of the Great Tree where he landed on silent paws.

She was the largest and oldest tree in Durga. Many believed she might be the oldest tree in the world. She possessed all knowledge of the past, the present, and the future. And it was she who allowed Pohevol to travel through time.

As if under a spell, Pohevol began rubbing his face and body along her thick trunk. He opened his mouth slightly and left an invisible trail of his scent along her pink bark. He pushed his Cat body into hers and let his tail curve as he made slow circles around her. He repeated this motion several times. He concentrated on letting her will transform his own, and as he did this, her thick wooden body began to move.

The Great Tree was moving!

Her body creaked and moaned as she turned in a slow circle. Dirt flew up from her roots. Grass and bits of tree were thrown from her base, as she strained to be free of the ground. Her branches tucked in and then moved up and down in a slow wave motion. A great crack and low groan tore through the forest.

Pohevol changed his direction and began moving with her. He kept his right side to her trunk, letting his whiskers brush her bark. They made many circles together, Pohevol staying right at her side. On the tenth circle the air began to buzz with a new shrill tone. The ground set free a subterranean rumble. The Great Tree began to turn faster, and Pohevol stepped away. He tucked in his wings tightly to his body and concentrated on his release.

The Great Tree's powerful spinning created strong winds that pushed Pohevol's fur flat against his body. They increased and cleared the forest floor of detritus—fallen twigs, leaves, and dirt. Pohevol stood steady, gripping the exposed ground with his claws. He braced himself against his hind legs so that the force of the vigorous winds would not carry him away.

Despite the forceful winds, the other trees in the forest started to lean in closer to the spinning tree. With a deep vibration, they began humming in synchronicity. Pohevol's pupils dilated, and he focused his vision deeply into the small crevices of her trunk. Her bright pink trunk turned iridescent and then quick flashes of color splashed behind her bark. He began to see twisting visions of the old forest and the present forest blurred together. In a rush of wind, sound, and pressure his body was pulled into the Great Tree.

Instantaneously, the tree came to a deliberate and immediate stop. Pohevol was gone.

⌘ 3 ⌘

ZUN

Zun was the same age as Lily, but he was an orphan. His parents were killed in the infamous battle against the Horse-riding invaders. He was only one Sun old when the Durgan people had to defend their homes and way of life for the first time in remembered history. Strange men who enslaved Horses, a grave offense to the Durgans, rode into the village brandishing bronze swords and shields. They had no women or children with them, and they seemed to have seen no more than twenty Suns apiece. They yelled and screamed in their foreign tongues and charged the Durgan Humans who stood in paralyzed shock.

Zun's mother was the first to run to the Dragons, screaming for help, "A strange tribe of Humans—they have come to kill us! Please help us!"

She was answered with silence.

Stunned and devastated, she rushed her infant son to

the nearest cave, tucked him into a shallow crevice deep inside, and then ran back to defend her home.

At first the Dragons did not want to interfere. Marii, the wisest and eldest Tree Dragon, had predicted a time when Humans would eliminate various tribes for inconceivable reasons. It was not the Dragon way to interfere with the conflicts of other tribes, and Humans could be particularly perplexing at times. But after two hours of witnessing the callous slaughter, seeing a small number of men destroy a peaceful group of Humans, the Dragons came together and decided to end the madness.

They descended upon the invaders, lifted each man off his enslaved Horse, and in a swirl of steam and smoke placed the unruly men in an immense Dragon satchel. Some invaders were killed as they tried to resist, slashing at the flying Dragons. A few Dragons were injured with deep gashes in their chests and tails. Yet despite the awful battle and various wounds, the Dragons decided to spare the lives of the captured invaders. The strongest Mud Dragon, a reserved Dragon named Ius who had incredible claws and a deep blue undercarriage as thick as stone, grabbed the satchel and flew the brutes back, far away to the Northeast—from which they had come.

The remaining Humans, overcome with confusion and grief, buried their dead as if in a trance and mourned for three full Suns. There were no celebrations and no festivals. The trees stood bare as they were not adorned with offerings, and the Humans went about living as if it were mandatory and not a blessing. The Dragons, who always showed great restraint in using their power, mourned their hesitant role in quelling the massacre. There were many meetings of understanding, forgiveness, and healing. Over time the sadness faded, and gratitude for life returned to the spirits of the Durgan Humans.

But any time a Human from a distant tribe approached Durga, fear swelled in many Human hearts. The elders warned against this prejudice. For as a seed of hatred had been sown the day the Horse-riders attacked, the elders warned the others to keep it buried without any ray of light or drink of water. The children who continued to spend their days cavorting, learning, and Dreaming with Dragons quickly healed and were spared most of this pain. But Zun was the only boy to lose both his mother and father during the slaughter. While the others could receive comfort in a familiar lap or strong embrace, Zun felt abandoned. He was the only child to be completely orphaned.

Losing his mother's milk and arms, Zun became an inconsolable child. He never fully bonded with his maternal aunt, Sari, who adopted him after the tragedy. As he grew up, he spent most of his days in and around the cave where he was left on that fateful day. He chose not to follow the other children to the Dragons, as he grew up thinking they were arrogant, apathetic, and absent when they were needed the most. He knew the story of being carried to the Dragons, of his mother screaming for their help, and of their absolute and utter silence, their complete lack of movement. If only they had listened to her immediately. Two hours was enough to make a massacre of his family.

No matter how many children begged Zun to understand the Dragons' decision that awful day, he would not budge. He would watch the children climb hills, swim lakes, and cross valleys going to meet the Dragons, yet he would remain close to his cave, drawing in the dirt, gathering food, and sleeping by the Lazuli River. It was during these long respites by the water that his first visions came.

In these visions he saw angry Dragons with fire streaming from their nostrils and mouths. He saw Humans crouching in fear, trembling under the shadows of these terrifying Dragons. He saw the Earth spinning out of control and trees standing naked as if burned alive. Humans crawled across the Earth like Ants, and multitudes of animals languished behind bars of metal and inside vast buildings of stone. There were epic battles between Humans and Dragons, and Humans suffered while Dragons were feared.

Lily was the only Human who knew about his visions and drawings. While other children scorned Zun for his hermit ways and fear of Dragons, Lily was curious about Zun. They became friends the day Sari asked Lily to bring a sack of acorns and hazelnuts to Zun. Lily was on her way to meet Caduceus, so she decided to Shift into a Squirrel. She thought the Shift to be slightly humorous, as she was transporting nuts.

She always made certain to Shift alone. Early in her training, Caduceus had warned her about the deep confusion and unease most creatures would experience if they were to watch Shifters transform their bodies. The change could be instantaneous and almost invisible for master Shifters, but for those just learning, it could be slow and awkward.

When Lily was learning to Shift into a Deer, one of the

easiest first Shifts, she would often have Deer legs and Human arms protruding from a twisted and curved torso. It was not pretty. On the day of their first meeting, Zun was watching from behind an oak tree when Lily made her Shift into a Squirrel. He watched her perform the Shift in silence and admiration. Unlike Caduceus's prediction, Zun felt an instant connection with Lily. As he spent most of his time alone, Zun did not trust the individuals of most tribes. But after watching Lily Shift into a Squirrel, after seeing her simultaneous power and vulnerability, he felt he could trust her.

∽ ∂

Now, while the other Humans reveled on the Midsummer night, Zun crouched in his cave and painted by flickering candlelight. His hands moved from a black pot to the gray walls. His arms were long and small scars appeared at the edges of his elbows and the backs of his hands. His fingers glowed with red and yellow paint. He stopped often to tuck his long hair behind his ears, leaving traces of color along the edge of his scalp and cheek.

Zun worked with a silent focus. He looked only to the pot and to the cave wall. He carefully drew his fingers along the wall's surface and then leaned back and stared at his work. Black shadows danced on the walls making the drawings of Dragons and Humans move in jagged starts. Lost in the image, he jerked his head to the right at the sound of a Human approaching just outside the cave's entrance. He cocked his head and narrowed his eyes. Zun concentrated on the soft footsteps, the steady breathing, and the Human's slow almost imperceptible heartbeat.

"You've come to tell me the festival has begun," he said without turning around.

Entering the cave, Lily replied, "Will you grace it with your presence this year?"

Zun turned to face her while raising an eyebrow, "Convince me."

Lily crossed her arms across her chest, "Once a year, you can watch from a distance. From a distance is the important part. You can observe the tribe of which you are a member—remember that? Those wily, strange Humans. You wear their skin and hair, you speak their language, and yet you don't seem to understand them very well. So watching the festival is kind of like, research. Research!" Lily looked around the cave and then lowered her voice to an intonation of conspiracy, "And, you can observe Dragon behavior from a safe distance, marvel at their disorderly fires, and listen to the coded messages in their strange songs. What do you think?"

"Not good enough," Zun replied turning back to his painting.

"And," she became practical as a last resort, "I can spirit away enough food to last you a week."

Zun leaned back to see Lily's questioning gaze. "Now that is the only reason to attend."

"Bring your biggest stone bowl because I heard Anippe is bringing enough leek stew to last a Dragon Moon," she added.

Zun let a half-smile escape his lips. Of all Dragons, he loathed Anippe the least. When he swam in the Lazuli River, he often caught her golden brown Horse-Dragon face staring at him from beneath the waters. She would raise her large almond-shaped eyes above the surface and blow bubbles from her delicate nostrils. The bubbles would lift out of the water and reveal shimmering rainbows inside. They would float all around Zun, darting in and around, flirting shamelessly.

Anippe never spoke to Zun, yet she could sense when he started to feel uneasy about her proximity. She would slowly swim away, leaving a soft trail of Dragon essence floating on top of the glassy water.

"Anippe is different," Zun said to Lily. "She is a loyal Dragon, a selfless Dragon. She would never abandon her friends."

Lily sighed. This again, she thought to herself, always this. "The Dragons never abandoned us," she tried to fill her voice with compassion, "they came to our aid just in time."

Zun stood up and walked over to a stone shelf nestled in a dark corner. He washed his hands in a bowl of water. "No," he voice broke, "they did not come just in time."

The tone in his voice hurt Lily's heart, and she looked down at her hands. She could not imagine losing her parents. She knew she would never truly understand the pain residing in her friend.

She did not know how to respond, so she walked over to look at his newest drawings. On the cave wall she saw a circle of huge Dragons standing menacingly around a small Human male. Their eyes were angry and fire shot out of their mouths. In another picture Zun had used charcoal to draw a mountain with jagged slopes. With red paint he showed bright lava spilling from the top. At the base of the mountain a woman lay dead, a wound in her heart.

"There is no hope in your drawings," Lily said sadly, turning to look at Zun.

"Let's go. I'm hungry," Zun replied, drying his hands on a piece of cloth.

"Why are they all so bleak?" Lily pressed.

"Let's go," Zun said again.

He laced on his sandals, grabbed a satchel, and stuffed it with candles, a fire rock, a blanket, and most of his food bowls.

"You forgot the big one," Lily said, pointing to a low shelf.

He grabbed it from underneath his sleeping alcove and shoved it into another bigger satchel. He took one last look around the cave and stepped out into the Midsummer night.

The air outside was cool, with the slightest scent of burning Alder and thyme floating through the trees. Darkness filled the forest, and the full Moon cast its glow throughout the branches. The boughs shimmered in the milky silver and white light. As Lily and Zun walked along the path, they listened to the burbling river. They heard the trees stretch and creak. Tiny leaves and needles fell from the branches. The darkness felt like a secret.

Small animals scurried across the path. A Chipmunk and Mouse stopped to look at the two Humans. Their bright eyes sparkled in the Moonlight and their tails twitched nervously. As they walked, Zun felt as if some of the trees pulled back their roots as they moved past. He would quickly look to the trees and search for movement, yet each time he looked closely at the base of the trees, the roots were still and motionless.

When they approached Alder Ring, Zun started to shift his bags around. He slowed his pace and coughed. Lily knew he was telling her he would go no further. He needed to remain at a good distance. She reached for his hand, "There is a space up here that will be perfect."

"I don't want to keep you from the dance," Zun pulled her hand back, "Look."

They both could see the great fire lighting the Human and Dragon bodies below. A spiral dance moved slowly around the fire.

"Don't worry, I will join it soon," she said.

Lily led him to a short cropping of stones nestled in the hill. From this distance they could easily see the clearing and all of the activity. They could also hear the bright music as it wafted up, high reeds, a sporadic pipe, and the cacophony of deep drums.

"Zor is drumming tonight," Lily said softly while Zun spread his blanket upon the ground. Her heart quickened and her worry about her friend's sadness and fear slipped away. She did a motion of the spiral dance in the dirt, turned in circles, and then said, "Give me your sack, and I will get enough food to make your wild hair tame!"

Zun pulled back his tangled curls and glowered at Lily. He thrust his satchels at her and said with derision, "Have fun."

He watched as she navigated her way down the hill to the festivities. She moved like a Deer, turning quickly back and forth in jagged zigzags to find the best footing. Lily looked back once and waved. He nodded his head and leaned back against a smooth boulder. How strange, he thought. Dragons and Humans dancing so close together, dancing as if there were never any questions. Never any regret. Never any anger. It made him feel sick inside.

❦ 4 ❧

The Midsummer Celebration

In Alder Ring incense filled the air with exotic spices, sweet fruits, and scented woods. Drums punctuated all movement, trees throbbed, and the Moon swelled. Dragons thumped their tails against the forest floor, and the deep vibration traveled to the feet of each Human. The Humans, linked and twirling under the stars, felt alive and fresh. White Owls flew low over and around heads, diving out of trees and swooping back up to land on low boughs. They sang out low staccato calls and blinked their round eyes in unison.

Then the Moon Dragons arrived. These rare Dragons communed with others only with the light of the full Moon. They had silver skin, white eyes, and were as big as small Deer. They had silver manes of hair and long elegant limbs. Their faces were shaped like Turtles and their bodies were smooth and glistening as if wet.

Moon Dragons made no sound when they flew or walked. It was as if they were weightless. So when they approached Alder Ring, only the most attentive Dragons realized they had come. After landing, they linked tails with the other Dragons and whispered signs of greeting. A Moon Dragon named Tyr carried a tiny Moon Dragling nestled on her back. The news spread like spilled water, and all of the Dragons quickly gathered around to look at the newborn. She was silver with tiny gold horns along the ridge of her tail. She was curled into a tight ball at the base of her mother's wings.

Tyr clutched a silver bag in her claws and held it out to the gathering of Dragons. Reaching inside she pulled out rare stones one at a time. She gave an opal to one Dragon, a garnet to another, and a diamond to a small Bush Dragon.

As Tyr called out to the Dragon gathering, a Human boy translated for the adults, "The Dragling's name is Braan!"

A chant began, and the Humans bowed to Tyr, who in turn, blinked her luminous white eyes and gracefully bowed to reveal the curled baby. Firelight danced on the Dragling's silver skin. She remained tucked in her safe position, but her fair eyes glowed from beneath her shimmering mane. Zor moved slowly towards the new Dragling and pulled out a small cloak. He unfolded it with ease and reverently placed it upon the baby. The cloak was red with flecks of silver and had a braided edge of gold. He lowered his great body and breathed upon the Dragling's forehead. He then pulled out one of his red feathers from his Eagle-shaped head and placed it between her eyes. The feather glowed bright and disappeared into her skin.

After welcoming the Dragling Braan, attentions turned to the growing hunger. Quite a few Dragons became cranky. Some started butting heads against innocent trees, some let out high-pitched screams, and others began gnashing their teeth and hissing steam. No other animal in Durga went without food so poorly. Unfortunately Dragon hunger did not creep upon the stomach like in the Human tribe. At one moment the Dragon was fine, going about his business without any desire for a morsel of sustenance. At the next moment he could bite an innocent boulder in two. This is why most Dragons were encouraged to snack throughout the day, even if not truly hungry. It was a well-known adage that a hungry Dragon was an unhappy Dragon. No one wanted to witness the experience of a famished Dragon.

"Food! Eat! Food! Eat!" The chant began, and everyone quickly realized it was almost midnight and the feast had not begun. The Humans made room for the rush. Dragon bodies were not to be waylaid upon their movement toward nourishment.

The best cooks of the Human and Dragon tribes spent all day preparing the Midsummer feast, and many young Dragons and Humans had been scolded for sneaking a morsel or two from the pots. But now they could eat with abandon. Each tribe sat upon either side of the clearing crowding around the tables, filling their plates with aromatic delights.

It was a memorable sight to witness from above. On the West Side of the Ring one could see a table the size of a small lake filled with huge pots and serving plates, with a circle of Dragons hunched around, greedily filling their colossal oval plates. On the East Side of the Ring, one could view a modest table set with seemingly tiny pots and miniature serving plates from which the smallish Humans would dip.

But each side had ample amounts of delicious, mouth-watering food. They dined on magnificent mounds of roasted garlic potatoes, steaming spiced bread, baked oats and Maple sweets, and of course Anippe's famous leek stew. The Draglings munched on candied pears and nuts dipped in sweet cider. The children delighted in sugared apples and the rare Dragon fruit, cinnamon quobloon.

Everyone drank jhul, the special Midsummer drink. It was a warmed Dragon wine served in spiced and sugared mugs. No Human was allowed to know the recipe of the wine, but each Sun one was sure to hear fevered debate about which fruit comprised the base, which was secondary, and how long the fermentation had to be. Many a Human fell asleep against a tree mumbling and laughing about the ingredients of the very wine spilling in her lap.

Above the feast, the trees shimmered with Dragon candles. These flames would not set fire to the branches because of a steadfast charm, and thus Alder Ring sparkled with miniature fires throughout the canopy of wood. Below the tapestry of tree and fire the clearing was filled with eating and drinking, laughing and cavorting. Yet, as the bellies filled and hunger melted away, more and more bodies began to itch with the desire to dance.

The first spiral dance of the night was informal, but now that the evening was coming to its apex, both tribes felt the need to perform the more serious dance of Midsummer. Long ago, Humans learned the dance from the first Dragons, and for generations the dance was a reminder of the promise made between the two tribes. Prophetic visions came out of a properly performed spiral dance, and each participant could feel the pulse of life residing within Earth.

As the spiral dance began, magic swept into the forest and spun around the dancing forms. The Humans and Dragons slowly interlocked hands, tails, wings, and legs and a humming began to rise. A large group of Dragons and Humans remained on the outside, beating a pulsating rhythm on the many drums. Bush Dragons, tiny Dragons who skittered on the forest floor like miniature Horses, thumped their tails on the ground. The Mud Dragons beat their front legs against tall, skinny drums that stood thirty feet tall. The drumming seemed to both contain and release the spirit of the forest. The Human adults sang about the blessing and beauty of being alive. The Dragons sang about the Journey of Time, the Great Remembrance, and the Splendor of Birth. The Human children sang translations of the Dragon songs—each silently promising to never forget the enchanted language.

After an hour of dancing, the forest began to rustle with a new type of movement. Tree branches bent and snapped, bushes shook, and a heat bristled at the edge of the clearing. Those inside Alder Ring felt the bodies of numerous animals moving toward Mount Calyps for the Midsummer meeting of tribes. Now the air seemed charged with a new kind of fire.

Since the first memory, at each Midsummer festival

Dragons requested a meeting of all tribes who lived together and yet were often separate. As each animal depended upon the existence of another, the Dragons believed a communal meeting was one way to honor the circle of understanding. Sophia, a Dragon born with the magic and skill of translation, would share the gift of empathy and wisdom to all animals who wished to understand another.

Midsummer was the only time of year when the recently split tribe of Dogs and Wolves came together to commune. The Rodent tribe gathered to share ideas and learn more about their ever-present predators. The Bird tribe came together—Raptors, Song Birds, Sea Birds, and River Birds, shrieking and singing of both positive and negative news. The Feline tribe used the meeting to formalize mating rituals, as they preferred a solitary existence throughout the rest of the year. The Deer came to remind the Humans about the many compacts regarding foraging and gardening—sometimes errant Human children would leave a wild asparagus patch bare, without even considering the elaborate agreements made the previous year. The Reptile and Amphibian tribe enjoyed the deep respect they held at Midsummer's meeting, for they were the closest relatives of Dragons. All Durgan tribes were represented, even the Fish tribe who counted on Anippe, the River Dragon, to voice their multiple wills.

The spiral dance slowed as the Dragons heard the buzz in the trees.

"The time has come!" a pounding Dragon shouted from outside of the circle. He beat his drum two forceful times and all drumming came to an immediate halt. "The tribes have arrived!" he looked down at all the Human faces turned up to him. "Let us not keep them waiting!"

The Dragons began to speak quickly in their silvery speech. Their words were familiar to the adults, yet just out of reach. Children whispered to their parents and guardians, translating the Dragon tongue.

"Zor just told Ius to hurry up," one boy said to his father.

"Anippe just said, 'Why must we rush? There is plenty of time,'" another girl said to her mother.

While the translating continued, the Dragons packed away their food and musical instruments. Zor collected the sacred Dragon Drums and immediately encircled his grip around the torso of one Human who mistakenly put a small Dragon Drum in his own bag. Zor tightened his claws and raised the rigid body up to his stern, feathered face.

The man shivered as Zor nodded his chin toward the bag.

"I'm so sorry," the words tumbled from the Human's lips. "Honestly, I thought it was my drum."

Zor lowered the man back to the ground and pointed at the clutched bag. The man quickly took the Dragon Drum out of his bag and held it up to Zor. The red Dragon swept the drum from the man and then tapped one claw against the man's forehead. The Human whispered, "Never again."

Zor nodded his head.

As the Dragons and Humans prepared to move to Mount Calyps, Labrys walked back into the clearing with the elder Human woman. The pink and gold Dragon placed another necklace around her old friend and used her tail to gently pat the woman on the shoulder. Labrys then tossed a handful of gray pearls into the air. She blew a gust of fire, and the pearls flew over the heads of the Humans. Each pearl twisted and turned seemingly on a deliberate path to find a certain person. At her command the pearls flew softly into the base of each Human's neck. They rested softly near the skin and shimmered in the Moonlight.

The Humans felt a distinct warmth form at their necks, and they instinctively reached up to touch the pearls. As soon as their fingers brushed against the gray spheres, a large thunder clapped in the sky, and a thousand stars shot out across the blackness.

꿍 ꩜

Lily quickly gathered food for Zun. She scooped up Dragon biscuits, three loaves of her mother's delicious clove bread, a full sack of lion fruit, and a bowl of roasted potatoes. She filled his largest pot with Anippe's stew. As she ladled the last bit of creamy leek and potato into the pot, she felt Dragon eyes resting on her back. She turned her head and found Zor watching her closely. He lowered his red-feathered head to her, and she nodded back.

Lily's mother walked up, and Zor turned to walk with the other Dragons making their way to Mount Calyps.

"Let me guess, for a certain lonely boy who lives by himself in a cave?" her mother asked.

Her face became warm, "Yes, Mama, this is for Zun."

"He's lucky to have you as a collector," Lily's mother pulled a package out of her satchel. "Here, give these cookies to him. They're raspberry lutes, I know he likes them."

"You remembered," Lily smiled with gratitude and hugged her mother. "Thank you for understanding him. I know some of the adults don't like his reclusive behavior."

"I certainly don't feel comfortable judging him," her mother said. "I don't believe any Durgan has been orphaned twice."

Lily squeezed her mother, and then let go so she could secure the lutes. "I'll see you at the meeting!" she called out as she made her way through the trees and up the hill to Zun's hiding place.

"Don't be late!" her mother called after her. "And be careful in the dark!"

Stepping carefully around the rocks and bulging tree roots, Lily traversed the hillside that seemed wet with Moonlight. Even though she could not see him, as she came closer to where she left him, Lily could feel Zun's eyes on her. When she finally saw his crouched form, she noticed how easily he blended with hillside. His skin had a grayish-brown hue, like stone and fallen log, and his hair was wild and tangled. Even when he pulled it away from his face, it seemed to creep back with a life of its own. His eyes were black, and his arms and legs were long. He enjoyed sitting still. He could wrap his legs inside the protective cover of his arms and sit this way for hours without moving.

"The dance didn't last very long," Zun said.

"No, the other tribes came earlier this time, and some Dragons are whispering."

"Whispering?" Zun asked.

"That something is different. Pohevol was not there." Lily looked back down the hill and then turned to peer into the black forest. She tried to adjust her eyes to see the hidden forms. She looked back at Zun and set his sacks down on the ground. "Enough food to last you a week!"

"Thanks," Zun stood up and put one hand on her shoulder. He gripped her muscle, and a slow smile formed on his lips, "Your arms are changing, you're getting stronger." His eyes rested on hers.

Embarrassed, Lily flexed her muscle and pointed her arm straight as a Bird's wing. "I've mastered the Raven," she paused, wondering if he would understand the significance. "I'll receive my Name and Necklace soon."

Zun stared at her for a few moments in silence. Then, as if remembering who she was, he blurted out, "Congratulations, Lily," and gave her a quick hug.

Lily and Zun separated from each other awkwardly. Lily looked back to the clearing and said, "We must get moving, they've packed up everything."

Zun looked down and saw the procession of Humans walking to the mountain. Some Dragons took off in flight, and the air thundered with the flapping of enormous wings. Others pounded the ground with their heavy steps, and the forest resonated with Dragon movement. This made Zun shiver.

"You go on ahead. I want to take these back home," Zun said.

"Zun," Lily began.

"Go on, I'll be quick."

Lily looked at him for a moment and then nodded. There's no use fighting him, she thought. When she started back down the hill, Zun picked up his sacks and slung them over his shoulder. He carried the pot of stew in his arms and made his way back to the cave.

The only one to remain in Alder Ring was Labrys. The air was still sweet and filled with aromatic food smells. As the last one to leave, Labrys was in charge of putting out the Dragon fires. Labrys, a master jewel maker, was also a master of fire tending. The Dragon candles were easy to extinguish—she needed only to reverse the steadfast charm and they would be magically drawn to her candle satchel. Hundreds of candles flew from the trees, still alight, and when they entered her bag, they instantly went out.

The Dragon fire around which they had danced was an entirely different matter. Dragon fires are massive and often have a will of their own. Dragons understood if a Great Fire does not want to be extinguished, it will decide to remain hidden. The blackest of coals and tiniest wisp of smoke could burst into flame if fire willed it so. Thus, Labrys had to woo the fire, sing to it, and lull it into a deep sleep.

As Labrys caressed the erratic flames with her smooth voice and sang soft lullabies to the Midsummer fire, the flicking orange and red blaze gradually disappeared without the aid of water or smothering. Labrys offered a few of her gray pearls to the ashes and rising smoke.

Lily watched as the tendrils of smoke curled around Labrys's pink and gold head and horns. The Dragon smiled and snorted, and then gathered up her bags of jewels and took off for flight. Her double wings brushed along the trees, and when she reached a clear spot of air, she corrected her position by making a sharp twist to the left. Labrys flew off to the Midsummer meeting.

Lily wondered why Pohevol had not been at the celebration. She made her way toward the mountain. If he were not waiting there, something was wrong.

∽ ∾

Sophia waited at the base of Mount Calyps. She felt the tribes converging upon her realm. She whispered Dragon incantations asking for clarity, patience, wisdom, and fluidity of speech. She blessed her mother before her and prayed for the spirit of all translators to be with her on this Midsummer evening. Each of her heads sat unmoving with their eyes closed.

As the tribes arrived, the ground hummed with movement and anticipation. The Midsummer gathering was a time of stillness. Each tribe honored the rules of tolerance—no fighting, no past grievances, no predation, no infighting. Greetings could be heard in numerous languages. Old friends hugged, rubbed heads, sniffed bodies, kissed, and danced various steps of meeting. Thousands of animals converged near the base of Mount Calyps, each tribe nodding to the members of the next tribe nearest them.

"Welcome," a multiplicity of voices called out from Sophia's various heads.

Each tribe listened for its unique language, and when

heard, they responded, "Blessed Midsummer!"

Sophia bowed her heads and reached into her bowls of Dragon Dust. She raised a handful to each of her seven mouths and blew the shimmering Dust over the bodies of the gathering animals. Everyone sparkled in the mountain Moonlight.

Her voices began speaking to each tribe in a succession of words, "Durgan tribes, those who walk, fly, swim, slither, and crawl, welcome to our Midsummer meeting. Now is the time to come forward and share concerns, dreams, problems, and solutions," Sophia leaned back and her heads searched across the sea of bodies.

Lily was almost to the center of the Human tribe when she heard a loud flapping and awkward landing in the middle of the Feline tribe.

It was Pohevol.

Forest Cats, Mountain Lions, and Cougars encircled him and spoke in Cat tongue. They rubbed against him and sniffed his fur. They stepped back and gave him room to stretch. As he extended both his front and then back legs, the other tribes leaned in to get a better view.

His feathers were ripped and torn, half of his white whiskers were missing, and his fur was strewn with bits of rough tree bark.

As he made his way to Sophia, the various tribes began chattering. They understood the urgency of his haphazard arrival. He had been inside the Great Tree. Pohevol had traveled through time. What news would he share? Would he reveal visions from the past or from the future?

Sophia lowered one head to Pohevol, and he spoke

into her ear. She raised the head and said, "Pohevol will speak first."

Everyone buzzed, leaning into the ear or body of a neighbor. Sophia raised her large wings, and a hush fell over the crowd.

"Speak, Pohevol," she said, "and listen tribes of Durga."

"Tribes of Durga," he spoke as Sophia translated, "the Great Tree summoned me on the way to our celebration," Pohevol paused. "She sent me to the future."

Everyone became silent as stone.

"Thousands of Suns had passed. The Earth was older and moaned under a strange kind of heaviness. The air was thick with smoke and dirt, and despair filled the atmosphere, the plants, and the animals. Large metal and stone structures sat near damaged rivers and lakes. Roaring boxes tore through the sky and over the land. An invisible current passed through the air—it felt like a lightning storm without wind, rain, or thunder.

"I thought the Great Tree must have sent me to another planet, perhaps she transported me to a different Universe, for surely it could not be the same Earth as ours. But the Moon was slightly smaller, the mountains were slightly larger, and the ground spoke the same language. It was our Earth—only she was older.

"The Earth cried out to me, and I tried to understand her pain. I began searching for the Dragons of this future. They would help me comprehend this grief. I flew thousands of miles. I searched for many weeks. I searched in caves, on mountains, throughout deserts, over snow. I flew around the entire planet," Pohevol stopped. "There were no Dragons to be found."

The Dragon tribe came alive.

"Preposterous!" shouted a Tree Dragon.

"No Dragons in the future?" a Mud Dragon exclaimed.

"Impossible!" a River Dragon roared.

"It cannot be true!" shrieked a Bush Dragon.

Anippe lowered her voice, "Pohevol, are you feeling well?"

A Moon Dragon retorted, "He cannot be well, this is madness!"

Zor raised his eyebrows and turned to Ius with a piercing look in his eyes. Ius sharpened his claws on the nearest rock, closed his eyes, and nodded his head slowly.

With deliberate clarity Pohevol said, "I am healthy and well. Please, let me finish."

Many Dragons grumbled. A few Humans whispered. The eyes of all tribes were wide and full of disbelief.

"I spoke to many animals, and they could not remember any type of Dragon. I spoke to the Lizards and Frogs, I spoke to the Snakes—they could not remember Dragons.

"I asked them to go into Dreamtime, and even then they could not remember a time on Earth with Dragons. They asked me, 'What are these Dragons? Did Humans make them? Are they fueled by the Black Remains? Are they machine?' And I could not respond, for I was speechless."

"What are 'Black Remains'?" a Woodpecker called out.

"What is 'machine'?" cried an Opossum.

"Did you speak with the Great Tree? Surely she could

explain," a Sparrow called out.

"That was the most confusing part," Pohevol began, "I entered this future time standing next to what appeared to be a disfigured stump of her. Every part of me said this had to be her remains. The stump was larger than any tree I have ever seen, the rings suggested the age she would be, yet how could she be cut down? Who would do this? Who could do this? How could I be in the future without her presence?"

"Then it is impossible!" shouted a Raccoon. "If this were our future Earth, the Great Tree would be there. No one could possibly cut her down."

The Beavers all nodded saying, "Yes, yes! Raccoon is right!"

"Wait," said an Owl. "This must be our Earth's future. The Great Tree would not send Pohevol to another Universe. What would be the reason, the logic? This journey was portentous. We must allow the meaning to appear."

The Owls hooted in agreement, and other Birds chirped and cawed in concord. Sophia mimicked the movement of the Birds in her translation. With so many animals speaking, her seven heads went up and down rapidly, listening and translating over the different tribes.

A Bush Dragon spoke up, "Did you speak with the Fish? Perhaps there were Dragons living under water or sleeping in Dreamtime?"

"I spoke with many Fish," Pohevol replied, "and they knew nothing of Dragons. I flew over the vast seas, and there were no Dragons. I even went to the land of ice. I spoke to Whales, Tuna, Salmon. They knew nothing of

Dragons." His voice became tentative, "But they knew much about one tribe."

"Which tribe?" Lily asked Pohevol aloud. Her voice quavered, tightness spreading across her stomach.

The Humans turned their faces toward Lily. She was the first Human to speak. She felt uncomfortable, as if this Human silence were a suggestion of guilt.

Pohevol looked at Lily, "The Whales spoke of Humans."

The tribes quieted.

"What about Humans?" Lily asked Pohevol silently.

"Lily," he quickly thought, "it is not good. Brace yourself."

Speaking aloud, Pohevol continued and Sophia translated, "They described the history of Humans with profound sadness. They said Humans broke the circle, abandoned Earth's ways, and upended balance. They described thousands of Suns where Humans took more than they gave, destroyed more than they created, and enslaved tribes who were not Human. Eventually, they enslaved their own kind—they enslaved other Humans."

"This is absurd!" shouted one Human female. Another young girl added, "Humans could never do this, we would never do this!"

An exasperated air rustled about the Humans, as they all began speaking at once. They argued against the vision, they pleaded with Pohevol saying he must be mistaken, they nervously laughed at the inconceivability of Humans having lost the essence of what made them a part of the animal clan, the essence that bound them to Earth.

Lily blurted out, "We would not be so foolish! We

wouldn't allow such a path to be taken!"

"Wait," an elderly man walked up to Sophia who was deep in her translating meditation. He reached up both arms to one of her heads, and she lowered herself to him. It was Thorn, Lily's great grandfather. He was the eldest Human male of Durga.

"Thorn says we must continue listening to Pohevol. He says there have been recorded visions and warnings. He says to remember the men who enslaved the proud tribe of Horses. The men who brought the first sadness to Durga."

Everyone became quiet. A few heads meekly turned to the small area where the Horse tribe stood. After the horrific invasion, only a few Horses continued to come to the Midsummer meeting. On this night there stood three young Stallions. The elders stayed away, and the Mares dared not go near Humans. The Humans understood the Horses' fear, as certain memories had not faded. Many of the Horses who had been once enslaved still wore black scars on their hides. The once-captured Horses had black triangles with two intersecting lines in the middle permanently burned into their flanks. This was the brand of the men who ripped them away from their families. These men forced the Horses to bite iron rods fastened to their mouths and had straddled their strong backs. To keep from being thrown, the men had lashed the Horses with painful whips and beaten them with the flat of their swords.

"We remember," Thorn bowed to the Horse tribe, "we have not forgotten."

"Yes," a Squirrel added in a quavering voice, "in

honor of the Horses, give Pohevol the chance to continue."

Pohevol lowered his head and stared at the forest floor in front of him. He extended one wing and looked at the jagged tears and rips. He then tucked the wing close to his body.

"I noticed something else," he began. "There were no Dragons to be found, and the only tribe to carry wings were Birds."

The Hawks and Eagles looked nervously to the Dragons. A Frog instinctively stretched out his wings to make sure they were still there. A mother Deer began grooming the soft purple wings on her fawn's back, and a small Black Bear nervously tucked his tiny blue wings deeper into his thick fur. He was a Durgan Bear born with unusually small wings, wings that could not lift his body to fly.

"I spoke with the Cats, and they laughed at me, asking why Cats would wear the clothes of Birds. I spoke with the Frogs, and they told me how their tribe suffered horrendously under the follies of Humans. They described how their children were born with five legs and missing eyes. They pleaded to know who I was and from where I came."

"This still makes no sense," a silver Wolf with golden wings stepped forward. She continued, "What about the Wolf tribe? What about the Aurochs and the Bears? What about the tribes from the Land of Beginning, the Elephants, Tigers, and Giraffes? How could Humans decide the fate of multiple tribes, tribes who are stronger and who outnumber Humans?"

"Yes," other Wolves barked, agreeing with the elder. A few Dogs barked too, and the Wolves whipped their heads around and glared.

"You ask a good question," Pohevol cleared his throat. "In search of answers, I went to the tribes who surround us, but who choose not to commune."

"Insects," the murmur spread across the tribes. A little girl brushed away a Mosquito who chose at this very moment to land upon her cheek.

"I went to the Insects and Arachnids and begged an explanation. The Roaches laughed, and the Ants ignored me. The Butterflies bewildered me. Finally, some old Spiders took pity on me and tried to answer my questions.

"They told me of the Age of Cold and Sadness. They believed strong imbalance was born there and continued to grow. Food was scarce, and many Humans died. They could not gather enough foods to feed their tribe, so for sustenance they turned to flesh. Humans forged metal into shapes meant only to kill. These Humans killed to live, thus killing became similar to birthing. These Humans began worshiping death, and they created elaborate rituals honoring death and destruction. This new belief commenced a coordinated attack upon other tribes. In order to control their food supply, some Humans began to force coupling inside other tribes. And then after the births, to gain the most power over procreation," Pohevol paused, "they separated babies from mothers and created subservient tribes."

The female animals looked around at one another. Sensing tension and fear, babies began clinging to their mothers' skin, feathers, or fur. A few began nursing more emphatically, and maternal arms, legs, and wings clutched for evidence of sweet babies' breath.

Pohevol continued, "One Spider told me to fly over the distant plains to view the vast farms, smoking shelters, and stone prisons. I cannot fully impart what I witnessed. Few tribes lived freely in this future. Prisons held animals in cages for Humans to use, view, or torture. Docile Aurochs, animals the Spiders called Cows, hairless Pigs, Chickens, Dogs, even Horses were imprisoned and then led to merciless slaughter. A small group of Humans killed and cut apart some of these animals, so that a multitude of Humans could feast upon their flesh."

"This is not true!" a child shouted.

The Canines and Felines looked about themselves in wonder. Humans acting as carnivores? Then what of us, they thought. In the future will we graze on the fruit of trees and dig for roots in the ground?

"But these Humans would die," a Dragon said. "This imbalance could not last long."

"At this point in time," Pohevol replied, "they seemed alive and prolific to me."

The tribes muttered amongst themselves.

"But what of the Dragons?" A voice called out behind the tribe of Humans.

The Humans turned around to find Zun standing at the farthest edge of the circle. His dark hair was pulled away from his face, and he stood trembling under the light of the full Moon.

"What happened to the Dragons?" he demanded.

Lily moved through the crowd and reached for his hand. Zor's feathered face twitched, and he flashed a look of concern at Ius. Ius stiffened his chest and turned to look at Zun. He stretched out his wings, curved them in to make a shield around his body, and caught the Moonlight in this pocket. The silver light pooled inside the spaces between his armored scales. His eyes began to glow white.

"No, Ius," Zor whispered, "not yet."

Ius lowered his wings, and his eyes lost their white fire.

Pohevol looked up at Sophia. She was tired from her work. Her heads drooped closer to the ground, straining to hear all of the tribes' chatter, and her mouths grew slack from so much translating.

"We must give Sophia a chance to rest," Pohevol said. "She has been translating for over an hour. Zun brought us back to the original discovery. In the future the Earth is in turmoil, the tribes are in peril, and for some inexplicable reason, Dragons no longer exist. We have much to discuss."

⌒ 5 ⌒

POHEVOL'S PLAN

Trembling, Lily stood next to Zun. Clouds passed in front of the Moon, and shadows passed over his face. His eyes were hard and filled with anxiety. Lily looked around and saw the circle of Humans numb with shock. The news was difficult to comprehend. A world without Dragons? What would happen to Dreamtime? Who would instruct the children? Who would sing the remembrances?

Sophia twisted her seven heads into a spiral and lowered herself into a large brown mass at the base of the mountain. Zor walked over and placed one of his capes around her body. She said something to him and then tried to place herself in a deep sleep. Despite her efforts, Pohevol could feel Sophia's heartbeat pounding rapidly through her thick skin and scales. He lay in a tight ball curled next to Sophia, his tattered wings tucked in. He concentrated on trying to breathe slowly, committing the trip to the future in his permanent memory.

No Dragons, he thought. What will we do?

The Dragon tribe was active. Baby Draglings bounced from back to back, peering over shoulders, trying to listen to the adults talk. Steam and rare fire snorted from nostrils. Wings quickly shot up and down creating gusts of wind. Dragon words burst forth and eyelids darted up. Horns lay flat and tails lashed and whipped. A few Dragons motioned angrily toward the Humans while others quickly slapped their wings and told them to be quiet. Nine elder Dragons moved away to form a tight circle at the Western edge of the mountain.

The Humans glanced over with curious eyes and asked the children what the Dragons were saying. They strained to listen but could not decipher the meaning. The Dragons were too far away, and they were now using the Old Tongue—the special language—unknown to Human children.

Zun looked to Lily, "You're shoving your nails into my skin."

"I'm sorry," she said, dropping his hand.

"This doesn't make sense to me," Zun said. "My dreams show Dragons fighting Humans and hurting them, not the other way around."

"Zun," Lily said, "I can try to understand your pain, but I cannot trust your visions of Dragons turning evil."

"That's because they've never hurt you."

"And they've never hurt you," Lily reminded him.

Zun's voice was caustic, "They sat and watched Durgans die."

"And then they ended the massacre," Lily grabbed Zun's shoulders. "The Dragons defeated the invaders! I can't believe you. You ignore the memory, you deny the beginning and the history, and you toss aside your chance to learn from them, to understand why they did what they did, why they made certain choices—all because you lost your birth parents." Lily's temple was throbbing, and she felt exhausted.

"They were taken from me," his words tumbled from his lips.

"By Humans! Not Dragons!" Lily screamed.

"You can Shift!" Zun yelled back at her. "You can escape, you can see from another side. I can't!"

Lily sat down on a boulder and crossed her arms. She tried to slow her breathing, and she pressed her fingertips into the coursing blood on both sides of her forehead.

"You could choose to see from a different side," she said softly. "Your visions are wrong, Zun. I feel it in my blood. I know I'm right."

Zun looked back to the Dragons. The nine elder Dragons walked back to the larger group, and he saw many heads nod in unison. Zor went to Sophia and whispered near one of her long, coiled heads. As her many eyes opened, she uncoiled her necks and stretched. Zor gathered in his cape and stepped back to give her room. The Moon had moved across the sky, and many of the animals began yawning as they huddled closer to keep warm.

"Sophia is ready to begin again," Zun said.

"Are you coming to the circle?" Lily asked.

Zun replied stonily, "Only to hear better."

When they walked over to join the Human group, Ius followed Zun's every step. His eyes began to glow white.

Zor's red tail flickered against Ius's back, and in response Ius again controlled the white fire.

Pohevol stood and turned to Sophia. She uttered a jumbled succession of words and sounds. Her brown Dragon scales fluttered and then flattened themselves. Then her seven mouths opened and began a symphony of music. She was singing in several languages, bringing in different harmonies both high and low. She closed her eyes and continued for ten minutes. The animals became caught inside her circle of voices, lost inside her art of sound.

Lily, enraptured with the moment, opened her eyes to see Pohevol staring right at her. He thought to her, "Lily, imagine a life without Dragons. Their absence will hurt us all. Speak to the Humans and guide them. We must not allow this future to come."

Sophia stopped singing and said, "My family, my tribe, the Dragons will speak now. Elders, come forward."

Marii, the eldest Tree Dragon, came forward and wrapped her eight wings around herself. She looked at Pohevol and the many tribes staring at her, waiting for her words.

"Pohevol speaks of a future in which our tribe is no longer present," she began. "The Great Tree would never send him on a false journey. She is warning us. It is obvious. A horrific future awaits us, and we must heed her wisdom and prediction. For this is what Pohevol's trip represents. Our future is in jeopardy—the Dragon tribe will be destroyed, taken away from this Earth—unless we decide to do something."

The Moon Dragon, Tyr, walked over to Marii, her

Dragling on her back, "We must decide what to do now, so that we can change the future vision. The Great Tree would not show us this if she were not certain we could do something. We must not allow this future to exist, or if it is fated, we must prepare for its inevitable path. We believe the Human tribe must work with us, as they exist with too much power and imbalance in the future. They must also help to unravel this mystery."

Thorn spoke, "I agree with Tyr and Marii," he said. "Something horrible has happened in this future, and our tribe is covered with guilt and shame. We must join the Dragons in making sure this future does not come to pass."

"No!" Zun shouted.

"Don't do this," Lily whispered under her breath.

"This is wrong," he continued, even as Lily motioned for him to stop talking. "The Dragons will turn on us. They already believe we are at fault for their disappearance. If we work with them, who is to say this isn't how we begin to destroy ourselves?"

The Dragons mumbled and shot angry glances at the Humans. A few young Dragons grumbled, "He will never understand," and "Zun is the one we must watch."

"Zun, you are filled with anger," Marii said, "and your skepticism is unwarranted. Now, more than ever, you need to experience Dreamtime with a Dragon. We will need your knowledge and your visions to help with this important decision. You must put aside your fears and join us."

"Zun, you must have faith," Anippe's soft voice added. "We need you."

Zun looked to Anippe and found himself drawn to her sloping Horse face, her smooth skin, her gentle eyelids that could be touched with outstretched fingertips. Why didn't she scare him? What was it about Anippe that made him want to move closer instead of farther away?

"How can we help, Anippe?" Zun stammered. "What can we possibly do to change the future?"

"Yes," another Human offered, "isn't the future determined?"

Menet slapped her strong tail on the ground, "Absolutely not!" Even though she was over a thousand Suns old, she had hope and optimism running through her scales as sweet and persistent as Dragon wine. She had two thick stripes of white fur running along the ridges of her back and over her thick chest. Some said her magic came from flowers braided into her thick Dragon fur. Menet curled her claws around her tall walking stick and stood up on her back legs. In this position, she became the tallest Dragon at the meeting.

Her voice boomed and echoed against the rocky face of the mountain, "The future is always in flux! We have been given a gift!" She pointed her stick at the tribes beneath her, "Pohevol has placed a jewel at our feet. A jewel that is buried in solid rock and covered in thick mud," she paused and dropped down with a heavy thud to stand on all legs and peer carefully at everyone under her huge head, "But it is a jewel nonetheless."

She continued, "We must collect our gifts of prophecy and open our eyes to the change that is already happening—a change that some of us have viewed from a distance," she shot a quick look at Ius and Zor. Unless one had the speed of a Dragon's neck, one never would have noticed upon whom her glance was focused.

"The Great Tree is offering us a chance to save our future descendants and possibly ourselves," Menet said. "What a gift—to have the chance to remove protective mud, to break open solid rock, and to find a jewel of hope waiting inside. We must believe in our power to change our world."

"But what can we do?" a Human asked impatiently.

"Action is necessary," Marii answered, "but planning is essential."

"I have an idea," a calm voice spoke from the Feline tribe. Everyone looked to Pohevol who sat proud and still. His wings were tucked neatly away, and his white chin seemed to glow. "The future was without any Dragon presence. The skies were empty and the mountains were quiet, as if they were sleeping, but I had the strangest feeling. Felines enjoy hiding. We love small spaces, and we enjoy looking out at the world from a safe and secure spot. After my journey around the planet, I felt like there were numerous beings," he paused and then said, "who were hiding and waiting."

"What are you saying, Pohevol?" Marii asked.

"Perhaps, we can protect Dragons, by asking a few of them to retreat into hiding."

"Hiding?" a Dragon repeated.

"Only until we can understand why the future exists without Dragons, only as a last hope, a last hope for survival," Pohevol looked around at the elder Dragons.

Marii and Tyr came together and spoke in soft voices.

"You cannot ask this of us," one Dragon called out.

"These chosen Dragons would have to give up flying, or swimming, or roaming free on the Earth. To ask this of a Dragon is to ask him to destroy everything that makes him a Dragon."

"But they could have extended Dreamtime, which might offer up ideas as to how to solve the future problem," a Raven offered.

"This is easy for you to say," another Dragon added, "Ravens are not being asked to hide away, to be in a vault away from the open sky!"

"This is true, Pohevol," Tyr added, leaning away from her discussion with Marii. "To ask this only of the Dragon tribe is too much."

"But if we do not protect some Dragons, how will we prevent the tribe from being destroyed?" Lily found herself mouthing these difficult words.

"How do we know that going into hiding is not what sparks the disappearance in the first place?" Marii offered.

Many Dragons agreed.

"But, Dragons can survive," Pohevol stressed. "If they are in a safe place, they can live for thousands of years. If their eggs are in safe places, they too can survive and live for thousands more. It is an act of compromise and an act of safety. We protect a few to ensure survival of the generations to come."

"There is a serious problem," Zor's deep voice entered the discussion. The Draglings whispered and pointed at the powerful cloak maker.

"In order to protect the entire Dragon tribe," Zor said, "we would have to place into hiding Dragons from all over the Earth. Our tribe survives because of diversity.

Pohevol's Plan

Durga is full of Tree, Mud, River, and Bush Dragons. But we need the wisdom and presence of the Ice, Sand, Vine, and Sea Dragons—as well as the Moon and Spirit Dragons who live not in one specific place."

Tyr and Saja nodded to Zor for his consideration of their rare tribes.

"Convincing these Dragons—some of whom we have not seen in ages—would be a task," Zor continued. "Why should they trust our Great Tree and Pohevol? The Great Tree's reputation might be known across Earth, but Pohevol's time travel might not be believed. Even if it is possible to save our tribe from extinction by hiding, how can we convince enough Dragons to make this sacrifice?"

They will never agree to do it, Zun thought. Believing no one would hear him, Zun whispered aloud, "They are too proud and selfish. They don't understand the meaning of sacrifice."

Zor flashed a stern look at Zun. Zun had forgotten about his sharp hearing. He could hear an Ant crawling upon a twig in the middle of a thunderstorm. Zun, acting as if he were just as powerful as Zor, stared back at the red Dragon. Zor opened his eyes wide and snorted a puff of steam from his nostrils. Zun crossed his arms across his chest and forced himself to look away. Inside his chest his heart beat like a hammer. Tiny droplets of sweat formed on the edge of his scalp.

Stretching out his battered wings, Pohevol stood up on four legs and proclaimed, "I will go to each and every Dragon across the Earth and personally tell them my story."

"I doubt that will be enough to move Dragons of this

Earth," a voice came out of the woods. A long purple and green Dragon emerged from the trees.

"Caduceus?" Lily whispered. Caduceus never came to the Midsummer festivities. He hated communing with any tribe—excepting only Serpents.

"One flying Forest Cat will not convince the diverse Dragons of this world," his voice was full of derision. Caduceus slithered into the clearing. His Alligator head looked left and right at the tribes assembled. Arching their bodies from the safety of his neck, Caduceus's Snakes smelled the night air, their tongues flicking in and out. "Neither will the finest Dragons of Durga. You will need representatives from many tribes to attempt this feat. You will need numerous Snakes, of course," he chuckled at the obvious necessity. "And you will need Dragons who already enjoy the many benefits of hiding. Smart Dragons who already prefer the dark. Dragons who distrust the present time and its dastardly inhabitants."

A few children giggled as Caduceus spoke. He was so grandiose. Their parents hushed them with stern glares.

"I agree with Caduceus," Pohevol said, "we should choose a group, a diverse family to travel the Earth in hopes of convincing Dragons to accept this challenge."

"We have not agreed to this idea," Tyr stepped in.

"We must discuss this further and come to an agreement before we continue," Marii added.

The other tribes started to fidget. The Rabbits complained about the time, wishing they were at home asleep. The Dogs were upset, as the present events seemed to take immediate precedent over an important planned discussion with the tribe of Wolves. The Bears wanted to dance again, and the Deer wished to speak to the Humans about a group of young boys who continued to disrespect their secluded thickets. A few Mice had already left, as no one seemed to ever notice if they were happy or not, and the Birds were concerned, knowing their tribe would be the first to suffer from lack of sleep.

Sophia listened to all of the voices and knew what to do. She raised her seven heads high and hovered over the various tribes, "Durgan tribes, each Sun you come to honor the Midsummer meeting. Tonight a grave message has been delivered to our minds and hearts. The Dragon and Human tribes have been dealt a heavy blow. While every tribe will feel grief if this horrid future is true, the Dragon and Human tribes will bear the weight of responsibility." Sophia's heads paused.

"Let us come together for the end of Midsummer and agree to honor the spirit of community by wishing each tribe peace and harmony," she said. "The Dragons and Humans shall continue to commune and messengers will be sent to keep all tribes informed of the final decision."

There was an audible sigh of relief as the tribes were given their leave. Animals linked hands, paws, wings, and legs saying goodbye and goodwill to one another. Yet as Sophia hovered above the groups, translating the various calls of parting, she observed a strange pessimism lurking among some. The links seemed not as strong, and the words of a few individuals were forced and insincere.

Like the sudden change in wind, tribes began walking, flying, hopping, and crawling back into the woods. All moved except Dragons and Humans. Sophia lowered her body to the ground and tried to find comfort. She arranged resting spots for six of her heads and kept one hovering near the Humans. Zor walked over to her again and placed a cape over the resting necks. The heads nodded their appreciation to him.

The air warmed and a soft breeze swept through the clearing. In the East, a faint and distant promise of light began to soften the black sky. The Moon Dragons felt the early moments of dawn and began to gather their belongings.

"Midsummer night is almost over, the Sun will soon rise," Tyr reached out for her baby who was resting in another Dragon's neck feathers. She placed the Dragling on her back and covered her with Zor's gifted cloak. "We must leave soon, yet I fear this matter will not be settled by morning. What shall we do my family?"

Marii spoke, "We must practice deep reflection upon Pohevol's idea. We should consult the ancient books and spirit worlds."

The Dragons agreed and began stretching their limbs and wings.

"Shall we agree to meet tomorrow night at Mount Calyps to make our decision?" Tyr asked. "Humans, does this meet with your approval?"

The Human tribe leaned into each other and conversed.

"Yes," Thorn replied, "we will meet with your tribe tomorrow evening."

"Let it be so," Marii bowed to Thorn.

The Humans bowed to the Dragons, gathered up their belongings, and began walking back to their village.

There was a palpable heaviness in the air. Although

dawn was approaching, both Dragons and Humans went their separate ways carrying the invisible weight of uncertainty.

Lily found her parents and begged them to plan a meeting with the Human elders and Pohevol, "They need to ask him more questions, to learn more about his visit to this future!"

"It is almost morning, Lily," her mother whispered, "we must sleep and meet later in the day."

"This is too important," Lily pushed, "they should meet now!"

"Lily," her father said, "listen to your mother. We're all shaken and confused. We must give our bodies rest, so our minds can be creative." He reached for his daughter and drew her close. "Sleep, my dear. Pohevol needs you to be rested."

Lily looked over to find Pohevol. He was sitting near Caduceus with his head pointed up listening intently to the Shifting Dragon.

"Yes, father," Lily said and then kissed him quickly.

"You will come home now?" Her mother asked.

"Yes, but may I say goodnight to Pohevol first?"

Her parents looked at each other, worry lines crept across their foreheads.

"Quickly," her father said.

Lily walked over to Pohevol and Caduceus. Zun, who stood with his arms crossed leaning against a tree, watched the three of them closely. His eyes were dark and focused. Lily seemed too small and fragile when standing next to the Dragon. She looked like a wildflower, easily picked or trampled. Zun didn't like the way Caduceus peered down at her. His Dragon tail moved slowly and cautiously upon the ground, just like a Snake.

Lily bowed to Caduceus and spoke the Shifting words of greeting.

He nodded his head and motioned to his heart.

"You Humans will most certainly make a mess of things," Caduceus began and then paused, "Wait, you already did." His nostrils fumed, and he dragged his claws upon the ground.

"Caduceus," Pohevol said, "it is not her fault, do not assign blame indiscriminately."

The Dragon moaned and threw his head back. "Fault!" he bellowed. "Fault! Humans are full of fault. Durgan Humans care nothing about the rest of the Earth. There are tribes who already suffer. There are changes in the wind, and it seems that Dragons will suffer the most—and Humans, so selfish and concerned only with singing and dancing—do not care!"

"We do care," Lily whispered.

Caduceus whipped his head down lower and peered into her face.

"Yes, little one, you appear to care," he blew steam into her eyes, "but do all of you care?"

Lily blinked away the steam and felt a chill descend upon her shoulders and arms. Gathering her cloak tightly around herself, she turned to find Zun. Had he already left? She knew the Dragons worried about Zun, especially as he grew older and more steadfast in his beliefs.

"Instead of looking to the Northeast, instead of searching his own spirit to ask the proper questions about the loss of his parents, Zun blames us." Caduceus made a sweeping motion to his chest and outward to the remaining Dragons still huddled next to the mountain.

"Instead of studying with a Dragon, a blessed and selfless gift my glorious tribe shares with your youth, Zun turns his back upon us and whispers ill things when forced to be in our presence."

"He has visions," Lily started.

"Of course he has 'visions,'" Caduceus interrupted. "All of the ones who have caused the greatest harm have 'visions.'"

"Dragons have visions," she protested.

Caduceus was silent. He then replied, "We do not judge others because of our visions, and we do not act capriciously and use our visions as an excuse."

"I can think of a Dragon who acts unpredictably..."

"Stop Lily," Pohevol quickly interrupted. She was beginning to forget her manners, and she was talking to Caduceus, a Dragon who would not forgive easily this temporary slip. Lily bit her lip and stopped speaking.

"We are all tired and frustrated," Pohevol said. "But let us not forget we will have to come together if we want to change this future, right?"

"Earth help us," Caduceus walked away grumbling.

"You need to go home and sleep," Pohevol thought to Lily. "Your tribe needs you well-rested and in good form."

"We need to talk more," Lily thought.

"And we will," He lowered his eyelids at her, which always provided Lily with comfort.

She reached out and touched Pohevol's fur. He rubbed against her waist and let his tail linger around her back. He then brought his feathers close to his body, made a powerful Cat leap, and disappeared into the forest.

Lily looked around for Zun but could not find him. The first rays of light pierced through the trees to the East. A few members of the Bird tribe started to sing in the warming air. The Sun's rays pawed through the branches and climbed up over the horizon releasing soft heat across the forest. The mountain warmed and delicate flowers opened their petals to allow the Sun's warm fingers to caress their small bodies. Lily pushed her cloak back behind her shoulders and called out for Zun. She listened but could not hear his response.

He's angry, she thought. Well, so am I.

She decided to let him be. She would go home to do as her father and Pohevol advised. Lily quickly made her way through the trees, looking for the familiar stands of wildflowers, pathways lined with enormous rocks, and trickling streams that marked her way home.

As she approached the village, she noticed a different kind of silence. A few homes had small pockets of light coming from inside the windows and a few wisps of smoke exiting the chimneys, but most of the dwellings were dark and motionless.

Lily came to her home and softly pulled open the door. She saw her parents huddled over a small book in their bedroom. She heard the words, "prophecy," and "invaders," before they realized she was standing outside their room. They became silent and closed the book.

"Good morning," her mother called out. "You were gone longer than we expected," she raised her eyebrows at Lily.

"I know. I'm sorry," Lily answered, "good morning,

I'm going to sleep now."

Lily stumbled into her room and looked at all of her things. Her walls were covered with colorful tapestries painted by her mother. The fabric captured beautiful Dragons, Flying Fish, flirtatious Butterflies, and Mountain Lions running up Mount Calyps. She had a wooden shelf on which she kept stones, pressed flowers, the silver amulet her father designed for her, and a large white whisker trapped in hardened amber. The whisker had belonged to Pohevol, and he had gifted it to Lily on her tenth birthday. He told her one day it would come to good use.

She thought about what Pohevol said earlier that evening, about traveling to all the Dragons of the world to convince some of them to go into hiding. She thought about Zun as he listened to the description of the future. She thought about his angry, distrustful eyes. She thought about Caduceus's accusatory words and his arrogant insistence regarding Human fault.

She thought about her individual role in what was to come. She had often questioned her Humanity, as she worried about her Shifting ability and how it separated her from other Humans. But now, the worry turned into fear. This fear exhausted her, and bed seemed a sweet escape from her pounding mind. Lily climbed into the soft covers, nestled into a comfortable position, and let her eyes close. She saw dancing points of light and swirls of bright colors, and then she was asleep.

⊰ 6 ⊱

SAJA'S CAVE

Lily awoke with a start. She had slept only a few hours, and her dreams were abstract and foggy. Rubbing sleep from her eyes, she admonished herself for not thinking clearly earlier that morning. She needed to see Saja. Why waste precious time sleeping in her Human bed when she could be with her Dragon mentor? Lily knew now more than ever, children needed to harness their strength and knowledge, and enter Dreamtime with Dragons.

Lily washed her face, used her cinnamon stick to scrub her teeth, changed into fresh clothes, and quietly crept out of the house. The Sun was directly above her, and she scolded herself for being so dense. Many Humans were awake, bustling around the village, gathering the afternoon fruits and vegetables, grinding leaves and roots, baking bread.

A small group entered the village transporting the

stunning skin of a Rainbow Snake. They were grateful to live near such generous and giving Snakes. Not only did they shed their useful skins often, but they also left them close to the village. The Humans could make clothes, satchels, bedding, and medicine from the discarded scales. Zun's aunt was one of the many carrying back this recent offering. She looked over to Lily and waved.

"Lily, how is Zun doing today?" she asked. "I know he was upset last night."

"I don't know," Lily replied. "I haven't seen him."

"I'm worried about him. I think he should come home and be with me during this difficult time."

"I agree," Lily said, "but you know how stubborn he is."

Zun's aunt smiled and reached into her basket, "Would you bring him this for me?" She held out a loaf of sweet apple bread.

Lily took the loaf and promised she would. Zun's aunt hugged her and whispered into her ear, "He needs your friendship now, Lily. Don't give up on him. The Dragons are upset with him. He is trying to balance on a river log—no easy task."

Lily gave her a goodbye kiss on the cheek and continued walking along the edge of the village. When she came to a clearing near the river, she knelt to gather a satchel of strawberries. She watched as a small Spider crawled over the dark green leaves. She picked the ripest fruit only and thanked the Earth for her sustenance. Once clearly out of sight of the village, she hid the loaf of bread in a cluster of stones and prepared herself for a Shift. She wanted to impress Saja by approaching her mentor Dragon as a Raven.

Saja was a Spirit Dragon. Her body was long, thick, and serpentine. Like Caduceus, she had both Dragon and Snake qualities. Unlike Caduceus, she had no legs. Her body shimmered purple and gold, and her wings were thin and segmented like the fins of Fish. She had a flap of skin that spread out around her neck like a fan, long feathered ears, and a slender horn jutting from between her violet eyes. Spirit Dragons could create lightning and thunder with this long, thin horn, and they were protective of them. They could become invisible and performed this type of magic more than any other Dragon. Saja also was a master at Shifting.

Unlike most Dragons, Spirit Dragons did not enjoy settling in one place. They were often accused of being nervous and flighty, but those who came to know them understood they heard a distant call. The world was too small for their comfort, and frequently they had to break free in order to soar beyond the known realms. There were rumors that Spirit Dragons could travel to other planets in the Universe, but no Spirit Dragon would speak of this ability, if it were true.

Saja had traveled to numerous places on Earth, but lately she had begun to settle down, at least for a while. She had an object that was suppressing her nomadic lifestyle. Saja was protecting her first egg.

Since Saja would hatch a Dragling soon, Lily and Saja traveled through Dreamtime in a secure and isolated place. Saja picked an abandoned cave at the base of a roaring waterfall on the Alys River. It was loud and wet on the outside but secluded and dry on the inside. One could travel deep inside the mountain and find comfort and security. When hidden in the belly of the mountain, the cave was warm and quiet.

Saja began secluding herself when she felt the egg first forming in her deep abdomen, many Suns earlier. Since Dragons only laid eggs every 50 Suns or so, nesting was not to be practiced lightly.

Detailed preparation went into nest building, and Saja had been hard at work, collecting all of the necessary items. Lily had traveled throughout Durga with Saja, watching as the Spirit Dragon searched for the perfect growth of golden river reeds. She watched Saja enter the caves of Marduk to gather topaz and emeralds. Saja told Lily about the gift of fidelity topaz would offer, and how emeralds would help to establish a lifetime of love and success for her new Dragling.

Jewels and divine metals were crucial to mother Dragons, as they were vital for sleeping eggs. Dragons understood the vulnerability of the developing tissue, growing gradually, slowly, patiently inside the delicate shell. They knew the Dragling must be wanted, cared for, sung to, and protected at all costs. Jewels transferred different abilities to the resting egg, and every Dragon mother had to meditate and journey through Dreamtime to learn which precious stones were meant for each individual Dragling.

A Dragon mother waited until her perfect time to have a Dragling. Some Dragons felt the call at a young age, while others like Tyr, did not feel the call until later in life. Some female Dragons never desired a Dragling and instead nurtured other aspects of Dragon lore such as studying medicine and healing, honing different forms of art, or practicing to be the smartest and strongest at Dragon sports.

Saja was a young Dragon, only 78 Suns old, but a few Suns ago when Lily was only six, Saja felt the intense desire to lay an egg. Her body glowed bright whenever she wrapped her body around little Draglings, and she knew Durga would benefit from more Spirit Dragons. She found the father, a gentle Mud Dragon who studied healing arts, and they courted for eleven Moons. At the beginning of the twelfth Moon, she felt her egg forming in her abdomen. After creating the nest, Saja spent most of her time positioning various jewels around the egg, guarding it, and waiting for the Dragling to emerge.

∽ ∾

Lily, impatient to reach Saja's cave, tried many times to make the Shift. The release was difficult as she kept thinking of the night before, the Midsummer meeting and the anger in Zun. After the fifth attempt, her Human body let go and she transformed. Her Raven body broke free and climbed its way into the sky.

Lily flew over the trees, following the Lazuli River until it met the Alys. She quickened her pace when she saw the tall waterfall in the distance. A few small Woodpeckers flew beside her and tried to entice her into a game of chase. She opened her humped black beak and cawed at them. The Woodpeckers seemed to laugh at her voice and darted away. When she approached the deafening cascade of white water, she slowed her flapping and lowered her feathered body. The roar was much louder in her Raven's ears, so she adjusted her internal organs to compensate. She navigated herself around the waters and landed on a rock near the entrance.

The water splashed roughly against the wet rocks, and foam sprayed up around her. Lily tried to move behind the water to enter the cave, but still not used to her Raven body, she slipped and fell into the cold water.

Fear exploded throughout her body. How could she swim as a Raven? Her feathers were weighed down and useless to move in the strong current. She gasped for air and took in water. Her lungs burned and tightened.

She cried out in vain. She tried to Shift back into her Human body but fear gripped her. Her mind was jumbled with thoughts of death, water, Zun, her mother, Saja, and death again. Lily began sinking in the water, she flapped and kicked, came up for a moment, but then sank down as the river carried her away.

The current continued to pull her under, and she felt her lungs become smaller and smaller. No one knew she was here, so no one could save her. The river, so peaceful and cooling in the hot summer, now surrounded her in all its terrifying might. She opened her eyes and saw the white rush of water and air mixed together with the occasional rush of colorful fin and dark stone. Lily thought about death—the passage seemed close and inevitable, almost as if she were ready for the transformation—but then fear came back and pierced her lungs.

I am not ready to die! Inside her body, which felt like it would explode, she screamed.

Fish, she thought, to be a Fish. She thought of the

Trout in this same river, their smooth bodies, and their willing acceptance of water. This receptivity was so profound they breathed it in and desired it to glide across tiny gills. Lily calmed her pulse and concentrated on the cooling blood. Fish blood. She slowed her racing mind and let her eyes focus on the world beneath the water's surface.

A Trout swam near her and came inches from her Raven's eye. He flicked his strong tail, and Lily collected this image of a powerful water creature and willed her Shift. Her body released the Raven feathers, turned lungs into ribs and muscle, transformed legs and talons into a slippery tail, and changed wings into fins. Lily was now a Fish.

Lily turned her new Trout body left and right and allowed her gills to breathe in the oxygen, magically present in the rushing water. Filled with relief, she realized how close she had come to drowning. Through careful thought and by controlling her panic, she had saved herself.

She had saved herself!

Lily swam around in circles, thrilled with her ability and full of pride, until suddenly she felt a sharp pain in her back. She darted around and focused her Trout eye up to the water's surface. She saw a dark shadow hovering over her.

Simion, the Black Bear and her Shifting peer, was hunting for Fish—hunting her! Quickly Lily swam as fast as she could across to the other side of the river. Simion was strong and agile in the water. He followed, crashing through the water, constantly batting at her. His claws were now the longest, sharpest claws Lily had ever seen, and her insides quaked at the thought of being eaten alive by the very Bear who trained at her side, learning the magic of Shifting under Caduceus's tutelage.

Lily wanted to Shift again, but she had to use all of her focus to escape Simion's slashing claws. They both darted back and forth through the water, Simion causing a great commotion, leaping and twisting and jabbing at the water. He dove into the water headfirst and almost caught Lily's Fish body in his mouth, but slammed into a rock as she slipped herself into a crevice made by underwater reeds and boulders.

Simion peered into the reeds and looked patiently, waiting for movement. He was a persistent Bear, one of the reasons he was so good at Shifting, and also one of the reasons other Bears didn't particularly care for him. Instead of crashing through the waters, leaping after the numerous Fish who filled the rivers, Simion insisted on chasing after one Fish. One Fish only. Until he caught it. Then he would pick another, catch it, and then another in this careful and deliberate way. He found the indiscriminate rushing from one to another and then another to be confusing and random. Where was the skill?

Lily realized Simion was waiting her out, so she knew she had to Shift immediately. Safe in the river reeds, she plunged into thoughts of her mother. She willed her Human form so quickly that Simion jumped back roaring as the reeds burst open and Lily appeared coughing and gasping.

Wet and shivering from fear, Lily held up her hand in the shape of a claw, the sign of friendship and respect that all Bears understood. Simion shook his head and looked back into the reeds. Lily pointed at the reeds, made the sign of "Fish," and then pointed at her chest. She then made the spherical sign of the Shift, and watched as Simion tried to understand her message.

His eyes became wide, and Lily smiled meekly. He had just realized what almost happened. Simion lumbered over to Lily and placed one paw on her head, his offering of deepest apologies. In return, she placed her hand on his large belly, the Bear sign of forgiveness.

Lily nodded to Saja's cave, and Simion motioned for her to go. He trudged out of the water. Dejected and no longer hungry for Fish, he went to look for a clump of blackberry bushes.

Lily climbed out of the river and collapsed onto the muddy bank, taking in shallow breaths of air. Despite her necessary diplomacy with Simion, she was scared to death about what had just happened to her. She thought about Caduceus's warnings. "Arrogance will destroy us all," he grumbled every time she Shifted improperly.

Arrogance will destroy us all, she thought. She let tears come as her body shook. What was happening? Pohevol seemed distant, his news was horrifying, and somehow she felt Humans were guilty. She cried, thinking about Zun's fear and anger. She cried, thinking about growing older. She would soon become a woman, and her Dragon world would be lost. She cried, thinking about Shifting. At times she felt Shifting was a blessed power, but other times she feared it. Why was she the only Human who could Shift? Was she strange? Grotesque? What did her parents and the other children really think about her ability? Were they truly impressed, or did they secretly believe her to be a hideous and peculiar thing?

As she lay there sobbing on the banks of the Alys River, a golden light flittered behind her. Lily felt her shoulders become warm, she felt a soft body incasing hers, and she smelled a sweet smoke encircling her body.

"Saja," she whispered to the air.

As Lily said her name, the Spirit Dragon became visible. Saja coiled her violet body around Lily, her head lowered next to Lily's face, and her collar flapped slowly. A golden light pulsated around the two.

With sadness in her voice Lily said, "I wanted to come as a Raven." She told Saja the story of slipping into the river, Shifting into the Trout, and escaping the fate of becoming Simion's mid-afternoon meal. Desolation filled her words, as tears rolled down her cheeks.

Saja used her feathered ears to rub away the tears on Lily's face. "Shifting is like breathing. When you are stressed or worried, angered or nervous, your being is affected without you even realizing it," Saja's soft voice sounded like wind moving through the highest tree branches. "It is dangerous for you to Shift casually right now, Lily, with all that is happening in Durga."

"I am so tired," Lily nestled herself deeper into Saja's warm coils.

Saja was silent for a moment, "Let us go to my cave. I too am tired, and now is the time for all of us to sleep more than usual. We need to Dream."

Saja uncoiled herself and rose into the air, hovering beside Lily. Lily stood up, brushed the wet river mud off of her legs, and mindfully followed Saja to the entrance in the side of the mountain. Every step she took was measured and precise. The slippery rocks were beautiful, but she now knew they could be deadly. They passed a family of Rabbits huddled inside the base of a fallen tree, and Saja motioned for Lily to look inside a Hummingbird nest. Two tiny eggs lay nestled in wisps of purple Dragon fur, black Dog hair, and bright blue Jay feathers.

"Two sisters," Saja said as she used her tail to discreetly drop a small opal in the nest. "For hope," she whispered.

As they approached the opening to the mountain cave, Saja looked around with concern. Her floating body coiled and uncoiled in the mist before the cave entrance. Her neck flap moved up and down in a steady pulse. Dragons were cautious when caring for an egg. They did their best to create the safest nest possible, as mother Dragons could leave an egg alone for many days at a time. Saja had no legs or claws, so her lightning horn was especially sensitive and ready for use.

Confident that they were the only creatures present, Saja said the words of entrance. In response, the mountain door opened. Lily tried these same words on many occasions but could never get the door to budge. Saja ushered Lily inside, and then turned to watch as the door shut behind them. Rock slid against rock. The cave echoed when the door came to a final stop.

The passageway to Saja's cave was long, moist, and dark. An occasional Dragon candle nestled into small nooks along the walls revealed her colorful paintings. Many Dragons were accomplished artists, and Saja was known for her skill with tree oil paints. She painted images from her travels, and this was how Lily learned about the lands far away from her forest home of Durga.

On Saja's walls, Lily had learned of the great desert, the Sands of Ochre, and the epic games of the Sand Dragons—the DragonBall race, the SandLuge and the difficult RiddleQuest. She loved the images of the large Sea Dragons with their Whale companions, and the miniature Vine Dragons who lived in the jungles of Jha'mah, the Motherland.

But most of all, she loved staring at the paintings of the Ice Dragons. Lily could not imagine a land covered with ice. Mountains, lakes, and valleys—all ice. She would listen to Saja speak of the great sleepers, Ice Dragons who would lie under a sheet of clear ice, content in Dreamtime. She said one could walk over them and watch them sleep—and if one were silent, one could place an ear to the ice and hear the Dragon hearts beating beneath.

Saja promised to take Lily to Iceloch, the land of the Ice Dragons, but that was before she had an egg to protect. They both now knew this would have to wait.

Lily walked down the dark passage and found Saja's sleeping space decorated with glowing gems and flickering candles. Then she saw the egg. Saja had fashioned a beautiful nest for the pale white egg. All of the reeds, fur, and feathers she had collected earlier made a soft bed for the sleeping egg. Saja had placed numerous jewels around the shell, but Lily noticed many new ones Saja could not have found by herself.

Saja, sensing Lily's question, moved to the nest and gently touched the different jewels, "Yes, Labrys came by this morning."

Lily let her gaze fall upon the jewels and said

reverently, "They're beautiful."

"And powerful," Saja added, "the diamonds are from Zor—for innocence, the bloodstones from Ius—for courage, the sapphire from Marii—for clear thinking, and the moonstone is from Tyr—for health. Of course, the platinum—a transition metal—is from Sophia."

The egg seemed to hum in the middle of such power and protection. It was a large egg, almost twice the size of Lily, and it was perfectly oval, fat on the bottom and slightly smaller at the top. Saja had placed red Dragon candles around the nest and also a bowl of incense. This incense had been burning for five Suns.

"When will she hatch?"

"Very soon," Saja slid around the cave, using her horn to light more candles, moving blankets and pillows. She then looked to Lily, "Are you ready?"

"Yes."

Lily and Saja moved over to the incense and fanned the smoke over their faces. They watched the curls and swooping circles of smoke dancing in the candlelight. Lily watched as different shapes emerged. The Raven trapped under icy waters, Zun kneeling inside his cave, Pohevol staring up at the Great Tree. She saw Dragons and Wolves with open mouths, calling out to the night.

Saja flew to her egg and coiled around it softly. She then glided over to the sleeping alcove and nestled herself in the blankets. Lily followed her and curled her body inside Saja's waiting coils. Saja expanded her neck fan, and Lily placed her hand on the warm scales. They both closed their eyes and lay silent for a few minutes. Then they allowed the pillows and blankets to mold to their bodies, and they fell into a deep sleep.

∽ ∾

Hearing a loud drum beating in the distance, Lily floated with Saja on the waves of a large orange sea. Creatures not known on Earth flew through the pale green sky. They saw plants with beating hearts, round eyes, and smiling mouths. They saw animals who looked Human and Lion or Bear and Chameleon.

Hundreds of Dragons floated on their backs, letting the orange waters lap over their exposed bellies and undertails. Lily watched a group of River Dragons practicing their dives. Two would fly straight up hundreds of feet into the green and gold sky, and then turn their heads down, tails up, and dive as fast as possible into the water. The splash created splendid rainbows, and baby Draglings would suddenly appear, sliding down the arcs of water.

Lily spoke to Saja, "Are any other children here?"

"Yes, look over there," the Dragon replied.

Lily saw a whirlpool with nine children standing on their hands. A few Draglings bounced on the extended feet, screeching and whooping, quickly flying up whenever a child moved his toes. Lily looked into the middle of the circle and saw some elder Dragons having a conversation with the children. She moved closer and listened.

"Never give up hope," the Dragons said.

"Never give up hope," the children repeated.

"You hold the answers to all questions."

"We hold the answers to all questions."

"Have patience and embrace wisdom."

"Have patience and embrace wisdom."

"Dragons are not your enemy."

"Dragons are not our enemy."

One child looked up, "What's an enemy?"

The scene shifted, and Lily found herself walking across a steep and rocky cliff. The air was cold and the wind bit at her face. Her hair flew around her head in large gusts, blocking her vision. Lily pulled it back and reached in her pocket for a band. She looked around for Saja but could not see any Dragons nearby. She could only hear the high-pitch whine of wind.

A mountain towered over a patch of trees in the distance. She saw smoke coming from the snow-covered peaks. She stumbled over the rocks, making her way closer to the edge of the cliff. When she came to the very edge, she looked down and saw a band of bright haired men taking heavy axes to a thick cropping of evergreens. She sucked in her breath and fell to her knees.

The scene shifted once more, and she found herself witnessing an immense fire burning bright in the dark of night. She was in the desert as there were no trees, only sand and dry foliage in small clumps as far as the eye could see. Hundreds of Humans chanted in a circle around the large fire. When she looked closely, she saw a figure move inside the flames. She adjusted her eyes to the darkness and peered closely. It was a Dragon. . . it was Zor, trapped in the flames!

Lily pushed through the people and jumped into the fire. She felt no pain, and she was not burning. Lily screamed at Zor, begging him to explain, but he only crossed his front legs across his red chest. He extended his wings and bowed his head to Lily. The flames consumed Zor and Lily in a flash of light, and they were transformed into a field of fragrant roses.

The roses moved together in a slow dance. Then the flowers sprouted tiny legs, stood up, and walked away revealing a lake in the middle of the field. Zor and Lily looked into the water and saw their reflections. Zor's reflection changed, and in its place he saw his entire Dragon line looking up at him. Lily's reflection changed, and in its place she saw Zun, reaching out and grasping for her. The lake changed from blue to white, and soon wispy Dragons began floating over a thick sheet of ice. Zor disappeared, and Saja appeared in his place. Saja touched the tip of her tail to Lily's shoulder. They watched as Ice Dragons, Sea Dragons, Vine Dragons, and Moon Dragons began fighting, cursing, and breathing flames of gas and smoke at each other.

The Dragons fought with such exertion that Lily and Saja could see their hearts pounding through their chests. Horns twisted in anger, claws extended beyond retraction, eyes blazed, and teeth grew longer. The Dragons moved cautiously, side-stepping like Felines. Claws pierced flesh, and fire scorched feathers and fur.

Saja turned Lily's face to hers and blew. Lily closed her eyes and felt the Dragon's steam cover her. She inhaled and allowed her own will to surrender to Saja's.

And then they both woke up.

∽ ∾

A few miles to the East Zor, Ius, and Pohevol stood together on the top of Mount Calyps. The air was cool and thin, and a gathering of Vultures flew above them in slow circles. Their brown bodies blocked the Sun at different intervals, and Pohevol watched as their wings remained perfectly still.

"It is happening," Ius picked up a large boulder and threw it down the mountain, "I knew it would." The jagged rock crashed through a cropping of evergreen branches. Zor cringed as a gathering of Ravens flew out of the trees that suffered Ius's anger.

"We have to do this," Pohevol said.

"I do not wish to go back to that land," Ius said quietly. He began methodically filing his claws against a sharp piece of flint.

"We seem to have no choice," Zor said, "we are a part of this mess, and we have to fix it."

Pohevol stretched his front and then back legs and paced around the rocks. Looking across the vast forest, he then turned to Zor and Ius, "There is always a choice, and you both are not a part of the problem." He stretched out his wings and began flapping them vigorously.

"But we are," Zor argued. "Ius knows what other Dragons do not know."

Ius stopped filing and looked at Zor.

"Whom do you think you are protecting?" Zor stared back at Ius. He counted his claws one by one, "The Humans? The Dragons of Durga? The world's Dragons? We both know evil can exist in the least likely tribes." Zor paused and then snarled, "Even in our own."

"I do not want to talk about it, and I do not want to

go back there," Ius slammed his front leg down and made the ground quake. He threw the file at Zor and thrust himself into the air. Pohevol and Zor watched as Ius's blue armored body became smaller and smaller.

"Zor, what did he see?" Pohevol asked.

"I cannot say. I gave him my honor," Zor reached for his gold cape with red embroidery. "I can say that Ius witnessed a truth most Dragons would not be able to tolerate. He is burdened by this weight. But he knows this journey is right." Zor lowered his head towards Pohevol's and rubbed his face in Feline fashion, "He will participate."

"Only if he desires," Pohevol stressed.

"He desires," Zor sighed. "He is also afraid, as the wisest of Dragons would be."

The two looked down at the forest below them. They saw the Sun gradually move across the valley, burnishing the trees in golden light, and then the village. They watched the Humans go in different ways, some to the Cave of Waters, some to the Circle of Stones, and some to Dragon Hill. Each clan gathered for a separate meeting. The final decision would be made tonight, and there were only a few more hours before the final setting of the Sun.

❧ 7 ❧

DRAGON HILL

The Durgans walked through the village with intent and purpose. The women of age went to the Cave of Waters, the men of age to the Circle of Stones, and the children to Dragon Hill. Each group walked silently, as they all knew what was being asked of them.

They knew they were not alone on this spinning planet. They were respectful of the elders and paid heed to the visions that appeared in times of sacred ceremony. They knew a time would come when the demands of being born Human might interfere with the blessings.

The adults learned it well when they came of age and lost the ability to commune with Dragons. The Dragons would hold the Sacred Ceremony of Life each year, blessing the boys and their new hair, muscles, and voice—blessing the girls and their new hair, softness, and blood. The Dragons would bestow upon the girls and boys gifts of precious capes and stone. During each ceremony the

Dragons offered up words of hope—they wanted the children to remember and not forget.

But every year it was the same. Something changed inside the children. They not only became adult, they felt adult—they felt different. They felt powerful. The Dragons had honored the children's change and instead of letting the admiration roll off, letting it fall like a stone into water, pride took root. Pride buried itself inside the children's hearts like a sleeping seed, and they found they liked the way it felt. They felt special and different. The following morning, when the children tested the language, as they did each and every year, they found it was no longer there. Suddenly, as if they never had the ability at all, they could no longer speak with Dragons.

Tongues would twist and stumble. Ears would ring, and Dragon words and speech became incessant, annoying, and incomprehensive screeching. And then the warnings of the elders became clear, and the children-now-turned-adults found themselves listening to elder words instead of Dragon tongues.

The lesson was always the same, and the adults made them repeat it over and over again: We belong to a tribe of those who left, who walked away from pain. Why we left, we do not remember. We only know that to stay would have meant death. We came to Durga in search of shelter, food, and peace. We found Dragons who accepted our children and guided them to remember the first way. We forgot our past in order to remember the present.

Despite the passing of this message from elder to adult, the message remained vague and distant, as if these words were for other Humans living in other lands. Yet years ago the Horse-riding men had come, and for the first time in Durgan memory, pain had a face.

As the Humans walked to their various places of meeting, this lesson weighed heavily upon their minds. Each knew this quest, this call to action, would reveal more pain. They feared it, and they worried. Yet many secretly craved it. Many saw this journey as a chance to right the wrong. If they could find the secret that erased the Dragon tongue, perhaps they could bring back the speech and commune forever in the company of Dragons.

∽ ∾

The children walked to Dragon Hill, the center of Dragon sport and game. Most Dragons came to this hill to argue and debate, or to compete physically when Dragon words would not suffice. Wrestling tournaments occurred on this hill, as well as eating and fire competitions. Covered in bright green clover, the hill had soft slopes, shallow basins perfect for wrestling and rolling, and an abundance of natural springs filled with cool water to quench the thirst of active competitors. There were few trees, so if the fire of any Dragon became disobedient or unchecked, little damage would be done. The springs were also useful in this rare case.

Because Dragons allowed children to watch their competitions, they also allowed children to use Dragon Hill for important meetings. It was safe and comfortable, and because of its history, it carried the spirit of justice and honor.

Lily and Zun walked to the hill, each coming from a

different direction. Unbeknownst to either, they each thought of their diminishing role in the children's gathering. Soon they would no longer be accepted, as the signs of adulthood were appearing. They both felt a bittersweet melancholy sweep over them.

Sefani, the moderator of the children, was already on the hill. She sat in a field of green near the Stone of Remembrance. The Dragons used this stone to remind debaters and competitors to keep perspective. It was also located near a clear and deep spring of water.

Sefani was blind. Unlike the other Durgan Humans, her eyes were bright blue and her hair a golden yellow. She was also slight and thin-boned. People whispered that she was actually the child of Fairies. There were many tales of forest Fairies, small Human-like creatures who still possessed wings. Some claimed to have seen them flying through the trees. Supposedly they flew only on the brightest of days when the light of the Sun flashed off water and leaves, danced through the air, and partially blinded observers.

Ten summers earlier, Sefani was found crawling naked through the forest. She was only an infant, just under eleven Moons. Not upset, she crept slowly, sniffing dandelions and nosing Beetles in the dirt. A Durgan Dog named Perjas followed closely behind her. When she stopped, he stopped. When she nibbled on a leaf, he would lick the leaf. When Sefani would crawl, he would track her, marking his scent along her wake. A young woman, Rianne, who did not want a life-long mate, but who had longed for a child, found Sefani and Perjas in the woods that summer day. Rianne felt an unspeakable joy.

She gathered the baby up in her arms, and Sefani turned her face in the direction of Rianne's voice and smiled.

When Rianne brought the infant to the village, the Durgans stared at the strange baby. Her bright eyes and hair were so different from theirs, and the healers could not bring sight to her eyes. Not even Adrianne, the healing Spider, could bring sight to Sefani's eyes. So Rianne kept the baby and waited for the birth parents to come back to Durga, as she felt they most certainly would. Rianne waited with a dull ache in her heart. As the child grew to love the smell of Rianne's skin, the cadence of her voice, and the feel of her soft hands, Rianne waited. She waited many Moons for someone to come and claim the child.

To Rianne's joy, no one ever did.

Sefani now was eleven Suns. She was quiet and focused. Her sense of hearing and smell were acute. She loved to cook and could speak rapidly with Wolves and Dogs without the aid of translation. Instead of following behind, Perjas now walked beside Sefani. With one hand on his back, Sefani spoke to him in Dog tongue. Through this communication, Perjas became Sefani's eyes. There was one other special attribute of Sefani's. She was the only Human to ever ride a Dragon.

Before Sefani, Dragons never entertained the idea of allowing a Human to sit upon their backs in Realtime. During Dreamtime anything could happen, and so many children cajoled their mentors into allowing them on their backs. But it never seemed fully satisfying, because it was a Dream. After Sefani joined the Durgans, the Dragons felt drawn to her. They sniffed her wide-open eyes that did not react to movement. They watched her tilt her head to listen to the sound of a falling leaf. They allowed her searching and questioning fingertips to move over their wings and scales. Sefani was an enigma to the Dragons, and they wanted to understand her better. After they consulted the elder Dragons and ancient books, they made a decision. They wanted her to be with them in the air. They wanted to fly with her.

The Dragons asked Sefani to climb upon their thick bodies. They built an elaborate seat with a thick harness for her to attach herself. But on the first day when Sefani agreed to go up on the back of Zor, she refused the seat. She said she would ride without the device. When they took off flying almost vertically into the air, she clutched at his red feathers and pressed her arms around his strong neck. As they cleared the trees and began soaring horizontally through the air, she let go. Hair blowing in the wind, her body merged with Zor's. Her eyes flashed and seemed to look around at the world above and below her.

Unfortunately, many children became jealous over her ability to ride Dragons, so Sefani had few companions. Yet with every disappointment there often comes an attached blessing. Because she was blind and had few Human friends, she spent a significant amount of time alone. Therefore, she became a good listener. Because of this skill, she was chosen to be the children's moderator. She could discern when the smallest, most quiet child wanted to say something, and she always knew when the most boisterous child had spoken too long.

As the children arrived, they formed a tight circle around Sefani. She turned her head in slow sweeping circles and began sniffing for Perjas. He was marking his scent along nearby rocks nestled in the long grasses. When he felt her movement, he raised his snout to sniff the air. He picked up Sefani's scent and trotted back to her. She reached out for his fur and brought him close to her face. He licked her and nuzzled her neck.

Sefani smiled and spoke to him. He curled up by her side and placed his head in her lap. More children came, and there was the rustling of bodies and the smell of Sun-warmed clover as everyone found a spot. Lily sat close to Sefani while Zun sat on the opposite side. Their eyes met, and Lily felt her face grow hot as Zun stared at her.

"Is everyone here?" Sefani asked.

The children looked around and searched for any missing faces.

"We're all here," Lily said to Sefani, relieved to break free of Zun's searching eyes.

"Let's begin," Sefani said. She sat with her legs tucked, and her hair carefully draped over one of her shoulders. Her fingers were long and slender, as she caressed Perjas's fur. "Do we agree with Pohevol's idea, this plan to convince Dragons to go into hiding?"

"Only until we learn more about their disappearance," Lily added.

A little girl replied, "I think Pohevol is smart." She had just turned four and tried to be very serious at the children's meetings.

"And he is furry," added a boy.

The older children giggled.

"Fur is important!" the boy turned deep red, "And he is strong too!" Sefani nodded in the boy's direction and reminded the others to respect all opinions.

"I would like to go," Bridget, a tall girl of twelve Suns called out. Her black hair was pulled back in a tight braid, and her dark eyes flashed. "I can climb any mountain and swim faster than any Human, and I will never forget the Dragon language!"

The children deflated at the mention of their inevitable fate. Zun picked up a stick and threw it into the center of the circle. "Save the Dragons!" he blurted out. "Why are we so concerned with saving their skins? I'm already sick of this talk."

"Zun, watch your words," Sefani turned her head to face his direction, and Perjas began a low growl. "You don't understand your power of influence. When you speak so casually like this, the youngest ones get confused." She carefully formed her next words, "Dragons mean everything to the young ones because they've experienced such wonderful moments in Dreamtime. Your words contradict what they feel and know in their hearts." When she finished, she touched Perjas on his back. He barked once and stopped growling.

"The children are trapped in a fog, a fog created by selfish, cold Dragon thoughts," Zun replied. "They need to hear words that aren't tainted by the Dragon tribe!"

"You are the selfish one!" Bridget shouted. "You are the only one who hates Dragons—we shouldn't have to hear your words!"

Bridget's ire rose even further, "Why are you here anyway? You hide away from us, sulking in your little cave, swimming alone in the river, sneaking food from the village. Why don't you stay in your precious cave and let us speak without your blistered heart getting in the way?"

Bridget had a quick temper. She lived with her father and aunt because her mother had died in a violent lightning storm. Bridget had seen only five Suns when she lost her mother, and she thought Zun was ungrateful. Yes, he had lost both mother and father, but he had an aunt who loved him. He should know better.

Zun stood and put his hands on his hips. He looked around the circle and saw Lily look down at her folded legs. She would not meet his eyes.

"Fine. I won't be a part of this. You're right, Bridget, I'm not a part of this village. I wouldn't want to be. These Dragons are masters of trickery and illusion. This so-called 'Dreamtime' is dangerous magic. It isn't real."

Lily looked up to him, "Are your visions real?" she asked softly.

Zun was caught off balance. He opened his mouth to speak and then stuttered, "Yes, they are because they're not influenced by others."

"But are you sure? How do you know that you aren't being influenced by some dangerous magic, that which is not Dragon?" Lily shook with emotion. She did not like this current path, and she did not want to lose his friendship.

Zun shook his head, "I know what I've seen, and I must believe it."

"As we must believe what we've seen," Bridget added, her voice was full of confidence.

"We've heard the voices of Zun, Bridget, and Lily. What about the rest of you?" Sefani asked.

The children took turns speaking. Each child agreed with the advice of Pohevol and wanted to support the quest. Some were fearful and did not want to leave the village, while others were excited and argued passionately why they should be allowed to go.

Sefani listened and absorbed the words. She gently stopped a child if she spoke on and on about her skills. She encouraged a silent child to speak if she sensed his desire to contribute to the conversation. She held the hands of toddlers, especially if they struggled with the ability to form words accurately to express their thoughts. Sefani had a special gift that allowed her to help those who had few or no words to somehow speak their will.

The children came to a consensus that they would support Pohevol's quest, and that Lily, Bridget, and Tomal would be the best ones to accompany Pohevol and the Dragons.

Tomal had seen ten Suns. He had red hair and was the only Durgan to have dark green eyes. Many thought his eyes looked like those of a Dragon. They were deep and piercing. He was also the only child to spend not only days but also nights with Dragons. He helped at the Dragon Games, and he worked in the heavily guarded Dragon gardens, tending to the sacred soil fruit.

Soil fruit was dear to Dragons because it provided a never-ending supply of food. Dragons often went on long trips and journeys that passed many days and nights. As most Dragons preferred food that was grown in the soil of their homeland, and as a hungry Dragon could be a dangerous Dragon, they always carried provisions in their baskets or pouches.

Soil fruit, grown in the Misty Gardens at the edge of Durga, was a delicious, oval-shaped, red and yellow spotted fruit with a sweet rind one could eat. As long as a Dragon kept at least one fruit tucked away in a bag filled with the special soil, a new fruit would appear every hour upon the hour. All of the fruits were connected. If one Dragon ate the last fruit in his private bag, a chain reaction would occur and all of the other soil fruit would shrivel up and perish. No Dragon ever ate the last fruit in his bag.

Dragons honored soil fruit. It represented moderation, thoughtfulness, and a revulsion to greed.

There were ancient tales of Dragons who ignored the prohibition and almost destroyed the species of fruit. These tales prevented any Dragon from eating her last fruit. Soil fruit was too precious to mishandle. Every Dragon made sure there was at least one fruit in his bag at all times. There were no exceptions. Tomal loved tending to the soil fruit and hoped he would never come of age. He could not imagine a life without Dragons sleeping nearby.

The chosen ones—Lily, Bridget, and Tomal—stood up and formed a circle inside the larger circle. The rest of the children stood, linked hands, and began moving around the three in the middle. A chant began:

Luck and speed,

Good will and safety,

Mother Earth shall protect you.

Lily looked outside the circle to find Zun, but he was gone.

❦ 8 ❧

STONES AND WATER

At the Circle of Stones a palpable uneasiness permeated the air. Located in the shadow of Mount Calyps, this Circle was made by the first Durgan Dragons. The slabs of rock were over twenty feet tall and at least ten feet wide. Some had small notches carved into them. No foliage grew on the ground inside the circle. Only fine, cool black dirt rested in this shade of the mountain.

The Dragons made the Circle of Stones to commune, to celebrate, and to track the positions of stars. The Circle measured seasonal shifts, and the calendar—first imagined by Dragons and then shared with children—was thought of here. The first Sundial was envisioned here, and marriages occurred in this Circle, Durgans barefoot and palms open. During times of need, the Circle also became the hallowed place reserved for Human men of age.

As the men gathered in the Circle, eyes darted about and muscles began to twitch. The men were nervous, and they were upset about being nervous.

"The children cannot shoulder this burden alone," one man called out before the meeting was officially blessed.

"Shhh!" another man quieted him as the Circle continued to fill.

"Let's begin this!" another called out.

"We aren't all here," a voice answered.

"It's taking too long, there isn't enough time. Let's begin!" a loud voice countered.

"We aren't all here!" a stronger voice persisted.

And so it continued as the males of age gathered. When all had finally arrived, Thorn blessed the stones and opened the discussion.

Thorn, the moderator, had seen almost 90 Suns, yet he had a strong and lithe body. A studied magician, he could turn Snakes into Lizards and Lizards into Turtles. These transformations only lasted a short amount of time. He was fascinated with Shifting animal bodies but knew that imposing his will upon another species was not polite. Of course, it was often necessary to entertain cranky babies, distract fighting children, and cheer those with broken hearts. Consequently, a few representatives of the Reptile and Amphibian tribes visited Thorn every odd Moon or so, requesting he keep his magic in check. To this end, Thorn knew the exact location of the best fields and ponds sheltering the most abundant Insects. It was his way of saying thank you to the disgruntled subjects of his magic.

Following Thorn's lead, the men of age took turns sharing concerns. Voices raised and a growing tension reverberated in the Circle. The majority of males wanted to convince the Dragons that one strong male of age, one accomplished representative, should accompany the children upon the quest.

Thorn warned them that the Dragons would view this as a sign of impudence, "They do not, nor will they, trust any of us. We are too old."

"But these faraway lands are different. There might be danger too difficult for a child to bear," a young man countered.

"But the children who are chosen will be strong, wise, certainly clever," Lily's father added.

As the discussion continued, the light of the Sun inched slowly across the Circle. The men looked to the sky and saw dark clouds in the distance. A storm was brewing, so their decision had to come soon.

"Zun should go," said a young man named Divar.

The men became silent.

"Zun is not trusted," Thorn said, "the Dragons would never permit it."

"But the group will need balance and skepticism. He is unlike the other children," Divar continued, "he asks difficult questions."

The men discussed the idea. Some argued that Zun was patient, and he could survive with the least provisions. Others argued against this. If they offered up Zun, the Dragons would assume the clan of men supported his anger expressed the previous night. They discussed the merits of sending other children, but their words kept coming back to Zun.

"All this talk doesn't matter," Lily's father added, "Zun would never agree to go."

Thorn detected a feeling of helplessness spreading

over the men as they spoke of the choice. Although they were arguing over whether or not to offer up Zun, many of the men secretly wished they could be the ones to go.

The men knew Dragons shut all Durgan Humans of age out of their everyday lives for a reason, but they had too many fond memories of lazy Dragon days, Dreamtime, and the teachings of Dragon wisdom. It seemed wrong to be shut out so completely.

Thorn placed a finger in the dirt and brought a few flecks to his tongue. They were cool and bitter. The younger men of age had compassion and reverence for the wise ways, but as they aged and grew further from the memories of Dreamtime, questions and doubt slowly sank in and gnawed at their hearts.

"The majority of men want Zun to go," Thorn finally said, "so we shall offer up his name alone."

The men crossed their arms across their chests and nodded to Thorn.

"We must accept the Dragons' decision," Thorn said, "and we must place our faith in the children."

The men turned toward the tall stones and began a deep chant. They pounded the dirt with steadfast feet and began to walk around the Circle in a slow, side-stepping march. As their voices grew louder, they knelt down to touch the ground and then rose up to touch the boulders in quick successions. This movement from dirt to stone transferred a warm energy through their hands. As they moved faster, the stones began to vibrate, and if one closed his eyes slightly, he could see their blurry movement as if the stones were moving with them.

Following Thorn, the men slowed their legs and made

their chant even deeper. Each man released a final sound, as if releasing all of his lungs and belly to the Circle.

When the last voice came to an end, Thorn looked to the sky and said, "It is time to go."

༄ ༄

On the other side of Durga, the women of age sang softly as they strode through a light rain to the Cave of Waters. Some carried infants in slings and others held hands with the elder women, helping them gather up skirts and navigate across the slippery rocks and rushing water. Clouds moved into this part of the valley, making the air milky and gray.

The Cave was in the shape of a Horned Bull, and it had a steep shelf around the edge of a dark pool of water. The water originated from a small spring buried beneath the gray rock. It was custom for women to lead females who were coming of age, heavy with child, or seeking answers to difficult questions to this Cave. Once lowered into the water, pain diminished and a clarity of thought soothed troubled minds.

As they entered the Cave, the women touched their fingertips to the carved image of a Bird goddess on the rock wall. They then dipped one finger into a bowl of black ash and dabbed a smudge somewhere visible upon their bodies. They edged their way around the shelf, walking down the gradual slope with careful steps, to come to the entrance of the shallow water.

Neva, an elder who had seen over 100 Suns, was the moderator. She took her time gathering the needed energy and spirit for the meeting. "The time has come for swift action," she began. Her hands clutched a carved walking stick made from cherry wood.

"The prophecy is revealing itself," Lily's mother said. "We must gather strength and wisdom to give to our children who will make this journey."

The women undid their hair, setting loose their tight braids and restrictive bands. They entered the water in a slow procession, carefully moving through the coolness to form a circle around the edge of the pool. Once the circle was complete, each woman turned to the woman on her left to find and touch her spot of ash. After finding the spots, they clasped hands and raised arms into the air. They stood thigh deep in the black water.

After a long moment of silence the women simultaneously began to make a concert of unique sounds. One started softly, with a Bird-like call. Another joined with a deeper, resonating chant. One woman began a low whooping like that of an Owl. One more lowered her body into the water until only her head remained above the surface—her voice seemed to harness the sound of the old Humpbacks. A few women created drum-like rhythms, building patterns on top of each other. As the women joined voices and allowed the sounds to fill the cave, the water began to bubble and churn. The women continued, diving deeper into their singing and chanting. Then they turned to Neva to watch for her signal. With a sweeping hand gesture, Neva stopped the singing abruptly and slowly lowered her ear to the frantic, frothing water.

She raised her head toward the cave's entrance, "Lily is the chosen one, and Zun must accompany her, no matter how much he resists."

The women turned to look at Lily's mother, their eyes wide with wonder. She held her head up high and smiled at the others. Inside she felt her stomach tighten into a ball of rock.

The two women standing on either side of Lily's mother took her hands and squeezed. They took turns kissing her cheeks and forehead.

"So let it be," the women began to chant, "So let it be."

"So let it be," Lily's mother whispered to herself.

When the women stepped outside of the cave, they heard a clap of thunder that tumbled through the valley. Amazed at this summer storm, only one day after Midsummer, the women watched as rain poured down upon the forest and Mount Calyps.

⊰ 9 ⊱

THE BURIAL WATERS

The sky darkened. Ominous clouds settled over the forest, and winds began to blow. The smell of rain filled the air. The trees swayed, and the sound of branches cracking punctuated the moments of stillness. The first drops of rain began, washing the dry dust off the summer leaves. The shower released a faint perfume into the air. Lilac, rose, and evergreen mixed to create a heady aroma. Then a heavy rain came down, hitting the rocks and ground with persistence.

The Dragons flew through sheets of rain to gather at the ancient burial waters. Few animals knew how long Dragons lived—while new Draglings hatched every other season, it seemed like no Dragons ever died. Sometimes a Dragon would fly away and be gone for ten or twenty Suns, but he always returned. Someone always remembered him. Many whispered that Dragons were immortal. Despite all of the rumors, Dragons refused to talk about their questionable longevity. The truth was this: Dragons did live for over a thousand Suns, and they did indeed die. Despite the magnificent stories of the contrary, they also could be killed.

Unbeknownst to most animals, especially Humans, there existed an old riverbed that ran through the center of Mount Calyps. The Lazuli River flowed from the melting glaciers at the summit, but deep inside the mountain, buried in a ravine that was bordered by treacherous red cliffs and jagged glaciers, there flowed a deep river originating from the Narool spring. This river eventually mixed with the Lazuli, but its waters were kept private and most revered by Dragons.

It was here where Dragons went when they felt the death transition approaching. And it was here where living Dragons secretly carried the bodies of those who died unnaturally. The bodies, when lowered into the river, would lay rigid in the tumultuous flow. But after a few minutes, the scales, armor, feathers, or fur would melt and disappear into the water. Only the bones remained, like white elongated rocks, sparkling under the rushing water. It was here where Dragon elders received their most vivid visions. It was here where Dreamtime was born.

Despite the connection between Dragons and children, the burial waters were kept secret from all Durgans. Rarely would two or three Dragons, let alone a group of Dragons, ever risk meeting at the location, for fear of causing a loud disturbance. But this evening was unique, and the elder Dragons reminded everyone of the urgency.

With night approaching slowly, the Dragons came

stealthily. The rain acted as a cloak, muffling the sound of beating wings, protecting the Dragons in a gray mist and fog. Each Dragon came alone, except for the ones who were carrying Draglings upon their backs. Each flew North, as if to make for Steem Lake or the Valley of Florine, but just as they approached the highest glacier, a dark and shadowy place, they did a swift nosedive and entered the ravine with a sharp turn to the East.

Despite the awkward flying, each Dragon corrected his approach and landed directly at the banks of the river with a resounding boom. The sound of rushing water and rain pelting the rising river filled the air as every Dragon lowered her head to sip from the frigid waters.

The mountain groaned under the weight of so many Dragons. Hundreds had landed in the river, near the banks, and some even hung from trees like Bats. Dragon wings stretched out and water dripped from them steadily. Above the thick clouds encircling the mountain, the setting Sun hovered along the edge of the mist, bathing the peak of Mount Calyps in a softening light. Multiple rainbows could be seen in the distance, strange orange-hued rainbows, changing and moving with the descent of the Sun. Underneath the clouds, each wet landing and splashing step caused by a Dragon made trees cringe, rocks groan, and Fish scatter.

One young Dragon who soared above the clouds and then chose to dive headfirst back into the stormy mist, landed clumsily on a slippery cliff jutting 100 feet above the river. Stumbling and scratching his way to find a clawhold, he shouted to the Dragons below when his grasping foot set loose a heavy boulder. The rock, the width of three Horses standing head to tail, came crashing down dragging small evergreens with it. The Dragons below, including four young Draglings, whipped their heads up to locate the object screaming down the cliff.

"Watch out!" yelled the offending young Dragon, with an apologetic, "I'm sorry!" trailing behind.

The wind whipped branches around and the erratic movement made it impossible for the lower Dragons to dodge the crushing rock. Zor, sensing the impending danger, swooped down and flew directly under the heavy stone. With a dull and awkward thump that sent steam out of his nostrils, Zor caught the boulder between his shoulder blades. He lunged to the left, crashing into a jagged cropping of trees.

Three Draglings flew to the broken mess of branches and leaves, gasping and blinking with wide eyes. They tucked their wings in, and maneuvered hesitantly through the wet foliage. They found Zor lying on his stomach, legs splayed out, head turned to one side. His eyes were closed. The boulder lay next to him in a perfect nest of broken trees. The three stood in a row peering down at the immobile Dragon.

"Are you all right, Zor?" the first Dragling whispered.

"He's not moving," said the next.

The third Dragling stuttered, "Did…he…die?"

"Of course not!" shot back the first.

"Zor, are you OK?" the second pressed.

"His wing is broken!" the third cried out, pointing. "He's hurt!"

The young ones pulled away torn branches and tried to get closer to Zor's closed eyes. The rain slowed and after a few long seconds, it stopped. The forest was now silent except for an occasional breeze and the sound of dripping rain coming from heavy boughs.

One of the little Draglings climbed atop Zor, gingerly stepping around his slippery spikes along his long, crimson back. He lifted one of Zor's horns and watched with horror as the red spiral fell to his head in a weak lump.

"He's dead!" the Dragling gasped.

The group gathered in closer to peer at the motionless Dragon. The older Dragons, who happened to be viewing the charade, quickly stifled their laughter. For as the small Draglings peered closely at Zor's sleeping face, he was ever so carefully lifting his red tail over their wet, hunched bodies. He moved it back and forth like a Cat would, teasing their young wings. The Draglings, too concerned with Zor's apparent demise, flicked their wings as if to shoo an annoying Fly.

"Oh, this is horrible!" moaned the third Dragling who had purple and gold stripes along her chest. "Zor was the best, the very best!"

"Was the best?" Zor opened one eye and pointed a horn at the worried Dragling.

"Zor!" All the Draglings screamed in unison.

They jumped around, flapping their wings and nudging him with joy. Hearing the cheering, other Draglings flew over to join the celebration. The red Dragon sat up in the middle of his happy chorus and examined his broken wing closely.

With a booming voice Zor said, "Now watch this my little lovelies." He pulled one of his red feathers from his cheek and held it in front of his mouth. He formed his

Dragon lips into a precise O and blew a thin stream of fire into the feather. Instead of bursting into flame, the feather began to blush a fiery bright orange. Zor then took the glowing feather and placed it upon the broken wing. The red wing began to glow, and the young Draglings watched, their mouths agape, as the brilliant feather revealed a snapped skeleton beneath the skin. Zor pressed the feather deeper into the wing and closed his eyes.

The glowing spread evenly across the broken bone, and gradually the bone mended itself as the feather was absorbed into his wing. The Draglings gasped and began jumping around again. The excited bodies sent wet duff flying through the air.

"Teach me, teach me, Zor!" the Draglings with feathers began screaming.

The ones without feathers began looking at their own bodies, peering at the many textures that until now had seemed so simple and boring.

"Can my furry claws do that?" asked a Mud Dragling.

"I've got peeling scales like Lin," said a River Dragling. "Can I do magic with them?"

One tiny Bush Dragling with smooth skin and wings looked desperately at her body, searching for any slight feather, patch of fur, or peeling scale. Finding none, she said rather meekly, "I've got a lot of teeth?"

She opened her mouth and revealed a double set of gleaming white teeth. She had at least fifty teeth on the top and bottom.

Zor nodded and placed one of his red claws on a tooth. The Bush Dragling's eyes glimmered as she felt the tooth grow warm. She looked down past her flat nostrils to see a golden light emanating from her mouth. The other Draglings looked in awe as Zor pulled his claw back and showed how it glowed from the magic in her teeth.

"Never forget, little ones," Zor said with deep sincerity, "Dragon magic resides in each of you. You all have different powers, and you will learn exactly what you can do, when the time is right."

Satisfied with this lesson, and feeling the need to get back to the older Dragons, Zor lifted himself up, shook his wet body with force, and guided the Draglings back to the ancient river. He neglected to notice a small group of Mice gathering around the fallen evergreens next to the offending boulder.

"Again!" one Mouse grunted while scampering around the bits of detritus.

"I thought you said they didn't come up here anymore!" another Mouse screeched at his partner.

"Don't yell at me, I haven't seen a Dragon up here in Suns!"

The Mice went about salvaging their broken nests and muttering how they would never in their lives escape the pounding of gigantic Dragon feet.

When Zor reached the rushing river, a few older Dragons asked him if he were truly healed. Before he could answer, a muscular blue Dragon walked over and bumped him on the shoulder.

"A bit of a rough landing, hmm?" Ius raised his eyebrows.

Zor quipped, "My dear friend, I would like to see you navigate that descent with a boulder on your back." He shoved his feathered face directly in front of Ius's, "In the rain."

"I do not believe a little rock would send me crashing into some twigs."

Anippe slid in between the two male Dragons and placed her wings around each, "It seems to me that both of you spend too much energy comparing strength, when you could be discussing speed." Anippe bent down and in a burst of energy flew straight up into the sky. Zor and Ius lifted their faces to the sky while intoning monotonously, "Dragon one…Dragon two…Dragon three…Dragon four…Dragon five…" Their faces moved down while watching her body come careening back to the mountain.

She landed and threw back her head. "How fast?" Anippe asked, quite pleased with herself.

"Six seconds this time," Ius said shaking his head.

"No," she snorted heavily, "five and a half, I think."

"A full six," Zor countered. "But streamline and," he released a gruff cough, "graceful."

Anippe furrowed her brow, "I do not care about grace," the word hissed out of her mouth, "I care about speed."

"Yes, but strength is, of course, the most important," Ius replied.

"Forever we will have this argument," Anippe sighed, "but I think this trip will establish once and for all what is truly important." She smiled, narrowed her eyes, and the horns near her nostrils lay back, "And that is speed."

Zor said with intrigue, "Why are you so confident that our tribe will agree with Pohevol's idea?"

"Because we all know this is the only way," she replied.

"What has he told you?" Ius glared at Zor.

"Absolutely nothing," Anippe said. "There are a few Dragons who still listen to Human prophecies…despite our distrust."

Zor flapped his wings, released a loud snort of steam, and smiled, "Well, if we go on this quest, I am positive my endurance will outweigh Ius's strength and your speed combined."

"Whatever you say, Zor," Anippe droned.

Ius said with mock sincerity, "If only we could be more like Zor."

It was Anippe's turn to smile, and she winked at Ius.

Zor leaned down to playfully ram his red-feathered head into Ius's blue-armored chest. When the elder Dragons called the meeting to begin, the three became quiet and moved closer to the river.

Menet and Marii extended their wings and looked around at the hundreds of Dragons gathered in the remnants of the first summer storm. Dragon scales glistened in the setting Sun, huge claws gripped exposed tree roots and river boulders, and Dragon eyes glowed toward their elders' direction.

"The ancient Dragon prophecy is correct," Marii spoke first. "We must join with the Human children in preparing for the First War."

The younger Dragons, confused, looked around at each other.

"What prophesy?"

"First War?"

"What's happening?" a Dragling whispered into her mother's ear.

"Just listen little one," the mother responded.

Marii lowered herself into the river and sank until the water completely covered her form. No bubbles appeared. She was gone. Staring into the water for signs of her body, all the Dragons became silent. A strong wind swept through the trees. It sounded as if the river were flowing through their branches as well.

With a large splash, Marii emerged from the water clutching a massive green chest. The chest was covered with rust and river moss. Two small Dragon bones lay fastened to the outside of the box.

She moved to the edge of the river and set the chest down on a large slab of rock. Water dripped off the moss, and the chest looked old and decrepit—as if it should be left alone. As the Dragons drew around, stretching to get a better look, Marii turned around to face the gathering.

"The revered Dragon elders, who lived here long before the Durgan Humans, wove tales of the future into our ancient books and songs," she said. "They spoke of missing wings, an age of frigid cold that would last many Suns, an attack upon the circle, and a hatred of all things Dragon. They entrusted us to preserve the books, to introduce Dreamtime to the children, and to honor the bones. They also charged us to prepare for the cold and for a journey far and wide to protect the circle and Dragons, at any cost."

The Dragons looked around in bewilderment. There would be no discussion. The elders had already agreed upon the quest. Pohevol's idea was accepted in full, without question.

Marii, feeling doubt rise over the river, spoke with

clarity, "Yes, my sisters and brothers, the decision is already made. If you join us in the river now, you will understand the secret we have been carrying for hundreds of years. Our race is in danger. We must act now, for the Great Tree has set this in motion."

Leaving the chest on the stone, Marii led the others into the river. As the Dragons stepped into the river, watching the white bones sleep underneath their heavy feet, a silver and gold light began to form around them, filling the air right above the water with a light mist.

Saja and the other Spirit Dragons were now present at the river. They looked like ghosts, floating in the air over the water, the sparkling light pulsating around their iridescent bodies.

Marii nodded at Saja. The Spirit Dragons started to beat their wings in unison. Like stationary Osprey hovering above the water, their wings moved slowly together at the pace of a Dragon's heartbeat. One and two. One and two. One and two. Beating on like this, the Spirit Dragons created a whirlpool of vapor that encircled the Dragons below.

To shield their eyes from the spraying mist, the Dragons turned away from the Spirit Dragons and instead looked down to the river's surface. Amazed at what they saw, they peered closer. Atop the smooth water, as still as glass, there lay images spread out like a reflection. Yet unlike Dreamtime visions, these figures did not seem real. They were warped and hard to discern. As they continued to stare, the pictures came into focus.

The reflections were repeated over and over. They saw the invaders. They saw the Horse-riding men pour into the forest and set their rage upon the peaceful Durgans. They saw Zun crying in a cave as his mother screamed for help. They saw the invaders try to escape Ius and the Dragons' final retribution. They saw the eyes of the invaders flash with fear and anger as they were carried back to their far away home.

And then they saw the dying. Dragons both old and young were stretched in impossible ways—torn, broken, and bleeding. Fire raged around the ravaged bodies, and black smoke filled the sky for as far as the eye could see. The reflection did not show what caused the horror, only that it was real.

As Ius stared at the images, his back muscles twitched, and his claws began to crush the stones under his grasp. In the reflection he saw the black eyes and wings of gold. Steam began to seep from his skin, and his wings started to expand. Saja sensed his growing agitation and motioned to the other Spirit Dragons to lift the spell.

The Spirit Dragons pointed their noses to the sky and linked wings as they beat their tails in unison. They rose away from the river just as Ius let out a tremendous Dragon roar. He ripped himself away from the river and crawled his way into flight. As he soared away from the mountain, the stones he had crushed into powder fell like ashen rain.

Zor immediately took off after Ius. He could not see Ius in the blinding setting Sun, so he concentrated on smelling the powerful blue Dragon. Come back to me my friend, he thought as he flew through the air.

Zor whipped around in the air currents, following the faintest scent of Ius. Around two miles ahead of him, he saw a flash of blue and silver. To eliminate all drag, he stretched his front legs as close to his undercarriage as possible and pumped his wings with increasing velocity. After a few minutes he could see Ius's body clearly ahead of him. His friend was flying with clenched claws.

When Ius sensed Zor behind him, he screamed, "Let me be!"

Zor pushed himself to fly faster. When the moment was right, he dove underneath Ius's body and flew upside down so that Ius could hear him clearly.

"Come back," he pumped his wings, "my good," another pump, "faithful," another pump, "friend!"

Ius continued to fly as if he heard nothing. He looked straight ahead and flew harder and faster.

Zor had to turn on his belly to keep up with Ius. He changed his position and now flew above Ius, "It is over, you are safe!" Zor had to strain himself to keep up with Ius's unbelievable pace.

Ius looked up and saw Zor's familiar feathered face.

"I cannot do this," Ius said, his voice slow and full of exhaustion.

"You will not be alone."

"I do not have the strength," Ius said. "I am too weak."

"Ius!" Zor's voice boomed, "You are the strongest Dragon I know. Your courage will save our tribe. Come with me. Come back down to the mountain."

Ius looked at Zor, and his eyes glistened. There were no tears, but Zor could see his obvious pain. Ius felt feverish and tired, but he also felt the power of belief. Zor believed in him and that would be the strength to carry him through this difficult day. He followed Zor back to Mount Calyps.

When Zor and Ius returned, Marii and Menet began opening the heavy Dragon chest. On the outside two Dragon bones were set into a locking puzzle. Menet placed her claws upon the bones and closed her eyes. With five distinct moves, the bones unlocked and the chest opened.

Inside the chest lay seven silver necklaces. At the base of each necklace there lay a large amulet encasing a red stone.

Picking up one of the necklaces, Menet revealed, "These are for the children who will make the journey."

The necklaces were called Ochrets, old Dragon amulets of fidelity. Now that the journey would indeed happen, the Dragons felt they had to do everything in their power to protect the children who would be risking their lives.

Ochrets were forged for those who had established a sincere trust with Dragons. Many Dragons, who were prone to believing other tribes trustworthy, had been hurt by trickery and lies. Thus amulets were used when faithfulness could not be doubted. The foreign Dragons would need proof of fidelity residing in the children. The Ochrets would prove their conviction.

"Who shall wear these?" Menet asked the group.

"One must be for Lily," Zor quickly stated. "She will accompany the Dragons on this journey."

Tired and obstinate, Caduceus decided it was now time for him to speak, "She is not ready."

"Caduceus," Marii replied, "we will need her powers, and…"

"They are still developing," Caduceus interrupted coolly. "She has received neither her Necklace, nor her Name. I cannot promise she has full control over her ability. She might compromise this quest."

Zor walked over to Caduceus. "I believe she will earn her Necklace and Name on this trip," he said with confidence. "Think about our choices, Caduceus. We must have faith in her. She is Pohevol's chosen one."

Caduceus looked off into the distance and harrumphed.

Zor tapped a red claw on Caduceus's chest, "Just as we must have faith in you. You are going on this quest, are you not?" A Snake, who was wrapped around Caduceus's neck, hissed and flared her hood at Zor.

Caduceus whipped his head around and glared at Zor, "Of course I am! How could I risk this improbable journey to just anyone? How can these children accomplish anything without a Dragon who has seen the world, who appreciates the world, who respects all creatures who are different?"

Zor used his tail to touch Caduceus's shoulder, "I was only asking."

Menet pulled all of the necklaces out and handed them to Sophia. Sophia ducked her heads under each necklace, one by one, and stood up tall once they were in place.

Marii said, "Sophia must go, as she will be our mouths and ears to the Dragons with whom we have lost contact. She does not want this charge, but she is gracious and selfless in accepting our request. Those of you listening to me now have a choice—you may stay, or you may go."

The Draglings began to twitch with excitement. "No

little ones…Draglings must stay in Durga. We need seven Dragons of age to join Sophia. Those Dragons who would like to go, please step forward and claim a necklace," Marii raised her wings and flapped them in the thin mist.

Zor grabbed Ius's leg, and they both moved to take a necklace from Sophia. Caduceus was next. Anippe went forward and bowed to Sophia. She whispered into one of Sophia's ears, and when the seven heads bowed back, Anippe carefully slipped off a necklace. When Labrys stepped forward, Marii dropped her wings.

"No Labrys, you will soon be an elder. We need you here."

"Marii, I am going. I may be older, but I am the only one who can navigate the sea."

Marii replied, "This journey promises to be dangerous, and you are the holder of the sacred stones. Labrys, you are too precious to Durga…we cannot allow it."

Labrys lowered her head, and the gathering of Dragons grew restless. A Bush Dragon said, "Marii, I am studying under Labrys and have been through the testing already. I can hold the sacred stones if something were to happen."

"We cannot take the chance," Marii began.

"I will make sure she comes home safely," Zor brought a claw to his head and heart and then bowed to Marii.

"And I will make sure Zor keeps his word," Saja spoke suddenly.

"No!" Menet thundered. Her stripes of white fur bristled, and her heart began pounding so fast that the other Dragons clasped their chests thinking it was their own. "Saja, you must stay in Durga," Menet implored. "My daughter, I cannot allow both Labrys and you to leave our home in this time of fear!"

"Mother," Saja touched her own heart, "I mean only to use my spirit power from the safety of Durga. I have no intention of leaving now."

Menet let out a sigh of steam and relief. She then blinked in intimate recognition. Rarely did full-grown Dragons acknowledge their progeny. But sometimes the bonds of egg blood held fast and tested the discretion of a Dragon mother's love.

"No one must worry about me, and no one need watch over me. I am a Sea Dragon!" Labrys's curved teeth flashed. "Be assured, I can remember the waves and tides and storms as if I were swimming through them yesterday. I have strengths others have never witnessed. I have no intention of coming to harm."

Marii bowed to Labrys in supplication, "What will be, will be." She raised her head and continued, "We need two more Dragons. Who will complete this group?"

Guldrun and Lin both stepped forward, and both were covered in large clumps of mud.

"Oh no!" cried Labrys. Had they just left Lapis Lake? She wondered if they had even attended the Midsummer meeting. "Indeed not! They are crazy and foolish, far too attracted to mud. They must not go!"

"Oh Labrys," Guldrun moaned, "please don't ruin it for us!"

"We will be solid," Lin promised, "the group needs Mud Dragons!"

Menet offered, "Are there any other Dragons who

would like to go?" All of the Dragons looked around at each other. No one stepped forward, so Guldrun and Lin shivered with anticipation.

"See Labrys, we should go! Mud Dragons are sturdy and strong. We will do good things on this trip!"

Ius stared at the two young Mud Dragons with disbelief. Labrys blinked at Guldrun and tried to smile, "I shall try to have faith in you two. I shall try. Let us hope where we are going the mud lakes are few and far between."

Guldrun and Lin whooped and went to Sophia to claim the last two necklaces.

"Let us leave this sacred spot," Marii called out, as she lowered her wings and looked to the evening sky. The stars began to appear, one by one. "Let us go and meet the Humans," she said. "Night is here."

∽ 10 ∾

THE FINAL DECISION

Deep in the Durgan forest, in a large cropping of rocks, down a dark and dry hole, a Rat was busily packing a bag. He was looking around his home, grabbing a few dusty vials of liquid, shoving in glistening rocks, and tucking away cakes of toasted almond and hazelnut.

Muttering while he packed, he stopped every once in a while to sneeze. Dust filled the small hole and after every sneeze, which was a violent and loud event, he gathered himself and shook his head, as if to remember what he had set about to do.

"The quest!" he cried, and then he went back to the task of packing his bag. "They must allow me to go," he muttered. "I am small, I am crafty, I can mend anything." He kept talking to himself in a small and crackly voice.

His name was Mortoof, and he was the most adventurous Rat one could ever hope to meet. At least, that is what he hoped others would think. Unlike most

Rats, he did not feel connections or ties to any one place. Of course he appreciated a tidy and snug Rat hole or nest, but he grew wide-eyed and sometimes unpredictable when an adventure lay around the bend. He wanted to be unpredictable. He desired it. Many animals spoke of the Rat tribe with criticism bordering on contempt. Dirty, sneaky, toothy, pointy, ravenous with hunger and greed. So unlike the Mice, they would say. So big and awkward, not at all cute and sweet, they would say. These comments were said with such predictability, and it was this that disgusted him most of all. Not all Rats were alike…not all Mice were alike either! So Mortoof made it his work to convince everyone of this little-known fact.

Mortoof was a fine looking Rat. His furry body was brown with a white stripe down the center of his back, and he had a tiny purple wing on each of his front legs. He was fond of mornings, and always the first Rat to emerge into the Sunlight. He could predict that other Rats would sleep away the cool mornings, so he made sure to rise with the earliest hint of dawn. He preferred to eat ripe breeberries and spring corn, and he enjoyed tender asren shoots that grew on the edges of the forest. Unlike other Rodents, he made his temporary nests near Dragons, and one particular unpredictable Dragon was his favorite.

Mortoof lived near Ius's cave. While Ius slept, he spent many afternoons munching on corn nearby. Mortoof enjoyed the sound of Ius sleeping. The Dragon would snore heavily and on each puff of wind blown from a nostril the size of a small boulder, Mortoof would stretch out his wings and float on the exhalation. No one would expect a Rat to do this, he thought. It was thrilling.

Mortoof believed his life was meant for more than just scurrying from hole to hole, scrounging for scraps dropped by Dragons and Humans, procreating new Rats, and securing the warmest sleeping space. He knew from firsthand experience that the world was vast and full of mysterious happenings. He had been on many small adventures of course. He had rescued a Mouse from certain death in the Lazuli river, freed a Brown Bear who was trapped in a thicket of brambles, and crossed the Shiri Falls walking only on his front legs. But he desperately longed to see what it looked like beyond the Durgan forest. In his long, long life of two Suns, he had merely traveled to the edge of the forest. He never had any excuse to go further.

Now, he had his chance. If only he could convince the others of his courage.

Mortoof remembered the night before. While everyone was shocked with Pohevol's news, he shivered and quaked with anticipation. He was determined to go on the adventure with Pohevol and the other Dragons. It was his purpose. It was his destiny. He had much packing to do.

❦ ❧

A good mile away, a large brown Spider began disassembling her elaborate web. She started at the bottom, delicately untying the silken threads from the branches of a young elm tree. She gathered up the threads and whispered words into the growing bundle. She undid the two center threads and moved up to collect the loose top threads. She carefully wrapped the web into a large ball, and then secured it onto her back.

Adrianne was a Horned Silk Spider. She was one of the oldest Durgan Spiders, having seen 98 Suns, and she had birthed over 500,000 children. She was as big as a Cat, a little under 20 pounds, and her body and legs were green with triangular flecks of gold. She had four golden horns protruding from her abdomen, and she used these horns to spin elaborate webs. Unlike other Spiders who had only one set of spinnerets, Adrianne was born with two. She used her regular spinnerets to wrap Insects for food and to travel from tree to tree. But she saved her horned spinnerets for making homes and for healing the sick. Her mother had warned her about using these horns too carelessly. Once a Horned Silk Spider ran out of her special fluid, she would begin a rapid descent toward death.

Known throughout Durga, Adrianne was a venerated healer. Many animals, including Humans, came to her with their sick family members. If Adrianne felt the cure existed within her, she would wrap her special webs around the injured or sick individual. Most often, in a matter of minutes, the injury would fade or the illness would depart. Sometimes her cures would not work, as with Sefani's blindness, but she continued to try even with disappointing outcomes. She also was shy about using her webs, and only felt comfortable sharing her ability with animals who were just as shy as she. Too many times a boisterous Squirrel or loud-mouthed Jay would come begging for help. Adrianne would scurry up high into a tree and tuck herself away from the commotion below.

She would remain crouched in the tree and not move for ten or twenty minutes, silently willing the animal to leave her alone. Move away you loud beast, she would think. Find your own cure.

Disturbing dreams of the future troubled Adrianne, and during Pohevol's revelation at the meeting she recognized his images and descriptions. Adrianne's mother, before she died, had shared similar dreams with Adrianne. The same black smoke and perpetual imbalance that Pohevol spoke of came in her mother's dreams and now in her own. Adrianne noticed the trees were talking more with each new Sun, and their words were filled with a haunting premonition. The Great Tree was sharing truth with the forest tribes, and Adrianne knew she was fated to go along on this journey to lands far away. When the Dragons said they would think over Pohevol's plan of hiding, something moved inside of Adrianne, and she knew this plan to hide in the dark would protect the tribe of Dragons. She began preparing to leave Durga.

Night moved over the wet forest, and the Dragons flew down to the base of Mount Calyps. The afternoon storm left the air heavy and moist. One could taste sweet evergreen in the air. The Moon rose high into the sky, and its muted light spread across the tips of the trees and colored the mist a pale silver.

The Dragon tribe landed with powerful thuds, each moving to make room for the next descending Dragon. Zor and Ius flew together, swooping in and around each other, riding the other's wake and grabbing a tail to elicit a quick snarl. Labrys came next, using her large iridescent wings. Guldrun and Lin swooped in, still muttering with excitement. Anippe landed softly, lowering her thin head to the ground as balance. Caduceus's wings shook as he landed with three large Snakes coiled around his neck. Sophia was the last to arrive. Her heads were loose, and her numerous eyes revealed no gleam or sparkle.

The elder Dragons were forcing Sophia to go on this quest. She did not want to go, as she did not like to travel, and she hated to fly. Imagine coordinating seven different minds to one direction, one altitude, and one position of landing. Instead of discussing elaborate flying instructions, she simply preferred to walk everywhere she went. They are asking too much of me, she thought. I am not right for this quest.

Sophia wanted only to roll around on the ground and breathe in land smells. While it is true that Dragon nostrils were made for the rush of wind, the fast passing of scent and odor wafting inside delicate passages, Sophia's nostrils—all fourteen of them—shrieked with the high odors of Earth. The low odors, the soft grasses and streams, the wildflowers and mushrooms, these she could manage. She also coveted silence. With so many heads and ear openings and so much of her time spent translating, she sought silence with diligence.

The other Dragons respected her desire to stay close to Earth, as they understood it must be difficult to fly or talk, or do just about anything with seven different heads. Despite what others presumed, Sophia did not talk amongst herself often. Translating so many different tongues made her tired of animal voices, even Dragon words. When given the chance, she spent her free time moving quietly through the green fields at the foot of Mount Calyps, smelling flowers, rolling in dew, and nibbling sweet tulis berries. She preferred the silent language of plants.

But she also knew she had no choice but to go. Most Dragons of Durga had not seen other world Dragons for thousands of Suns. The forest was intoxicating and sheltering. Once one lived inside the tree canopy for two or three hundred Suns, the forest convinced the inhabitant there was no other possible place to feel as safe or happy. The forest was so vast a Dragon could fly for a full day at top speed and still be within its expanse. And of course there were always the rumors.

Rumors about distant lands where peace was not normal spread across Durga. The Human invaders were the first to confirm this story. But a few Dragons, the ones who had recently traveled, had witnessed strange lands where Dragons interacted with adult Humans. Going against the agreements of old, these Dragons continued to commune with Humans after the children came of age.

These Dragons and Humans made decisions together, ate together, and often fought against one another. Some had witnessed angry fights, where a long and brilliant metal stick would be pulled out and thrust angrily at a Dragon, only to be snapped in pieces. The huge Dragon would blow steam at the tiny Human and sometimes thump it on the head. The Human would scowl and slink away, only to bring back more Humans with more shiny metal sticks. The Dragon would snap all the sticks and snort fire. He would turn away with a huff, swinging his heavy tail around and leaving a cloud of dust to sting the Humans' eyes.

A few Durgan Dragons tried to commune with the strange Dragons who lived so closely with adult Humans, but language was always a barrier. They would spend hours rolling words around, hoping to find an ancient dialect held in common, but it was in vain. If the Dragons of Durga were to be successful, Sophia would have to come. How else could they convince a few of these Dragons to give up everything they knew and retreat into hiding?

⚜ ⚜

Darkness wrapped its arms around the forest, and so the Dragons built another fire. Labrys sung a soft melody to the first sparks and lulled the flames to grow. The light danced around the circle of Dragons, and the group murmured as bodies moved in closer to feel the spreading warmth.

Then the stomping began. Slowly a single beat resonated throughout the group. Boom. Boom. Boom. Then a double beat rose up, louder and harder than the first round. Boom boom. Boom boom. Boom boom. Dragon wings went up and down, while Dragon legs pounded the ground with forceful bursts.

Boom boom boom boom boom boom boom, the beats grew until the ground shook as if the drumming originated from the belly of the Earth.

The Dragons continued drumming with their feet for a long fifteen minutes before the Humans approached the mountain. The men and women wore dark cloaks with green sashes tied at the waist. The children wore the same cloaks but with white sashes. Every third Human carried a burning torch. The men, women, and children came in their separate clans—Neva led the women, Thorn led the men, and Sefani and Perjas led the children.

At the call of Zor, the Dragons abruptly stopped pounding the ground. They opened the circle to invite the Humans inside. A distant Owl hooted twice as the Humans walked into the circle.

"Where is Pohevol?" Zor asked Ius. Ius lowered his head and peered into the small Human group, searching for a large black Cat.

"Over there," Ius pointed one scaly claw to a dark image flying at the very end of the Human procession. Lily walked before him, carrying a brown satchel across her shoulder.

When everyone was finally inside the circle, the Dragons sealed the opening. The fire sent up red and orange flames, and shadows moved along the tiny circle of Humans and giant circle of Dragons.

Menet was the first to speak, "We accept this quest. The Dragon tribe will send eight Dragons to travel all four directions of the Earth."

"Which Dragons will go?" asked Neva.

"Those wearing the sacred amulets," Marii bowed to the seven Dragons with silver around their necks. "Sophia will go as well, as our translator," she looked to Sophia who responded by nodding one of her heads.

Marii added, "The Dragons are wearing necklaces forged by our ancient elders. These stones will protect the children who are chosen to accompany our sisters and brothers." She stood on her back legs and extended her wings, "Have your clans made their decisions?" she boomed into the darkness.

Neva raised her gnarled walking stick to Marii's large Dragon head, "We have chosen Lily."

"A wise and expected decision," Menet said. Steam snorted from many Dragon heads, as they nodded to each other in agreement.

Lily looked to the female clan, searching for her mother. They chose me, she thought. Did she choose me? With heat moving to her cheeks, she stepped forward and pushed her hair back, away from her face. Anippe removed her necklace and placed it over Lily's head. Lily closed her eyes as the heavy stone rested at the nape of her neck. She saw the slightest movement of fire dance in Anippe's brilliant Dragon eye, but then it was gone. It was just a reflection, she thought. But the memory of Dreamtime with Saja came rushing into her mind. Lily searched the circle of Dragons to find Saja. The Spirit Dragon was not there.

"Who else has been chosen?" Marii thundered.

"Marii," Sefani called out. Everyone stepped back to reveal the girl. "We choose Lily, Bridget, and Tomal."

Bridget stepped forward in her full regalia. Her chest jutting out and both hands on her hips, Bridget stood proud with bright ribbons woven into her two black braids. She wore blue pants of shed Snakeskin and an embroidered white shirt. Instead of a dark cloak like the other Humans, draped around her shoulders was a hand knit cape made with a hundred different hues of blue. One

Sun previous, Zor had taught Bridget how to knit a few Dragon stitches. As Zor only wove capes for Dragons, Bridget decided to knit capes for everyone else.

Ius took off his necklace and lowered it over Bridget's head. The tip of his strong blue head nudged her cheek, and then he carefully raised a claw to tap once on the amulet. Bridget held her arms up to Ius, and dropped her body into a deep bow. She then pulled two beautiful capes out of her bag and placed one around Lily and one around Tomal.

His dark red hair pulled back into one long braid, Tomal's face shone in the firelight. His small chest swelled as Guldrun moved close to place a necklace around his neck.

Before Marii could ask if the men had chosen other children, Caduceus stepped into the circle and took off his necklace. Holding it high into the night sky, he blew fire through the oval space, and then brought it back down. He motioned for some Humans to move aside, and then with sincere thoughtfulness he lowered the amulet around Sefani's neck. The stone immediately began to glow, pulsating a deep red.

The Dragons bowed to Sefani, as she brought her fingers to the necklace and turned her head in different directions, trying to sense those beings who were bending toward her. She bent her head to Perjas, and he whined and barked gently into her ear. After a few seconds, Perjas sniffed the amulet and let out a loud bark.

"Yes, I will go, "Sefani smiled, forming her hands together in a shape similar to that of the amulet. "And Perjas will come too."

Caduceus molded his claws into a similar shape. The Dragon draped in Snakes and the blind child lowered their heads to each other.

The other children started to speak in quick bursts:

"How can Sefani go? She's blind…"

"She is wise."

"But won't she be a burden?"

"It's because she can ride the Dragons, I bet."

"She can't go. This isn't fair!"

"If she can go, why can't I go?"

Sefani lowered her head to her chest. Her hands fell from the necklace to Perjas's back. Her face flushed and tears pooled in her lower lashes. Perjas leapt up on all four legs and began to growl. He arched his lips to reveal sharp Canine fangs. He began pacing in stealthy circles around Sefani, snarling and barking at the hurtful children and their mean words.

"Silence!" Caduceus growled. "You ignorant and inconsequential little whelps!" He turned to his own tribe, baffled and perplexed. "You choose to share Dreamtime with these irreverent creatures?"

Whipping his head back toward the children's clan and pointing one claw to Sefani, he bellowed, "This one child has more strength than twenty of you combined! She will add a perspective to this journey greater than anything any of your miniscule minds can imagine! To think my tribe bothers with the likes of you!" Caduceus's Snakes were arched around his neck, hissing and spitting as his words tumbled out in resounding blows, "Keep quiet young Humans and learn! Shut your inconsiderate mouths and open your puny brains!"

The children, wounded by his verbal tirade, hushed immediately. Caduceus was ornery, but he was a Dragon.

Caduceus fumed and crossed his front legs. Sefani raised her head up and wiped away the small patches of wetness on her cheeks.

Marii looked down at Sefani with compassion, "We agree with Caduceus. Sefani is a wise choice." She then turned to Thorn, "Have the men decided?"

Thorn looked around to catch the glances of other men before he spoke. He was hoping to glean their conviction and strength, "The men would like the Dragons to accept one more child."

Neva looked at Thorn and a smile began to spread across her lips. He felt her warmth fill his heart, as her smile grew larger and more sincere. Neva's smile filled him with courage.

"This child might say no, and he most certainly will fight, argue, and demand to be released. The men ask that Zun go on the quest."

A stunned silence fell over the gathering of Humans and Dragons. Lily turned to look at Pohevol and then back to Thorn, her great grandfather, in disbelief. Pohevol did not blink an eye or twitch a feather.

"You knew," Lily thought.

"Yes," Pohevol replied.

Breaking the hush, Caduceus, Zor, and Ius roared in unison, "Absolutely not!"

"Quiet, Dragon males!" Marii exclaimed. "This offering is most interesting and we accept!"

Now the Dragons turned and looked around at each other. What was going on? Allow Zun, the one who hates

Dragons, to go on the quest? He would jeopardize the plan. He could hurt other world Dragons. He would destroy everything.

"Learn closely what is feared, and the answer is revealed," Pohevol thought to Lily.

"How on Earth are we going to convince Zun to go with us?"

"Sophia," he thought, "she does not want to go either. Sophia will convince him to go."

Suddenly there was a whipping of wind overhead, and a brilliant winged body flashed over the circle. A huge brown Hawk soared above the group with his large black eye peering down at the Humans and Dragons below.

"Doren!" Zor called out.

The Hawk spoke in Dragon tongue and told Zor in numerous high-pitch shrieks, "Look to the woods, the Dogs and Wolves come to war!"

Zor's brow furrowed as the other Dragons turned around to see a moving mass inside the thick trees. The Moon shone on sleek furred bodies and hundreds of eyes glowed pale yellow. They heard barking, howling, and growling. Now the Dragons of Durga knew exactly what they had forgotten.

Zor pounded the ground with his back leg, "Good Earth, we forgot!"

The Dog and Wolf tribe had come for battle.

At the Midsummer meeting the two Canine tribes did not have their grievances heard. With all the talk of the future without Dragons, the two disparate tribes were neglected. Of all discordant tribes, the Dogs and Wolves needed to discuss problems rationally, calmly, with the aid of neutral moderators.

Now it was too late.

Hundreds of Wolves paced at the Southern end of the woods howling an endless chorus of discontent. To the North an equal number of Dogs snarled and barked at their furry cousins. Their voices echoed across the forest.

"Sophia," Menet called out, "can you do something? Can you help them at all?"

Sophia was already moving toward the grove of evergreen and oak, but she was full of apprehension. She knew both tribes were in a dangerous space. Animals who sat calmly on their haunches only one night ago might lunge at her necks tonight.

She heard the words muffled in the trees, so she stretched one head closer to the ground, to pick up the language.

"Traitors to the Canines, weak and spineless, you grovel at outstretched hands!" the Wolves snarled.

"Trapped in your old ways, unable to change, always suspicious of something you do not know!" the Dogs shot back.

"Stupid!" the Wolves shouted.

"Proud!" the Dogs barked.

"Slow!" the Wolves sneered.

"Arrogant!" the Dogs retorted.

"TAME!" the word pierced Dog hearts.

When the Wolves released this dreaded insult, the Dogs' lips pulled back and white fangs gleamed. Sophia felt the air in the grove contract, as if the trees were holding their breath. She braced herself for battle.

Why did these two tribes grow to dislike each other so

viciously? The elder Wolves spoke of a time long ago when a small pack of Wolves decided to leave the tribe.

Was it because of the gray pup lost in a snowdrift, the mother Wolf searching for his scent everywhere? When she found him, he was in the arms of a Human male. The man was scared and immediately put the Wolf pup down in the cold snow and stumbled backward.

The mother showed her fangs and growled at the Human, but the Human did not move. His eyes were motionless and reserved as he brought his fingers to his lips. The mother Wolf stared into his gentle eyes.

Or was it because of the broken Wolf? An elder Wolf chasing a spring fawn, tripped over a concealed tree root and broke his leg. Two Human females found him whimpering on the forest floor.

When they approached the wounded Wolf, he let out a deep growl that brought up the hairs on the women's arms. When the Wolf sniffed the thin fur and unique scent of both women, he let loose a howl that made the forest shiver. The women would not walk away, so he let them move closer to his broken body.

The women laid their hands upon the Wolf for two days. The Sun rose and set, rose and set, and the women did not move for food, drink, or rest. On the third rising of the Sun, the bone break had healed, and the Wolf never left their side.

Or was it the lost litter? A sick Wolf, a male Wolf the tribe had once wanted to banish—but foolishly did not—killed a mother of four pups. The tribe did not realize this horrific deed until two Suns later when a pack found four thin creatures who did not recognize the sign of the Wolf.

These four spoke of Humans as companions, and they spoke in high-pitched voices that smacked of trust and reverence. The Wolves urged these lost four to come back to the tribe, to learn the sign again, and to abandon the Humans. But the four did not come back. They raised their tails high, let the wind catch their scent, and ran off back into the woods.

Thousands of Suns later, there were two distinct tribes—the Wolves and the Dogs. Tradition had settled in and neither tribe had a clear memory over why the split was difficult for both. Some spoke of jealousy. The Dogs allowed Humans to touch them, to caress and handle their aches and pains. Some Wolves wanted this attention too, but if they admitted this desire, the other Wolves would mock and howl over their weakness.

Some Dogs spoke of regret. Being separate from the Wolf tribe, most Dogs had forgotten the Canine histories—the numerous stories, songs, dances of courtship, and the special ways to mark. Some whispered a dreaded and horrific idea late at night—Dogs were losing their sense of smell.

Every Midsummer, Dogs and Wolves came together to talk about hunting rules, water rights, mating rituals, and the Rites of Puppyhood. Puppy talk was most agitated. How should they raise Wolf and Dog pups? How could they stay fair and neutral about the differences between the pup cousins? How might they be both honest and respectful?

Missing a meeting was like missing a stream when one is parched and trembling with thirst. The Canines were panicked, filled with frustration and discontent. And now they readied themselves to do battle in Durga.

Before Sophia could intervene, the Wolves and Dogs started to fight. Lithe bodies ran into the center of the grove and met with a rush of fur, saliva, and teeth. Hackles raised and tails were erect. Two Canines, cousins almost identical by sight, locked eyes and assumed fighting positions. Growls rolled out of throats, teeth flashed, and then they sprang upon each other.

Numerous fights commenced, side by side, fur by fur. Wailing barks rose out of the middle of the fights. Twisting bodies arched and snapped and lunged for necks. Neither Wolf nor Dog would go down and admit defeat. The many Moons of pent up aggression were now released into the waiting, watching forest. A heat bubble formed around the mass of Canine anger and aggression, and Sophia knew she must do something immediately if lives were to be spared.

"The puppies!" all seven heads bellowed in Canine tongue. "Remember the puppies!" She then closed her eyes and willed Saja to come to her aid. In a few seconds, a shield of mist raised between the two groups of fighting Canines, separating the Wolves from the Dogs. Saja's serpentine spirit body flew into the clearing and hovered above the fog. Her lightning horn was pointed and alert.

At the edge of the wall of mist, the Dogs and Wolves stepped back and pricked their ears. Where had their enemies gone? Their coats were matted and dirty, clumps of fur fell to the forest floor, and many Dogs and Wolves had blood staining their necks. Despite all of the anger and frustration, both Canine tribes were ready to sacrifice anything for the safety of their pups.

The panting, sore bodies realized Dragon magic was at work when they saw Saja slinking through the trees above them. They lowered themselves to their haunches and watched as Saja swept back into the clearing and used her horn to illuminate the floating mist. Images slowly began to form in the droplets of water. The sound of panting, coughing, and retching filled the night air.

One of Sophia's heads cried out, "Continue on this destructive path, and you shall find only pain and suffering!"

The mist showed a pack of Wolf puppies howling over the bloody body of their mother. Small tongues licked her wounds, but the mother was stiff and lifeless. The Wolves outside of the fog closed their eyes, and a few solitary howls pierced the air. Then the mist shifted and revealed a heap of Dog bodies, bones broken in horrible ways, necks limp, and fur torn away from skin. Dog puppies curled into small balls and shivered near the lifeless forms. The Dogs in the grove, watching the images in the mist, now lowered their heads and tucked tails between nervous legs.

"Is this what you want?" Sophia roared.

"No," the Wolf and Dog tribe uttered this simple reply, but they did it together, in one tongue, as one tribe.

"Then fight against greater evils now, and agree to a new meeting," Sophia said. "There is no need to wait for next Midsummer. Preserve your linked tribes with communion and discussion. Do not allow violence to make final decisions you will regret the next day," Sophia raised her head and moved away from the mist.

An elder Wolf stepped forward. Peering through the mist, searching for a face on the other side, she stepped through the fog. As soon as she crossed through the wall of thin water, Saja sent a bolt of energy from her horn to the mist and the wall crackled, popped, and disappeared.

The elder Wolf walked up to a Dog who was licking a wound on his front leg. The Wolf stood before the Dog, who immediately snarled. But instead of raising her lips in response, the elder Wolf lowered her head and cautiously, never removing her eyes from his, began to lick the Dog's wound. The Dog looked around at the other Canines, his eyes asking the others how he should respond. He looked down at the Wolf, watched her in this act of supplication, and then licked the top of her head. They nuzzled necks and licked the sides of their mouths.

The Dogs sent up a howl of retreat, and the Wolves joined in the howl. The Durgan forest throbbed with Canine voice, and Sophia retreated to meet the waiting Dragons. We have avoided one catastrophe, she thought. But we are about to thrust ourselves into the midst of many others.

❧ II ❧

LEAVING DURGA

At the base of Mount Calyps the Dragons and Humans began making preparations to leave Durga. Pohevol asked a pack of Mountain Lions to inform the carnivores of the plan to leave the following morning. He asked a group of Deer to inform the herbivores. Midsummer was officially over, and he knew better than to send a Cat to a Rabbit with important news. Rabbit hearts would not respond well. The Dragons wanted to leave at first light, and everyone knew Dragons would not suffer anyone being late for an agreed upon date.

Lily wandered around the group looking for her mother and father. Would they be worried about her leaving, or would they be proud? She knew Caduceus would have warned the Dragons about her Shifting limitations, but he was not aware she had accomplished the Raven Shift. What would become her Shifting Name? What would the Necklace look like? She had to remember patience and humility. She had to prove to Caduceus she desired wisdom, not a reward.

"If you could share any advice with me," Sophia's words caught Lily off guard, "I would appreciate the attempt." Lily turned around and found Sophia's large heads looking in all four directions, but one peered down directly over her.

"About Zun?" Lily asked.

"Yes," said Sophia. "It seems there are two creatures who would rather stay at home, by themselves, but our tribes will not allow it."

"He won't go," Lily said. "I can't give you any advice. He will blister at the idea of traveling in a Dragon's basket. He'll never set foot inside one."

"Then I must use my own brains," Sophia replied. Sophia slipped into the forest, and Lily crossed her fingers, hoping Sophia would fail. Although she cared for Zun and had faith that he would one day learn the truth about Dragons, she feared this journey would only engender more hate inside his heart.

Lily heard a rustling in a pile of dry leaves to her right. She knelt down to look closely. A rather large Rat was dragging a bag over broken sticks and around a pile of stones. He looked up at Lily and signaled to her to come closer. Lily smiled and sat down cross-legged. Curiously enough, the Rat took out a piece of pressed paper and a tiny stick of charcoal. He began writing. When he finished, he scampered up her leg and into her lap. He thrust the piece of paper into her hands. It read: Good evening! Name's Mortoof. Here to join quest!

Lily was astonished. A Rat who could write in Human

tongue? He handed her a blank piece of paper and offered up the stick. Lily stared at the offering and wondered how to respond. Mortoof tapped the paper and motioned for her to write something. She wrote: Pleased to meet you, Mortoof. Name's Lily. Ask Pohevol.

The Rat read her words with a grave look on his face. As his eyes looked over her handwriting, his snout twitched. He turned the piece of paper over and wrote: Excellent advice. Thank you!

After he showed his new writing to Lily, he took the paper back and placed it and the charcoal back in his bag. With a miniature huff, he slung the sack over his shoulder. He then headed toward the smell of Cat. His long tail dusted the forest floor with resolve.

How brave, thought Lily. Pohevol doesn't prefer Rat for dinner, but he's still a Feline. How any Rodent could simply walk right up to a Forest Cat was beyond Lily. She watched as Mortoof approached Pohevol.

"Good luck," Lily said aloud.

"You will need more than luck," her mother's voice came from the darkness.

Lily first felt fear and then curiously enough, shame, as she saw her mother approach her. Ever since Pohevol's news, Lily had felt distant from her parents. She looked down at the ground and instinctively rubbed the four scarred puncture marks on the back of her neck.

"Mama," she said with lowered eyes, "I have to go."

"Your father and I would like to talk to you about this decision." She saw Lily open her mouth to speak, "Now wait," she interrupted Lily. "Before you say anything, you must hear me," she took her daughter's hands in her own and kissed the palms.

"You are twelve Suns old, and you are a Shifter. I know this, your father knows this, and we understand this ability can help our tribe and the Dragon tribe. But you are still a child," her mother stressed this last word. "You haven't even gone through the Moon rites yet."

"But I will be with Pohevol and Zor," Lily protested. "And Anippe and Labrys," Lily tempered her voice to a more reserved and respectful tone. "I will be safe with them, and we will not be gone long."

"Pohevol said it could take at least two full Moons," her mother replied.

"He doesn't want me to go?" Lily felt dejection spread across her chest.

"No, he wants you to go. He just wanted to prepare us for your absence."

So there's hope, Lily thought. Her heart leapt.

"Lily, we are prepared for your leaving," her mother looked deeply into Lily's eyes and waited for recognition. "We just want to sit down with you and talk about it."

Lily realized her parents would not hold her back. They just wanted to know where her heart and mind was. Was she scared, nervous, excited, or worried? Lily reached out for her mother and buried her face in her warm body. Her mother's smell sent small spasms down into her heart. She hoped she would make her mother and father proud.

※ ※

Sophia walked through the forest slowly, taking in the various smells and sounds. When she approached

Zun's cave, she lowered herself to the ground and slid one head to the opening of rock. She heard a dull, persistent scraping noise coming from inside. Carefully she stretched her head closer and closer to peek into the cave. She saw Zun sitting on the ground by the light of a candle, forging a knife out of two sharp rocks.

She wondered about her duty. Her tribe wanted this wayward boy to accompany them on the quest. This angry boy, this stone-faced, hard, scarred boy was desired on this journey. None of her heads could truly comprehend.

"Why do you hate us?" Sophia's stretched head spoke into the cave.

"Mother, help!" Zun jumped to his feet and crouched in the corner of his cave. His heart pounding, he waved his crude knife in front of his body and peered out into the darkness. Because of the candle, Zun could not see clearly. Sophia blew out the fire and watched as his eyes slowly adjusted. When Zun saw Sophia's long sleek head peering at him, he let out a sigh of relief.

"Why are you relieved?" Sophia asked. "Am I not a Dragon?"

"You're like Anippe," Zun worked to breathe normally, "You have feelings."

"And Zor and Ius, they do not feel?"

"No, they're cold-blooded, ruthless, and…" Zun stopped abruptly.

Sophia's second head looked into the cave and said, "I am cold-blooded."

Zun looked at both heads and shivered. Two separate Dragon heads with four eyes blinking at him. She could kill him right now. No one would know. She could eat him, she could take him to the river and drown him—no one would know. No one would care.

"I can't explain it," he focused on the first head that spoke to him. "I don't hate you…" he paused. "But I hate the others."

"I think you hate male Dragons," she said.

Zun looked at Sophia and furrowed his eyebrows. He allowed his eyes to travel over her long necks and her piercing Dragon eyes. Though they were gigantic animals covered in thick muscles and scales, Sophia and Anippe seemed benign and gentle. Zun didn't believe they would hurt him. He knew it made no sense, but he tried to explain.

"You care for the Draglings," he stammered, "the other ones are too quick to breathe fire."

"We breathe fire just as often as the males," Sophia replied, "and Dragon males nurture and protect Draglings alongside females." She blinked her two sets of eyes and moved closer to him, "Why must you be stubborn? Why must you hate that which you do not understand?"

Zun looked at Sophia's body in the darkness. Her two heads were brown with deep ridges along the sides. Her eyes looked like polished stones, and her mouths seemed old—but also known—like forgotten memories.

She holds a blind allegiance to her tribe, Zun thought. At least he knew that enemies resided within one's own group. The men who killed his parents were Human, so he would never believe in absolutes. He would never express unconditional fidelity to anyone. The possibility of deception always lurked in the shadows.

"I understand pain, and I understand the failure to

act," Zun said. "I understand friendship, and I understand selfishness."

"No my child," Sophia said. "You might understand what it means to be selfish, but you do not understand true friendship. Perhaps one day you will." She raised both heads and said with authority, "Despite all of this, the Dragons and Humans ask that you go on this journey."

Zun looked at the cave floor, as if he had not heard her request. He was lost in his own mind, seeing images of fire and destructive Dragons. Loneliness and fear spread across his chest, heart, and found a secure space in his gut.

"What did you say last?" his eyes looked back to her faces. He could have sworn she said something about Dragons wanting him to go on the quest.

Sophia said softly, "You must come with us."

"You cannot be telling the truth," Zun's voice was filled with astonishment.

"I, myself, do not want to accompany this group," Sophia said. "I hate flying, and I fear what is to come on this journey, but I am going because those whom I love have asked me to go."

Zun shook his head and brought the back of his fingers to his mouth, "What did Lily say?"

"She was shocked and certain you would never agree."

"Then tell everyone I accept."

It was Sophia's turn to look bewildered. Her two heads shot within inches from Zun's face. Startled, he backed into the cool cave wall. Her eyes opened wide, and he saw the pupils grow large revealing something strange inside. Zun squinted to see the image slowly forming in the black portal when suddenly she snapped her eyelids shut and pulled back her heads.

"As you wish," she whispered and quickly pulled her heads out of the cave. He heard her body moving through the trees and away from him. Suddenly her long tail slithered into the cave's entrance. It dropped something onto the stone floor, and then the Dragon tail was gone. He saw a faint sparkle and a flash of movement. Zun crawled to the object and warily reached out to touch it. It was a silver necklace encasing a red stone. The amulet lay cold and hard on the cave floor.

He stood up, lit a few candles, and searched for a cloth with which to pick up the necklace. He feared touching it with his bare skin. Zun peered closely at its intricate metal work. Bringing the amulet closer to the light of a flickering candle, he saw faint triangles, spirals, and Dragon eggs carved into the silver surrounding the red stone. When he looked again, the spirals started to move. Frightened, Zun used the cloth to smother the jewel.

But something stopped him, and he opened the cloth to look again. He brought his eye closer to the necklace and looked deeper into the red stone. In a flash, in a blink, in a skipped heartbeat, in a moment of time that cannot be quantified, he saw the face of his mother. Zun blinked and the image disappeared. He dropped the necklace to the floor and brought both hands, trembling, to his heart.

� ɞ

Lin and Guldrun could not be contained. They bounded through Durga, racing each other, tripping over their tails, scrambling to reach their home before they missed anything. The egg brothers were glowing so brightly the nearby sleeping Birds raised their wings to cover their eyes. One Sparrow trilled, "Turn it down! It's nighttime!" but since Sophia was nowhere near, the brothers just beamed at the sweet chirping sound and glowed even brighter.

"Think of the new mud, Guldrun," Lin gasped.

"New mud, thick mud, thin mud, OH MUD!" Guldrun roared.

They flew up through the trees, breaking branches and sending a few Squirrel nests crashing to the ground. Before they could hear the screaming Squirrels chastise them for their inconsiderate flying, they burst through the canopy and flew in circles, grabbing hold of each other and spinning even higher into the sky. The Moonlight landed on their bodies and made the shadows look like waves across the forest below. Lin flew under Guldrun's belly and attached himself like a baby Opossum, "What should we bring?" he asked his brother who was now panting because of the extra weight.

With a serious and stern expression, Guldrun replied, "Mud."

"But we will have all the new mud!" Lin exclaimed.

"But what if when we travel to Iceloch and the Sands of Ochre, what if there is no mud?" Guldrun asked. "The land of ice will freeze all mud, and the land of sand won't have enough water to form mud."

Lin shivered under Guldrun and suddenly let go, falling to Earth like a rock. He then swooped up and flew beside Guldrun, "No mud? We must bring mud!"

Guldrun nodded his head, "And soil fruit."

"Oh, yes," Lin murmured.

"And mud," Guldrun said.

"And our marbles."

"And mud," reminded Guldrun.

"And a drum," Lin offered.

"And more mud."

"Mud, mud, mud!" Lin shrieked.

The egg brothers flew faster when they saw the tops of the trees that signaled their home. At the edge of a small marshland in the middle of Durga they had made their home. Fashioned out of dried mud and long grasses, Guldrun and Lin had constructed a Dragon lair for the two of them. Inside the mud hut they assembled two sleeping platforms decorated with mud collected from all over the forest. In the center of the hut, there was a raised well with a gold water dipper hanging from a hook. Whenever guests wanted to see the full beauty of the various mud piles, they need only dip up some water and pour it over the mounds. The true color of mud would slowly emerge, and the Dragons would gasp, sigh, and sometimes roll on the ground next to the piles in bliss. Sleep would overtake them, and one could hear soft moans coming from pleasant faces streaked with traces of drying mud.

Guldrun and Lin now approached their home with anticipation. They landed with a thud and rolled their heads in some nearby pink mud. For almost an hour they lost themselves in rolling, breathing, and digging their claws into the thick and wet mud. Then Guldrun seemed to snap to attention, "Bags!" he screamed. "We must get ready!"

"I shall find bags!" Lin screeched.

While Lin looked, Guldrun collected their marbles and picked the most suitable drum for travel. Lin brought in two sturdy bags and sat them in front of Guldrun. He had a look of worry spreading over his Dragon face, "Which mud should we bring?"

"We're going to need another bag." Guldrun replied. "Two is not enough."

"Ius isn't going to be happy," Lin's shoulders shook. "You know he thinks we are too dependent on mud."

Guldrun's shoulders began to shake as well, "But he doesn't have to know. You see, we'll just bring the bags and say something like, 'Well, all ready!' and then throw them in the basket, and we'll be off. He won't look, will he?"

"I don't know," Lin's eyebrows furrowed, as he looked around at all of their mud mounds.

"We won't bring three bags then. We'll just bring one, and we'll carefully fill it with different kinds of mud."

Lin thumped his tail, "Yes! And we'll put a drum at the top, and everything will be fine!"

"Yes!" Guldrun began thumping his tail, and the matter was settled.

Guldrun and Lin spent most of the night deciding which mud to take and how much. Raccoons jumped up to the lair's windows sneaking looks inside, and Deer peered in through the cracks, snorting at the hunched-over Dragon bodies that were scooping, smelling, and lovingly packing away the many piles of mud.

༄ ༅

Anippe lowered her golden brown body into the Lazuli River and floated on her back. The Moonlight brushed her scales, and the scent of wet evergreen filled the air. She heard the call of Owl and the wings of Bat swooping above her. Anippe felt the moment had come. Ius and Zor knew a secret kept hidden from the Dragon tribe. Now they would embark upon a quest that might reveal this secret. As she lay musing over the future, a small Bat alighted upon her belly. He preened his fur, and then crept near her snout. Anippe lowered her eyelashes at him and blew a ribbon of steam from her nostrils. He closed his eyes and allowed the steam to bathe him in warm vapor. A tiny Bat smile spread across his mouth, as he let out a sigh of pleasure. He lowered his head and rubbed it against her soft belly. Afterward, with a high-pitch squeal, he took off in search of evening Insects.

"Floating instead of packing?" a deep voice crawled across the water.

Anippe raised her head and saw Zor's massive red body standing on the edge of the river. He was extending his wings, testing each one, pointing it straight out before allowing it to settle against his back. His basket sat beside him, and next to the basket sat a silver bag.

"It will be hard to leave this river," Anippe said.

"We will not be gone long."

"What if the Dragons refuse to hide?" Anippe felt small Fish coming up to catch water Insects who were hovering near her body.

"We will convince them," Zor answered. "Do not worry."

"I fear your steadfast confidence will waver before this journey is done," Anippe sighed.

Zor released his wings and flew up, hovering above his basket. Dragon baskets were used to carry heavy objects that might interfere with long-distance flying. As they must carry Humans, other animals, and provisions, baskets all over the forest were being unpacked, cleaned, repaired, and decorated with ribbons, flowers, and plant stems. Zor picked up his basket and flew above Anippe, flapping his wings in slow forceful strokes. Swells began to form on the river. The drone of his beating wings punctuated the darkness.

"It is not a matter of confidence, Anippe," said Zor. "We must succeed, as there is no other choice." Zor then raised himself higher into the darkness and flew away.

Anippe lifted herself from the turbulent waters and blew warm air around her body. She moved along the water's edge until she found her cave entrance. She had fashioned a sleeping alcove right by the opening of the cave. When it rained, she could hear the slight trickle or steady onslaught. She loved the smell of rain, the heady perfume of plants drinking, and the sound of water upon water. River Dragons laid their eggs underwater surrounded by brilliant gems, jewels, and gold. And so for the five Suns where Anippe lay inside her egg gathering strength, speed, and wisdom from the precious stones and metals, she listened to the continuous rush of swift and steadfast river currents.

As she stepped inside her cave, she knew she must bring soil fruit, her cooking pot, a sack of medicinal herbs, and her rain cloak. This cloak, a gift from Zor, was designed to attract rain. It was silver and blue and had sapphires sewn at the base and around the neck. She then picked up three glass flasks. One was filled with a dull yellow liquid. Another held a thick black liquid that moved slowly when jostled. The third flask was empty. She carefully wrapped the tip of her tail around it and lowered her tail into the Lazuli. She gathered the river water and brought the flask back inside the cave. Anippe stoppered the flask and tucked all three bottles into a small sack, which she then placed inside a larger sack.

She layered many cloths and blankets upon the small sack, placed her pots in next, then the herbs, and finally the bag of soil fruit. This last bag was bulging, so she took out a piece of fruit and ate it.

Anippe looked around her cave and used her tail to stroke every corner and crevice. It lingered upon her sleeping alcove and the delicate blankets that would lie untouched for many days, perhaps many Moons. She would take other coverings, of course, but she would leave her most treasured sleeping blanket here. Her heart pounded, as she remembered why they were leaving. A surge of energy excited her blood, and she tied up her sack, attached it to her back, and went out into the approaching dawn.

∽ ∾

The agreed upon meeting spot was Alder Ring. No predatory behavior was allowed in Alder Ring, and no fighting. As the night slowly faded away, the trees began to stir with the song of morning. A chorus of Bird song rose out of the canopy. Layer upon layer of Chickadee, Mourning Dove, Woodpecker, and Hummingbird filled the soft air. Wings were stretched, the first quick swoops were made from close branches, and feathers were preened.

As the Sun spilled into the Durgan forest, the children arrived. Lily came alone, dressed in comfortable pants, a short tunic, and purple boots made from a Rainbow Snake offering. She carried on her back a pack stuffed with clothing, her journal, Pohevol's whisker caught in amber, and one of her mother's tapestries. She chose the small one of three Dragons sleeping around a child. On her neck she wore two necklaces—the Ochret and her father's silver amulet.

The talk with her parents had gone better than expected. They had asked her to send letters home as the Hawks had agreed to send three of their strongest to accompany the group. They had also asked Ius to physically bring the children home if it became too dangerous.

"But, that'll make us look weak!" Lily had exclaimed.

"He agreed immediately to our request," her mother replied with raised eyebrows.

Lily crossed her arms, looked to her father, and then looked back at her mother. She slowly nodded her head, "If that is your request, I must honor it." She grabbed her mother's hand, "But we won't be in danger. The Dragons will protect us—you needn't worry. And Pohevol will be there."

"Yes, Pohevol," her mother paused, raising her hand up to feel the back of Lily's neck. The raised puncture wound scars were still there. "But he prefers a solitary existence. I wonder how this trip will affect his need for seclusion."

While most Forest Cats desired the presence of other Cats, to lean into, sleep against, and groom occasionally, Pohevol craved privacy. He tolerated the proximity of others, but it was a test of his endurance. If one found him sleeping under a bush while sheltering from the midday heat, with four Cats or kittens sprawled around him, their feet, whiskers, and legs covering his eyes, belly, and tail, it was not his idea of pleasure. He could tolerate only so much of this intimacy.

In fact sometimes in the middle of a sleeping session, when he had many heads leaning on him and a few legs draped across his torso, he would spring up grumpily and lope off to another patch of comfortable shade. He would collapse grumbling, and stare at the bewildered group he had just left behind. As his eyes would slowly close, the other Cats would try to situate themselves into a comfortable pile again, but would eventually give up because the one who had pulled them all so close had broken the spell. Because his close proximity was precious and rare, whenever Pohevol graced the others with his touch, a strong purring could be heard a Dragon's length away.

Lily reassured her mother that Pohevol would rise to the occasion and suffer the close proximity of so many animals for this important cause.

"And Lily," her father added, "you must listen to Caduceus. We know you are close to earning your Name and Necklace, but you still must pass his test."

Lily nodded, "I know, father. I will remain humble."

"Please don't do anything dangerous," her mother added. "Don't Shift when you are nervous."

Lily's face grew warm, and she quickly looked away. She had not told them about the incident by Saja's cave. If they had known how close she had come to death, they would never let her go on this journey.

She kissed them both, ran to her room to pack her sack, and came back to give them each a long hug. They then hugged as a trinity. They often did this when saying goodbye for extended periods of time. They hugged as three, each kissing the one to the right and then left. Lily closed her eyes and breathed in their scents.

∽ ∾

The other children and Dragons entered Alder Ring. Sophia came without a basket. Considering her aversion to flying, the other Dragons agreed she need not carry any cumbersome object. Instead she clutched a bunch of wildflowers. When Labrys came, Sophia planned to ask her to carry the flowers in her basket.

Zor and Ius arrived carrying separate baskets, sacks, and back satchels. Ius dropped his bag to the ground from fifty feet in the air, and landed with a loud boom next to it. His landing was unsatisfactory, so muttering to himself, he pulled out a file and went to work sharpening his claws.

To the West of Alder Ring came Mortoof. He scurried into the clearing wearing his pack, whispering to himself in a rough, yet squeaky voice, "Clear the trip with Dragons. Clear the trip with Dragons." He stopped and brought a paw to his forehead. "Logical. Makes sense. Of course I shall do it." He continued to scurry, but then halted and paled when he saw Zor and Ius standing like mountains in the distance. Pohevol, by way of Sophia's translating, said that Mortoof could go if the Dragons agreed—small bodies were always useful. What a wise Cat, Mortoof thought, very unpredictable. I like him. Yes! No one would expect a Rat to like a Cat!

He smiled to himself and continued scampering and muttering, "Find Sophia. Introduce myself to Ius. Display my abilities. Beg for acceptance," Mortoof suddenly stopped again. "But how is that unpredictable? Everyone would expect a Rat to follow the rules and be scared. To scurry when ordered. No!"

A sparkle began to form in his eye, "I shall not clear the trip with Dragons. I shall surprise them. Yes! That is what I will do!" He quickly slid behind the trees and approached the clearing stealthily. Crouching behind rocks and in piles of leaves, he ran to the Dragon baskets and dove headfirst into the first open bag he saw.

Mortoof landed in a pile of fabric and thread. Zor's bag, he thought. He nosed his way around the bag and felt the cool slipperiness of golden thread, linen cloths, and silver Dragon yarn. He rolled around in the softness and contemplated taking a nap.

"No!" he quickly muttered. "They will expect that of a Rat. Sneaking into a bag and falling asleep before the adventure even begins. How predictable!" Mortoof climbed around the bag searching for more interesting items. He found a bag of soil fruit, a small satchel of stones and gems, three completed cloaks, and a book with an elaborate metal lock on the outside. Mortoof tried to pry the lock open, but it would not budge.

As the Sun rose along the edge of the forest, Zor looked to his bag and saw a shudder of movement inside. He heard a slight rustle and a squeaky voice. He walked over, opened the bag, and looked inside. Mortoof dove under a cloak and held his breath. Through tiny holes in the fabric Mortoof could see Zor's giant eye peering in at him. A stowaway, Zor mused to himself. How interesting. Zor's eye blinked once, twice, and then went away. Mortoof was so relieved he immediately fell asleep.

Bridget arrived with her father, and Tomal came with his extended family surrounding him. Bridget's father kissed her and held her tight. He whispered something in her ear that brought tears to her eyes. She nodded her head and told him to go. He slowly walked away, only turning back once to look at his young daughter. Bridget's aunt refused to come to the clearing, as it was too painful for her. She had packed Bridget a full satchel of food and medicine, but she would not say goodbye in front of everyone.

Tomal's entire clan was present at the clearing. He had four brothers and three sisters, seven aunts and five uncles, all of his grandparents and even his great grandparents at Alder Ring. His dark red hair was pulled back into multiple braids, and each lock held a slender ribbon or tiny charm gifted to him from a family member. They hugged him many times and nodded at the other Humans and Dragons. Their pride was contagious, and soon Alder Ring was filled with a sense of urgency.

Anippe, Caduceus, and Labrys arrived in a flurry of

wings, baskets, and wind. Labrys had decorated hers with thousands of sparkling gems and stones. Anippe wove ribbons in multiple shades of blue throughout her basket, and Caduceus came with his decorated with the sign of the Shift. Inside his basket sat Sefani and Perjas. Around his neck were two glistening Tree Snakes.

All Dragons except Guldrun and Lin were ready and waiting.

Zor nodded to Sophia, who then raised one head above the Dragons and another above the Humans, "Where is Zun?" she asked.

Lily looked around at the group of Humans and could not see any shape that looked like him.

From a nearby hill Zun sat watching the scene unfold before him. All children were present. All Dragons, except the young brothers, were present. Where were the Hawks? Where was Pohevol? Why weren't all the Durgans present? This is wrong, he thought. Look at all of them wearing those necklaces, trembling with pride. I can't be a part of this.

As soon as he allowed the thought to enter his mind, he felt movement behind him. Adrianne, the green Horned Spider, crawled near him and used one leg to tap his back. Zun jumped and let out a small cry before he recognized Adrianne. She waited patiently for him to calm his racing heartbeat. This often happened to her. She did not understand why Humans were so jumpy around her kind. Spiders did not hunt Humans. Sometimes Spiders would attack, but only when Humans went looking or stepping into dark places they should not see or go. Sometimes smaller Spiders would bite, but these were only small nips, and only because Mosquitoes would brag and carry on about how sweet Human blood tasted. Spiders never drank too much Human blood.

When Zun finally calmed himself, Adrianne walked in front of his sitting form and undid her web. She carefully laid it out before him. She placed one furry leg on his left hand and then touched the center of her web. As if she had asked him plainly, Zun lifted his hand and placed it in the middle of her web. He trembled slightly, but kept reminding himself that Adrianne was a healer and a respected member of Durga. Adrianne crawled over and around his hand and the web as if she were constructing a shelter. She spun more web and tied and untied it until it was in the shape of a jagged mountain.

Zun felt his hand become warm and suddenly knew he would find answers if he journeyed on this trip. Willing the silk to speak, Adrianne focused all eight eyes upon his hand resting in her web.

"You must go," the web spoke to Zun.

Without hesitation, Zun nodded his head. Adrianne quickly undid all of the ties, knots, and loops. She packed her web away and placed it onto her back. She crept down the hill and entered the clearing. Zun followed the large green Spider, tracing her exact steps.

Incredulous, Zor and Ius watched as the Horned Spider and Zun came walking into Alder Ring.

"Interesting," Zor whispered to Ius. "The little whelp does not fear her."

"He is shaking," Ius replied, "look at his bag."

Zor looked, and indeed where his hand met the satchel, one could see trembling.

A commotion broke out behind the group, and everyone turned to the noise. Guldrun and Lin were attempting to fly through the trees while carrying one basket between the two of them. Tree branches crashed to the forest floor, as the brothers jostled and fought to navigate the shared flight. Inside the basket stood Pohevol, looking annoyed. His wings were splayed out for balance, and his front claws clutched the edge of the basket. Mud covered his white paws and when they finally landed, he leapt out of the basket and immediately began cleaning his feet.

"Sorry to be late!" Lin cried out.

Sophia moved one head over the egg brothers, one over Pohevol, and another over the Humans.

"Labrys," Guldrun began, "we're really sorry!"

Labrys lowered her eyes at them and shook her head.

"We had to give Pohevol a ride," Guldrun said. "He's just a Forest Cat, and we all know he can't fly forever, so we had to prove to him that we could carry him."

"To give him a rest," Lin added.

"To give him a rest," Guldrun repeated.

Pohevol pulled back his ears in frustration and continued to clean himself.

"But the basket was too heavy," Lin said, looking at all of the Dragons, "so I wanted to carry him because I'm stronger,"

Guldrun interrupted, "But really I'm stronger, so I wanted to carry him, but then Lin wouldn't let me, so we both had to carry him, and now we're here," he gasped for a breath of air, "and we're really sorry."

Everyone looked at Pohevol, who was now clean after

the long explanation. "And now we are here," he agreed.

☙ 12 ❧

FLYING NORTH

Pohevol addressed the gathering of animals ready to embark upon the journey, "We will begin in Iceloch."

"Ice Dragons are notoriously cranky," Zor interjected. "Perhaps we should save them for last."

"I agree," Ius added, "we should save our energy."

"You might be right," Pohevol replied, "but if we can convince the Ice Dragons, we will have a better chance convincing the others."

"We should listen to Pohevol," Anippe said. "The Sand and Sea Dragons will be impressed if we have the Ice Dragons' commitment."

Zor and Ius exchanged glances. Would Pohevol have the ultimate power on this trip? They both respected Pohevol and considered him to be as close to a Dragon elder as any non-Dragon could be, but would this journey have consensus or a leader?

Ius asked, "What about the children? Can they manage

the sudden drop in temperature? It will be far below freezing."

Pohevol looked to Caduceus for support. The cranky Dragon snorted and tapped his claws on his belly, "If the Human children cannot withstand the challenges of Iceloch, it is better to know at the beginning. I say we travel North."

The Dragons agreed, and Caduceus whispered something to one of the Snakes wrapped around his neck. The Hawks began stretching their wings, and Anippe did a final check on each Dragon basket. These baskets were normally for carrying fruit, drums, and jewels. If one snapped carrying those items, it would not be devastating. Now Anippe felt deep concern about their new cargo. Lily and Zun would travel in one basket, while Bridget and Tomal would fly in the other. The Dragons would share carrying the children, Perjas, and Adrianne. Pohevol would ride in a basket only when he needed to rest. The only Human to ride on the back of a Dragon would be Sefani.

The children climbed in the baskets, and Caduceus helped Sefani straddle Zor. Perjas would ride with Lily and Zun under Ius. Guldrun and Lin would take turns carrying Adrianne, Bridget, and Tomal. Everyone seemed ready to go. The time to leave Durga had come.

"Goodbye and goodspeed!" the adult Durgans called out. Tears appeared in the corners of eyes, and hands outstretched as Dragon wings began to beat. With a rush of wind and sound the Dragons lifted off the forest floor. Pohevol took off and flew around the rising group of Dragons. He peered into the Northern distance and looked down at the straining necks of Humans.

"We shall return!" he cried out. "We shall return triumphant!"

Zor banked to the left to converse with Pohevol, and then flew ahead of everyone to take the lead. Sefani sat with simple calm as he swerved and dipped. She leaned her head back and allowed the cool morning Sun to bathe her neck with soft light. Bridget and Tomal clutched their basket while Lin pumped his way to assume position behind Zor. Lin's path was choppy and the children jostled around, stumbling and falling to one side and then the other. Adrianne spread her eight legs across the circumference of the bottom of the basket as best she could. This is going to be a long trip, she thought.

Guldrun flew to the right of Lin and gave his brother a worried look, "Need some help, brother?"

"Shhh!" Lin snapped. "I'm fine!" He lowered his head to his passengers, "Sorry about the choppy start, things will get bettttttteeeeerrrrr!" The basket lunged down and to the right. He whipped his head back up and turned pale.

Labrys flew next, keeping a wary eye on the twins. Ius flew behind Labrys, yet he kept his eyes on Zor. He carried his basket as if it were a small twig—he was unaware of the silence residing in the basket's occupants. Anippe flew after Ius. She flew with little exertion, and yet she turned often to see the Lazuli River, now only a thin blue ribbon on the forest floor. Sophia was behind Anippe. She concentrated on watching Anippe fly. All seven heads were fixed on Anippe's wind wake. I am a Dragon, she thought. I am meant to fly. I can do this. One head dipped to seek out a whiff of wildflowers, and her entire body veered left and fell from the group.

Caduceus, traveling behind Sophia, dropped down and nosed her wayward head.

"I know this is hard for you," he said. "We will manage this together. Pull up," Caduceus whispered, "pull back up."

Sophia let the flower essence go and flew back in line with the others. Caduceus resumed his role as the final Dragon at the end of the group. The three Hawks, with Doren in the lead by Zor, flew in a triangle formation around the group. Pohevol flew far away from the Dragons and Hawks, almost five Dragon lengths to the left.

From Earth the party looked like Geese flying in an arrow. Zor led the group high where the air became thin, as this was the fastest altitude in which to fly. Pohevol could be seen thrumming through the air, his Cat feet stretched out straight behind him, his front legs tucked out of sight. He was prepared for a long flight.

Lily kept her back to Zun. She stood at the edge of the basket and stared at the forest below, trying to count the different shades of green. She had never left Durga. It was beautiful, yet so small from this distance.

She looked up at Ius's strong chest and noticed he was using only one leg to hold the basket. If only she could Shift into a Dragon. Lily would love to feel the strength, the importance, and the sheer magnitude of such a being. Caduceus said this Shift was impossible for Humans. But Simion the Bear had told her once that it was actually forbidden. Lily looked at Zun from the corner of her eye and saw him staring at her. She pretended not to notice and looked back at Durga below.

After many hours of flying Mortoof woke up. He sensed an immediate chill surrounding him, and so he squirmed, yawned, and tried to burrow himself deeper in the folds of fabric. He mumbled to himself, "Ius. Too chilly. Make a fire. Breathe on me. Cold in here." The chill remained, and he groaned and opened one eye. Where was he? He sniffed. The smell of soil fruit wafted into his nose. He nosed the fabric around. What was that sound, and why was the cave floor moving? Mortoof quickly gathered his wits, pushed the fabric aside and came snout to snout with the brown weave of Dragon basket. His eyes adjusted to the tiny holes, and he saw clouds soaring by.

"Great Malooks!" He shrieked at the top of his tiny Rat lungs, "I'm flying!"

He scrambled to the top of the basket and peered over the edge. The roar of wind knocked him back, and he flew to the opposite side of the basket. He jumped up and held on tight to the side.

"Whoopeee!" Mortoof's small body shivered in the gusts. He strained to look at the bodies flying in the short distance. When he saw Lin, the purple Mud Dragon pumping his wings and staring directly at him, Mortoof gasped.

Tomal, riding in Lin's basket, saw movement at the top of Zor's basket and nudged Bridget.

"What is that?" he asked.

From their basket they saw a small creature straddling the tip of Zor's basket, struggling along the edge. Zor's powerful red forearms held his basket lightly, and his wings flapped rhythmically. He was unaware of the stowaway. The right flying Hawk named Rowan saw the creature too. She flew close to Zor's basket to take a look.

"Zor, I think you have an unexpected passenger," she called.

"Really?" Zor mused.

"Would you like me to introduce myself?" she smiled.

"Be my guest," he replied.

Rowan lowered herself to the basket and stared at Mortoof with her sharp yellow eye. Mortoof's shrieks of joy abruptly changed.

"Aacckk! Don't kill me! No meat on me! Skinny! Look at me! Skinny bones!" Mortoof tried to bury himself in the pile of capes.

Rowan clutched the basket with her talons and used her beak to push items around, searching for this interloper. She had not understood anything he said, but she did need to tell Zor why this Rat was riding inside.

Mortoof scrambled about the basket, burrowing deeper every time Rowan uncovered his hiding spot.

"She won't find me here!" he screeched, nosing his way into a bronze cape with green tassels. He sat shivering, twitching his nose and ears. She merely lifted one tassel.

"Aacckk!" he screamed.

Mortoof dove into another sack and scrunched his body deep into the very bottom. He whispered, "Impossible to find me here…"

Rowan used her free leg to open the sack and tap him on the back.

"No!" he yelled, dodging her exploring talon.

Mortoof climbed out of the sack and began searching for his paper and charcoal stick. "Find paper! Only way," he pushed things to the left and right. His body became entangled with silver and gold string used for Zor's cape weaving, making it hard for him to move. The harder he struggled, the more difficult it was for him to escape.

"Great Malooks!" he screeched. He found his paper and stick, but they were now two arm lengths away. The strings wound around Mortoof like a bandage. He stretched his arm out to reach his writing implements but could grasp only more string.

Rowan saw what he was trying to do and carefully encircled her talons around the desired objects. Mortoof's eyes grew wide. Maybe she didn't want to eat him. What a glorious and unpredictable day!

"Give them to me! Let me explain! Let me write!" he motioned for Rowan to give him the paper and charcoal.

She adjusted her wings and cautiously handed the objects to the shivering Rat. What was this little Rodent saying? Rowan wondered if she should entreat Sophia's help. Mortoof quickly wrenched a paw free and scribbled some words on the paper. He thrust the paper out and shook it at Rowan, "Take to a Human!" he cried. "Take to a Human!"

The Hawk took the paper and brought it close to her yellow eye to peer at the strange marks. What did this creature want her to do with this tiny wisp of paper?

Zor without warning shifted his position and careened to the right making Rowan falter. In order to balance herself, she let go of the paper to grasp the edge of the basket.

Mortoof let out a wail and climbed up to the edge of the basket to watch his precious paper float away. Bridget saw the little piece coming fast toward her. She stuck out her left hand and caught it.

"Nice work," Tomal marveled.

"I wonder what it is," Bridget said as she looked. A thoughtful wrinkle appeared over her brow.

Tomal looked with her, and they both smiled when they found the tiny scratches of writing. The hand was bumpy, but they could just make out the message: Do not eat! Here to help Dragons! Excellent abilities for quest! Name's Mortoof!

Tomal looked ahead at Zor's basket. The Hawk remained attached, still peering in at the little, furry Rat. Tomal took out his seeing glass and focused on Mortoof. With the glass he saw the wind-blown body struggling to hold on to the edge of the basket. He also saw the miniature purple wings on his forelegs, almost invisible because of the wind. They were there though, Tomal was sure of it.

"He's a friend!" Tomal shouted. He immediately took out his horn, blew hard to catch Rowan's attention, and made the sign of translation. She flew away from Zor's basket and went straight to Sophia. When Sophia flew alongside Lin, he quickly became defensive.

"Don't take them away just yet," he pleaded. "Please let me carry a little while longer!"

"Do not fret, I am not here to relieve you," she whispered.

Sophia lowered herself to basket level.

"What do you need," she asked.

"Tell Rowan, Pohevol, and the Dragons that we have a new member of the quest," Tomal said. "His name is Mortoof, he's a Forest Rat, and he can write in Human tongue!"

"Intriguing," she mused.

"He says he has 'excellent abilities'," Bridget added.

"Quite intriguing," Sophia smiled.

Sophia flew to tell the others of this new traveling companion. Tomal looked into his satchel and found his fire rock. He scratched onto the paper: Welcome to the group! He then signaled for Rowan. The Hawk swooped to his extended hand and took the fluttering paper.

As she soared back to Mortoof, he had to squeeze his eyes shut. The image of a giant Hawk aiming straight at him was the exact picture Rat younglings tortured each other about during extended winter nights under the full Moon. When he opened one eye to peek, he could not see her anywhere. Where did she go?

He felt an insistent tap on his head. He looked up and saw Hawk talons one whisker-length away from his beady eye.

"Great hidden hole!" he squeaked as Rowan dropped the wind-ragged paper in his paw. He began panting as she flew back to her original spot. This was most certainly unpredictable. A Hawk helping to deliver communications for a Rat! Mortoof scrunched himself down out of the wind to read the letter. His panting made little puffs of air, which continued to ruffle the paper. This puzzled him. He scrunched down lower to escape the wind, but the ruffling continued. It took his reflection in one of Zor's mirrored capes to explain the continued movement. He saw his white stripe of fur trembling, his purple wings stiff as twigs, and his tongue hanging out like a Dog's. He realized he was a bit out of sorts.

"Pull yourself together!" he screeched at himself. "Any common Rat would be frightened by these events. You are uncommon! Act like it!"

Mortoof, with a contrived measure of calm, forced his stripe of fur to settle, relaxed the tautness of his wings, and snatched his tongue inside his pointed mouth. He then opened his eyes wide to read the important note. After he read the first word, he shrieked and began clapping ecstatically.

"Welcome! Welcome! Welcome!" Mortoof sang. "They want me, wheeeeeee!"

Mortoof immediately began planning. After a full five minutes he fell asleep, exhausted.

∽ ∾

When the Sun began to set after their first full day of flying, Pohevol decided to fly next to Zor. He pointed to a purple and pink canyon to the Northeast. He noticed deep crevices that indicated possible caves along the rim.

"We should stop there for the night," Pohevol said.

"We could fly through the night," Zor offered.

Pohevol objected, "We are not ready for that."

Zor turned to look at Guldrun and Lin, slightly pale. Sophia's heads were struggling to remain straight and focused, and Caduceus had a scowl on his face.

"Yes, we should stop for the night," Zor said. "We must build stamina for night flying."

Pohevol flew to the Hawks, and everyone slowly began the descent from the sky.

Sefani, who slept for most of the trip, gradually awoke and lifted her head from Zor's soft feathers. She turned her head left and right, and then turned her body completely around to hear the others. She waved to the children below in the baskets, and they looked up at her amazed.

It was as if she could see them! How could she stay on Zor without holding on? She didn't even grab one of his spiraled horns, perfect for gripping. Sefani just smiled and turned back around. She peered around as if she were watching their descent into the canyon. Perjas let out a bark, and Sefani nodded her head. She then made a pointed shape with her arms raised above her head. Perjas began thumping his tail. Lily, who was standing next to Perjas, wondered what was going on between the girl and Dog.

As they came closer to the canyon, Lily noticed how the chill of the high air did not go away. We must have traveled far North today, she thought.

The canyon lay on the edge of a mountain. Beside the tall cliffs of rock lay a dark blue swath of river. It looked deep and frigid. Pohevol and the Hawks flew ahead and cleared two full circles around the perimeter before motioning the Dragons to land. They picked a butte near the Eastern rim to land. Labrys tried to discretely warn Zor and Ius about the adjacent mud flats, but Ius convinced her that the wayward brothers would be too exhausted for a mud roll.

The first thing Lin did when he saw the flats was dump his basket roughly on the butte and dive into the mud. The basket tipped over dumping Bridget, Tomal, and

Adrianne onto the ground. Lin lay in the nearby mud oblivious of his coarse behavior. A stupendous sigh escaped his mouth, as he rolled on his back flapping his wings. Sending huge chunks flying everywhere, he thumped his tail with joy. One chunk hit Caduceus as he landed. Another smacked the middle of Rowan's chest, and most egregious, a pelting of mud drops rained down on Labrys just as she was flying over to scold him.

Labrys, wide-eyed and hissing fire, shook the offending mud off her skin and used her two sets of legs to lift the overjoyed Lin out of the messy bath. Lin opened his eyes and turned his head to find all of the Dragons shaking their many heads at him. Even Ius and Guldrun were scolding him with their reproachful eyes.

"Wait, Labrys!" Lin cried out.

"Do not speak!" she shrieked. "Did you see your basket? Did you see Tomal and Bridget falling over each other? Did you see Adrianne stumbling to extract herself from your shoddy landing? For Earth's sake Lin, she is a Spider, and your blunder of a landing left her on her back, legs in the air!"

"I'm sorry," Lin hung his head, although because she was carrying him high in the air it looked as if it were flapping in the wind.

"You should be!"

"Where are you taking me?" he moaned.

"Do you see that small island out in the river?"

Lin craned his head and saw a lonely clump of land with a few trees in the middle of the water.

"Yes," his voice fell.

"You are going to sit over there for a few hours…by

yourself," she scolded. "Then you can come back and apologize to the children and Adrianne."

"Yes, Labrys."

Labrys dumped him on the island, and he fell in a dejected lump. The only thing Lin and Guldrun loved more than mud was food. He sat staring at the butte. Dragon one, Dragon two, Dragon three, Dragon four. . . only 7,200 Dragons to go.

After the entire party landed, they went about preparing the meal. Everyone was famished. Zor and Ius searched in their baskets and bags for clove bread and cinnamon quobloons. Caduceus lowered his head to the ground so his two Snake companions could uncoil themselves to search for food, while he ate a sparse meal of oats and potatoes. Labrys blew the beginnings of a roaring fire, and Anippe went along the river bank looking for wild leeks. She returned with her tail full of aromatic greens. The children set about making their meals, sneaking looks at Lin across the water on the little island. They could hear him mumbling, see him pacing, and every so often falling upon the ground in a huff.

As the Dragons ate their meal on one side of the butte, the children ate theirs on the other. The Hawks and Pohevol were absent from the group, obviously hunting for their dinners. Adrianne crawled under an adjacent rock and unpacked some dried Flies. Mortoof was still asleep.

"Will we have enough food to last the trip?" Tomal asked the others.

"No," Lily answered, "but Pohevol says that is the other reason we must go North first. When we run out of food, we will be in the warm lands—perhaps even in the

Motherland."

Sefani and Perjas ate quietly, listening to the others speak.

Bridget raised her head, chewing on a dried maple sweet, "What do Ice Dragons eat?"

"Flesh," Zun said with clear disgust.

"They have no other choice, Zun," Lily gave him an exasperated look.

"Well, if they're as smart as everyone says they are, why did they migrate up North to the freezing lands in the first place? I thought Dragons were supposed to," his voice raised in mocking derision, "'seek the path of least harm'."

"They haven't shared the reasons with us, Zun," Tomal added. "I'm sure it was necessary for them to migrate."

Bridget looked at Lily, "What kind of flesh do they eat?"

Zun smirked, "Worried they might enjoy a bit of Human thigh?"

"No," Bridget snapped. "I'm interested in reality, unlike you, cave boy."

Perjas growled, and Sefani rubbed his back, whispering to him.

"Enough, you two," Lily sighed. "We need to get along. We've yet to see one day pass."

"I've heard that Ice Dragons eat Seal and Polar Bear," Tomal said softly.

All children were silent, pondering the idea of carnivorous Dragons feasting with blood staining their mouths and claws.

"I don't know why the Dragons of Durga don't eat animals," Zun continued. "They certainly were made for ripping and devouring helpless creatures. Why else have fangs, claws, and fire?"

Bridget crossed her arms and raised one eyebrow, "If you traveled through Dreamtime, you'd understand a lot of things you puny, little, cave…"

Both Lily and Sefani interrupted now, "Bridget, stop."

Lily answered Zun's question, "Saja shared this with me during some of our first trips in Dreamtime." Lily closed her eyes and an idea came to her. Why not? This was going to be a long trip, and she would most likely perform numerous Shifts. "Let me try to show you." Lily stood up and looked to see where Caduceus was. His back was to her, so she felt safe.

She took off her cape, and in a flash Lily transformed into an Auroch, muscles rippling and a chest wide and proud. She snorted and stamped the ground with her hoof. Zun laced his fingers and rested his chin upon them. The other children stopped eating and stared.

"The first Dragons were smaller than the Dragons we know now, and they were omnivores," Lily said. "But the elders began noticing the strength of the herbivores. All of the largest land animals were herbivores, and they were larger than Dragons." Lily then transformed into a Bull Elephant, a Rhinoceros, and finally a towering Giraffe.

Bridget's mouth opened, Tomal's eyes widened, and Sefani smiled in the direction of Lily's Shifts. Zun continued to watch as if he were calculating something.

"You know how much Dragons love being big," Lily spoke with pursed Giraffe lips. She lowered her head to the children and pawed the ground.

She then Shifted into an elderly Bonobo, "All the herbivores lived longer than the omnivores as well." She stared at the children with eyes that looked Human. After a few deliberate moments, she transformed into a wise tropical Parrot.

"Lily," Bridget gasped. "You can Shift into a Bird!" Bridget jumped up and pointed at Lily, now preening her colorful plumage.

The Dragons turned to see what the commotion was, and Caduceus stared at the Parrot. A slow smile spread across his Alligator face. He then quickly removed it.

Lily said, "And so, desiring longevity and the massive bodies we're used to seeing, the Dragons decided to give up flesh—as a test. Each generation grew larger, lived longer, and soon it was considered foolish to eat animals like carnivores do. They were better without eating flesh."

All of the children clapped, except Zun. Now he was staring at the Parrot as if in a trance.

Feeling brave, she flew over to Caduceus, who held out one of his short arms. His purple and green body glowed warmly, revealing deep joy, despite his effort to deny any semblance of pride. Lily alighted on his leg and side-stepped closer to his shoulder.

"You have accomplished the final Shift?" he said dryly.

"Yes, master Dragon," she replied.

"And I am to assume you would like your Name and Necklace now?"

Lily hesitated. A Shifter should remain humble always. Admit the desire for a reward, and the gift would not come. Yet she must remain truthful or else Caduceus would sense her dishonesty and deride her for deceit.

"I would welcome my Name and Necklace," Lily whispered.

Caduceus peered deeply into her Parrot eye. He blew smoke around her shivering body, as she had forgotten how cold the canyon was. She had Shifted into a tropical Bird who was used to a moisture-laden heat.

Lily became worried. Was he going to do it? Would he give her the reward she thought she deserved? And that is when it happened. Her worry and coveting made the Shift falter. Her Human face flickered behind the Parrot beak. Her wings suddenly became arms, and in seconds Lily—the Human—sat perched on Caduceus's shoulder. She blushed and buried her head into his large, thick scales.

Caduceus lowered Lily to the ground, and she stepped off. Her head hung close to her chest.

"Do you believe you still deserve this honor?" Caduceus raised his eyefolds.

"No, master," Lily replied, fighting back tears.

She turned away and walked back to the children's fire. She saw Pohevol now, sitting far atop the canyon wall. His magnificent wings were spread, making him look like a statue.

"Why is this so hard?" she thought to Pohevol.

He thought nothing in reply.

Bridget, Tomal, and Zun stood waiting for her. Sefani sat facing the flames.

"Fearn!" Caduceus called out. The Name roared across the canyon. Everything remained silent. "Fearn!" he cried again. This time when the Name echoed off the dark canyon walls, Lily turned to see Caduceus standing tall. His Serpents were coiled around his neck again. From where had his Snakes come so fast?

"Come Fearn, kneel at my side," he motioned to his left.

Lily walked cautiously back to Caduceus. She looked to Pohevol, but he was no longer on the ridge. When she came to Caduceus, she knelt by his side and closed her eyes.

"Lion!" he called.

She became a growling Lion.

"Mouse!"

A twitching Mouse scurried in front of the Dragon.

"Turtle!"

With wise eyes, a green Turtle looked up at Caduceus.

"Horse!"

She reared back on her haunches and whinnied, kicking the air.

"Raven!"

A dazzling Raven began preening her feathers.

"She's done it," Zun whispered.

Caduceus bellowed, "Let all who can hear my voice know!" He paused and put out his leg for Lily to sit upon, "Lily of Durga is now Lily Fearn!"

Caduceus motioned for Lily to fly. As she took off flapping, he Shifted into another Raven and they flew together, sending out deep caws that echoed off the mighty canyon walls. With every beat of a wing, Lily's heart pounded with elation and joy.

⋇ 13 ⋇

DRAGON'S LAIR

After a night of rest, and after Lin ate his cold repast in stone silence, the Dragons and children traveled two more days to the land of cold, to Iceloch. The children pulled on their warm leggings, hand-knit sweaters made from spun Dog cardings, thick Snake shedding boots, and hats. The Dragon amulets lay under the clothing, pulsating against their skin.

The Durgan Dragons, not used to the encroaching cold, blew puffs of steam and smoke through which to fly. This would provide a temporary moment of warmth that soothed their wind-chapped scales. Perjas, in the basket with Zun and Lily, seemed to welcome the frigid air. Unlike the children, who spent most of the flight huddled inside the baskets, Perjas stood up on his hind legs, front paws perched on the edge. He often would call out to Sefani, who would then turn her head toward his sound and call back in response.

The Hawks and Pohevol flew hard, but as they approached the glaciers, looming massive and stately in the distance, Pohevol took brief respites perched between Ius's shoulders.

Adrianne curled into a tight ball and wrapped her web around her for warmth. Mortoof remained asleep, only awaking to scrounge for bits of food. He knew he was being utterly predictable, but everyone would expect a Rat to eat through all of the provisions. The only way he could keep himself from attacking the scrumptious Dragon treats with wild abandon was to sleep. So he would be predictable by sleeping, but downright surprising by nibbling.

Ice was everywhere now. The sky was a blinding blue, so Sophia tucked four of her heads in to shield her many eyes from the glare. Many of the Dragons flew with their eyes shut for minutes, concentrating on the swell of the air currents and the sound of their hearts beating, just to escape the blazing light of the Sun's reflection off the ice. The children, sensing a shift in light, stood in the baskets and leaned over the edge to witness the vision. There were deep fjords adjacent to white and blue glaciers, and purple mountains capped with snow. Some of the glaciers even had stripes of bright green.

When Sefani sat up and made a sign with her long slender arms, the children saw it. The bright blue of the sky above was mirrored below. A sea of blue appeared, and the Dragons dropped down out of the sky to fly above this endless lake of azure.

"The ocean," Lily whispered. None of the children had ever seen the ocean before. They only knew of it from stories and travels through Dreamtime.

Zun looked down and saw the vast expanse of water. Something inside his stomach pitched, and he had to look away.

Bridget and Tomal peered down at the massive blue, and while Tomal looked in silent wonder, Bridget began squirming in the basket. "We are almost there!" she cried. "It's about to begin!"

Bridget began moving about in the basket, searching for her satchel, yet being careful not to disturb the large Spider still curled into a ball. Tomal remained quiet, simply staring at the ocean.

Lily resembled Tomal, taking in the sight without words. She and Perjas saw icebergs floating like jagged teeth in the water, black and gray forms along the edge of the ice that could possibly be Seals. They saw occasional spouts of white water that must be the Blue Whales, and sometimes Lily thought they saw a white ghost move across the ice. The Polar Bear, she thought, the great white Bear of the North.

Zor called out to Pohevol, who was again flying after a short break atop Ius, "We are here, where shall we land?"

Pohevol look below at the frozen land and felt a shiver run through his wings. Could they convince Ice Dragons to go into hiding? In a land this cold and seemingly barren, without a tree in sight, could he convince these giants to believe his ominous trip to the future?

"They are your cousins," Pohevol replied. "I will follow your lead."

Zor nodded his red-feathered head at Pohevol and dropped back to fly alongside Ius.

"My friend," Zor turned his head to Ius, "where shall we land this party of ours?"

Ius looked at the sea of blue, the choppy icebergs, and the sharp glaciers. He then saw a long strip of white resting between two glaciers.

"There," Ius pointed one claw toward the strip.

Zor nodded, informed the other Dragons and Hawks of the decision, and led the descent.

There was tension in the wind, as everyone knew the task was about to begin. When would they find the first Ice Dragon? Would these cold beings remember the stories of the Dragon amulets? Would they listen to Pohevol's story? Most important, would they believe it?

Zor was first to land, lowering his basket to the ice, before landing himself. The ice popped as Zor's heavy legs touched down. He kept his wings outstretched, ready in case the ice could not hold his weight.

"Wait!" he roared to the others who were approaching the strip of ice. Ius and his followers swooped back up and flew in slow circles, waiting to see if the ice would crack. Pohevol and the Hawks landed with ease, yet when their feet registered the full chill, they began hopping around trying to adjust to the cold. Lily saw their discomfort and grabbed a few blankets to throw on the ice.

The Hawks flew to one blanket while Pohevol flew to the other.

"Thank you," Pohevol thought to Lily.

"You can't walk on blankets the entire time," Lily thought.

"No, we will get used to it or ask Zor to make us coverings."

When Zor realized the ice would hold, he signaled for the others to land. "Spread out," he warned them, "it will hold if we stand far apart."

Labrys flew to Guldrun, who was now carrying Adrianne, Tomal, and Bridget.

"No funny business!" she scolded. "Every decision you two make will affect the success of this trip! Best behavior Draglings!"

Guldrun's eyefolds shot up. He turned to Lin. Had Lin heard that? When Labrys flew away, Guldrun said, "Did you hear that?"

"I know, I know," Lin mumbled.

"She called us 'Draglings' all because of your foolishness!" Guldrun yelled.

"You're just angry because you didn't get to the mud first!" Lin yelled back.

"You," Guldrun hissed, "are going to have to control yourself!"

Lin looked dumbfounded, "How can Ius be so controlled around mud?"

"Quit avoiding the point!" Guldrun screeched. "Labrys is going to tell the Hawks to watch us if you don't control yourself!"

"Yes, yes," Lin conceded. "Look down below, Guldrun," he tried to change the subject, "there isn't a spattering of mud in sight. How do Dragons even live here?"

Guldrun looked at his brother and then at the ice. No mud. It did make him wonder.

The Dragons flew down one by one, watching to make sure they kept at least three Dragon lengths between them. The ice cracked and popped when they landed, but it held their weight. Pohevol flew to Zor while the children began climbing out of the baskets. Zor nodded his head and began unpacking his basket and satchel. When everything was out, he quickly set to work with his materials. He began tying and knotting. Three long silver and gold needles came out and flashed in the afternoon Sun. Zor made large capes for the Dragons and coverings for all of their feet. It was colder than Pohevol had anticipated. The Hawks could not withstand the ice on their feet, even after many attempts. Sophia was shivering too. Zor finished her cape first and asked Doren to fly it over to her shivering necks.

In a matter of minutes the coverings were finished, and just as the last gold trim was attached, Mortoof flew out of a bundle of thread and rolled across the ice. As he was in the deepest of sleep, when he awoke slipping across the smooth ice, his body shook, scampered, and rolled in every direction.

"Great Malooks!" he shrieked. His furry brown body slid fast, as he tried to stop and gain his footing. He finally became upright, but each attempt to grab the ice with his four paws made him slip and tumble. When he became upright for the last time, he jutted out his wings and furiously beat them so he could flee the infuriating ice.

Mortoof flew awkwardly at first, as if it had been many Moons since his last flight, but after a few minutes he was more adept. He flew in circles around the Dragons until Ius shot his front leg up and caught Mortoof mid-flight. The blue Dragon motioned for Sophia to stretch one of her heads to him. He would need translating to speak to this creature.

"Are you not the sneaky Rat who lives near my cave?" Ius asked.

"Rat, I am," Mortoof replied, shaking like an autumn leaf in a cool breeze. "Sneaky, I am not."

"Do you not sleep near my home?" Ius held Mortoof by the tail.

"Ius," Zor began, "go easy on him."

Ius transferred Mortoof to his other leg and carefully cradled the Rat inside a gleaming set of sharpened claws.

"Thank you," Mortoof settled a bit in the Dragon's familiar company. "Yes. It is true, majestic one. I happen to live just outside the great Ius cave." Sophia translated the words and tone precisely, mimicking Mortoof's reverence and formality. Zor and Anippe had to stifle their chuckles.

Anippe mouthed silently, "Great Ius cave!"

Ius blew steam at the Rat and was intrigued to see the little face brace itself in the warm, moist air. Mortoof closed his eyes and smiled. This little Rat likes me, thought Ius. Immediately Ius softened to the furry Rodent with wings.

"Mortoof is my flying companion," Ius announced. "He shall ride atop my back whenever he wishes." Zor shook his head, and Mortoof beamed and began blowing kisses to Ius. Ius turned bright blue and stood a bit straighter.

"I will not let you down, great Ius!" Mortoof pronounced.

Anippe and Zor laughed. Caduceus and Labrys stood perplexed. Guldrun and Lin wondered why this was so strange. Ius was the best Mud Dragon of Durga. He was great.

Now that the cloaks and coverings were finished, the group set about moving the baskets and satchels to a secure cave. Doren and Rowan found a suitable one nestled at the bottom of a nearby glacier. In a slow and steady procession, making sure not to follow too closely behind each other, the group traversed the ice. Zor reminded them, "Three Dragon lengths, at least." The children walked together in the middle of the procession. With a hand on his back, Sefani walked alongside Perjas. Adrianne, with protective web coverings for her eight legs, seemed to skate across the ice. They stowed their materials in the cave, ate a quick meal, and set out to find the Ice Dragons.

As they moved across the lake of ice, Pohevol reminded the children to take out their amulets, lest the Ice Dragons distrust them. Zun pulled his amulet out and looked down at the stone. It did not glow. He tucked it back inside and decided to walk behind the others. With hope, the Ice Dragons would see the unfailing devotion of the others and overlook his dull gem.

As they walked, the Sun began to dip slightly in the West. Lily and Tomal yawned. Although it was still light out, the air became colder. The landscape turned a shade darker, as if an eclipse were happening.

"Remember, night is here, though the Sun will not set completely," Pohevol thought to Lily.

"That's right," Lily said out loud.

"What's right?" Bridget asked.

"The Sun never sets during Midsummer in the farthest

North."

The children looked at the Sun, and then looked away as the blinding light filled their vision with white. They looked at the surrounding glaciers and the lake of ice before them. Flashes of black danced across the white. Whenever they blinked, the Sun's ghost would remain against their eyelids. It was fun to play this game. Look at the Sun for one second. Then look at the snow, the glaciers, or anything white. Then close one's eyes. The Sun would become a companion, a playmate, a constant. This far North, the Sun would never go away. No wonder the Ice Dragons chose to live in the land of ice and light. They could even sleep under the Sun.

"Will we never see the Moon?" Bridget asked, her voice filled with worry.

"Don't worry," Tomal pointed. "There she is, hovering above that glacier."

Bridget followed Tomal's finger and saw the waning Moon, a smooth white pebble floating in the sky.

As they continued to walk along the ice, every few minutes Anippe and Labrys would release a low purring from their throats. Sometimes Sophia would lower her heads to the ice and make the same purring vibrations, pitching each mouth at a different tone.

What are they doing? Zun thought. He watched the Dragons ahead of him and turned often to watch the ones behind him.

All of a sudden the children's amulets ceased to glow. Ius stopped in his tracks. Mortoof sensed Ius's muscles tensing and gripped the Dragon. Zor stopped too and felt the ice for vibrations.

Lily and Bridget clutched their amulets and then dropped them when they burst into a firelight red that made their faces glow.

The Ice Dragons were here.

Caduceus was the first to feel it. The beating. Boom, boom. Pause. Boom, boom. Pause. Boom, boom. He looked down and peered at the ice. His nose was less than an inch from the ice. "Listen!" he whispered. "Listen with your feet."

Everyone listened. They felt the beating.

Boom, boom. Pause. Boom, boom. Pause. Boom, boom.

Lily felt the strength of the beating. Something deep inside her told her to Shift, that her Human shape would not be safe now. She looked to Caduceus and Pohevol, but could not meet their gaze. They, too, were staring down at the ice floor.

Lily lowered her gaze to the ice beneath her feet.

Staring up at her, from underneath the icy depths, was a tremendous green Dragon eye.

≼ 14 ≽

ICELOCH

Lily stood still and held her breath. The eye below the ice blinked once. It blinked again and opened larger, moving and looking all around the surface of the ice.

Lily thought, "Pohevol," and said slowly and clearly, "Zor, could you come here?"

Pohevol flew over at once, and Zor strode across the ice, making sure not to cause any breaks. When Pohevol peered down, the Ice Dragon merely blinked again. When Zor looked down, his pointed spiral horns stood straight up, and the Ice Dragon below let out an enormous rumble.

The entire Dragon body appeared under the ice, a glorious, pulsating greenish blue. Like magic, the other Ice Dragons appeared beneath the ice simultaneously. Multiple bodies began to glow, and the Dragons from Durga realized they had stumbled upon the Ice Dragons' sleeping lair.

"Everyone back!" roared Zor.

Lily stumbled away, finally catching Caduceus's eye. She made the sign of the Shift, and he shook his head, no. Everyone moved back and stood watching. Zor and Sophia remained in the middle of the ice.

Streams of fire shot up from below. Like rays of Sunlight, the precise bands cut through the ice, making large circles. A strange salty smell filled the air, and steam rose in plumes around each circle. The loud sound of ice popping and straining filled everyone's ears. The Ice Dragons were coming. After each circle was completely cut, the flames stopped. Silence tip-toed through the frigid air.

At once, the Ice Dragons burst through the holes, sending thick chunks of ice flying. The Dragons closest to the children put out their wings to protect them from falling ice. Mortoof put his paws up over his head, closed his eyes, and did his best to press his furry body deep into Ius's blue scales. Adrianne climbed a vertical wall of ice and pressed her body flat against the frozen water.

As the ice fell in deafening crashes, the Ice Dragons hovered above the fresh holes. They encircled Zor and Sophia, so Sophia spread her heads out in a circle. Zor whipped his head around to see how many Ice Dragons had him surrounded.

Ius, sensing Zor's flash of worry, sharpened his claws surreptitiously against his stone and flew to land by Zor's side. He did not care if the ice cracked—he would always protect his friend. The two Dragons stood taut, ready for a fight.

Sophia was the first to speak, "We come in peace. We are sorry to arrest your slumber."

The Ice Dragons landed beside the holes and tucked in their wings. One would think their weight would compromise the stability of the ice, but when they landed, no straining was heard.

The green and blue Dragon, who had first seen Lily through the ice, spoke first, "Whence do you fly?" His voice was deep and quizzical. He was the same size as Zor and had segmented wings with extra skin folds. His skin changed color with his breathing. During inhalation his scales were green, during exhalation they turned a deep blue. The children had never seen a Dragon do this.

Relieved that he could understand and speak their language, Sophia said in her own tongue, "We come from the land of Durga, West of the Gray Mountains and North of the Motherland."

"Why are you here?" the Dragon continued.

"That story requires time and patience to tell," Sophia replied.

"Interesting retort," the Ice Dragon looked to the children huddling under Dragon wings. He saw Zun by himself, pressed against a cleft between rock and ice. "Why do you voyage with them?"

"Dragon cousin," Zor began.

The Ice Dragon stopped Zor, "I am not assured we share the same egg lineage."

Zor slid his eyes toward Ius, who gripped the ice with his sharpened claws. Mortoof looked up and decided he would pounce if necessary.

"I mean," Zor continued, "brother from our Dragon tribe, do you not remember the amulets of time? The Human children with whom we travel wear them. If you do not trust them, the amulets will comfort your suspicions."

The Ice Dragon searched to find the glowing amulets. Once observed, he seemed to ponder Zor's words.

"Why are they…apprehensive?" the greenish Dragon stared at Zun's stern face.

Ius now spoke, "Because they have known only the Dragons of Durga. They are cold and tired, and our voyage is not one of pleasure."

The Ice Dragon now turned to look at Ius. He scanned each part of the blue-armored Dragon. His green eyes crawled across the battered scales and sore muscles. Something about this Mud Dragon made the Ice Dragon muse, "What is your name, Mud Dragon?"

Lily strained to hear the Dragon speech. Did the Ice Dragon just reveal he knew Ius was a Mud Dragon? How would he know?

"My name is Ius," he replied, outstretching his wings and forming the symbol for mud with his claws.

In synchronicity, Guldrun and Lin formed the sign and bowed to Ius. "Mud Dragons!" they both roared from the edge of the icy strip.

"I am Dett," the Ice Dragon said, and he released his wings to make the sign for ice. The other Ice Dragons did the same.

"Ice! Ice! Ice!" their Dragon voices filled the air.

A lavender Ice Dragon flew to Dett and whispered something in his ear.

"The amulets are glowing," Dett said, "so logically you are welcome to sojourn with us. Follow me."

"We are drained from our travels and not used to

sleeping in the light," Sophia began.

"Do not worry," Dett said with a slight chuckle, "we know about Mud Dragons. If you are comparable to their tribe, you will relish our sleeping caves. They have not been used in many Suns, but they will suffice. Of that, I am sure."

The Ice Dragons led the others along a narrow strip of ice. At first Pohevol was skeptical of the children walking over the frozen lake next to so many holes. He was about to say something when Labrys stopped him. She felt the pull of the icy waters.

"They are just leading us to darkness," she said. "The children will be safe. Because we have disturbed their slumber, we should feel lucky the Ice Dragons are not furious."

Pohevol thought about this. He flew above the children, specifically watching Lily. Lily felt her puncture wounds throbbing and looked up to find him. She smiled, and he felt better. As she walked by the large holes, Lily looked down at the water and wondered if she could Shift into an animal who could withstand such cold temperatures. To be a Seal, she thought. A ripple of desire moved across her body, and then it suddenly vanished. She remembered what Ice Dragons feasted upon.

With Zor's new feet coverings and extra capes, the trek to the sleeping coves was not as painful as imagined. Zor, Ius, and Anippe walked in front, watching the Ice Dragons slide. They could even glide across the holes without using their wings, as if skating on the water. Perjas was next, guiding Sefani around the dangerous openings.

Bridget and Tomal walked hand in hand, careful to

remain steady. Adrianne, grateful to have her web coverings, but also worried that she did not pack enough dried Insects, navigated the ice, stopping frequently to stare into the deep pools. She loved the cool rains of the forest that dripped on her furry green body and beaded on her web. But this kind of water scared Adrianne. How could Dragons sleep in the freezing liquid?

Lily followed the Spider, with Pohevol flying above her. Guldrun and Lin walked behind Lily, and both Dragons were pale and silent. Labrys walked to the right of the Mud brothers, "Cheer up, Draglings. An absence of mud is good for you sometimes."

Guldrun thought about their Durgan mud stowed away in the cave they were now leaving behind. When would Lin and he be able to unpack the mud and lounge in its deliciousness?

Zun followed the two brothers and Labrys. He was sullen and still full of a silent fear. Lily had abandoned him. A gulf appeared between them, and he was not certain they would survive this trip, let alone be friends again. Sophia and Caduceus walked at the end of the group, watching and listening. The Hawks flew as sentries to the left and right.

The group followed the Ice Dragons, marveling at the freezing world surrounding them. There were strange black Birds flying in the distance. Sometimes a flash of pink, green, purple, and blue light would fill the air over the white glaciers. The children, warm in their many coverings, felt tired and yet lucky to be witnessing such a unique sight. All, except Zun.

A few Ice Dragons began yawning. The Sun, low in

the sky, turned the ice a dull shade of blue.

Labrys fell into step next to Sophia, still keeping a close eye on the egg brothers. An interesting thing was happening to Labrys. The sea was calling her. While she was not used to these frigid waters, her ancient lineage began swelling in her blood. Unbeknownst to Labrys, her blood began dropping in temperature. While the others shivered and reached for more of Zor's capes, Labrys felt flashes of heat and warmth flowing throughout her body.

Soon the procession curved around a rocky cliff, and they saw tremendous caves buried deep into the face. Guldrun and Lin let out a whoop of joy, and then quickly stifled it when Labrys and Anippe glared at them. Ius took notice and decided it was time to speak to his two wayward tribe mates.

Sophia breathed a sigh of relief, "This is wonderful. Thank you for your generosity."

"Feel free to sleep as long as you desire. We will commune in two or three Moons," said Dett.

The Durgans looked at each other. Did the Ice Dragons just say two or three Moons? The Dragons of Durga could sleep for two or three days during times of leisure, but this was too much. They could not wait this long to reveal their request.

Anippe said, "Dett, we realize your sleeping was disturbed by our untimely arrival, but our group needs only one night to rest." She bowed, showing her humility, "If we could commune within the week, we would be most grateful."

The Ice Dragons shared quick glances and watched to see how Dett would respond.

He said, "One solitary night to gather your wits and wisdom? To allow the blood to cool and flow without obstacle?"

The Ice Dragons nodded their heads.

Dett continued, "We must all sleep for at least one Moon to meet in Dreamtime and understand your strange arrival. Would you not have to agree?"

Anippe turned to Zor, who was now flanked by Mortoof and Perjas. These two looked like observers at DragonBall, their little heads turned to look at Dett, and then at Anippe. At Dett and then Zor. At Dett and then Ius. Anippe could tell Zor was thinking about how to respond to this fascinating Ice Dragon.

Then an interesting thing happened. Caduceus stepped up and introduced himself to Dett. His long Alligator head bowed slightly, as he revealed his covered Snake companions. They, too, were having trouble adjusting to the cold.

"I am Caduceus," he began.

"Stop," Dett said with a strange voice. "Say no more."

Caduceus felt a chill run down his spine, as he remembered something familiar from a long time ago.

"I shall tell you who you are," Dett began. He stared into Caduceus's eyes and into the eyes of the Snake closest to Caduceus's right ear. Dett brought his claws together and pressed them into the shape of a triangle.

"You are from mixed-blood. Your mother was the largest Snake in the shared reptilian story that dates back to the birth of the Moon. You have a modest appetite. You are a master of the Shift."

Everyone was silent, except for the Ice Dragons who

began to make strange clicking noises with their mouths, excited to see the wonder in everyone's eyes. The lavender Ice Dragon smiled and nodded her head at Dett. He returned the smile and bowed to Caduceus.

Next, Caduceus did something the children would talk about for many Suns—something he had never done before in their presence. He Shifted into Dett. He became the Ice Dragon standing before him. Two, identical green and blue Dragons stood face-to-face, nose-to-nose. Even Guldrun and Lin were confounded. No two Dragons were identical, not even egg siblings.

"Do you think you know me?" the identical Dragons asked simultaneously.

"I know you better than you think," they both responded.

"Prove it," they said.

"You are tired," said one.

"You are waiting," said the other.

"You are hurting," said one.

"You are bewildered," said the other.

"You are afraid," said one.

The two Dragons continued this process of declaration, both bodies stealthily walking in circles, eyes trained on each other, speaking with the same voice and the same intonation, as if one were talking to his reflection in a mirror.

Finally, the two stopped, and Caduceus Shifted into his true shape.

"We shall meet in Dreamtime at once," Dett said.

"And we shall welcome the opportunity," Caduceus replied.

Urgency filled the air. The Ice Dragons began clicking again, and they pushed off, flying back to their sleeping waters.

The Dragons of Durga flew back to the first cave to gather the baskets and sacks while Pohevol and the Hawks circled the rocks, looking for any small morsel of movement. Whatever magic occurred with Dett and Caduceus, no one wanted to question or delay the progress. Sophia, already fitted with extra coverings and capes, nestled into one cave. Labrys stretched out languidly in another. Caduceus stayed with the children, who could not stop staring at him. He eyed them, refusing to hide his disdain.

Yet one child was filled with rapture. Lily could not grumble anymore. Caduceus was divine. He was incredible, and he was her teacher. One day, she thought, I might Shift into a Dragon.

When the baskets and satchels returned, the Dragons and children set about making comfortable sleeping spots. As none of the children shared Dreamtime with the present Dragons, conversations turned to discussing who was a heavy or light sleeper, who snored, and who blew steam or drooled.

Everyone agreed Lily should find Saja in the spirit world to Dream with her. Bridget would Dream with Anippe, Tomal would Dream with Ius, and Sefani would Dream with Zor. Sophia would Dream alone, while Labrys, Guldrun, and Lin would be watchers. Caduceus would be a leader.

What do we do with Zun? Zor wondered. While he pondered this, Ius asked to see Guldrun and Lin outside the cave.

"Young Dragons," Ius began, "I understand the calling. I know how powerful mud is. In fact, I can smell the Lazuli mud, the dried mud, the red mud, and the rare fruited mud tucked inside your satchels.

The two egg brothers gasped and looked at each other in disbelief and fear.

"Please don't take it from us, Ius," Lin begged.

"I will not, but you have to learn to control yourselves," he warned them.

Guldrun said, "He's learning, Ius. You have to be patient with Lin."

Ius snorted, "You are no different than your brother. He just landed in the canyon mud before you did."

Guldrun pouted, and it was now Lin's turn to smirk, "See Guldrun, Ius knows. He knows."

"I want you to practice restraint tonight in Dreamtime. I am going to ask Caduceus to take us to the Mud Sea of Moren," Ius began.

"Oh yes, yes, yes!" Guldrun and Lin cut him off.

"And," Ius boomed, "you are to fly over the sea and dip your wingtips only!"

Guldrun and Lin looked as if he had just said they were to abstain from eating for a full week. It would be impossible.

"Yes," Ius smiled. "Dip only the tips of your wings and focus on how a little bit of mud can recharge the spirit. It can be enough, I promise."

"But," Guldrun started.

"Guldrun," Ius warned.

Lin whined, "Ius!"

"No, Lin, do as I say."

"Yes, Ius," they both moaned and walked back into the cave to prepare for the test of will and tenacity.

Zor, Ius, Caduceus, and Labrys conferred about the night's Dreamtime and looked to find Zun afterward. They agreed Zun should sleep by himself at the edge of the cave, as he was used to sleeping alone. The Dragons needed all attention to be focused on Dreaming, not watching his every move.

"What if he sneaks in and bothers a sleeping Dragon?" Ius questioned.

"We will ask Labrys to guard the cave," Zor said. "She sleeps lightly, and if Zun leaves the cave, she will awaken herself and control him."

Zor found Zun and told him the Dragons' desire. Zun, for a slight moment, acted as if he could not understand the red Dragon before him. Zor flared his nostrils and snorted.

"Do not make me bother Sophia, boy," Zor said. "I know you can understand my speech. You may hate us, but you still carry the lineage of your parents. You have not gone through the change."

"I wish I had," Zun mumbled.

Zor raised his voice, "What is that? Speak up!"

Zun shrank under Zor's command, "I said, I wish I were of age already."

"It will come soon enough," Zor said, looking away from the boy. "Soon enough."

Zun began making his sleeping platform and agreed to sleep at the edge of the cave. He was actually relieved. Exhausted from being around so many Dragons, his muscles ached. Labrys built a fire to warm and soothe his body.

The Hawks remained outside, hunting through the long, bright night. Adrianne nestled close to the fire and kept her many eyes on Zun.

The Dragons designed their sleeping alcoves and when they were done, they invited the children to join. Mortoof, still frightened from the earlier encounter with Dett, clung to Ius. He only let go when the blankets around Ius created a warm and secure space between fabric and Dragon skin. He was too scared to be unpredictable.

Gentle murmurs were heard coming from the caves, and soft light from Dragon candles danced on the walls. Small plumes of incense floated out of the cave opening, and Labrys settled herself outside, far away from the fire. The freezing temperature did not affect her. In fact, every few minutes she had to fan her wings to cool her body.

As a calm settled over Iceloch, Labrys placed one foreleg into her bag of jewels and allowed their cool smoothness to comfort her. She thought of Saja, guarding her egg in Durga. She also wondered when she might see the thick Durgan trees and Mount Calyps again. These Ice Dragons seemed potentially stubborn. Would they believe the story of a Durgan Forest Cat? Would they go into hiding? Then she thought of the sea and the cool blue waters that seemed to call her name. When would she dive into their inviting waters? She continued to ask questions as the Sun-filled night washed over her.

✥ 15 ✥

DREAMING IN ICELOCH

A booming could be heard in the distance. Flying Ice Dragons filled the bright green sky.

"Durgan Dragons certainly take their time," Dett commented, swooping in carrying a smooth glass sphere in his right set of claws.

"We bring children with us," Caduceus began, "they can be slow."

"Why do you bring them, then?"

"You do not remember?"

"It was a long time ago," Dett sighed, "refresh my memory."

Caduceus stared at Dett. Was he telling the truth, or did he want Caduceus to reveal something?

"While I see no logical reason for their decision," Caduceus grumbled, "the ancients swore harmony and peace could be maintained if the children were invited to Dreamtime. They were not to be excluded."

"What if they become scared by what they see?" Dett asked.

"We guide, and we protect," Caduceus replied. "They are never alone."

"And what would happen if one of the children made it here alone?"

"It is impossible," Caduceus snorted, "they do not possess the skill."

"I would be wary against absolutes," Dett mused.

Caduceus was about to say something when Guldrun and Lin appeared.

"Observe," Caduceus reminded them, "only observe."

"Yes, Caduceus," they both replied.

When everyone appeared, it was time to begin. It was strange to see Lily alone, but when Caduceus looked carefully he saw Saja's spirit shape floating behind the child. He nodded to Saja, and she nodded in return.

"Follow," he said.

A flash of bright light instantly surrounded the Dragons and children, and they were flying faster than a ray of Sun. They appeared before the Great Tree. She was in full bloom, and her smell of rose, lily, and lilac permeated the air and made a few Ice Dragons swoon.

Caduceus spoke, "Here she is. We adore her limbs, trunk, and wisdom."

The children flew into the branches, running their fingers over the smooth pink bark. Lily and Bridget plunged their noses into her flowers and inhaled deeply. Sefani could see in Dreamtime without the aid of Perjas, and she flew in many circles around the Great Tree. Tomal nibbled on a leaf.

The Ice Dragons looked closely at her roots, which were fully exposed. The Great Tree was floating in the green sky, and her roots were endless. One Ice Dragon said she was going to fly to the bottom, to observe the tips of the roots.

After many minutes she returned panting, "I cannot see the tree's end!"

Other Ice Dragons murmured, and Dett nodded his head. The Dragons of Durga looked on with pride.

"Quite impressive," Dett said.

"Follow me," said Caduceus.

The green sky faded and was replaced with a roaring sound of waterfall.

"Hear of our journey," Caduceus intoned, "listen and understand."

The sky began throbbing with a deep purple heartbeat. An expanse of white water formed in front of the floating Dragon and Human bodies. Inside the rushing water old Dragon bodies appeared, each with a heartbeat throbbing in rhythm with the purple light.

"Pohevol traveled into the future by means of this Great Tree," Caduceus continued. "He saw horrible things."

The elder Dragons inside the water turned to stone, their heartbeats frozen into heavy, gray rocks. With a sudden rush of pressure and light, they exploded into a million fragments. These rained down upon the heads of the floating Dragons.

Dett raised a wing to shield his eyes, and Lily noticed

that one of his eyes was not real. Instead of the piercing green in Realtime, Dett's left eye was a glassy rock of obsidian.

Just as she sucked in her breath, Dett turned and winked this brilliant eye at her. Immediately—so fast that Lily had to ask herself if he had truly looked at her—Dett turned back to the image of dying Dragons, took his wing that had been a shield and thrust it at the waterfall.

"Explain!" Dett roared.

Pohevol appeared in front of Dett, ten times his normal size and with enormous blue wings. He was as big as Zor.

"Blue wings?" Lily thought to Pohevol.

"There is a reason," he replied. "You will understand at another time."

"Dett, we come to ask the Dragons of Iceloch to make a dear sacrifice," Pohevol floated in front of the waterfall, which was now a cascade of rainbows.

"Explain!" Dett roared again.

"I shall," Pohevol said with measured calm. "Watch."

The waterfall turned into a sphere, and the Dragons and children began circling around its rush of waters. Pohevol hovered on the top of the sphere, his bright blue wings spread out and curled slightly inward at the tips.

Inside the sphere the observers watched as Pohevol's story repeated itself. The Great Tree spun, Pohevol flew inside, and the future appeared with its foul images—the belching brick structures, the gasping and dying tribes, the choking Humans, the misery, the suffering, and the absence. The absence of Dragons.

Dett peered into the sphere closely. His head turned,

as he used his eye of obsidian to search. It moved slowly, then rapidly. He shot his head up to Pohevol, "Where is my tribe?" he demanded. "Where are the Dragons?"

"That is why we are here, and why we need your help."

"The Dragons are gone in this future of yours?" Dett asked, his eyefolds raised.

"Yes," Pohevol said. "In the future, according to the visions of the Great Tree, Dragons do not exist."

The Ice Dragons spun away from the sphere of water visions and reformed in a triangle. Their tails pointed to the sky, which was now raining green mist.

Dett flew back to the Dragons of Durga and asked them to enter the triangle. Zor, Ius, Anippe, and Caduceus flew under the Ice Dragons and entered the triangle. The children encircled the sphere and joined hands. They turned their faces up to Pohevol and closed their eyes. The amulets pulsed, glowing bright red against their necks.

"Will they believe you?" Lily thought to Pohevol.

"We will know very soon," he replied.

Dett, back inside the triangle, whispered into the ear of Caduceus, "It is not logical."

"We must let go of logic for this decision," Caduceus turned his head to stare into Dett's shining eye.

"Logic is the only way to proceed," Dett said. "Always."

"What does your heart feel when you see the images?" Anippe asked the other Ice Dragons.

"I feel a tightening," said one.

"I feel anger," hissed another.

Another whispered, "I want to know why."

"What do you want us to do?" Dett asked Zor.

"We want two of your strongest Dragons to go into hiding, to reside for as long as it takes to understand this most dangerous future. We know we ask much of these two Dragons, as this time exists perhaps 1,000 Suns from now," Zor said, "but we believe it is the only way to preserve Dragons." He lowered his head, awaiting a loud outburst from the eldest Ice Dragon.

Dett surprised everyone. He remained silent and still.

Caduceus used this pause to shift the scene. A silver fog appeared. The Dragons, children, and Pohevol were now in Saja's cave.

Saja nestled in one corner of the cave, sleeping soundly. Her egg lay in the middle of the nest of precious stones and gems. Incense filled their nostrils, and soft music wafted around their floating bodies. Her cave walls had images of faraway lands, and her wall coverings seemed to dance to the music and cradle the billows of smoke.

Saja's Dreamtime spirit floated to her sleeping Realtime form. She lowered herself and nuzzled her own closed eyes. She then flew to her egg and hovered over it, blowing smoke and steam. She tapped the egg and watched as a small heartbeat glowed inside. A small Dragling spirit, identical to Saja, appeared beside the egg and Saja pointed her slender horn to meet the tiny Dragling's horn.

"Why did we come here?" Dett demanded of Caduceus.

"To show you that hiding is nothing new to Dragons," Caduceus pointed to the sleeping Saja.

"You dwell indoors when nurturing your eggs," Dett reminded him. "The Dragons of Iceloch protect their eggs in the freezing water beneath the ice."

"We are not asking you to hide in caves," Caduceus added. "You may choose any place, including the frigid waters of your sleeping lairs."

Anippe said with distinction, "The only difference is that you must remain in hiding."

"We might discover the reason behind this absence in just a few Suns…" Zor began.

"Or it might take more than 500 Suns," Dett interjected.

"We are asking you to agree," Ius entered the conversation, "because we cannot think of any other way."

"Mud Dragon," Dett pulled out his obsidian eye and held it up for everyone to see, "there is always another way."

The eye began to glow, pulsating in rhythm with Saja's sleeping music, and now everyone was bathed in a green light. They were no longer in Saja's cave. They were standing on a frozen ocean. The sky was pale green, and the ice floor was pink.

"The ancient Ice Dragons predicted this future many, many Suns ago," Dett called out. "Dragons and children of Durga, listen to and understand what we have to say."

Dett breathed a blanket of fire across the pink ice and created a large and inviting bed. The children crawled on top and watched Dett as if in a trance.

"No one has asked, and yet we feel the question on your lips. Why are we here? Why do Ice Dragons dwell in this land of bitter cold? Why do we feast upon the flesh of other tribes? Why would we choose this life? We could tell you our hearts beat with more vigor in the cold, and that would be true. We could tell you the blood that races through our veins prefers to be chilled, and that would be true." Dett took a deep breath and blew a stream of fire that cut into the green sky and revealed a painting floating on a golden pedestal.

"We could also tell you we are waiting for a battle—a war between Dragons and Humans. A war against those who have embraced only one aspect of cold and have ignored the full complexity of what cold truly means."

Ius felt his heart begin to pound, so he searched for Zor's eyes. When he found his friend staring intently upon Dett, Ius closed his eyes and tried to calm the drum inside his chest.

"What are you saying?" Caduceus approached Dett.

"I am saying that sometimes the best defense is to initiate a formidable offense," Dett revealed his sharp fangs. "The Dragons of Iceloch will not go into hiding. We are preparing to go to war."

"No! No! NO!" The children were the first to turn around.

From where did this voice come? The Dragons quickly searched the beating heart of Tomal. The loud scream, which was clearly from a young male, did not come from the throat of Tomal.

Pohevol turned to Labrys, and instantly her Dreamtime form disappeared.

"You seem to have an interloper," Dett turned to Caduceus. "I thought you said they did not possess the skill."

"Is Zun here?" Caduceus asked Lily.

Lily shook her head, "No."

"And yet his voice is?" Dett mused.

Dett turned to Lily and peered into her amulet, "Little child, do you know why this boy cries out with a voice that can reach our sacred Dreamtime?"

Lily knew this Ice Dragon could easily sniff trickery or lies. She carefully stood up on the bed of fire and bowed to Dett.

"He cries out because he's seen the same visions as your tribe," Lily replied. "He's scared of what Dragons can do."

Dett turned from Lily to Ius and then Caduceus. "The boy has visions of fighting Dragons?" Dett asked the two Durgan Dragons.

They nodded their heads.

"Then he must be present at the game," Dett smiled mischievously.

"Of what game do you speak?" Caduceus stared into Dett's black eye.

Dett lowered his eyefolds, "The only game, of course."

"Dragon chess," Anippe whispered.

"Yes, Dragon chess," Dett bowed to the Dragons of Durga.

"Why would we play?" Caduceus continued to follow Dett's sparkling roving eye.

"To see who holds the most wisdom," he began, "and to decide which strategy is best—hiding or fighting."

The children looked at each other. Was Dett considering their plan? A game of Dragon chess would decide whether or not the Ice Dragons would go into hiding? Lily immediately thought to Pohevol, "Who plays Dragon chess in Durga?"

Pohevol remained silent.

Lily searched the green sky and frozen pink ocean for the Cat. He was nowhere to be found.

Anippe whispered to Lily, "He went back to Realtime, to help Labrys with Zun."

Lily nodded her head and touched Anippe's slender tail, "Who plays Dragon chess, Anippe?"

Lily watched as a slow smile spread across the River Dragon's golden brown face, "I do."

～ ～

When Labrys awoke outside the cave, she saw Zun standing before her with his arms outstretched. His eyes were shut, and he held a small dagger in his hand. She watched as he crouched, made scratches in the rock near the fire, and then stood up again. He screamed, "No!" and the sound punctured the frigid air. Adrianne was awake and crouching near the cave wall.

Sleepwalking, Labrys thought to herself. I wonder if he knows?

Labrys reached for her satchel and pulled out azurite, a dark blue gem. She placed the stone under Zun's nose and told him to lower himself to the floor of the cave.

"Slowly," she crooned to the boy, "good, follow the stone."

Zun, drawn to the gem, got down on his hands and knees and lowered his head to the floor. He stretched out his body, and placed the dagger on a rock near the fire. He then curled into a tight ball and closed his fist around the azurite. Labrys let him keep the stone. She blew a puff of smoke over his body and motioned for Adrianne to keep him there for a few more hours. Labrys needed to go, now.

Adrianne edged her way over to Zun and placed one leg on his forehead. Sleep, she thought. Sleep. Labrys released a slow chuckle when she saw the Spider's furry green leg moving over the boy's face. Would he sleep so soundly if he knew how his slumber was created?

Labrys looked into the sleeping cave and saw the Dragons still actively Dreaming. Their eyes were moving rhythmically underneath the many eyefolds. They will remain in Dreamtime for at least four more hours, she thought. I must try.

Labrys leapt off the edge of the rocky cliff and flew to the ice. The cold air calmed her blood, and the smell of ice pulled her body to the ocean of blue and white. When she approached the Sea of Iceloch, she circled over the holes through which the Ice Dragons entered their sleeping lairs. She gazed at their floating bodies and marveled at how they held their breath in such frigid waters.

One hole in particular seemed to whisper to her. Labrys flew to it and stared down into the freezing water. She looked around and saw that no one had followed her. Without thinking of what may lie beneath, Labrys tucked her wings close to her body, pointed her two sets of legs, and dove into the sea.

❦ 16 ❧

THE UNDERWATER VALLEY

Once in the water, Labrys allowed her body to adjust to the freezing temperature. She swam around the sleeping Ice Dragons, peering at their gently swaying scales. There were at least fifty Dragons in this loch, and their bodies floated like underwater icebergs. Most were multiple shades of blue, green, and gray. Their claws extended and retracted in their slumber.

Labrys saw a Seal swim by Dett and poke his nose near the Dragon's tucked leg. Dett moved, and suddenly Labrys felt the need to breathe. She swam to a hole and raised her head slowly out of the water. Water droplets slid off her scales, as her curved face surveyed the land above the ice crust. She took a breath and sank back into the deep.

Underwater she felt a current pulling her away from

the sleeping Ice Dragons. Relaxing her muscles, she let the current take her. At first she moved slowly, but as she moved farther away from the sleeping lair, she began to glide through the water at a swift pace. The ice shelf above her became thinner and thinner, and then it disappeared completely.

She was in the open ocean, away from land, free in the midnight Sun.

Labrys swam as fast as she could and then soared for the surface. In a remarkable leap, she breached the water and flew through the air. Water sprayed and cascaded around her in a tremendous shower. She aimed for the sea and crashed into the blue ocean with a loud boom.

She was home.

Why did I ever leave? Racing through the water, she asked herself this question.

Using only her fin wings, she swam in large circles, creating a whirlpool. She then relaxed and allowed the force of the water to carry her. A group of Herring became caught in the vortex, and she watched as they frantically tried to escape.

Labrys stopped the underwater tornado, freed the Herring, and began swimming South as fast as her wings could take her. She passed a mother Blue Whale and her calf, a group of giant Sea Turtles, and then she saw him. Swimming to the right of her was another Sea Dragon.

Labrys came to a sudden stop. She swam in a tight circle and trained her eyes on him.

The other Dragon stopped. He mimicked her every move.

"Who are you?" the voice rumbled through the water

and surrounded her body and her heart.

She floated in the sea, staring at the other Dragon. She opened her mouth, amazed that she could speak through water, "I am Labrys of Durga."

"Durga," the Dragon repeated, "that is far to the South. How many Suns have you seen, and what are you doing here?"

He swam closer to Labrys and revealed his full black body, wings outstretched, glistening in the Sun-streaked water.

"I am 489 Suns and have come with others to Iceloch to reveal painful news," she searched his emerald green eyes and began craving her satchel of precious stones, tucked away in the Iceloch cave.

The black Dragon lowered his wings and pushed to the surface. Following him, Labrys broke through the water and breathed deeply. The two Dragons bobbed along the top, gently fanning their wings below in the icy waters.

"What is this news, Labrys of Durga?"

Before she answered, Labrys looked around at the endless expanse of sea. "Are there many other Sea Dragons here?" she asked.

Carefully watching her searching eyes, the Dragon replied, "No, most prefer the warmer waters near the Motherland." He watched his words sink in, "I am the only Sea Dragon to live near Iceloch."

"What is your relationship with Ice Dragons?" she was drawn towards his glistening black body, as she swam around him in slow circles.

"Would you like to know my name and age?" he

evaded the question.

She stopped swimming, "Of course."

"I am Merdon. I have swum the seas for 590 Suns."

Merdon, she thought. Merdon.

He continued, "We do not commune, the Ice Dragons and I. They are isolationists, and they do not desire my company."

Labrys lowered herself back into the ocean, and Merdon followed. Swimming for a few minutes like this, Merdon said, "Now it is your turn to follow me."

He dove down vertically into the depths of the water. Labrys chased him, keeping her eyes locked on his undulating tail. It was difficult to see him at first, but then her eyes did an amazing thing. They began to glow. A light encircled her pupils, and suddenly she could see Merdon as if it were daylight in the nadir of the sea. He looked back at her, and she saw his eyes were glowing just as brightly.

I remember, she thought.

Merdon stopped at an underwater canyon shelf. He floated to the edge and motioned for Labrys to stand beside him. With both of their eyes lighting the waterscape, Labrys marveled at the scenery. Similar to the iceberg promontories floating above water, mountainous ridges existed below. Expansive cliffs and canyons could be seen for miles. Large and small Fish swam in continuous lines and erratic patterns around the crags and valleys. Huge bowl-shaped creatures with translucent ribbons floated in the water.

"Jellyfish," Merdon pointed to the ribbons. "Do not touch those unless you want a jolt."

"How long can you stay under water without

breathing?" Labrys asked. She felt her lungs beginning to strain.

Merdon smiled and motioned for her to follow him, "Swim with me." He dove off the shelf, and she did the same.

They swam further into the underwater valley and came to the bottom of an iceberg, shimmering electric blue. Labrys followed Merdon to the edge of the ice shelf and noticed light green algae attached to the ceiling, like spring's first growth. They swam until they reached a skin of water. Pushing through this surface, Labrys emerged in an immense underwater cave. The first breaths of air were so pure and sweet, she had to go back underwater to keep from becoming dizzy.

She slowly came back up into the perfect air and looked around.

"This is the inside of Fionn Iceberg," Merdon said.

"It is incredible," she whispered. "The air is. . ."

"Sweet as honey," Merdon finished.

"Yes," she said, "even that."

"Come," Merdon motioned to her. "Come out of the water."

Labrys watched as Merdon climbed out of the water and began lighting Dragon candles in small niches around the cave. She pulled her body out of the water and lowered herself at the edge of the pool. The walls were slick and sometimes bulging. The top of the cave rose 300 feet and spiraled into a never-ending cone.

Labrys kept taking deep breaths, amazed at how the air slid over her lungs like evaporated sugar. Each breath made her hungry for another. As Merdon finished lighting the candles, the room appeared in all of its glory.

Like a Bear's ice den, the underwater cave smelled of Cod, Capelin, and Herring. She saw elaborate sculptures made from Fish bones. She saw bones of Skate and Shark, and bones from a sea mammal, the Gray Whale. The walls seemed to be dripping with luminous water, but she realized it must be a trick of the light, as it was far too cold for any melt. Looking back to the pool, she saw the water flickering with microscopic Flagellates, spinning and converging near the edge of ice. They, too, seemed to shimmer with internal light.

"How did you. . ." she began.

"Take more breaths," he gleamed.

The air was cool, sweet, and powerful. It filled her lungs and enlivened her blood. She continued to see new crevices in the walls and more shimmering lights. The ice seemed to be living. She was certain the walls were breathing with her.

She asked Merdon, "Is it alive?"

"In a way," he answered. "I found this cave hundreds of Suns ago," Merdon glowed. "When I found the valley outside of Fionn, I did not want to surface for many days. The underwater ice pulled me closer that day, almost as if it were calling to me. I smelled the air locked inside. I could sense the sweet oxygen trapped inside the cave. When I first arrived, it was intoxicating. I could not leave for many weeks."

Labrys smiled at him and nodded in agreement.

"Now tell me," Merdon said, lying against the smooth cave shelf. "What is this painful news?"

Labrys looked around at this underwater world. She

imagined staying beneath the waters for all eternity. She looked into his shining green eyes and felt comfortable and safe. He would do this, she thought. He could do this, and it would not cause him any discomfort.

"Can you imagine in 1,000 Suns a world without Dragons?"

He leaned his head to one side and watched Labrys. Her iridescent wings freely extended themselves behind her sturdy fin-shaped ones.

"Labrys of Durga," he sighed, "I have lived apart from Dragons for many Suns. Yes, I can imagine a world without Dragons. Tell me more of what you mean."

"In Durga there lives a Visitor, a great winged Cat named Pohevol, who has traveled to the future," Labrys continued with the story, explaining everything until the moment she saw his black body swimming in the sea alongside her.

"The Ice Dragons will never agree," Merdon said.

"The others are in Dreamtime with them now. They will do their best to convince them."

Merdon searched Labrys's eyes, "I believe you."

Labrys felt her blood chill, a cool and enjoyable sensation.

Merdon continued, "Some Dragons would accept this challenge." He looked around the ice cave, watching the flickering candles and the shadows made from their two bodies. "Some prefer to never surface. Some wish they could live forever underwater, away from the blistering Sun above."

Labrys felt the deep water pulling her body back to the open pool.

"Can we swim to the bottom of the ocean floor?" she asked Merdon.

"We can."

Labrys stepped off the shelf and dove into the pool. Merdon followed, and the two swam for five minutes, until Labrys saw the glow of white sand resting upon the underwater floor. Ice Crabs danced their sideways step to make room for the approaching Dragons. Fish with their own glowing lights darted in front of Labrys's shining eyes. When she touched the bottom, she turned to find Merdon.

He was right behind her. When he landed next to Labrys, he lowered his body until he was splayed out flat on the sandy floor. His wings looked like gigantic Rays, rippling along the base, waiting for something to come.

Labrys lay down next to him, spread her wings in a similar fashion, and watched the ocean currents move slowly above their resting bodies. She felt the sand under her wings and the water above her heart, and she knew this felt like home. After a time, she turned her head towards his.

He was staring at her.

They both looked at each other for a long time.

⚜ 17 ⚜

DRAGON CHESS

Shaking off sleep, the Dragons of Durga awoke with Sun-strained eyes. This land of ice was so bright, the Sun's light pierced even the deepest caves with probing rays. The children stretched and groggily rubbed their eyes, looking around for Zun.

Lily watched as Zor and Ius unfolded their sleeping bodies. Tomal crawled away from the blue chest of Ius, and Zor carefully nudged Sefani away from the blanket of his red wing. The two Dragons found a clear path and walked to the mouth of the cave, flapping their wings and calling to each other in low rumbles.

They found Zun asleep at the edge of the cave, shivering under his blankets and clutching the azurite. Sleeping next to Zun, Adrianne's furry body was curled into a ball. Labrys was nowhere to be found.

"Labrys!" Zor roared into the bright Sun-filled day.

His voice crashed against the icebergs and vibrated

across the frozen valley. Adrianne jumped to all eight legs, her many eyes flashing with anticipation. Zun's eyes flew open and he reached for his knife. Guldrun and Lin woke up with a start, frozen drool hanging from their faces like beards.

"What?" shouted Lin.

"Who?" shouted Guldrun.

"Where is Labrys?" Ius grabbed Lin's neck and squeezed.

"She's here," Lin squirmed, "right there!" He struggled to point where Labrys had been sleeping.

Ius let Lin go, and the smaller Mud Dragon looked perplexed when he saw no sleeping Sea Dragon at the mouth of the cave.

"She was there, I swear!" Guldrun tried to rescue his brother.

Zor growled, "We asked you to be watchers!"

Ius whispered, "We asked Labrys to be a watcher, too."

"Do we now need watchers to watch the watchers?" Caduceus chuckled, as he walked up next to Zor and Ius.

"You find humor in this?" Zor asked.

"She is a Sea Dragon, remember? Just like my father," Caduceus yawned. "I am sure she is just enjoying an afternoon swim."

Guldrun shivered, "In this cold?"

"She is adjusting," Caduceus replied.

The long Shifting Dragon stretched and looked back into the bright cave, "We must eat and prepare for the tournament."

"We are playing Dragon chess," Zor said. "Dett said

nothing about a tournament."

"Ice Dragons do not play just one game," Caduceus flexed his claws in the Sunlight. "They will settle for no fewer than three."

Zun stood up and moved away from the Dragons. His warm breath hit the cold air and made tiny plumes of fog. He looked inside the cave, searching for the children. As if in answer, Tomal and Bridget walked out of the cave, dressed in full ice coverings and nibbling on apple bread. When they stood by the Dragons, the yeasty smell drifted up and made the Dragon bellies rumble. Lily, who was guiding Sefani out of the cave, had to move out of the way as Zor and the three Mud Dragons raced back inside. She turned around and watched as soil fruit came flying out of bags. Juice dribbled down their chins and stained the flashing claws red. Numerous loaves of bread were shoved into ravenous mouths, and deep sighs of relief were released into the frigid air.

Guldrun burped, "I could eat all of the soil fruit!"

"But you wouldn't be that dense," Lin answered.

"I bet you couldn't eat it all," Guldrun turned to face his brother.

"I bet I could."

Ius picked up both of the brothers' bags and held them high above their heads. He muttered, "It is a wonder the elders allowed you two to come."

"Give it back," Zor cajoled, "they are only playing."

"Do not joke about this fruit," Ius chastised them, "Do you hear me?"

"Yes, Ius," Guldrun sulked.

Lin offered a loaf to Ius, "Have some more bread?"

Ius grabbed the bread from Lin and snapped the loaf in two. He tossed one piece to Zor, who caught it with his mouth. He tossed the other up and devoured it whole.

After the children and Dragons had enough to eat, the Dragons put on their protective coverings and went down the cliff to meet the Ice Dragons. Adrianne chose to stay by the fire, as she had not fully prepared herself for the intense cold. She wanted to absorb the fire's heat and trap it inside her inner core. Mortoof, still asleep, was snoring softly in the cave, fully relishing the remaining warmth and scent of blue Dragon.

As the children climbed down the jagged ice, carefully making their way to the frozen floor, the Dragons flew in wide circles, stretching wings and legs. Their protective capes rippled around them. Zor blew gusts of steam to clear his throat, and Caduceus flew upside down exposing his undersnout to the clear blue sky.

"Should I search for Labrys?" Anippe called out.

"Have you misplaced your brain?" Zor banked left to fly next to her. "We need you for the games!"

"I am the only Dragon comfortable in water," she swooped below Zor and used her tail to knock him off balance. Ius snorted.

Caduceus flew under Anippe and interjected, "Labrys will come back in good time. Stop worrying." He flew ahead of the Dragons and slowed when they were above Iceloch's sleeping lair.

Zor corrected the awkward flying caused by Anippe's interference and glared at Ius, "She has a strong tail."

"Yes," Ius nodded seriously. "I understand."

Zor looked back at the children in the distance. He

saw the five forms walking next to Sophia's giant body, "Sophia is alone with the children. I will go back and walk with her."

"I will go with you," Ius turned to accompany his friend.

"No, you stay with Caduceus," Zor replied. "Besides, I think Dett likes you."

The blue Dragon blew a gust of smoke at Zor, which again made him fly off balance and stumble in the sky.

"That is the second time today," Zor grumbled. "There will not be a third."

As Zor flew back to Sophia and the children, the rest of the Dragons landed near the sleeping holes. Guldrun and Lin pawed at the water, snatching up their legs and blowing warm steam over their freezing extremities. Anippe stared into the gaping holes, searching for Labrys's shadow.

Once again, a low booming began as the Ice Dragons woke up. In quick successions and with loud groans, the Dragons exited their holes and stood dry and clean on the frozen floor of ice.

Dett yawned, "We need more sleep." He looked at Ius and Caduceus, "How any of you can think after such short naps is a mystery. How can you hibernate with any success?"

"We do not hibernate," Caduceus answered and then quickly added, "unfortunately."

Blinking and yawning again, Dett looked around for the children, "Did you find your little magician?"

"Zun?" Anippe asked.

"The one who breached Dreamtime, the one with the

voice," he replied.

"Yes," Ius responded, "we are not worried."

"You should be." Dett located the dark forms moving across the ice and turned back to Caduceus, "Are you ready for the games?"

"Where are they to occur?" Ius asked.

"Do you see the glacier at the edge of my claw?" Dett pointed to a white mountain that looked as if a Dragon had sliced the top off with one powerful stroke.

"Yes."

Dett smiled, "That is where we play chess."

"We need the baskets," Anippe said. "The children will need to be carried to the top."

"Whatever is necessary," Dett said.

When everyone finally arrived, Zor and Ius flew back to retrieve the baskets. After they returned, Ius told the children where the Dragons would be playing the games.

"They will be formidable players," Zor looked to Anippe. "Can you do this?"

Anippe stretched her long neck and flared her nostril horns, "I can play Dragon chess in my sleep. Do not worry feather face."

Zor glared at Anippe, and Ius snorted again.

"Feather face," Ius repeated. "I like it."

When the children climbed into the baskets, the Dragons lifted off the ice in mighty jumps. They flew across Iceloch and headed toward the flat glacier. They could see waiting Ice Dragons on top. From this distance they looked like Dragling dolls atop a play mountain. Everything was white and blue, except the dark Dragons moving across the glacier's skin.

As they flew closer to the ridge, they could see the Ice Dragons dragging an enormous object from the other side of the glacier. The chessboard. It was a slab of perfect ice, almost the size of Lapis Lake. Attached were four sturdy legs. When the Dragons finished erecting it, it stood 20 feet tall, about the size of a Mud Dragon's drum.

The Dragons of Durga landed near the board. As the baskets crunched down on the ice and snow, Anippe quickly let go of hers and flew in circles around the board. So they can see under my moves, she thought. Interesting.

"Where are the pieces?" she asked.

"They have yet to be fashioned," a small Ice Dragon answered.

Anippe looked around at the Ice Dragons. She watched closely as they stared into the surrounded glacier walls. They moved carefully, peering into the white, shifting their heads to the left and right. Their snouts almost touched the ice. What are they doing? Anippe wondered.

Pohevol and the Hawks flew over the glacier. Lily looked up and remembered how small Pohevol really was. She had seen him last in Dreamtime, where he had been as large as a Tree Dragon with luminous blue wings. In reality, he was no larger than a Jaguar, and his wings were black as charcoal.

When they landed, Pohevol found Lily and rubbed against her body.

"Are you ready?" he thought.

"For what? Children cannot play Dragon chess."

"The Dragons will need your abilities," he thought. "Of this I am sure."

Lily looked at Anippe and watched her concerned eyes. She looked to the Ice Dragons and wondered why they were staring into the glacier walls so intently.

"Dragons of Ice!" Dett called out. "Are you ready?"

Tails began thumping the ice mountain.

"Dragons of Durga," Dett began, "here are the rules."

Anippe, Caduceus, and Zor walked over to Dett and stood straight with their wings tucked upon their backs. The other Dragons stood behind them. Guldrun and Lin were trying their best to be serious while Sophia was carefully wrapping each head in Zor's extra capes.

The Hawks, Pohevol, and the children stood in a group outside of the Dragons.

Dett said, "The first game will commence when the last piece is cut, fire is used only during an opponent's turn, players have one chance to discuss a move with an outside player, and blocking is allowed with only one leg." He paused, "Children, feel free to move about under the board."

Anippe blinked her eyes slowly, "Did you say the chess pieces are cut?"

"Of course," Dett stared at her. "We have new ice pieces for each game."

"They are made of ice?" Zor asked incredulously.

"Of what else would they be made?" It was Dett's turn to be nonplussed.

Anippe moved toward Caduceus and whispered into his ear, "It is much easier to capture a piece if it is made of ice."

He whispered in response, "And to be captured."

Anippe addressed Dett, "You said only one leg is

allowed for blocking. I assume we can fly during our turn?"

"Of course," Dett nodded.

"Fine," Anippe said. "I see nothing wrong with these rules. I am ready to begin."

"Dragon chess with ice!" Tomal elbowed Bridget in the ribs. "Only one leg allowed during play. This is going to be exciting!"

"But won't it go much faster?" Bridget worried. "I mean, the pieces can melt!"

"Sure," Tomal replied, "but think about the blocking. And we can move under the board!"

Anippe positioned herself on the West side of the board and Dett moved to the East. The Sun beat down on the glassy surface and made the grooved squares sparkle. The air was freezing, as puffs of breath came from everyone's exhalation. The sky was a piercing blue.

At Dett's motion, the Ice Dragons began cutting chess pieces out of the glacier. They used their fire to melt the ice, and their claws to carve and mold the intricate shapes. The Dragons on Anippe's side cut into blue ice and the Dragon's on Dett's carved into pieces of white. When finished, they pulled out elaborate columns, pyramids, spheres, and the two most precious pieces of the game—the Dragon king and queen.

In a synchronized procession, each group marching to the appropriate side, the Ice Dragons carried the heavy pieces to the board. They placed all of the pieces—except two—in the appropriate squares. Then they stepped back. Two Ice Dragons flew above the board and hovered in the air.

The children moved closer to see the expansive playing surface. The pieces stood as tall as Human men and gleamed in the Sun. From beneath the board the ice pieces looked as if they had wills of their own.

"When the first queen touches the board, the game begins!" an Ice Dragon shrieked.

All eyes turned to the two Dragons holding the Queens.

Dett tapped the board with his claws and nodded to Anippe, "My guest shall have the first move."

Not taking her eyes off her queen, Anippe said, "Thank you."

As soon as Anippe's queen touched the board, Dett shot a stream of fire to attack her right-front pyramid. She calculated the severity of the attack and decided to let the piece go. When a Dragon spent mental energy focusing on attack offense, he might also miss a future move and block. She swiftly flew above the board and mentally planned her series of future moves. Right three, back nine, she thought. Diagonal eight, left four, left two, back twelve.

Just as Dett was close to melting all of her pyramid, she swooped above her left column and moved it to capture Dett's left-front pyramid. The Dragons of Durga had other ways of attacking pieces during an opponent's turn. One could use mental diversions, stealth by tail, or claw-to-claw combat. But these techniques took time, allowing the defending player to concentrate on future moves. Fire fighting would take too much concentration from the end game, so the speed of play was intense.

The children ran underneath the board, watching the

pieces melt into pools of steam and evaporate into the air. They watched Dett and Anippe fly low over the board, attacking with thin ribbons of fire. They saw blocks executed judiciously, the Dragons hovering over the ice board, only using one leg to fight.

During one move Dett said to Anippe, "Strange to use the Nool defense when you have already lost your third sphere."

Anippe did not reply. She knew verbal tactics were serious and deadly assaults. They could easily distract a player and lead to a hasty defeat. She focused her eyes and wings on the game, forcing Dett's voice to become inconsequential chatter. Sensing a future move, she flew to the opposite side of the board closest to Dett, and focused her fire on his corner-right pyramid.

Unwilling to let this important sentry go, Dett swooped in front of the attack and opened his mouth wide. Anippe's fire went inside his throat and before she could retreat, Dett had swallowed her fire whole.

Amazing, she thought. Durgan Dragons could not swallow another Dragon's fire. Dett possessed a formidable defense. But when she went back to begin another attack, she saw Dett stifle a slight cough.

Zor saw the cough as well. "He is skilled," he whispered to Ius, "but it comes with a price."

As the game continued, the Ice Dragons walked around the edge of the board, craning their heads to understand Dett's logic and watching with fascination as the River Dragon executed her many moves. Sometimes Anippe seemed under duress, yet other times she displayed a confident demeanor.

The Sun slid across the sky, and the temperature dipped a few degrees. Anippe started to shiver, her thin body rippling against the white landscape.

Zor called out, "Anippe!"

In a quick pass she flew over to him, and he threw a cape over her back. She flew back to the game. Dett, attempting an early capture of her queen, had unfolded a two-tiered attack against her remaining column and king.

Dett then flew to her corner and began moving his final pyramid back and forth, as if he could not decide upon a resting space. Anippe found herself drawn into his indecision. If he captured her column, she could counter-attack. Dett would have no remaining pyramids, a severe loss. But if she took his pyramid, that would leave her king wide open. He was trying to trap her.

She blew test fire at his pyramid, and Dett moved a piece on the opposite side of the board, directly placing her queen in jeopardy.

He flew to the ground and landed in silent satisfaction.

Her queen was in immediate danger. If Anippe lost this piece, Dett would be the winner.

Anippe called for a one-minute break and conferred with Zor.

The two Dragons bent into each other, passing quick words in a hushed succession.

After her minute was over, Anippe flew back to the board and started to move her king. As soon as her claw touched the king, Dett attacked her queen. Fire poured from his mouth and the ice queen began to melt, losing all of her intricate Dragon features.

Anippe roared to Dett and used one leg to knock his

mouth away from her queen. Dett caught this leg with his strong grip and arched his head back to the queen.

The struggle continued for many minutes. The two Dragons, both interlocked, wings flapping against and alongside each other, fought to destroy and save the queen.

Anippe kept looking down at the board, trying to plan her next move, while physically defending her queen. She saw a clear winning move, if she could only stop this attack.

The Ice Dragon employed mind diversions during the struggle in the air. Anippe began to feel insecure about her intelligence. She saw other Ice Dragons laughing at her and throwing their heads back in disbelief.

No, she thought, he is only making pictures in my mind.

She countered. She flooded her mind with images of control, strength, and precise mental acuity.

But Dett's mental diversions were enough to arrest her physical prowess. Dett, with a fast swipe of his left front leg, knocked Anippe off balance. He blew a river of fire at the queen. Anippe righted herself and hastily circled back to a defensive posture. But she was too late.

The queen was gone.

The Ice Dragons sent up a loud cheer, and the Dragons of Durga stared at the square that had no queen.

↭ 18 ↭

THE END GAME

Anippe flew to the ground and looked bewildered, "She is gone."

Ius walked over. "There are two more games," he reminded her.

"He won," she said in a daze.

"Let worry evaporate," Zor comforted Anippe. "You are playing in frigid air with ice pawns, thus the first game was bound to be difficult." He used his claw to lift up her chin, "You will win the next two games."

Anippe looked at the other side of the chessboard and the gathering of Ice Dragons raising wings and congratulating Dett on his win. Two more, she thought.

Anippe walked to the edge of the glacier and looked down at the endless white distance. She could see the ocean far to the left and the rising icebergs, floating like silent ships.

The children watched as Anippe stood at the glacier's

edge.

Zun pulled his coverings closer around his neck and scowled, "She's losing confidence."

Lily replied, "It sounds like you care about her." She turned to Sefani, "She'll win the next two games, right?"

"She has to think like an Ice Dragon," Sefani answered. "That's what I'd do."

Lily thought about this. She looked to find Pohevol and saw him perched on Sophia's back, preening his feathers. She caught his green eye. "How can I help her?" she thought.

Pohevol looked at the celebrating Ice Dragons, "Think cold thoughts."

Lily looked around at all of the ice. She looked into the sky and saw the Sun-washed blue expanding in an incessant reach.

After fifteen minutes the Ice Dragons started to converge around the board again.

"They do not require much rest now," Ius mumbled. "Do they?"

"They are confident this will be finished soon, and they want to go back to sleep," Zor answered. He turned to Anippe, "You can do this. I know you can."

Zun followed the red Dragon's movements. Zor looked at Anippe with obvious interest, but his eyes still seemed to mask some malevolent intent. Zun was certain of this. What would this red Dragon do if Anippe lost again? If the Ice Dragons didn't go into hiding, would the journey come to an abrupt end? Would they all go back to Durga, tails and heads hanging low? Zun secretly hoped this would happen. Lily always says I should hope, he thought.

After clearing the board and setting down the new pieces, the Ice Dragons hovered at the edge, holding out the new Queens. Dett and Anippe flew over to extract the prized possessions.

As he picked up his queen, Dett glanced at Anippe with a sparkle in his green eyes.

And then she saw it. Hidden deep in his right eye, she saw his doubt. I can do this, she thought. I know I can do this!

It was Dett's turn to begin, and when his queen touched the board, they flew into action. Anippe and Dett moved faster during the second game. Bridget and Tomal were out of breath, racing under the board and tracking each attack and block. Perjas guided Sefani to the open air, so she could feel and hear the swoops and dives and smell the pungent smoke floating on the remnants of Dragon fire. Every time she heard Dett blow his fire at one of Anippe's pieces, Sefani would clutch the Dog's fur.

Perjas barked in response. It was one of his barks that jolted Lily into thinking: What is similar to an Ice Dragon? She only understood Reptiles and Birds who lived in temperate forests. She had no extensive experience with animals who desired the cold. Wait, she thought. Yes I do! She could become the Trout in the Alys River outside of Saja's cave. Durgan Fish lived in frigid stream water for most of their lives. But how could she Shift into a Fish with no nearby water? And how would this Shift help Anippe? Dragon chess allowed no outside interference, and certainly Anippe would not ask for Lily's help. Help from a child? Lily remained at a loss.

The game progressed at an increasingly faster pace. Chess pieces melted so quickly it looked as if they were disappearing. Anippe and Dett used many mind diversions against each other, as they dared not look away from the board or each other's eyes. Their legs and wings became sore from the constant flying and blocking.

When the game neared the end, the Ice Dragons began clicking. They sounded like huge Beetles scraping their mandibles, or Grasshoppers rubbing their wings. Anippe forced herself to remove this noise from her ears. Concentrate, she thought. I can do this.

Dett was after her queen again. Destroying her pieces in a calculated march across the board, he remained on Anippe's side for many moves, fighting off her fire and moving his pawns in quick loops across and around her queen.

Just as he was about to capture her queen, Anippe focused all of her energy into her left front leg. When he lowered his head and moved in close to the board, she pounded him with all of her defensive strength.

Dett, unprepared for this force, flew backwards and hit the glacier floor next to the board. Anippe dove toward his queen and unleashed a flood of fire. The piece turned to vapor and vanished.

The children let loose cries of joy, and Ius and Zor roared into the blue sky.

Guldrun and Lin, who had been sulking earlier, flew up and did circles around the glacier, blowing fire back and forth at each other.

"Hey!" Guldrun yelled when Lin's fire came a bit too close to his brother's right wing.

"Toughen up, big brother!" Lin shouted back. "Be like Anippe!"

Perjas jumped up and began licking Sefani's face. Tomal and Bridget ran to Anippe and hugged her lowered neck. Anippe winked at Zor.

Ius whispered in her ear, "Strength knocked Dett away from the board."

"Speed got me to his queen," she wryly replied.

Zor interrupted them. "One more game you two," he smiled. "One more game."

Dett gathered with the Ice Dragons and moved far away from the chessboard. A biting wind began to blow, chapping the children's faces and making the muscles of the Durgan Dragons stiff. Pohevol lowered his body closer to Sophia's and shook ice crystals from his wings and fur.

Dett pounded the ice floor and looked back at the Dragons across the glacier top. His scales changed color with each breath—first a bright green, then a deep blue. A smaller silver and black Ice Dragon leaned into his neck and whispered. Dett smiled and nodded. He flew over to Anippe and the others.

"We are impressed, Anippe," he began. "You are clever and strong."

Anippe bowed to Dett, her cape fluttering wildly in the frigid wind.

"We are wondering," he proposed, "for this final game, if you would like to use a Fae?"

Ius pressed his claws into the ice, sending small fissures across the floor.

"You mentioned nothing of Faes earlier," Zor countered. "Why introduce them now?"

Confused, the children looked at each other. Worry lines spread across their brows.

"What's a Fae?" Bridget asked Tomal.

Tomal's eyes opened wide, "This is fine," he whispered. "A Fae is a second, an aid, someone to physically help you in the game."

"Why wouldn't Zor want Anippe to have one?" Lily asked.

"Because you can pick any Fae," Tomal replied. "And she's not home in Durga, so her choices will be limited."

"So Dett has access to any Fae he wants, any additional Dragon," Bridget added.

Zun looked at Lily, "You could be any animal she wants."

Lily turned to Zun. "She'd want another Dragon, I'm sure. She wouldn't want me."

"Are you so sure?" Pohevol thought to her.

Lily looked to Sophia and found Pohevol standing up on all four legs, wings outstretched, the Sun's rays rippling off his feathers. The Northern wind blew his fur taut against his face, and he braced himself against the onslaught.

Lily walked over to Anippe and touched her leg, "I could be your Fae."

"Perfect," Dett said quickly. "We accept."

"Wait!" Ius cried out, "This is moving too fast...Anippe did not agree to this!"

The Ice Dragons chirruped and clicked more loudly than before. Lily knew what they were thinking. A lowly Human child as a Fae? How laughable! The game would be over in seconds.

But the Dragons of Durga knew something the Ice Dragons did not. Anippe looked down at Lily, turned to find Pohevol, and ultimately, Caduceus. The Alligator face met Anippe's questioning eyes. He nodded his head and said, "Lily Fearn is a fine choice, Anippe."

Ius began to speak, but Zor grabbed his tail, "Lily Fearn is Human, but she is clever, Ius."

Ius focused on Zor's stressed speech. Lily Fearn?

"Fine!" Ius roared to Dett, as the meaning of Zor's tone suddenly made sense.

Anippe lowered her head in consent. "Lily will be my Fae," she said.

"Then I choose Varjus," Dett replied.

The silver and black Ice Dragon, half the size of Dett, stepped forward. Along his chest there were dull silver scales mottled like hammered iron. A row of black spikes marched along his back, and his wings were smooth and flat.

"Faes may be used at any time during the game," Dett informed the gathering.

"In any way?" Anippe asked.

Dett looked at her quizzically, "As long as they follow the rules established at the beginning of the game." He paused and lowered his large, Dragon head two inches above Lily's face. He sniffed her forehead and inhaled the air around her body, "Yes."

Anippe smiled, "Then I look forward to this final game."

The two groups separated and prepared for the final contest.

Caduceus flew over to the Ice Dragons and landed

smoothly, as a Snake might land on ice. He slithered to Dett and spoke clearly into the Ice Dragon's ear, "If you lose this game, you must agree to our terms."

"Now, we will not lose," Dett replied.

"You are sure of this?"

"I have my Fae," Dett said in an almost apologetic tone. "I cannot fail."

"You accept this Human child without question, without reservation?" Caduceus pushed Dett further.

"Yes!" Dett was exasperated, "We do!"

"So let it be," Caduceus pushed off the ice and flew back to the Durgan Dragons. Hovering in the sky, his wings flapping like an Osprey's, he called down, "I must check on my Serpent companions. The cold is increasing." He flew from the glacier and made for the snow-capped peaks on the edge of Iceloch.

Sophia watched as Caduceus became a small speck of purple in the distance. She looked around at the others and suddenly felt lonely. Labrys is still not here, she thought.

"I must find Labrys," Sophia said to Zor. "I cannot stay here any longer."

"Caduceus said she was fine," Zor reminded her, "and you hate flying."

"I will search for her after the game," Ius offered.

"I do not wish to wait," she said. "I will be fine, please do not try to discourage me."

"I will accompany her," Pohevol said from Sophia's shoulder. "I need to stretch my wings."

Zor turned to the ocean and searched the sea for any sign of Labrys. She had been gone for a long time, and Caduceus was no longer there to silence his worries.

"Fine," he said. "You both should find her." He reached out to touch one of Sophia's heads, "But please be careful."

Sophia's seven heads clenched with apprehension, but in a shudder filled with resolve, she burst into the sky. She awkwardly pawed her way up, forcing her heads to focus on flying in one direction. Pohevol followed her, pumping his wings to keep up with her deliberate pace. They both made a hazy arrow to the sea.

Below on the flattened glacier, the Ice Dragons stood waiting for the final game to begin. Anippe walked with Lily toward the edge of the platform. The River Dragon lowered her head and whispered, "Tell me everything you can become."

"You want animals who can withstand the cold, right?"

"Preferably," Anippe replied. "But at the right moment, I could use many types of skills and strengths."

Lily listed off all of the animals she could become. As she listened, Anippe's tail began to thump the ice floor. We can do this, she thought.

"We are ready to begin," Dett called over to Anippe. "You are taking too much time with your Fae."

Anippe turned her long neck around like a slow moving Snake, "We are ready." Her eyes pierced Dett's, and for a moment, Dett was worried he might actually lose.

The Ice Dragons took their positions above the board, hovering with the chess pieces. Zun walked from under the board to join Sefani and Perjas.

"What do you think?" Zun asked Sefani.

"I think Lily will be just fine."

"I wasn't worried about her," Zun began to protest.

Sefani stopped him, "Yes you were."

Zun looked at Sefani's face. Her eyes were open, but a milky cloud rested underneath the glassy part of her pupils. She used her hands to feel for Perjas, to touch her legs, and sometimes she held them in front of her body as if she were trying to catch a ball. Once she told Lily this was how she felt the movement of others. She could sense vibrations in the air.

"Well, maybe I am," he muttered.

Zun looked at Lily, who was standing and shivering on the ice. Was she shivering from cold or fear? He hoped the game ended quickly, as he wanted to go back to the cave. He needed time away from all of the Dragons.

"Begin!" Dett roared from below the hovering Ice Dragons. "You may start this time," he motioned toward Anippe.

When Anippe's queen skimmed the surface of the board, she whipped her head toward Lily and whispered, "Get ready."

Anippe pushed into the sky and flew around the board in three quick loops. Before Dett could blow fire, she grabbed her left-front pyramid and swooped to take his right column. As she flew low to make the capture, Varjus flew in front of her to guard Dett's pawn. He bared his teeth and lashed his silver tail.

Anippe retreated and realized Dett was circling her left-middle pyramid. She raced over to make an exchange. When Dett began his attack, she used her left leg to push him away. He countered by using his stream of fire against another pawn on the opposite side of the board. In a swooping glide, he arched his body sideways and blew fire toward a corner-sphere. Varjus flew to Dett's side and hovered as sentry in front of Dett's assault.

"Lily!" Anippe roared, "Falcon!"

Lily looked to the Sun and concentrated on a Falcon's eye. She would have to leave these warm coverings. She hoped the Falcon's feathers would keep her warm enough in the freezing cold. Faster than she thought possible, Lily made the Shift and burst into the air. She flew in a direct line toward Varjus and blasted him with her small yet powerful wing. He lost balance and dropped away from his protective stance.

Anippe, once again, knocked Dett away with her one leg and in a move faster than light, snatched the pawn he had attacked and made her own move, capturing Dett's right-front pyramid.

"Stop!" Dett cried. "Stop the game!"

The Ice Dragons flew to the air and encircled Dett. They turned toward Anippe and began roaring.

Dett emerged from the middle, "You lied! You have broken the rules! The Dragons of Durga have cheated the Dragons of Iceloch!"

Zor roared from the ice, "We have not! What is your accusation?"

"Your Fae is a Shape Shifter!"

Ius flew over and floated before Dett, "Faes were your idea! Caduceus spoke with you before the final game—he made sure you understood!"

"How could I question when I had no idea the child could Shift?" Dett roared.

"Why is it a problem?" Anippe flew over, "Caduceus is a Shifter, and he has played Dragon chess for many Suns."

"A Dragon Shifter is different," Varjus interrupted.

"You said we could use the child," Guldrun entered the argument.

Ius glared at the Mud Dragon, so Guldrun flew away, tail hanging low.

"Listen," Zor called from the ground. Lily flew away from the game and alighted on his shoulder. He continued, "Anippe asked if her Fae could be used in any way."

"If she followed the rules," Dett interjected.

"Are there any rules against Shifting?" Zor quipped.

"No," Dett said through clenched teeth, "but Humans are not supposed to Shift!"

"This Human does," Caduceus came soaring along the edge of the Sun's glare. Everyone turned to see his purple and green scales flashing in the light. From the air he called down to them, "You accepted her, Dett, without reservation. You cannot escape your words now."

Caduceus flew with his two Snake companions, who were wrapped in special coverings and coiled around his neck. He landed near the chessboard and pointed his wings vertically. He then tucked his wings upon his back and pawed the ground like a Dog covering his trail.

Caduceus raised his voice to a higher pitch, "Are you frightened of a small Human child?"

Dett glared at him, "Of course not!"

"Then let the game continue," Ius exclaimed.

Lily flew off Zor's shoulder and Shifted, in midair, into her Human form. With the Sun shining behind her body, the Shift looked like a trick of light or a wrinkle in the sky. She landed on the ice in a sprinter's crouch and peered up at Dett. She was ready for her next move.

Dett and Varjus stared at this new competitor. She was so small. She was so Human. How could she possibly beat them at their own game? Varjus knelt down and cut a large chunk of ice from the floor. He cut it into two pieces and blew fire upon them until they were perfect spheres. He gave one to Dett, and both Dragons held the globes up to the Sun. The ice shimmered in the light. Suddenly the Ice Dragons opened their mouths wide and swallowed the orbs whole.

Dett took a deep breath and said, "Let the game continue."

Anippe, Dett, and Varjus flew above the board while Lily, her hands on her hips, stood on the ice below.

Anippe smiled at Dett, "Your move."

With a formidable blast to the right, Dett grabbed his back-corner column and flew toward Anippe's king. What an arrogant Dragon, Anippe thought. She did a backward somersault to move into a defensive position. Varjus flew right behind Anippe so when she came out of the roll, he was waiting.

Anippe shouted, "Falcon, Giraffe!" and Lily closed her eyes for a moment's focus. Her Falcon body flew toward Varjus, and when she was right under his body, she Shifted into a Giraffe. She landed on the board with her legs splayed in four directions. Hastily adjusting her footing, Lily used her long neck to push Varjus out of Anippe's way. When Dett changed his mind and turned for her right-middle sphere, Anippe winked at Lily's brown

Giraffe eye. Lily lowered her neck and batted her long eyelashes at the brilliant River Dragon.

Varjus came back and flew toward Lily. She braced herself for impact but had to bend her long neck down, as he began flying under and through her stilted legs. Anippe was busy planning her next move, so Lily's awkward distress went unnoticed.

When Anippe collected her king and flew toward a powerful position on the board, she called out to Lily, "Tiger!"

Shifting at this exact moment was impossible. Varjus continued his loops through, over, and around her legs making Lily exceedingly dizzy. He looked like liquid mercury, weaving a silver chain of metal around her body. She tried to focus on a Tiger breathing—the warm fur, the fangs, and the muscle—but her Giraffe body kept adjusting its legs trying not to crash upon the board.

Dett took advantage of Lily's position and destroyed one of Anippe's pyramids. In response Anippe moved her king, taking Dett's middle sphere. In a moment of hesitation, Anippe looked back to check on Lily, and recognizing his chance, Dett made an ingenious move. He took Anippe's king without her defense.

"This will be over soon!" he roared to Anippe.

She flew to the square where her king used to sit and floated back and forth. Her brown, Horse-shaped head looked at the empty space. Her nostril horns flattened against her head, and she turned to face Dett. "There is plenty of time," she snapped.

Zun ran under the chessboard to where Lily was struggling against Varjus. He shouted up to her,

"Concentrate, Lily!"

The Giraffe looked down through the transparent board and focused on Zun. Varjus continued his loops and swirls. Dett and Anippe continued the game without their Faes.

"Caduceus!" Zun cried. "Do something to help her!"

Caduceus sat back on his hind legs, "She will decide if she wants to win, or if she does not want to win."

Zun furrowed his brows and glowered at the indifference of Caduceus. Tomal and Bridget joined Zun under Lily's struggling Giraffe body. "Lily!" Bridget shouted. "You can do this!"

Lily curled her thick neck into a tight ball and closed her eyes. Don't think about Varjus, she thought. Think about a Tiger. She focused and focused and allowed the smell of warm fur to enter her mind. She pushed the loud buzzing of Varjus away and instead allowed the sound of tangled jungle trees, tropical Birds, and Feline purring to fill her thoughts. The Giraffe body collapsed, and a splendid Tiger sprang out.

Lily bounded across the board, making sure to avoid the huge chess pieces. When she neared Anippe, she stopped and assumed a defensive posture. Varjus flew toward Lily, but had to dodge her massive swipes. Lily extended her Tiger's claws, opened her mouth, and roared. The crushing sound shocked everyone. Lily sounded indomitable. Varjus realized she may not be a Dragon, but her Tiger claws were just as dangerous.

Without the assurance of her king, Anippe had to concentrate on her many defensive moves. Her strategy had to revolve around protecting her queen. Lily concentrated on erecting a mental barrier to keep Varjus from entering her mind. *He's just an annoying Mosquito,* she thought. Anippe had Lily Shift into a Hawk, a Snake, and for one glorious minute, a Spitting Lizard. Varjus received a wet offering right in the eye, and Anippe captured Dett's king as a result.

It was now down to the two Queens. As long as they remained standing on the chessboard, there would be no winner. Lily did not have to worry about the freezing cold, as she was hot and exhausted from flying, running, and leaping.

Dett tried to help Varjus by turning his mind toward Lily, but Anippe kept him busy. He could not focus on the young Human Shifter.

After twenty minutes of queen chasing queen, pyramids setting barricades, and evasive strategies, Anippe saw her opening. Dett's queen stood flanked by a pyramid and his last sphere. If she could distract him by sacrificing her last pyramid, she might be able to take the royal Dragon down.

Anippe knew how she could distract Dett. She flew by Lily, now a tiny Mouse on the board, and grabbed her furry Rodent body. Flying in circles, too fast for Varjus or Dett to catch, she whispered into Lily's ear, "Become a Dragon. Think of your magician grandfather, and ask Saja for help."

Anippe flew down to the board and dropped Lily with a tremendous pass, soaring back to the sky and to her evasive moves.

How can I Shift into a Dragon? Lily thought. *It is not possible.* But her tiny Mouse ears heard a low humming her Human ears would have never perceived. Caduceus was humming. She scuttled to the edge of the chessboard and peered at the Dragon. With her Mouse perspective, Caduceus was now bigger than ever. He made the sign of the Shift in her direction, but he added a new claw position she had never seen before. Thoughts flooded her mind, He's helping me Shift into a Dragon!

Zun, Bridget, and Tomal ran to the edge of the chessboard to where Lily sat perched as a Mouse. Perjas led Sefani over, and she turned her ear to the towering ice board above her.

"Grandfather Thorn," Lily whispered. The children heard only tiny Mouse squeaks.

Lily looked at the children below and remembered how Thorn used illusion to make rocks disappear. She thought about Saja in Dreamtime and looked back to Caduceus who continued to make the new sign. His dazzling claws reflected the rays of the Sun.

She could Shift into a large Hooded-Lizard, and with the help of illusion and Saja, perhaps she could look like a Dragon—at least to those with weary eyes.

Lily focused all of her mental energy. She stared at Caduceus and longed to look anything like his huge Dragon body. She called out to Saja, begging her for help in the spirit realm. She prayed to her great grandfather, asking all the cells in her body to channel his revered magic. She stood on her hind legs, clutching the ice board with her Mouse claws and using her front legs to reach for the sky.

Anippe saw Lily's Mouse body standing and shivering in the wind. She shouted to Dett, "My Fae will capture your queen now! Watch!"

And then, exactly where the tiny Mouse stood, standing at the edge of the huge chessboard, quaking in the wind, an enormous explosion occurred. In the middle of the nexus of light, Lily transformed into a massive red Dragon. The air around her seemed to undulate in thick waves, blurring her form so that one had to look closely to see the red Dragon. She was hovering as large as Zor. She had thick armor covering her shoulders and legs, spikes protruding along her back, and a huge triangular spear at the end of her tail. Her face was serpentine, and her eyes glowed like fire. She screamed a piercing Dragon screech, and through the cold atmosphere it rippled toward Anippe and Dett.

Dett froze. He watched as Lily's blurry Dragon shape came racing toward him, intent upon him and him alone. He could not move. He was transfixed. Seeing Dett's immobile form, Varjus sprang into action, but Lily's tail rose above the black and silver Dragon. Something like a clap of pressurized wind hit him on the head. His lithe body careened to the right.

Anippe dove for Dett's queen and unleashed a cascade of rippling fire. The Dragon queen vanished in a puff of steam.

The Dragons of Durga won the game.

✧ 19 ✤

RESCUE

Tomal and Bridget cried out in joy and started jumping up and down on the thick ice floor. While they celebrated, Zun watched Lily. Unable to maintain her Dragon form, Lily began to collapse into her Human shape. Zun strained his eyes and saw Saja's spirit shape hovering directly behind Lily's shimmering Dragon body. Then both Saja and the red Dragon disappeared. Lily stood tall in her Human skin.

So that's how she did it, he thought.

Shivering and slightly blue from the cold, Lily walked to the edge of the board and looked up for Anippe.

The River Dragon swept down through the wind and gently lifted Lily off the edge. She carried her to the ice floor and let her go near the other children. Bridget and Tomal grabbed extra coverings and enveloped Lily in warmth and hugs.

"You did it!" Bridget beamed.

Tomal's eyes were glistening, "You became a Dragon."

Lily looked to find the Ice Dragons, huddled in a group near the edge of the board. She whispered, "It wasn't a pure Shift. I had some help."

Zun walked up and a slow smile appeared on his face. She could not remember the last time he had smiled at her. He moved his arm in a slight Snake ripple, and Lily knew he had caught a glimpse of Saja.

"It's good to have friends," Lily whispered.

"I agree," said Zun.

Sefani said, "The Ice Dragons must now choose those who will hide."

The children walked over to the Durgan Dragons and tried to hug some part of Anippe. Even Zun reached out to touch one of her legs. When he saw his fingers tremble as they neared her scales, he pulled his hand back and tucked it into his warm coverings. Lily saw this action as did Ius.

Caduceus, carrying a small chain that glinted in the evening Sun, walked over to Lily and thrust the gold into the sky.

"Kneel," he said.

Lily instinctually knelt to the ground. Zor, Ius, Anippe, and the two Mud brothers also knelt against the frozen ground. As if pulled by imaginary threads, the children came to their knees as well. When Sefani knelt, Perjas lowered his body to the floor.

Caduceus placed the Necklace around Lily's neck. It was a simple chain of gold link with a small sign of the Shift.

"To become a Dragon, no matter how much magic came to your aid, is nigh impossible," Caduceus said. "You are an accomplished Shifter, Lily Fearn. You are now in possession of your Necklace."

Anippe rose and roared, "To my Fae!"

Ius rose, "To the warrior!"

Zor rose and winked at Lily, "To a kindred spirit."

Guldrun and Lin rose as one, "To Lily!"

Caduceus spoke last, "To Lily Fearn."

The children stood up, and Lily smiled at all of them. She felt different, as if she were no longer tied as closely to their Human world. She wondered if this was what the coming change would feel like.

"Remember child," Caduceus's words came from above her like dropped thunder. "You are still under my tutelage. You are still an apprentice. Do not allow your Name or Necklace to become your identity. They are mere symbols of power," he lowered his Alligator head and peered into her eyes. "Symbols," he repeated, "of a power that must be revered…always."

Lily bowed her head with deference, "I understand."

"I hope so."

The Dragons of Durga looked over at the Ice Dragons and drew their capes closer to their bodies. Zor covered Anippe and whispered into her ear, "Nice game."

"Thank you," she replied, flaring her nostril horns.

Dett left the Ice Dragons and flew to Anippe.

Bowing to Anippe and Caduceus, he said, "We accept our loss. We shall agree to your terms."

"We thank you for your steadfast agreement," Caduceus answered with a reciprocal bow.

"But we ask for one caveat," Dett turned to his clan who remained on the other side of the glacier. "Tonight we would like to hold a gathering. We would like to say goodbye formally, with a proper feast."

Zor turned to Ius and raised his eyebrows. Ius shivered under his cape, "We are cold, Dett," Ius began. "We would like to begin our journey South."

"We ask only for one more night with the Dragons of Durga," Dett pushed. "You are asking two of us to give up hundreds, perhaps thousands of Suns. The least you can do is give us one more night."

Caduceus raised his front leg, "Yes," he boomed. "Of course we will stay for your feast!"

Lily turned to Anippe with worry lines etched into her forehead. She silently mouthed, "They will eat animals!"

Anippe nodded her head and solemnly closed her eyes.

⁓ ⁓

With slow and steady focus, Sophia and Pohevol flew toward the sea. Pohevol kept looking back at Sophia, who was counting in rhythm with each wing beat. The low Sun spilled around the snow-covered ice, and the craggy mountains jutted away from the ocean like broken teeth. Pohevol could see sleeping Bearded Seals on the edges of the drifting ice islands. Pohevol remembered Saja calling these areas of open water that were surrounded by ice, polynyas.

Sophia focused on the vast sea. Her heads fought the biting wind and kept dropping, then lifting. One head caught sight of a white shadow loping across the ice. The Polar Bear saw his world go momentarily dark. He looked up into the sky and reared back on his hind legs when he saw the seven-headed Dragon. Hoping to soothe his startled state, one of Sophia's heads began to fly toward him causing disagreement with her six others who were bent on reaching the sea.

Pohevol swooped down and flew under her wayward head, "The sea," he reminded her. "We must find Labrys, remember?"

"Forgive me," Sophia's wayward head muttered. "Did you see the Bear? He acted as if he had never seen a Dragon."

"He has probably never seen one with seven heads," he offered.

"Oh," Sophia said, as if remembering something. She then pulled her one head back to fly with the six others.

As they came to the edge of the thinning ice, they saw the lake of blue stretching endlessly toward the setting Sun. Pohevol saw a pod of Orcas breaching near the coast and a group of Caribou moving slowly across the frigid white landscape. They were traveling in the direction from where Pohevol and Sophia had just come.

"How will we find her?" Pohevol asked, swooping near Sophia and landing for a quick moment upon her back. Although his claws pinched into her scales, she could not feel the Feline points.

"If I allow one head to lower near the waters, I might smell her scent."

Pohevol's voice filled with concern, "But how will you fly straight?"

Sophia's head looked around at the intense blue glistening in the yellow Sunlight. "If I fly low, and you fly near my lowered head, I should be able to convince myself that I am walking on the water, not flying."

"What if you have trouble?" he asked. "Can you swim?"

Pohevol sensed that Sophia was scared. He felt her muscles tense under his claws, "No," she said flatly.

"Why are we even here?" Pohevol exclaimed into one of her ears. "You should not be out here without other Dragons!"

"I have you," one of her heads smiled at him. "I will be fine."

Pohevol let go of her back and flew alongside her. He looked down at the glassy surface below and saw small swells moving the water up and down like a breathing beast. Labrys, he thought, come back now.

"If we cannot find her soon," Pohevol warned, "we must fly back to the others."

"Everything will be fine," she replied.

Keeping the shore in sight, Sophia and Pohevol flew over the water in straight lines, approximately three miles at a time, out toward the Sun and then back to the land of ice. Sophia's lowered head hung loose and sniffed the waves below. As they traveled this way, back and forth across the sea, the waves began to increase in size. Sophia had to adjust her flying to stay just above the growing swells.

Like a Vulture riding heat currents emanating from land, Sophia rode the ocean swells, flying high and then low to keep her sniffing head close to the waters.

"I can smell her!" Sophia cried out, swooping low with the waves. "She was here earlier!"

"We must mark the spot!" Pohevol yelled back, as he realized the sound of the swells was beginning to overpower their voices.

"How?" Sophia questioned. "How can we mark water?"

Pohevol thought. He could squat on the water, leaving his pungent Feline odor. Perhaps Sophia could pull out some of her scales. No, I cannot ask her to do that, he thought.

"I will squat," he flew to one of her heads and told her his plan. "Let me know if you can smell me."

He flew above the swells and flapped his wings powerfully so he could tread the air. He marked the waters, and then flew back to her head, "Try to find me."

She rode the winds above the waves and sniffed, "Yes," she said, pulling back her nose and raising her eyebrows. "Your scent is quite strong."

Pohevol puffed out his chest and nodded his head. Felines were haughty about their ability to scent mark, "Now we can fly in circles from this spot. We will find her!"

As they flew in slow circles from Pohevol's scent mark, Sophia's heads stretched out desperately looking for Labrys's pink and gold scales.

Unbeknownst to the two, Sophia was not only soaring just above the swells, but she also was creating a small whirlpool within her flying circles. The waves grew higher and higher and began encircling Sophia. When Pohevol realized what was happening, it was too late.

"Pull up!" he screamed to Sophia, "Pull up!"

But before Sophia could fix all of her heads on the sky above, a huge wave came crashing over her sniffing head. The force of the water pulled the rest of her body under. She gasped and roared, fighting the waves, her wings flapping uselessly above and under the swells.

"Pohevol!" she cried, waves rolling over her heads like amorphous boulders. "Help me!"

Pohevol darted over the waves, diving low and grabbing her scales with his many claws. He pulled with every muscle he had, as his wings beat at the air trying to lift just one of her heads.

"Move your legs underwater!" he directed her.

"How?" she cried, terrified at what her body felt like thrashing under the crushing weight of the sea.

"Like a Horse runs on the ground," he called out. "Run under the water!"

Sophia tried to move her legs, but they felt like swollen forest logs. The waves continued to pound over her, roaring and clogging her ears. Two heads went under and did not surface.

"Pohevol!" Sophia screamed, "I am drowning!"

Pohevol let go of her scales and flew over the ocean shrieking and crying out in sheer Feline horror. He frantically searched for any nearby iceberg, Whale, Dragon, anyone who could help the struggling, seven-headed Dragon drowning in the sea.

There were no icebergs, and the ocean immediately surrounding them was void of any discernable life. There were no Dragons to be seen.

Three more heads went under, so Sophia thrashed

against the waves with her two remaining heads. She shrieked and cried and roared into the sky. Her wings came up for a few seconds and then plunged back under when a swell crashed over her. Her eyes rolled in their sockets, and she blew a river of fire around her that turned the waters red.

"Save your breath!" Pohevol cried down to her. "Do not release your fire!"

Sophia looked up at him with terror filling her eyes, and then her remaining heads crumpled. She slumped and allowed the waves to drag her under.

Pohevol flew to the waves, grasping in the water for one of her heads, grabbing only empty clawfuls of salt water. He hovered above the water and looked blankly at the empty swells. Sophia was gone, sucked into a watery grave. He rose into the sky and circled above the barren sea.

Suddenly, in a roar of force and cascading white spray, a Narwhal the size of a Blue Whale ruptured the surface carrying Sophia on her back. One of Sophia's heads was wrapped around the pointed white horn at the front of the Whale. Her other heads were draped around the Narwhal's back. Her wings splayed out immobile.

"Sophia!" Pohevol cried out, "Sophia speak to me!"

Two eyes opened from the head around the horn, her mouth parted, and water gushed out, "I am alive," she whispered, her voice barely audible over the roaring of the sea. "But my lungs are filled with too much water."

The Narwhal looked at Pohevol with her bright black eye. She then made a low, echoing sound, and Sophia mimicked the tongue.

"What did she say?" Pohevol asked.

"She is taking me to the ice," Sophia said with effort. "It is hard to breathe," she coughed up more water. "I am not sure if I will live."

Pohevol looked to the shore. The ice shelf was many miles away. The Narwhal would have to swim slowly, keeping Sophia's seven heads above the water. He feared Sophia might not survive the trip.

"I will fly to get the others," he shouted. "Zor and Ius can carry you back!"

"Go," she whispered, "go."

Pohevol stared at her water-crushed body. Her many heads lay slack, still as weighted stone. "Do not give up!" Pohevol said forcefully. "I will return with Dragons!"

Pohevol attacked the wind with his wings and legs, flying as fast as possible, aiming for Iceloch. The Narwhal swam through the waves, straining to keep Sophia's seven heads in the air. Sophia concentrated on breathing and closed her eyes against the white water spray.

❦ ❧

Hundreds of feet under the water's surface, Merdon and Labrys swam along the ocean floor. They had gone back to the ice cave for more sweet air, as Merdon wanted to show Labrys two more things before she returned to her group in Iceloch.

Floating along the bottom, their bright eyes lighting the way, Merdon and Labrys came to a seafloor geyser. Every few minutes a blast of boiling water belched out of the hot vent. Surrounding the opening were colonies of

Clams, Tubeworms, and sulfur-feeding bacteria. The colonies were brightly colored and moved in slow pulses, like mesmerizing dancers.

"They are beautiful," Labrys whispered.

"There is more," Merdon swam a few hundred feet and came upon multiple underwater mountains with white caps. "Mud volcanoes," he said. "Look closely."

Labrys peered at the volcanoes and saw mounds of white sediment covered with bubbles and more bacteria. Eelpout, a long and thin white Fish, swam near the mud volcanoes, feeding on the orange and purple bacteria. The water near the hot vents and volcanoes was as warm as the Sun's rays.

"Other Sea Dragons do not know about these places," Merdon said. "Even in the cold seas, I can experience warm waters too."

Labrys felt dizzy. She was not certain if she needed air or if something else was happening, but she told Merdon she needed to breathe.

He recognized the urgency in her voice, so he shot up through the water, creating a channel through which she could easily swim to the surface. As Labrys neared the water's skin, her eyes stopped glowing, and she could see the pale light of the Sun filtering through the blue waves.

When her head broke through the surface, Labrys choked on the air that now seemed strange to her. The direct Sunlight blinded her eyes, and she whipped her head around to find Merdon. He remained underwater.

"Come up," she said to his blurry image.

"Now that you have more air," he replied with a slight pause, "come back down."

She turned to the ice shelf in the distance, "I must go back to my family," she said. "They need me."

"I understand."

"Can you not fly with me to meet my family from Durga?"

He swam around her and lifted his head above the water to speak clearly. "Labrys," he said, "there are many things I would do for you, but I cannot leave my home." The Sun gleamed off his black scales, making them look like slabs of polished ebony. "I will always remain here."

A high-pitched cry erupted in the distance, and Labrys arched her neck to hear it more distinctly. "Pohevol!" she opened her eyes wide in fear. "My friend is in trouble!"

She turned to Merdon who was already under the water, moving away from her. She dove under and swam toward his face, "I must go now."

"I must remain," he replied.

"Will I see you again?" she asked. "May I find you again?"

"You know where I choose to dwell," Merdon's eyes were as comforting as the midnight sky. "You can always find me there."

Labrys swam back to the surface, "I will see you again," she called back to him. With a giant leap she broke through the water and flew through the air, fixated on Pohevol's cry.

∽ ∾

By the time Labrys heard Pohevol's cry, the flying Cat had already landed on the top of the Iceloch glacier.

His body was covered with freezing ice, and his eyes were awash in dread.

"Zor, Ius!" he screamed. "Sophia may be dying! Fly to the sea!"

The two Dragons leapt to all four legs, alarmed, alert, and flapping their wings to prepare for abrupt flight. Like metal shot from the Sun's bow, they soared to the sea.

Pohevol flew after Zor and attached himself to the red Dragon's back. While Zor pumped his wings and fixed his feathered Dragon face upon the distant blue, Pohevol told him what happened to Sophia.

At the end of the story Zor said, "Go to Adrianne, now. Tell her exactly what you told me. My feathers cannot heal this wound."

Pohevol dove off the Dragon and made for the ice cave. His Cat wings ached from the flying and exertion, but his concern for Sophia released the needed adrenaline. He focused on the white glaciers and willed his wings to keep pumping.

When Zor and Ius reached the open sea, Ius scanned the blue water, searching for her large brown body. He saw her just two miles ahead of them, floating on the Narwhal's back. Sophia's head looked impaled upon the horn.

"No!" screamed Ius.

When Zor saw Sophia's head, he knew what his friend must be thinking. "No, Ius!" he screamed in the wind. "The Narwhal saved Sophia! She is resting upon the horn!"

Ius blinked again at the image. As they came closer to the Whale, he saw Zor was right. The beast was carrying

Sophia's limp body.

"Sophia!" Ius cried out. "We are here!"

Sophia did not respond. The Narwhal stopped swimming and looked up at the two flying Dragons above her.

Zor shouted down, "We are going to lift you up! Let go of the Narwhal's horn!"

Sophia gripped the horn even tighter. Zor and Ius hovered above her and reached for different parts of her heavy body. As they lifted her off the Narwhal's back, Sophia refused to let go of the horn.

"Sophia!" Zor yelled, "let go!"

Sophia would not release the horn. She opened one eye and saw the Dragons pulling her limp body and six heads to the sky. She opened her other eye and saw the kind Narwhal beneath her.

The Narwhal began the low echoing sound, and this time she added a few clicks.

"I will not survive," Sophia said to the Narwhal in its language. "Let me die with you."

The Narwhal arched her back and began a series of low clicks.

"No, the air is too cold," Sophia whispered. "I want to stay here, resting on you."

Just then, Labrys arrived above the mass of struggling Dragons. She craned her neck to understand what was happening. As Zor and Ius lifted the bulk of Sophia's body, Labrys shrieked, "What is wrong with Sophia?"

"There is little time!" Zor roared. "Labrys, tell her to let go of the Narwhal!"

Labrys followed Zor's orders and hovered above

Sophia's clutching head, "Sophia, I am here. I am with you. Let go of the horn!" she begged.

Sophia looked up at Labrys and sighed, "We found you." She then slumped against the horn.

Sensing the limp body, the Narwhal slid from underneath Sophia and cautiously removed her horn from the Dragon's grasp.

Zor and Ius responded in turn by lifting the massive Dragon from the sea. Water cascaded off her limp body, and the setting Sun made rainbows appear in the droplets. Ius clutched Sophia's wings, Labrys cradled some of her heads, and Zor flew under her stomach to carry the bulk of her weight on his back. Just as he had carried the fallen boulder in the Durgan forest, Zor pumped his resilient red wings with Sophia wedged between his shoulder blades.

Flying in a choppy tangle, Zor, Ius, and Labrys carried Sophia back to the ice shore.

When they approached Iceloch, they saw Ice Dragons stretching their necks to see the spectacle above. Anippe, Guldrun, and Lin were preparing to fly the children back to the cave. They signaled their intent from the glacier.

Caduceus and Pohevol waved from the cave where Adrianne, Mortoof, and the Hawks stood waiting.

As the Dragons flew to the entrance, the Hawks and Pohevol flew away to make more room for the landing. Mortoof also scuttled to the side. Caduceus moved backward into the cave, sheltering his eyes from the Sun. He watched as the huge form slowly lowered, as if a living shadow descended at the mouth of the cave.

When Zor touched the ground, he extended his wings into a taut hammock. Ius and Labrys carefully raised the pale brown Dragon and placed her on the floor of the cave. Sophia was not breathing.

Adrianne worked quickly. The large green Spider climbed over Sophia's many heads spinning webs over her nostrils and mouths. Her furry legs commenced a frenzy of spinning and tying, spinning and ripping of threads. She climbed onto Sophia's chest and used one leg to tap for the Dragon's heart. Crouching low to the scales, she splayed her legs out so her abdomen could feel the throbbing heart. Unsatisfied, she scampered back to the mouths and retied her webs.

Sophia began to tremble, and a fervent quaking was felt throughout the cave. Mortoof ran to Ius and climbed up the blue Dragon's leg to find his safe spot amid Dragon scales.

"What can we do?" Zor yelled out.

Caduceus's deep voice came from inside the cave, "Adrianne is healing her, Zor. Have faith."

Adrianne fastened her eight eyes on Caduceus. Then she looked back to Sophia. She ran over the Dragon again and began ripping the webs away from her nostrils and mouths. In great convulsions, Sophia started to regurgitate pools of salt water. A hideous retching echoed throughout the cave, as Sophia's seven heads released the liquid. Small Fish, expelled from Sophia's long necks, landed on the cave floor and began flopping and twisting. Pohevol and Doren flew in, gathered up the gasping Fish, and carried them away from the cave.

When Sophia was done retching and coughing, she looked around at the group of Dragons staring at her.

"Labrys," she called out weakly.

"I am here."

A plaintive cry escaped one of her mouths, "Where were you?"

The other Dragons moved closer to listen to Labrys and Sophia. Labrys looked at Zor and Caduceus and quickly lowered her gaze to the floor. Adrianne rested on Sophia's heart and fixed all eight eyes upon Labrys.

"I understand now," the Sea Dragon seemed to choke on her words. "My absence was wrong."

"Why did you not inform us of your leaving?" Ius demanded.

"You were sleeping," she explained. "I did not imagine I would be gone very long. The sea was calling me," her voice faltered. "I just wanted a taste of it, that is all."

Zor said, "Labrys...you were gone all day."

She lifted her head and looked into his eyes, "I am truly sorry." She turned to Sophia and knelt beside her, "From now until the end of this journey, I will always tell you where I am going, I promise."

Sophia closed her eyes and soft smiles crept across her seven mouths.

Adrianne crawled to one of Sophia's ears and whispered.

Sophia opened her eyes and said, "Adrianne says I need rest and hot tea."

Caduceus said, "Leave the tea to me." He leapt off the cave's edge and hovered in the opening. "The Dragons of Iceloch are preparing for their feast. I will explain what has happened and let them know we will attend." Looking down at Sophia he said, "And I will bring back the best tea you have ever sipped, my dearest Sophia."

When Caduceus flew away, Anippe, Guldrun, and Lin descended with the children in baskets. Lily and Bridget jumped out and knelt by Sophia. Tomal held Sefani's hand from inside the basket. Zun stared blankly at the seven-headed Dragon's labored and shallow breathing.

Bridget was the first to speak, "Sophia, are you all right?"

Sophia turned a head toward the children and tried to smile, "I think so."

Zor spoke next, "She must rest. Adrianne has healed her, but she is still too weak to talk. Let us prepare for the feast and allow her time to sleep."

Feast—this was now the second time Mortoof had heard the word. The small Rat began to pace, running left and right across Ius's massive blue back. He had not had a proper meal in days. If he were going to be of any decent assistance during this trip, he knew he must ingest a suitable dinner.

Guldrun and Lin gingerly moved their large bodies closer to Sophia. Guldrun lowered himself to one of her heads, and Lin knelt by another. When she cracked her eyelids open to see the two brothers, they simultaneously began peeling their scales off one by one. Guldrun squinted dramatically at Sophia and with a sharp flick of his right leg, fingered a scale and slowly removed it like a banana peel. Lin flashed his huge double-set of teeth at her other head and with both legs, grasped two scales and pulled as if he were revealing a covered work of art.

They continued to peel their scales. When they were done, they left a pile where Adrianne had hovered most…right over Sophia's heart.

Sophia whispered to the brothers, "Thank you."

They blushed bright orange and purple and slid away from her.

Sefani could feel Sophia moving her multiple heads, trying to find comfortable positions. She climbed out of the basket, and Perjas jumped out to take his place by her side. He guided Sefani around Sophia's heads and helped to place coverings under each one to provide comfort.

Zun watched with curiosity. Lily walked over to Sefani and placed a hand on her shoulder, "No one thought to do that. You couldn't even see her discomfort, and yet you knew."

"I can feel agitation more easily than peace," Sefani looked up to Lily. "Unfortunately."

The wind began to howl outside the cave, and a scented smoke drifted inside, tickling everyone's nostrils. Labrys, still grieving her role in Sophia's near death, peered down the cliff and saw an orange fire staining the sky.

"The Ice Dragons have started their feast," she told the others. She remembered the bone sculptures in Merdon's underwater cave. *Now we will see what they eat and how they nourish themselves*, she thought. She looked at Lily and Zun. *He will surely hold this against us.*

Nervous, the children looked toward the fire. Everyone was thinking about the Ice Dragons' food. No trees stood in Iceloch. No plants pushed up out of the ice. The animals who resided in this land fed off other animals. In order to survive, the Ice Dragons ate the largest animals under and on the ice.

Bridget wondered, *How will they bring the animals to the feast?*

Tomal doubted, They wouldn't kill them in front of our eyes, would they?

Lily shivered and thought, How many animals will it take to fill an Ice Dragon's belly?

Sefani pondered, Will they share some bits with Perjas?

Zun glowered, Will the Dragons of Durga remember the taste of flesh?

"We must go," Zor interrupted the children's silent thoughts. "Make sure to bring enough food."

"No," Pohevol flew over and landed on Zor's shoulder. "We must ration our food. What is left must last until we reach Jha'mah."

Guldrun moaned, "I don't think I can fly without a full belly."

His brother reminded him, "You might not have the stomach to eat when you see what the Ice Dragons will have on their plates."

Zor looked at Ius, who was standing with his mouth slightly open. His nostrils were inhaling the sweet smoke wafting in soft plumes. Zor turned to Lin, "We will manage to participate in this feast. Remember Lin, the Dragons of Durga chose to forgo animal flesh." He flashed his sharp red claws at the Mud Dragon, "We did evolve to kill."

Ius looked directly at Zun, "And yet we do not."

The tension was palpable in the cold air. Anippe turned to Zor and Ius and said, "Well, I am famished. Would anyone enjoy some leek stew? You know, leeks, a member of the onion family? A plant?"

Lily stifled a laugh, and Sefani said, "I'd love some

stew."

"Well, then," Anippe sighed, "back in the basket!"

As the children clambered back in the baskets, the Dragons collected the food supplies and made sure Sophia was asleep. They decided Adrianne and Labrys would stay, and Anippe would fly back with the food.

After watching the Dragons and children vanish into the sky, Labrys unwrapped the wildflowers Sophia had asked her to carry before they had left Durga. Gently placing various bundles around Sophia, making sure a small bundle was tucked under each nose, Labrys knelt by her friend and sobbed.

20

ICE FEAST

Near the edge of the Halvard Polynya, a sliver of blue water carved out of the ice, the Dragons of Iceloch stoked their fire. The Ice Dragons abhorred any type of heat except the kind emitted from their throats. But this Dragon fire was different. Inside the glowing castles of flame, ice boughs shimmered. Instead of giving off heat, this fire burst forth a gale of cold.

Dett and his Fae, Varjus, walked around the fire, muttering incantations and sticking their legs into the flames to adjust the ice boughs.

"They will not enjoy this type of fire," Varjus grumbled.

"We will split it," Dett replied, fastening his green eye on the middle bough. "That one," he pointed at an ice bough about to fall. "We need to move it higher.

Varjus stuck in both of his front legs and lifted the bough. Leaning it against another, he found the right spot and pulled out his legs. They were glowing so brightly, his silver legs looked like elongated Suns.

"Why must it be you?" Varjus asked his friend.

"I allowed the loss to occur," Dett said simply. "I should be the one to pay the price."

"But we could choose a younger Dragon," Varjus implored. "Perhaps Yamuna would agree?"

"No, it will be me and Riema," Dett answered. "We are the strongest, and she is my mate. We will survive."

Varjus looked into the fire and watched the ice glisten in the orange and yellow flames. He cooled his legs over the flickering light, "We will miss you."

"You may visit us as often as you like," Dett smiled at his Fae. "The Durgan Dragons said we must hide, but they said nothing about other Dragons staying away."

Varjus raised his eyefolds, "That is true."

Dett walked over and clapped his friend on the back, "And I have another idea."

"What?" Varjus said quickly.

"You can always fly East."

Varjus looked into Dett's green eye and saw a mountain, a plume of smoke, and a great battle.

"Yes," his word slid out like thin smoke, "I can."

They heard a loud flapping and saw the arriving Dragons and Pohevol. As soon as the baskets set down, the children began to cough and shiver.

"What's happening?" Sefani asked.

Tomal looked around the basket, "It's colder here than in the air!"

Lily looked to Pohevol and thought, "We can't survive this cold!"

Pohevol flew to Zor and alighted on his arm. After a few words, the red Dragon spoke to Dett, "I have heard tales of your ice fires. We appreciate the cold welcome, Dett, but we cannot withstand this chill."

"Please do not think we would be so rude as to freeze our guests," Dett exclaimed. "We have yet to split the fire."

At Dett's command, Varjus signaled three Ice Dragons who were carrying something wrapped under their wings. When they neared the fire, Varjus whispered into the flames and a column appeared. It broke the blaze in two.

The flames nearest the Ice Dragons, consuming the ice boughs, roared and continued to release the freezing wind, but the flames on the other side were devoid of ice and began to die. The three Ice Dragons came to the fire and revealed their secret gift. Huge wooden logs from some distant taiga were carefully lowered into the dying tendrils of flame. Upon contact, the flame came back to life and devoured the wood. An eruption of smoke crawled into the sky, and the Dragons and children of Durga felt a welcome blast of heat pour over their bodies.

"So," Dett spoke to the entire gathering, "Riema and I have agreed to do as the Dragons of Durga have asked. We shall sequester ourselves in the ice caves along the Northern-most edge of Iceloch. We shall only leave the cave to sleep and hunt, and only during the Winter Solstice, under the cover of the longest night. Our bodies should survive without food and sleep for the rest of the Sun," he paused. "We hope."

He turned to Riema, a lavender Ice Dragon with gray

eyes and two powerful teeth jutting from her bottom jaw.

"Dett and I have courted for many Suns," she revealed to the group. "One day I will desire an egg. I will welcome the seclusion."

An Ice Dragon asked, "How will you obtain the necessary jewels and stones?"

Anippe answered, "Labrys brought sacks of gems. She will give to Riema as many as she would like to claim."

Riema thanked Anippe and looked to Dett and then Caduceus, "Your Dragons have won, Shifter. I hope you are happy."

Caduceus walked over to Riema. He bowed to the lavender Ice Dragon and said in a deep yet agitated voice, "I am not happy. I cannot remember the last time I was happy. I believe we must do anything and everything to save our race." He searched her eyes, "I sincerely appreciate your sacrifice."

Dett came over to Riema and took her claws into his own, "Tonight we make our departure. Let us feast until the Sun climbs upward into the sky!"

The children looked to the West and saw the Sun hovering just above the smooth lake of ice. It was only a few days after Midsummer, and the Sun still refused to set in this land of cold. Bridget reminded them that in Durga, the night would be black and the stars would be shining like scattered gems.

Ius, Guldrun, and Lin brought out their drums and began to pound a steady tattoo. Pohevol sat next to Ius, preening his feathers and grooming his thick black fur. Anippe pulled out her pot filled with leeks and started her stew. Zor took out cakes of clove bread, sugared apples, and sacks of soil fruit. Mortoof scampered around the Dragons, snatching little pieces of bread and fruit. The Ice Dragons watched with curiosity. While they had heard tales of Dragons who did not eat animals, they had never witnessed the practice firsthand.

The children sat near their side of the fire, as their eyes absorbed the Dragons of Iceloch.

Bridget whispered in Tomal's ear, "Where's their food?"

"I don't know," he replied.

Sefani unwrapped a sweet cinnamon quobloon and took healthy bites. She sniffed the air for any sign of animal flesh. Perjas lifted his nose in the air and began to whine. Sefani called out to the Ice Dragons, "May Perjas share in your meal? He is tired of my oats and fruit. He would love to eat some flesh."

Bridget wrinkled her nose. Tomal nudged her, "He is a Dog, remember."

"I know," she said, "but it's still disgusting."

"I can hear you," Sefani said softly, "which means so can Perjas."

"Sorry," Bridget apologized. "It's just hard to imagine…"

"I know. But just because I could never chew on a dead animal, doesn't mean I should belittle another animal's choice."

Varjus walked over to Sefani and lowered his head to sniff her hands. He also looked at Perjas, who seemed to become passive under the silver Dragon's gaze.

"Will he hunt Seal or Polar Bear?" the silver Dragon inquired.

Sefani whispered to Perjas and shook her head, "They are too large for him to catch."

"Will he try some type of small Fish?"

After a quick interchange, Sefani nodded her head, "He would love to hunt Fish."

"He may join our hunting party," Varjus motioned for Perjas to follow. "We should be gone for only a few minutes."

When the Durgan Dragons lowered themselves to eat on the ice floor, the Ice Dragons launched themselves into the air. Careful to not puncture his skin, Varjus grabbed Perjas and flew behind the exodus.

Dett shouted back to the Dragons and children by the fire, "We shall return with our feast," he looked to Zun. "We apologize in advance." The children heard the green and blue Ice Dragon laugh for the first time.

Bridget stood up and watched the Ice Dragons fly toward the other side of the polynya. In the distance she could see a small spot of gray. Seals, she thought.

"Where's your seeing glass?" she murmured.

Tomal searched through his satchel, "You sure you want to watch?" he said.

"Yes, I want to know."

Tomal handed her his glass and watched as she held the device to her eyes and searched the sky for Dragons. She saw them clearly with the help of the glass. They were only two hundred feet from the Seals. She focused on the gray shapes and clearly saw a few heads jerk up to the sky. As their mouths began to open and close, she imagined their quick barking cries. The oval bodies rushed to the water, but the Dragons were too fast. Darting like

Mosquitoes over the Lazuli, the Ice Dragons descended upon the Seals and scooped them up like strewn stones.

She saw Varjus with two claws grasping Perjas over the polynya and two others clutching a dead Seal. As they returned to the feast, Bridget saw two Herring dangling from the Dog's mouth.

"It happened so fast," she uttered, her mouth remaining slightly open.

"Are they already dead?" Tomal asked.

Bridget continued to watch the returning Dragons.

"Bridget," Tomal asked with a louder voice. "Are they already dead?"

"Oh, sorry," she dropped the seeing glass from her eyes. "Yes. They must have suffocated them or broken their necks. They're just dangling from their claws." Her eyes lost some glimmer, "They aren't moving."

"Good," Tomal lowered his head. "I didn't want them to suffer."

Lily asked, "How many do they have?"

"Most have four or five Seals."

"That's not too bad," she said.

Zun cried out, "Not too bad? What could be worse? They just murdered innocent Seals!"

Lily turned to Zun, "Do you get angry at Pohevol when he hunts? Do you not want to fly with the Hawks because they eat animals?"

"I didn't want to come on this trip at all," he reminded her.

Lily glared at him, "When we're home, do you blame Perjas and Pohevol and the other carnivores for hunting?"

"I don't think about it."

"Well maybe you should," she said. "Just because we were made to forage, does not mean others were made to." She pointed to Perjas flying in front of the midnight Sun, carrying the fat Fish in his jowls, "I won't begrudge that Dog for his craving. He risked the polynya to catch his dinner. You shouldn't judge him."

"The Dragons risk nothing when they scoop up defenseless Seals!" he shouted.

"They have nothing else to eat here!" she shouted back.

"Then why don't they leave? Why don't they give up this bloody practice?" his eyes were blazing.

Zor walked over and lowered his red feathered face over Zun's shaking body, "That is exactly what our ancestors did, boy." He thumped his tail. "But then, you would not know the tale, would you?"

Refusing to look at Zor, Zun glared at Lily and the others. He stormed off into a patch of snow and dropped in a huff.

Just as Zun dropped to the snow, the Dragons of Iceloch returned to their side of the blazing fire. They released the dead Seals onto the ice and landed next to the limp gray, black, and speckled bodies. Varjus lowered Perjas to the ground, and the Dog loped over to Sefani and began eating his small catch of Fish by her feet. She ruffled the fur around his neck, but after a few minutes she had to turn away and plug her nose.

The Ice Dragons pushed the Seals into a mound and blew plumes of smoke over the dead animals. The smoke encircled the mound and settled over the wet skins.

Dett turned to the Durgan Dragons, "Would you like

to taste what you have missed all these many Suns?"

Varjus added, "There is nothing as delicious as fresh-smoked Seal."

Caduceus replied, "No thank you, Dett. We are quite satisfied with our food."

Dett nodded and sank his teeth into a chunk of flesh.

The Ice Dragons grabbed up the bodies and tore into the Seals as if eating soft bread. Bright red blood dripped down their faces. Lily turned to Zun, who was still sulking in the snow. Don't look, she thought. Please don't look.

As if he heard her thoughts, Zun turned to watch the Ice Dragons. Horror inched across his face, as he brought his hands up to his parted lips. Blood covered the Dragons' claws and teeth. Great belches roared, as Seal bones were tossed in the air. Laughter poured from their feasting bodies. Zun kept his hands planted over his mouth and tried not to gag.

Anippe, sensing the discomfort, asked the children to come gather soup. After filling everyone's bowls, she gathered the remaining soup and bread to take to Sophia and Labrys. She also searched through one of Adrianne's bags and located a clutch of dried Grasshoppers.

"I will bring back gems for Riema," she told Zor. To Dett she bowed and tried not to focus on his blood-stained teeth, "It was an honor to play against such a wise competitor, and I..."

He stopped her in mid-sentence, "Do not humiliate me with your humility." Using an ice pick, he loosed a piece of Seal muscle caught between his teeth, "I will practice with Riema in the cave and will work my leg muscles until they are harder than your river boulders. I hope to play you again."

"As do I," Anippe said.

"I hope to win," he smiled.

"I hope not," Anippe rose in the air and hovered above Riema, "Before we leave tomorrow, I will leave a sack of jewels outside your cave."

Riema nodded her thanks.

Anippe took one last look at the gathering of Ice Dragons and flew toward the ice cave. Her long and thin body found wind currents in the frosty air. She sped toward the cave like a ribbon of lightning.

As the Dragons and children finished eating, the Sun sat full and hazy in the distance. Sleepiness filled the minds of everyone, especially the Ice Dragons.

"We must sleep before our journey South," Pohevol said to Zor.

"Yes, it is time to say goodbye."

The children packed up the remaining food, and the Mud brothers put away the drums. Mortoof jumped atop Ius and patted his round belly in satisfaction. Pohevol flew to Zun and encouraged him to come back to the others. Finally the children climbed into the baskets, and Guldrun and Lin positioned themselves above, flapping their wings in a steady hover.

Dett and Riema stood on all four legs and extended their wings, "We are ready for our seclusion," he said. "Varjus, Riema, and I will hunt more Seal to fill the cave, then we will continue our deep sleep near the ice shelf."

"Hopefully it will not be for long," Caduceus said to Riema and Dett. "We will do everything in our power to stop this future."

"We believe you," Dett said. Varjus moved into Dett's line of sight, and the two Dragons stared icily upon each other. "We too have faith that we will not be in hiding for long," he said.

"Goodbye Dragons of Durga," Riema called out.

"Goodbye Dragons of Iceloch," Caduceus replied.

"Until we meet again?" Dett lowered his head to Caduceus.

Caduceus Shifted into a Seal three times the size of Dett. He looked around, using his soft black eyes to stare at the Ice Dragons below. Dett sucked in his breath, gripped the ice with his claws, and lifted his lips in an attack snarl.

"Until that meeting, ponder this," Caduceus unleashed a Seal's bark that echoed off the nearby glaciers and shook the ground. He roared and roared and bellowed toward the bleeding Sun.

When he Shifted back into his Dragon form, he stared into Dett's glimmering green eye. "Are we not all brothers?" he asked. Then with an effortless push, he rose into the sky and flew off to join Sophia and Anippe. The Dragons of Durga followed his lead.

✥ 21 ✥

JOURNEY SOUTH

After many hours of sleep, void of any activity in Dreamtime, the Dragons and children began to rouse. The air seemed warmer and the Sun less piercing.

Labrys sat at the edge of the cave's mouth, staring out to the sea. Her eyes darted from the low mountains that rose precipitously from the waters to the ocean itself. Land or sea, she thought. Trees or water. We are asking other Dragons to go into hiding. Why not me?

"Yes," she said aloud, "why not me?"

Zor sat down next to her and asked, "Why not you?"

"Zor," Labrys turned to face him. "The Ice Dragons have agreed. Next you will convince the Vine Dragons," she paused. "You also need Sea Dragons to volunteer."

"And...?" Zor prompted her.

"I am a Sea Dragon."

"A Sea Dragon who fought with Menet about going on this journey in the first place," Zor's voice was terse.

"What are you saying, Labrys?"

"I met another Sea Dragon yesterday," she searched Zor's eyes. "That is why I was gone for so long."

"Ah," Zor sighed, "are there many in the Sea of Iceloch?"

"No. That is what makes him unique," her scales rippled. "He already hates coming above water, and he has found a way to stay under for many Moons."

"That is impossible," Zor replied. "I know your kind. You cannot go without air for more than an hour at a time."

"He has found a way, Zor. I cannot explain, but he can stay under."

"Are you saying you want to join him?" A wave of worry flashed over his feathered face.

"I think so."

Zor turned to look outside the cave. The ice stretched across the landscape until it reached the blue sea. Drift ice floated near the polynya ribbons. For the first time, Zor saw sea Birds flying in a straight line, heading toward the jagged glacier where the chess tournament had been.

"I swore I would protect you," he said.

"On the journey," she patted his leg. "If I agree to go into hiding, I will need no protection."

"When?" he asked. "When would you leave?"

"I would like to join him now."

"But we need you. We will be flying over oceans and lakes to arrive in the jungle. We will need your skills."

Labrys thought about the long flight to Jha'mah. She thought about the children and the promises she made under the canopy of trees in Durga.

"You are right," she said. "I will stay with the group until we reach the jungle. But then, I will turn back and fly to this sea."

"What about your divining skills and your fire skills? This feels wrong, Labrys."

"It will take a full week to fly South," she motioned to Anippe. "I could teach basic motions and practices to Anippe. There is no need for fire in the jungle or desert." A smile formed, "In fact, you will wish you had an Ice Dragon to cool your broiling skins."

Zor watched Anippe sleeping and thought about the journey without Labrys.

"Zor," she lowered her voice. "I am tired. I miss the sea. When I am with this Dragon, I feel like I am truly home. I want to stay with him, and I want to do this for our tribe. Please Zor, give me your blessing."

"It cannot be my blessing alone," Zor nodded to all of the rousing Dragons. "They must also agree."

A rumbling was heard as the other Dragons began rousing and shaking their groggy heads. Deep within the cave, Adrianne uncurled herself. She was sleeping tucked near her Dragon patient, far inside the belly of the ice cave, away from the frigid cold and wind gales. Her green legs crawled over Sophia's brown body listening and probing.

Sophia raised one head and spoke to the Spider in the Arachnid tongue, "Can I fly?"

"No," Adrianne answered. "They must carry you."

Sophia looked around to find Zor and Caduceus, "I am too heavy. I will be too much of a burden."

"That is foolish," the Spider said. "You need only a few more days of rest. They can easily carry you that distance. Now tell them, so they can prepare."

Sophia sat up and felt a rush of dizziness propel her back to the floor. Her lungs felt as if they had been ripped apart, and her many throats burned. She felt like movement was impossible.

"I cannot fly," she groaned.

Labrys walked inside the cave to kneel by Sophia's side, "Do not worry dear friend, we will carry you. You are still hurt."

"I am cold," Sophia whispered. "I want to go back to Durga."

Labrys nodded and lowered her head, "I understand what you are feeling, but we need you."

"There might be another translator in the jungle. Please let me go home."

Labrys felt burning shame rise from her heart and color her chest, neck, and head, "This is my fault. If you had not looked for me, you would be fine. I am sorry," she said. "I am so sorry."

Zor came in and knelt by Sophia, rubbing his pointed beak against one of her legs, "We were given seven amulets for a reason, Sophia. While we are eight Dragons now, this journey is far from over. Who knows what remains ahead of us in the Motherland and the Sands of Ochre? Please stay with us. Labrys is right, we need you."

Sefani, curled next to Perjas on the other side of the cave, heard this pleading. She called the other children to come and listen. As they heard the Dragons begging Sophia to stay with the group, a chill moved over them. Sefani called out to Sophia, "I wouldn't feel safe without you."

Bridget walked over to the Dragon and bowed, "I couldn't continue without you."

"Neither could I," Tomal stood up with his arms crossed on his chest.

Lily touched one of Sophia's necks, "It's not just Dragons who need you, Sophia. We need you too."

Lily's amulet began glowing a deep and pulsating red, which also made her new Shifting Necklace shine and sparkle. Sophia concentrated on the two necklaces and felt warmth enter her cold body, "I will stay."

The children climbed around her huge body to find a neck to hug. Sefani walked over and stroked the Dragon's smooth scales. Even Zun breathed more calmly. During the discussion, he kept thinking about her head speaking to him in his cave back in Durga. He did not have the will to stay if she were not there.

"I will carry her," Caduceus boomed from the front of the cave. The Sun's light filled the spaces around his form, so that all the children saw was a black shape of a Dragon, surrounded by white light. He looked like an enormous eye at the cave's opening.

"Are you sure?" Zor asked.

"Do not waste time questioning my intent," he snapped. He set down his bowl of tea, "We must leave Iceloch. I am tired of waiting."

Labrys whispered into Zor's ear, "He has slept in our company and with children for over five days now. He is more than grumpy."

Zor remembered. Caduceus, unlike other Dragons, preferred sleeping alone. The only companions to witness his slumber were Snakes. Zor walked up to Caduceus and stared at his scowling face. The veins in his eyes were swollen, his skin was pale lavender and light green, and his lips snarled whenever he saw one of the children move.

Zor leaned into the Alligator face, "Sophia is too large for one Dragon to carry, Caduceus. I will help you."

"I do not need your…"

Zor stopped him, "When we arrive at the jungle, you can sleep for a full day…by yourself."

Like steam from his tea, the idea of peace and quiet floated into Caduceus's brain. He squinted his eyes at Zor and muttered, "You must think I am strange, removing myself from Dragon activity, preferring to sleep alone."

"No," Zor shook his head in disagreement, "just different."

Caduceus took another sip of tea and sighed, "I need to breathe without interference." He nodded to the Snakes coiled together by a rock near the wall. "They do not speak in shrieks or incessant chatter. You are right. I am different. But this is something we must agree upon. We must leave this land of ice, now."

"I agree," Zor turned to the others and told them to pack, "Caduceus and I will carry Sophia."

Pohevol and the Hawks soared in, full from the early afternoon of hunting. The black and white Cat landed near Zor and shook his feathers and fur, "The wind is blowing South. It is the perfect day for flying."

Guldrun and Lin started wiggling with excited eyes. Lin said, "Let us carry the children this time!"

"Yes," Guldrun added. "We're experienced now. We didn't cause any problems in Iceloch. Please let us carry them!"

The Dragons conferred and agreed the egg brothers could carry the two baskets of children.

Guldrun and Lin flushed deep orange and purple and raced to the mouth of the cave. They had to check and double-check the baskets.

Guldrun looked at his claws, "I think I should file this one." He thrust it out for his brother to see. "Look how jagged it is," he continued. "It wouldn't be safe for grasping."

Lin looked at his own, "Oh," he fretted. "You're right." He noticed jagged edges on his own claws, "I need the file when you're done."

While Guldrun filed his claw, Lin began an elaborate routine of stretching. He stretched his front legs and took three deep breaths. He closed his eyes and stretched his hind legs. Guldrun eyed his brother and snickered.

"What?" Lin shrieked.

"You look foolish."

"I'm stretching," Lin hissed.

"Why?" Guldrun began filing another claw.

"Because it's an intelligent precaution."

"You?"

"Be quiet and give me that file!" Lin cried.

Guldrun threw the file at his brother. Instead of catching it, Lin ducked and the file fell off the edge of the cliff.

"See what you did!" Lin shrieked.

"Oh, I'll go get it," Guldrun groaned. "It's no big deal!"

"You're going to make them change their minds! Quit being foolish!"

Guldrun flew to the bottom of the ice cliff and retrieved the file. When he flew back up, he grumbled, "You are the foolish one," and refused to talk to his brother for a full five minutes.

Zor and Caduceus worked together to create a sturdy sling with which to carry Sophia. Zor's needles flashed, and Caduceus tested the strength of the threads. When they finished, the group was ready to leave. Everyone had eaten, all satchels were full, and the baskets were secure.

The Dragons carried Sophia out of the cave and rested her on the edge of the cliff. Carefully and with much effort, Sophia rolled her body into the sling. Anippe worked to smooth the fabric and secure the cords around her abdomen. Each neck had a reinforced pillow, and Zor had fashioned a soft support for her thick tail.

Guldrun and Lin lifted off the rock and firmly grasped the two baskets carrying Lily, Zun, Bridget, Tomal, Adrianne, and Perjas. The Hawks and Pohevol flew ahead of the Mud brothers while Zor looked down at Sefani.

Ius turned to Zor, "Let me carry Sophia instead. You should not carry Sefani on your back and hold Sophia's cords."

Caduceus grumbled, "It matters not to me."

Zor lifted Sefani to his back, "Very well, but do not use this to prove you are stronger than me."

Ius smiled and seized two of the cords. Caduceus grabbed the others, and they both lifted simultaneously, carrying Sophia away into the white Sunlight.

As the cave became a tiny dark opening in the distance, Zor heard a desperate cry.

"Stop! Don't leave!" a tiny voice called out.

"Do you hear a squeaking?" Zor asked Sefani.

"Mortoof," Sefani smiled. "We forgot Mortoof!"

Zor turned around and flew back to the cave. Standing at the edge with his satchel slung over his back, the Rat implored the red Dragon to land. He whipped out some paper and his charcoal stick, writing: Why did Ius leave me? What did I do wrong?

Zor studied the tiny words and allowed the symbols to register. He then bellowed, causing Sefani to almost slide off his back. She clutched his neck feathers.

"He thinks Ius left him," he told her.

Mortoof tried to understand what was being said, but since Sophia was away, the Dragon speech sounded like shrieking Eagles and hissing Snakes.

"My claws are too big to write on his paper," Zor mused. "And you cannot see to write."

Zor plucked the Rat off the edge and took off toward the others, already two miles ahead. Mortoof, not expecting this flight, screamed in delight.

"Most unpredictable!" he shouted.

All Sefani and Zor heard was, "Squeak!"

෯ ෨

The Dragons of Durga flew for three days over a changing landscape. Building up their endurance, they stopped only to eat and take short naps. The children slept in the baskets and ate most of their meals in the air. Mortoof, back in a basket with Adrianne and Perjas, began writing an epic poem about the journey to Iceloch.

"No one would expect a Rat to be a poet," he

muttered as he scribbled the words in small stanzas. "What rhymes with cold?" He thought of the alphabet. Bold. Fold. Gold. Hold. Mold. Old." He wrote with charcoal: The bold cold took hold. He swooned with pride, fell over, and clutched the paper reverently. "Poetry," he allowed the word to leisurely pass over his lips.

Guldrun and Lin were exemplary basket carriers, never swooping in dangerous turns or dropping below an appropriate altitude. Anippe continued to remind them of their progress, and Labrys had not called them Draglings, not even once.

When they flew within a short distance of Durga, Doren the Hawk collected letters from the children. He signaled to Zor and flew to deliver the news.

"Meet us at the Mountains of Lann!" Zor called out.

Doren said he would in less than a day and banked left toward Durga. As they passed, Sophia looked down at the distant ridges of green. Just over those hills, Durga lay waiting. She could just see the tip of Mount Calyps. Her body shuddered as she thought of the wildflowers and tulis berries.

Caduceus, sensing her despair, called down to her, "In good time, my dear friend. We shall return in good time."

Ius tried to focus on his Southern destination, but found himself looking East every few hours, searching for something. As the Dragon wings beat together in unison, he tried to concentrate on the steady mantra, the wind heartbeat in the sky. The jungle, he thought. Vines and flowers and safety. It is always safe in the jungle.

Pohevol spied a long ridge of mountains that looked, from a distance, like a Dragon's spine. "There they are," he told the others. "The Mountains of Lann."

The Hawks and Dragons pointed their heads to this ridge, and the children rose to look out of the baskets. No longer in the freezing cold, their arms were bare in the afternoon Sun.

Sefani, who had been sleeping on Zor's back, awoke and felt the breeze shifting. "We're slowing?" she asked the red Dragon.

"Very astute, little one," Zor replied.

The party landed in a dale near a lake surrounded by purple lupine flowers. Because the brothers had executed a smooth basket arrival, Labrys let them search for a fresh mud flat. They flew off in a race to bask in the cool and wet dirt. Ius decided to join the brothers, seeing as it had been a long time since he allowed himself this luxury. He brought his claw file as well.

The children took baths in the lake, and Perjas ran free through the flowers, rolling his furry back in the dirt and scratching his ears. Adrianne hunted for fresh Insects, and Mortoof strolled through the grass, reading his epic poem aloud.

After the children exited the lake, the Dragons took their turn bathing. Drying their bodies on the shore, Lily, Bridget, and Tomal watched as the huge bodies splashed and showered each other with torrents of spray. Dragon baths were athletic and long.

Once the water play was over, the true cleansing began. Aromatic Dragon-made vegetable soaps foamed over and under scales and were scrubbed along tails and spines. Once rinsed, the children realized how much the cold had dulled the Dragons' armor. Freshly washed, the

Dragons emerged burnished and gleaming. They seemed larger and stronger.

As they ate their evening meal, Doren flew back with two bundles of letters. When all of the food and materials were put away, the Dragons pored over the letters in a large group. Preferring to read in private, the children separated to read their missives. Zun was surprised to see Lily hand him a letter with his name printed neatly on the outside.

"It's from your aunt," she explained.

"She has patience with me," he said, turning the letter over in his hands. "I know it's hard sometimes."

Lily smiled and sat down in a soft clutch of lupine to read her letters. After Zun finished his, he watched Lily read. Her eyes darted over the words quickly, and her lips moved slightly as if she were reading aloud. She smiled at parts and furrowed her brow at others. Sometimes her body seemed to shudder or blur, as if she were about to Shift. He liked observing her.

After the letters were finished, the Dragons and children took a quick nap in the setting Sun. Anippe lifted her wings to make a long tent for the children, and Caduceus moved far away to sleep alone with only his Snakes. Some went into Dreamtime, but only for relaxation. They had no leader or watchers.

When they awoke, the stars were out and the waning Moon was low in the horizon.

"If we continue to fly through the nights, we will be there in three days," Caduceus said.

"Children," Anippe asked, "is this acceptable to you?"

No one disagreed, so they climbed back into the

baskets and set about making comfortable beds and sleeping spots.

Afraid of being left behind, Mortoof scampered as soon as he saw Dragon movement. He dove into his basket, dropping his poetry by mistake. He climbed back out and snatched the fluttering pages. Once collected, he dove back into the basket and began munching on acorns.

Anippe filled her basket with more food collected from Lann. She found a grove of rowanberries, hazelnuts, and Lann tubers that were rich and creamy. This food would supplement the remaining food from Durga. Once in the jungle, they would gather tasty delights of fruits, legumes, and nuts. She thought of the limp Seal bodies dangling from the Ice Dragons' mouths and wondered. Could the Dragons of Iceloch enjoy life as herbivores? Could they find pleasure in the assorted tastes and textures? Or would the fare leave them wanting?

When everyone was ready, they took off into the Moon-soaked night. The Birds were asleep, and the air was punctuated with silence. Lily could not sleep. She stood at the edge of her basket and watched the Moonlight reflecting off undulating Dragon wings. She had not Shifted since the Dragon chess tournament. What would she become in the jungle? As she watched Zor ahead of her, she followed his wing movement, his confident head, and his curved claws tucked near his body. She saw Sefani sleeping on Zor's back and Pohevol resting behind Sefani.

She had become a Dragon…almost. The Lizard blood had a spark of fire rushing through it, she remembered. And Saja's magic covered her in a wash of strength and vibrancy. It was a memorable feeling. She hoped she could feel it again one day.

❧ ❧

After another full day and night of flying, the group saw a massive blue sea in the distance. White and green hills flanked the Northern shore and small islands dotted the coastline. It was the Cerdwin-Askel Sea. When they approached the shore, Sophia lifted her heads in unison and breathed her first full breaths since before she sank into the Iceloch Sea.

"I can fly now," she said to Ius and Caduceus.

Ius bent his head to hear her better, "What did you say?"

"I said I can fly," and with a great ripping, Sophia severed the four cords keeping her safe in the sling.

Caduceus faltered in the air, unaccustomed to the shift in weight and pulled his wings down to compensate. Ius swooped below Sophia in preparation for her free fall to the sea.

But she did not fall. Her heads jutted straight out with muscular precision, and she flapped her wings with strength. She had healed. She flew to the basket carrying Adrianne and said in Spider tongue, "Let me carry you, my healer."

Adrianne climbed atop the edge of the basket and looked below at the deep blue water. The air was refreshing, warm, and sweet. White Gulls, brown Pelicans, and pink Egrets flew from island to island. The waves glistened near the shores and revealed smooth white sand when the water receded.

Sophia said, "Come, my friend. Please let me carry you."

Adrianne spread her eight legs far apart to firmly grasp the basket. She adjusted her many eyes to navigate Sophia's direct position, and then she leapt for the Dragon's body.

Her legs alert and searching for Sophia's back, she felt a rush of fear sweep over her. Before she could let out a scream, she felt Sophia's thick scales beneath her. She clutched the Dragon's back with relief.

Sophia flew Adrianne through the island channels and along the sparkling coasts. From a distance one would only recognize a seven-headed Dragon flying in a series of loops and circles. No one would guess a green Horned Silk Spider sat atop the Dragon's back, enjoying the ride.

When Sophia was finished and after the Dragons were assured she had truly healed, they flew South across the vast sea. The Cerdwin-Askel Sea separated the Northern lands from the Motherland. Once they crossed it, they would be in Jha'mah.

Labrys intuitively knew why she was needed on this part of the journey. Zor knew what awaited them. Without stopping it would take two days to travel over this sea, and as they moved closer to the equator, these waters would hold different surprises. Labrys knew a large swath of Sea Dragons lived in the Cerdwin-Askel. She also knew unexpected whirlpools would appear and engulf individuals with a grasp beyond the normal spin of water. Finally, she knew of the infamous Siir, winged creatures who were said to lure animals to their unwitting death in the most placid and temperate of waters.

To the flying travelers, it was hard to believe this sea could be so perilous. After a full day of flying, the warm breezes tantalized the senses. The honeyed air bathed the Dragons' membranes and relaxed their wingbeats so that they felt no labor moving through the setting golden Sunlight. Labrys scanned the water for movement, waiting and watching. Nothing appeared, not even a Dragon's shadow through the clear waters. As they flew through the night, she focused her senses on sound. She felt the slight pull of the Moon upon the water, and she concentrated on detecting other aquatic attractions.

When the Sun appeared in the East, a small golden egg resting on the water's surface, Labrys knew they had only one more day before reaching Jha'mah. She looked around at the others and knew this was the last day with her Durgan family. Looking down at the sea, she thought, This was simple. We are almost there.

Just as the thought escaped her mind's hold, she saw it. A small ripple in the water. She looked closely at the widening shape and she saw it, rising up, moving like a plume of white fire.

"Turn back!" she cried out to the others. "Turn back!"

⚜ 22 ⚜

THE SIIR

The Dragons of Durga heard Labrys's emphatic call and immediately changed course. Pohevol and the Hawks followed and pumped their wings to catch Labrys. Jostled awake, the children stood up and peered outside of the baskets. Behind them they saw the most beautiful sight ever witnessed in Realtime. White arches erupted from the water, revealing a gleaming jewel of an island. Stone columns, white with a hint of pale pink, encircled a pool of aquamarine. Waves of white and golden sand rippled around the columns, and immense orange, white, and black Tigers lay on the sand like royalty. Then they saw the tentacles.

Reaching up to them, calling the children with the sweetest song, was a creature they had never seen before. It was pure white and had the face of a Dragon, but its body was bulbous and continually changing form and shape. The only constant was its face, its color, and its tentacles.

Locked on the Dragons, the white arms reached up from the sea and beckoned the children to return. They looked soft, inviting, and perfectly harmless. Tomal shouted to the Dragons, "What are you doing? It wants us to come back! Why are you flying away?"

"Do not answer him!" Labrys ordered. "Keep flying, do not look back at it!"

Zor, Ius, and Pohevol kept their eyes fixed upon Labrys's tail. Caduceus and Sophia flanked Labrys's right and left and only turned to look at her determined face. The Hawks focused on the horizon and the meeting of sky and sea.

Anippe flew under the children's basket. "Listen to me," she breathed heavily. "Whatever it is, Labrys does not like it. We are not going back."

Lily, entranced with the beautiful Tigers relaxing on the sand, said, "It's a Dragon. Look at its face! Can't Sophia just talk to it? Can't we go back?"

Pohevol thought to her, "Do not listen to this creature. One cannot always believe one's eyes Lily. It is most certainly a trap."

Lily thought, "How could a Dragon trap a child?"

"I know not what it is, Lily," Anippe said. "But it is not a Dragon."

Zun looked down at the beckoning arms and started to climb over the edge of the basket.

"Zun!" Bridget called out. "What are you doing?"

"It's not a Dragon," he whispered. "It just told me. It says I'm not safe. It wants me to climb on its arm. It says it knows why my parents were killed."

"It spoke to you?" Lily asked expectantly. "When?"

"Just now, listen."

The children in both baskets leaned over and turned their heads to listen more closely. As the melodic sounds entered their ears, slow smiles spread across their faces.

Anippe flew to Labrys in a panic, "We must do something! This thing is speaking to the children in a way I cannot understand, and Zun is about to jump out of his basket!"

"Listen to me very carefully," Labrys shouted so the Dragons could hear her in the whipping wind. "Do not look at the Siir directly. If you must, use your side vision to mark its place. It will speak to you and promise outlandish things if only you return to its island." She roared into the brilliant sky, "Do not listen! It is lying to you! It will destroy you if you set foot on that island!"

Just as Labrys was directing the Dragons, Lin caught a glint of Sun flashing off a white tentacle. He turned his head, and though he remembered Labrys's order about only using his side vision, he disregarded her warning and looked the Siir directly in its brilliant face.

The Siir spoke to Lin, "I have the most rare mud elixir on my island, with warm baths, and chocolate mud creams." The eyes, so like a Dragon's, pulled Lin toward itself.

"Come sweet Dragon," the Siir beckoned. "Let me satisfy your every need. The others will never know."

The Siir's tentacle curled toward itself, and Lin found himself turning to follow its magnetic pull.

Bridget and Tomal were in Lin's basket, and they smiled up at the Dragon.

"Thank you Lin!" Bridget shouted. "It says there are different Dragons on this island, Dragons who can help us!"

"Labrys!" Guldrun shrieked. "Lin's flying back to the creature!"

"We will have to fight!" Labrys called out to the other Dragons. "Remember what I said, do not look at it directly!"

The Dragons banked sharply and flew toward the Siir. Sensing the change, the Siir pulled back and two other Siir, identical to the first one, appeared. More tentacles reached up to the sky with a symphony of sound that filled the warm air.

Speaking to Zor it said, "You will find all answers here."

To Anippe it cooed, "The rivers are sweet and warm."

To Guldrun it sang, "We have fragrant forbidden mud hidden beneath our shores."

To Ius it said, "We will release you of all pain."

Labrys and Caduceus heard nothing at all. To Sophia, able to hear a slight buzzing in all of her different ears, it spoke the truth.

"It is lying to you all!" she screamed. "It is saying it wants to devour you," she flew as fast as she could to the front of the group. "Do you hear me? It wants to kill us all!"

Zor replied, "How can we get away?" He looked down and saw they were just a few Dragon's lengths from the island's golden shores.

And then Zun dove. Like a Cormorant, Zun dove into the Cerdwin-Askel Sea. Lily was next to plunge into the waters, then Tomal, and finally Bridget. All of the children, save Sefani, were in the waters swimming to the Siir's shore.

Sefani, alert and riding Zor without any grip, listened carefully to her friends splashing in the waters below.

The voice was promising to bring vision to her sightless eyes. "Join them," it whispered a gentle song. "Let your body fall. As soon as you touch the water, I will save you. I will bring you to my island, and you will see me. Don't you want to see what the others see? Don't you want to walk on my pristine sandy beaches?"

Sefani answered, "You must look beautiful, but your words mean nothing to me."

She leaned down to Zor's ear, "Don't look at it, Zor. I can't hear what Sophia hears, but it's a liar. I know it to my core."

Lin, free from the children's weight, soared to the edge of the island.

Labrys cried, "Drop the baskets! Drop the baskets! Guldrun, save your brother! Caduceus and I will deal with the Siir! Everyone else grab a child!"

In a swirl of color and motion, the Dragons of Durga dove to save the children and themselves. Labrys and Caduceus attacked one Siir together, blowing fire and slashing their claws at its many tentacles. The Siir hissed, spit, and thrashed about, dodging the fire and sharp Dragon talons.

Guldrun flew in front of Lin and blocked his flight with a plume of smoke. Lin, coughing and gasping yelled, "What are you doing? This island is paradise, let me land!"

"It's lying to us, Lin! Turn away!"

Lin rolled out of the smoke and dove for the sandy beach. Guldrun shot after his brother and sank his claws into Lin's back.

Lin roared and looked up at Guldrun with astonishment and hurt flooding his eyes, "How could you?" Twisting and fighting the two brothers spun in the air.

Like Ice Dragons hunting Seal, the children were easy to pluck from the sea. While the Siir's white arms tried to grab at each child, the Dragons' fire made the tentacles shrivel and retreat. The children groaned as the Dragons lifted them out of the blue water. Zun had just reached the sandy bottom, crawling out of the surf, when Anippe flew low and snatched him up, clutching his writhing body to her chest.

"Let me go!" he screamed. "Release me!"

Anippe said nothing. She turned and flew away from the white shore. The children, dripping and yelling, struggled to free themselves from the Dragons' grip, but the effort was futile.

Staring back at a tentacle that was calling out to her, Lily began to imagine a Shift that would set her free. Caduceus, two Dragon's lengths away, sensed her focus. Fighting one Siir with his legs, he arched his body to face Lily, "Shift now, Lily Fearn," he growled, "and I will rip that Necklace off and never utter your Name for as long as you shall breathe!"

Lily turned toward Caduceus and saw his eyes flashing with disgust. She looked down at the Siir's arm and cowered. She wanted to follow the Siir. It had promised her many things, but Caduceus was threatening to take away what she had finally achieved.

Pohevol flew to Lily and beat his wings in front of her face, "Hear me!" He thundered in her mind. "You are stronger than this force. What you hear is an illusion!"

Lily looked into Pohevol's eyes. He lifted his face up so that she could focus on his white chin. As her eyes penetrated his fur, the Siir's words, which had been rolling in a repeating loop over and over in her brain, suddenly vanished. Lily saw only Pohevol. The Siir were banished from her mind.

Pohevol flew to the other children to force them into his hypnotic trance. While he worked on them, the third Siir joined the battle against Labrys and Caduceus. Like vapor, the Siir moved, collapsing and reappearing to jab and twist at the Dragons' limbs and wings. But Labrys sensed their motion and used her four legs to capture and control the arms. She ran the tentacles along her sharp bumps jutting from her spine and used her tail to slap the Siir's faces.

Caduceus thrust his tail around like a whip and cut into the Siir's arms with his silver spikes. His purple body fought against the three Siir, attacking one Siir with his fire and then another with his claws.

Above this battle, Guldrun and Lin fought each other tirelessly. Guldrun pleaded with his brother, "Look at Caduceus and Labrys! The creature is trying to hurt them!"

Lin turned to see the battle below and bellowed, "It hurts, Guldrun! It's calling me to land now!"

Labrys cried, "Do not let him touch the shores! They will leave us and attack him only if he touches the sand!"

Guldrun, fear exploding in his eyes, turned to his

brother and did the only thing he knew. He blew thick smoke into his brother's eyes. Horrified, Lin blocked his eyes and in that moment, Guldrun lunged his body at Lin's and drove them both into the sea.

With a torrential crash, the two brothers entered the Cerdwin-Askel Sea. Labrys saw the splash and turned to Caduceus, "The Siir will retreat soon. I must save Guldrun and Lin!"

"Go!" he yelled.

Caduceus continued to fight the three Siir while Labrys soared to Guldrun and Lin. Sophia, hearing the Mud Dragons' desperate cries from the waves, cringed as she remembered the icy waters of Iceloch. Mud Dragons would not survive long, even in this warmer water.

Guldrun gasped, "This is nothing like mud! It's too slippery, I can't move!"

Lin, still sore from the battle, screamed, "We'll die!"

Labrys focused on the struggling Dragons below and swooped down. Two sets of claws grasped Guldrun and the other two found Lin. She strained and beat her wings to lift the sopping Dragons from the sea.

When they had gathered their strength, she let go. Dripping with salty water, Guldrun and Lin flew in circles, looking down at the sea and shaking their heads in disbelief.

The Hawks released a piercing cry that caught the Mud Dragons' attention. Sophia flew over to Lin and said, "Follow Doren! Do not think, and do not look back. Just follow Doren."

The Dragons flew to the bobbing baskets, which were riding the slow swells of the sea, and dropped the children inside. Adrianne sat huddled in a corner, Perjas had his front paws on the edge, frantically sniffing for Sefani, and Mortoof climbed up the handle and was scampering back and forth squeaking to Ius.

Dazed and frightened, the children collapsed in the baskets. Now that their eyes were not fixed upon the Siir, they felt utterly used and taken advantage of. Zun slumped in his basket, and Lily tucked herself into a ball of shame.

Anippe stayed with the children and the Mud brothers while Zor, Ius, Sophia, and Labrys flew back to the Siir's island to help Caduceus. Seeing the long line of Dragons approaching them, the Siir retreated. They sucked in their tentacles and in a flash of light the bodies disappeared into the water. After the Siir were gone, the island flickered as if a mirage, and then vanished.

Seconds after the island disappeared, the sea erupted in new movement. Flashing under the water, in ripples of color and light, the Dragons of Durga saw the most amazing sight. Below them, drifting in tight groups of four and five, swam multiple pods of Sea Dragons.

Zor and Ius flew in circles around the swimming Dragons and watched cautiously as many breached the surface and dove back into the small waves. After multiple jumps, twists, and turns, the foaming water settled and the Sea Dragons drifted along the swells peering up at the Dragons in the air.

One green Sea Dragon, his long body breaking through the surface, attempted to speak to Zor. Flying low above the water, Zor craned his neck to listen. He could not understand the strange tongue.

"Sophia," Zor called. "I need your help."

Sophia flew over and translated for the two Dragons.

The green Dragon spoke, "We are pleased to see you did not fall for their trickery."

"What are they?" Zor asked.

Another Sea Dragon with golden webbed wings and sparkling neck flaps surfaced, "They call themselves Siir."

"Where did they go? Where did the island go?"

"We do not know," answered the golden webbed Dragon. "We have chased them all over the sea, and we have never caught them. Nor have we found the island underwater."

Ius flew down, "But they have Dragon faces, and they know our inner thoughts."

"They are an ancient species. Our elders say they can harness Dragon magic and merge Realtime with Dreamtime, but we are suspicious of these tales. We have lost many Sea Dragons to their lies and deceit."

The green Dragon added, "We believe they use sand magic."

"Sand magic?" Zor asked.

"The Sand Dragons of Ochre know of this magic. We have heard only tales, but the Siir seem to practice what the Sand Dragons describe. The forms and creatures on the island change, yet the sand remains the same."

Labrys dove into the sea and swam up to the two talking Dragons.

"You are of the sea!" The golden webbed Dragon exclaimed. "From which waters do you swim?"

"I hatched near Durga, in the Dendrite Sea."

"Yet, you have wings to fly through the air?"

"Yes," Labrys said flapping her long iridescent wings,

"I can fly in the air as well."

The Sea Dragons converged around the floating Dragon baskets. Their long curious necks rose out of the water, and their various heads peered at the children.

"Why do you travel with Humans?" a deep red Sea Dragon questioned Labrys.

"In our land of Durga, Human children share Dreamtime with us. We are on a journey to Jha'mah. They had to accompany us."

"Fascinating," she murmured. She saw Perjas, pulled away, and laid back her ear horns, "What is this creature?"

"He is a Dog. His name is Perjas," Sophia answered for Labrys. She was getting tired of hovering and translating at the same time. "Can you tell us how far it is to Jha'mah?"

"Can you not see the land?" The red Sea Dragon pointed her head to the South.

Everyone turned and looked carefully in the distance. Hovering at the end of the Southern sea was a deep rise of flickering green. If one did not focus carefully it seemed as if the waters had green waves. But it was definitely land. They could see the edge of Jha'mah.

"I would suggest you fly there immediately," the green Sea Dragon continued. "The Siir retreat when outnumbered, but always return."

Labrys swam next to him, and they rubbed bodies under the water. "Thank you," she said. "Hopefully we can meet again, without the presence of Siir."

The Sea Dragons moved away, and the Dragons of Durga flew back to sweep the baskets out of the water. Mortoof leapt from the handle onto Ius's back, and Perjas barked to Sefani. Zun stood up, and Lily wiped the tears away from her eyes. Bridget and Tomal leaned against their basket's edge, laced their fingers together, and stared at the distant land. That is real, Bridget thought to herself. That land is real.

With water dripping from the sodden baskets, they flew in a straight line towards the shore of magnificent green, the Motherland of all Dragons, Jha'mah.

᛫᛭ 23 ᛭᛫

JHA'MAH

The edge of Jha'mah was thick with trees of walnut, coconut palm, banana, and pineapple. Layers of dense tree canopy filled the Dragons' vision. As the Dragons of Durga flew over the first few miles of Jha'mah, they could smell pungent fruited wind. Lemon and grapefruit, date and fig entered the Dragons' nostrils and calmed their racing hearts. The children pushed aside their collective embarrassment and looked below at the pulsating jungle.

In Jha'mah the trees grew in abundance, seemingly with no spaces between trunk, limb, and leaf. The branches merged with each other and formed a massive body of foliage. Similar to the Cerdwin-Askel Sea, this jungle moved with a will of its own, and instead of blue waves, dark green swells rippled across the canopy top. Bird clamor punctured the green mass and rose up in billows.

Pohevol flew to Lily's basket, "Let the events fade from your mind, smell these trees and listen to the Birds. You must relax your mind."

"I'm ashamed," she thought.

"Everyone feels the heaviness. Let it flow from you, release the pain."

Lily inhaled the sweet air, "I'll do my best."

After the stand of dark green jungle, the Dragons reached a steppe dotted with Wildebeest and Zebra. Bridget watched the animals running across the light brown savanna, moving like channels of water around knobby baobab trees. As the Dragons flew them deeper into Jha'mah, Bridget felt the Earth releasing heat, drifting up to find her. She sensed a connection with this land, as if there were a distant rumble coming from the core. But because the Siir had tricked her, she knew she must be on her guard. Beautiful sounds and images could bring destruction.

They continued to fly for three more hours. Throughout the brown savannas they would see a copse of jungle green here and there, and in these verdant leaftops, Eagles' nests surfaced like small islands. Parrot shrieks permeated the air, great swooping calls and sharp twitters. The Cuckoo calls darted between branches with a medley of sound. Small Vine Dragons the color of deep viridian, darted sporadically from the canopy to peek at the traveling group. Before Sophia could speak to them, they would cackle and plunge back into the tree cover.

Excited by the Vine Dragons' emergence, Pohevol motioned for the Dragons to land. Lily saw a river to her left, cutting through the jungle like a dark Serpent. Dense foliage grew at the edge of the banks and reached into the still water. A small circular clearing appeared to the right of the river bank. The Dragons landed here.

As the baskets were lowered into the clearing, the children heard chattering in the trees. Thick, rope-like vines called lianas snaked throughout the large leaves. The lianas were woody climbing plants, seeking out Sunlight, grasping their way to the top of the canopy. Linking the trees, animals used these vines to travel quickly through the jungle without touching ground. The children saw brown furry bodies fly through the air, grasping and pulling the lianas for support. Moving too fast to be seen, they might have been Spider Monkeys or Lemurs. Parrots called from tree saplings and a variety of Monkey voices jabbered back.

When everyone had landed, the children climbed out and looked up and around. When they had been flying above the jungle, the Sun poured down and its heat shimmered on top of the trees in dry waves. Under the canopy, the jungle was humid and dark. Dead leaves lay everywhere and in the specks of light that managed to weave through the foliage, over-ripe fruit hung on weighted branches. Termites roamed the jungle floor, scavenging to find decomposing leaf litter.

The Dragons looked carefully at orchid pools, a type of flower designed to trap water, and drip-tips, leaves with spouts made to channel droplets of rain water in order to protect soil after turbulent storms. Bulging out of the loam were massive buttress roots. Because the jungle soil was very thin, only a few Dragon's nails thick, for survival the trees had to erect enormous roots that splayed out like twisted and overlapping legs. These interlacing roots breached the dirt and then dove underneath again, weaving in and around the trunks of neighboring trees and stretching throughout the jungle to create a firm mat of roots and leaves. This was the Jungle of Jha'mah.

Dragon bellies began to add a persistent groan to the cacophony of sounds, so the first charge was to prepare a meal. Caduceus sniffed the trees and smiled, "We will have fig pie this afternoon." He followed the scent and pushed his Alligator head into the tangle of lianas and buttress roots on a quest for figs and walnuts.

Adrianne, sensing the multiplicity of Insect bodies crawling over roots and hovering in the vines, crawled out of her basket and moved stealthily toward the jungle. She was tired of dried bodies. She craved fresh blood.

Mortoof scampered to the edge of Ius's shoulder, and took a deep breath. His purple wings fluttered, and feeling safe and free, he allowed his small wings to lift him in the air. Mortoof was not a practiced aviator, as his wings could just hold his weight, but if close to the ground, he could navigate small turns and dips.

The warm and humid air caressed his fur as he lowered to the ground. When his paws reached the jungle floor, he scurried to his basket and climbed inside. He poked his head out, jerking it left and right, listening to the sounds. He then jumped out of the basket with his satchel slung across his back. He was ready for serious adventure. In the jungle he would prove to be most unpredictable.

When Caduceus returned, a few lianas draped around his neck alongside his resident Snakes, the children and Dragons ate fig pies with crushed walnut crust. He also had found a grove of mango, guava, and pineapple. For dessert the Dragons and children ate the fresh fruit. Sweet juice dribbled down their faces and made their fingers sticky. Tsetse Flies landed on the Dragons' scales and skin to taste the remnants of sugar. After a few quick bursts of Dragon fire, the Insects abandoned the party in search of a safer meal to steal.

The fruit lifted their spirits, and even the dispirited Lin moved closer to his brother to comment, "You have guava peel on your nose."

After the Hawks, Adrianne, and Pohevol came back from their hunt, Labrys stood up to speak. With a slight nod from Zor, she said, "I am leaving the group."

Sophia turned one head to Labrys, "What do you mean, leaving?"

"Did anyone wonder why we did not ask the Sea Dragons to help us?" she asked.

The children pondered her question. After the battle with the Siir, they had been too overwhelmed to focus on the purpose of their journey. Except for Zor and Caduceus, a look of bewilderment spread over the faces of the Dragons. Why did they fly so quickly to Jha'mah without entreating the Sea Dragons for help?

Ius said, "We were preoccupied with the Siir. We were weak." His frustration was obvious. A Cuckoo cried out, its voice echoing off the trees.

"No," Zor said. "I think Labrys was speaking to our hearts throughout our journey from the ice. We knew what she desired."

Labrys spoke again, "I am going to fly back to…"

"Please," Sophia stopped Labrys.

"There remain no seas over which to fly. I am no longer needed."

"We will need you for other deeds," Sophia countered.

"No," Labrys smiled, "you will not. I will share the divining secrets with Anippe, and I doubt you will need any fire-tending in Jha'mah or the sweltering desert."

Guldrun stood, "Labrys, are you tired of reprimanding us? Because we'll change," he nudged Lin. "Won't we?"

Lin stood up and lumbered over to Labrys, his tail dragging low against the ground. He lay prostrate at her pink and gold body. Dragon tears rolled down his face, "I'm sorry I let you down. . . with that…" he gulped, "that horrible thing in the sea." Lin lay on the ground heaving, trembling, and sobbing into the dirt. "If you leave because of my awful behavior, I don't know what I'll do." His tears made a large pool of mud, and not one eyelid opened to relish the sight. No leg or wing moved to feel the wet coolness.

Labrys knew Lin was sincere. Lowering her head to his body, she nudged him to stand, "Get up, Lin," she whispered. "I am not angry with you, little one."

Lin released a small smile. She had not called him a Dragling.

"I attach no fault to you for listening to the Siir. Sea Dragons have spent generations learning how to defend ourselves from their captivating songs," Labrys pet his head with a wing. "No. I am not leaving because of you."

"Then why are you leaving?" Ius demanded.

Caduceus answered the question, "Because she is going into hiding."

Anippe's eyes flashed, "What? Where?"

Caduceus smiled, "In Iceloch."

Labrys nodded, "You understand."

"I have felt the pull too," Caduceus nodded to the North, from which they had just flown. "It makes sense. You are a selfless Dragon. You always have been."

"But why Iceloch?" Ius asked. "Why hide in that freezing sea?"

Labrys lowered her eyelids, "I am not purely selfless as Caduceus suggests. There is a Sea Dragon who will hide with me." She paused and blushed, "And he is special."

Anippe's golden brown body began to glow, and Caduceus chuckled, "Oh, I see."

Sophia pressed, "Are you certain? You will be giving up your home in Durga."

"My home has always been the sea," Labrys looked around at the Dragons. The jungle swelled with Bird movement. "The forest in Durga is intoxicating, peaceful, and a beautiful place to share hundreds of Suns." She turned to Zor, "But now it is time for me to go to my true home, the sea."

"And Labrys will help our tribe," Zor added. "Like Dett and Riema secluded in their ice cave, Labrys and her friend will be the necessary Sea Dragons lying in wait. They will stay in the frozen Sea of Iceloch for us, until it is safe to emerge."

A new wave of shrieking came from the trees as the children observed the Dragon discussion. Zor defended the decision and ultimately all Dragons concurred. Only seven Dragons would remain to navigate the jungle and sand.

Anippe and Labrys walked to the river's edge to

discuss divining secrets and to transfer the jewels. Labrys picked a bluish-white opal and a green bloodstone with orange spots from her bag, "This opal is for hope," the stone rose in the air and hovered in front of Anippe. "This bloodstone is for courage," it too rose and floated in the air.

Labrys spoke for hours about how to use the stones, how to keep them safe, but most important, how to listen to their wisdom. Anippe took the bag from Labrys and promised she would serve the jewels and listen well.

"I have no doubts," Labrys said. The hovering stones dropped into the bag, now held open by Anippe.

They walked back to the circle, and Labrys made sure she had enough food to fly to Durga, "I will leave my basket with Saja in Durga. She can unlace the jewels and nestle them around her egg. Already, they have encased a potent power from this journey."

Labrys rose into the air and hovered above her basket.

"Wait!" shouted Bridget. "Can we have a stone? For luck?"

The Sea Dragon looked down on the five children. Zun had been silent since Anippe plucked him from the Siir's watery shore. He stood staring into the moving jungle. His muscles were taut as if waiting to react.

"Yes," Labrys answered. "Each child should come forth and pick a stone from the basket. Any jewel that speaks to you."

Bridget found an oval piece of malachite. Tomal took an emerald. Sefani came to the basket and felt all of the raised jewels tucked into the folds and creases. Her hands rested on a square of burgundy jasper and her heart warmed. She carefully pulled the stone away from Labrys's basket.

Lily went to the jewels next and let her eyes search the shining cornucopia. A glittering jewel kept winking at her, its translucent face arresting her eyes.

"Take the diamond," Labrys said. "I hear it calling you."

Lily took it and tucked it into her pocket.

Labrys turned to Zun, "You are a part of this group, please take one."

Zun looked at Labrys and then at her basket. He knew which stone he wanted, but his legs felt like slabs of lead. He didn't know how he could walk to the shining basket and pluck this Dragon's stone.

"It is not mine," Labrys called out to the unmoving boy. "It is yours. I am only a guardian of jewels."

Zun saw a shining piece of topaz. It was a luminous yellowish brown with a hint of orange, like a smoldering Sun or dying fire. He pushed away a basket reed and took the small jewel from its home. Zun held the topaz up against the dark green trees in the background, and then quickly tucked it away.

Labrys now grasped the basket handle with her two front legs and began to lift it into the air.

"Goodbye and goodspeed!" Tomal and Bridget shouted.

"Goodbye children," she answered.

"Labrys!" Lily called out. In a flash of light and brilliance, Lily Shifted into a Raven and flew to meet the pink and gold Sea Dragon in the air. "We won't let you down!" She dove under the Dragon and flew in loops around Labrys's head. "And we'll change the future! You won't be long under the sea!"

"Diamond Raven! Absorb all that you can, dear Shifter," Labrys tracked Lily's steady loops around her face. "Use the power of the diamond to gather in the strength and energy of all life moving around you. Keep the diamond close."

Just as Lily flew down to the jungle floor, the seven remaining Dragons lifted off to say goodbye. They soared over the reaching trees and did elaborate loops and turns, screeching loud Dragon shrieks. They blew fire and smoke and then, in a sudden stop, the seven hovered in the Sun-soaked sky. Silently, they watched as Labrys, basket clutched underneath her powerful body, flew away from Jha'mah, and away from them.

24

CHILDREN OF JHA'MAH

The Dragons returned to the clearing and put away all of the remaining food. Each took two pieces of soil fruit, eating one and giving one to a child. Ius gave one piece to Mortoof who ate it in fast lines, up and down the rind as if he were digging trenches in the red fruit.

Pohevol looked to the thick vine-choked jungle, "We saw them fly in there."

Zor replied, "Then we must follow."

Sensing an imminent departure, Mortoof jumped atop Ius and squeaked.

"He says he is ready for adventure," Sophia translated.

Ius looked back on his shoulder to find the small Rat. He blew a soft puff of steam, and Mortoof closed his eyes and sighed.

Lily said, "It's so hot, should we bring water?"

"You children should," Anippe replied. "We can easily fly to the river and drink."

Zun and Tomal pushed their way through the branches to scoop flasks of water from the dark river. When they brought it back, Anippe tasted the water first and nodded to the children, "It is safe to drink."

Stripped down to the barest of clothes, and with enough water in satchels tied to their waists and backs, the children followed the Dragons into the thick foliage. Perjas led Sefani around the buttress roots and stopped often to let her touch the hanging lianas. Adrianne followed closely behind, her abdomen full of Tsetse Flies.

As the Dragons cut several vines to navigate the dark jungle passage, Zor heard a chattering deep in the trees. He told Sophia the Vine Dragons were near.

Sophia called out in numerous Dragon tongues, "We mean no harm, please reveal yourselves."

No Dragons emerged from the trees. They saw Monkeys swinging on lianas above them, and Lily spotted a Jaguar lounging in the branches of a fig tree, but there were no visible Dragons of Jha'mah.

They came to an intricate jumble of trees, interlaced and too complex to move through without destroying multiple vines and low hanging boughs.

Pohevol said, "Look at the Snakes."

Slithering easily through the maze of trees, vines, and roots were hundreds of Pythons and Tree Cobras. The Snakes were many shades of green, brown, and black. Some had vertical stripes, while others had diagonal lines moving across their scales. They slid through the trees without sound. Split tongues flicked out, smelling the air.

Caduceus smiled and his Serpents hissed their language to these jungle cousins. Lily felt an intense desire to Shift, so she focused on their razor-sharp pupils, their smooth and scaled bodies, their long and thin tongues. She Shifted into a Tree Cobra and slithered to Caduceus's lowered arm. She moved up his arm and coiled herself around his neck.

"He is so warm," she hissed at the two other Snakes.

"Nothing is warmer than Caduceus," a Snake replied.

"I see why you don't want to leave."

"We would never leave Caduceus," the other Snake said.

"Can you understand what the Jha'mah Snakes are saying?" Lily asked.

"Yes," the first Snake hissed. "If I were you, I would remain in Snake form."

Lily turned to Sophia who was trying to speak to the others. Just as the Snakes started to speak and Sophia could understand, the jumble of trees began to shift. Bark began to slough off the tall beings and, breaking the vertical rigidity so expected among trees, immense Snake heads with yellow eyes came crashing down from the canopy.

Caduceus screamed, "They are not trees! They are Snakes!"

What had clearly been trunks, standing perfectly still and regal, were really huge Snakes the size of trees.

Sophia choked as multiple heads shot at her necks and encircled her throats. One went after Zor and lifted him into the thick foliage above. The egg brothers were captured in two seconds. Ius tried to fight against the darting heads, careening down upon them, but was quickly captured, turned upside down, and entombed in a rising coil of Snake. Mortoof fell from his perch on Ius, and Caduceus snatched out his wing to catch the screaming Rat.

Bridget and Tomal pulled out their knives and raced over and through lianas, jabbing at anything that moved, vine or Snake. Seeing the Snakes surround them, the two children stood with their backs touching, slashing at the yellow eye slits and the glistening fangs.

Caduceus ordered, "Do not harm them, they will not hurt you!"

"I'm scared!" Bridget screamed. "Stop them!"

But before Caduceus could intervene, two Snakes caught them and swept Bridget and Tomal up into the canopy. Zun ran to Sefani and threw his body around her, but he and Sefani were raised into the air.

In a matter of seconds, they trapped Perjas, Pohevol, and even the diving and evading Hawks. The Snakes coiled around their helpless bodies and lifted them high into the canopy. The only ones to remain on the floor were Caduceus, his Snakes, and Lily, frozen in her Shift. Adrianne hid behind a buttress root calculating her next move.

"What do we do?" Lily hissed into Caduceus's ear.

"Be patient," he replied, slowly turning to look at the remaining Snakes. He looked up and saw dangling everyone from Durga. The Serpents had squeezed fiercely, thus all were unconscious, hanging like limp dolls in the trees.

Caduceus knew he had to act quickly, as Dragons

could not survive in this condition for long. He wasn't sure about the others.

Lily and Caduceus heard a scratchy whisper, as if air were escaping the pores of bark, "You, remaining on the floor of Jha'mah, are half Snake. Who are you? And why are you here?" Caduceus had no problem deciphering this foreign Snake tongue. He could understand their words clearly, the hissing, the cool silence, the waiting. They spoke a similar tongue to the Snakes of Durga, only with an elongated lisp.

He spoke slowly, "I am a Shifting Dragon from the forest of Durga. I come from far away to bring you a Visitor," his Dragon tongue hovered just on the edge of a Snake lisp. "We must speak to the Dragons of Jha'mah."

"They distrust Dragons from afar," the hiss whisper responded.

"We come from a land of peace."

"Prove you are not from the sand," many Snakes whispered in a loop of sound. "We do not trust Dragons from the sand."

Mortoof raced in circles on the ground, looking up at limp Ius and tracing the massive Snake who clutched him. His small lip snarled, and he released a low growl barely discernible. When he found the exact Snake who held Ius in its murderous coils, he climbed up the scaled body and unleashed a hefty Rat bite.

When his bite caused no immediate reaction, he screamed, "Let my Ius go!"

Seeing Mortoof's inadequate attack, Adrianne climbed upon the same Snake and sank her teeth next to the Rat's tiny puncture wound.

Another Serpent, his stomach rumbling after hearing the squeaking of Mortoof, slid his head down and opened his fangs in a wide attack. Just as the Snake was about to devour Mortoof and Adrianne whole, Caduceus knocked Adrianne away and snatched Mortoof in his claws, "This Rat is with me."

Adrianne tumbled amongst the roots and leaf litter. She crouched down low and did her best to blend in with the foliage.

The Snake arched his head back and hissed at Caduceus.

Caduceus hissed and arched back his head in a mirror movement, "Release them. They are my family, and they mean you no harm."

"These Humans who travel with you look nothing like the Jha'mah Humans," the Snakes hissed. "They look like the destroyers from the Northeast."

The Snakes lowered the children slightly, but did not let them go. Zun and Bridget were pale, Tomal's red hair looked lifeless, and Sefani's eyes were rolling underneath her eyelids. "They are almost identical to the destroyers," one Snake hissed. At this sound many fangs appeared, ready to strike at the children's dangling and exposed necks.

"No!" hissed Lily.

"Be quiet," Caduceus whispered in Dragon tongue. "Do not ruin my progress."

"They're going to kill them!" she spit back. Uncoiling herself from Caduceus, Lily leapt off the Dragon and Shifted from a Tree Cobra into a Python. She landed around the body of a huge Snake, still stiff from her subterfuge as a tree.

"We aren't destroyers! We know about those hideous people. We aren't them!" Her Python body was trembling, and the Snake around which she was coiled lowered her enormous head to peer at Lily. Staring directly into the eyes of this Snake, Lily whispered, "Please let them go. I'm a Durgan Human. My ancestors come from Jha'mah. We mean you no harm."

The Snakes whispered to themselves, and another Serpent's head moved closer to Lily to look into her Python eyes. Heart pounding in her chest, Lily thought only of escape. Raven, she thought, come to me now. She calmed her blood, focused her energy and Shifted into a blue-black Raven. She flew away from the Snakes and alighted on a true tree branch. As a Raven she could see easily the difference between plant and animal. Safe in the refuge of a true tree, Lily Shifted back into her previous Python form.

Caduceus hissed, "She is a Shifter as well." And then with as much emphasis as he could muster in Snake tongue, "She can be trusted."

"Please let them go," Lily pleaded in her Serpent's tongue. "One of the children you are crushing is an orphan. His parents were killed by destroyers!" Caduceus moved slowly from Snake to Snake. He then heard the familiar chattering coming from within the trees.

Rapidly, the Snakes released their captives. The limp bodies of Zor and Ius came rushing down through the canopy in a red and blue blur. Anippe and the Mud brothers slowly revived, as they passed a Snake audience surrounding them on their way down. Sophia was the last

Dragon to descend, as numerous Snakes had to navigate their relatives as they lowered the unconscious seven-headed Dragon. The Hawks, children, and Pohevol were easy to bring down.

Once upon the jungle floor, the Snakes released their coiled grip, and the Dragons and children fully revived. Coughing and hacking filled the jungle as the Dragons' lungs expanded. Adrianne assisted them, pulling her web from her back and touching it to their hearts and lungs.

Sefani and Bridget lay in a weak pile near Ius. Tomal scampered to stand underneath Caduceus's undercarriage. As soon as Zun regained his strength, he crouched into a fighter's stance. Turning slowly, his eyes darted between the many Snakes.

"We had to be certain," the Snakes hissed.

Zor managed to speak to Caduceus, "What happened?"

"Do not move," he spoke in Dragon tongue. "They will not hurt us if we show restraint right now." He saw Ius's claws extending, "Restraint, Ius."

With a rush of slithering sound and movement, an exodus occurred. The maze of tree, vine, and Snake slid away like circular ripples in water. The Dragons and children looked around themselves and saw they were in another spherical clearing. Tomal ran to Bridget and Sefani, and Lily Shifted back into a Raven. She flew with Pohevol and the Hawks to land on the Dragons. On guard, they turned around in slow circles.

As the Sun's rays flooded the clearing, they saw movement in the rim surrounding the open floor. Hundreds of Vine Dragons stood at the edge of the circle.

Chattering and flapping their small wings, these green and brown Dragons stood with curious eyes staring in at the group from Durga. At their sides, holding raised spears and taut bows and arrows pointed directly at the four children of Durga, stood the children of Jha'mah.

One Jha'mah girl, her dark brown skin shining in the Sun, stood with a blue-tipped spear raised in her hand. She spoke in a rapid tongue with many clicks.

Sophia lifted one head and translated, "We will kill anyone who comes to harm our Dragons."

Bridget stood up and walked with her hands high to reveal no malice, "We'd never harm Dragons." She touched her amulet, which began to glow a bright red, "We adore Dragons."

Lily flew from Caduceus's shoulder and Shifted into her Human form as she landed on the ground. The children of Jha'mah gasped and lowered their spears and bows. Lily stood by Bridget's side, "The Dragons of Jha'mah are revered. We're here to save their lives."

Zor flew to stand next to the Jha'mah girl. He turned in slow circles speaking to the Vine Dragons, "Look at the amulets upon our children. We do not lie."

All amulets, except Zun's, were a radiant red. Still crouched, body tense with anxiety, his Ochret flickered a dull pink. The dark girl from Jha'mah noticed the difference and raised one eyebrow. She said, "We recognize the amulets." She turned to the Vine Dragons, "Ura. It is safe."

A small Vine Dragon, the size of a grown Human, walked to the front of the circle. She had dark green scales, a thin body, four legs, and velvet wings shaped like a Bat's.

But what made the children from Durga stare were her hands. At the end of her legs, attached to five long and curved claws, were fingers that looked strikingly Human. Bridget, Tomal, and Lily looked at the many Vine Dragons. They all had the same Human-like hands. Tomal leaned in to whisper this description to Sefani. A few Dragons hung from lianas, and Lily could see their delicate fingers grasping the vines.

Lily felt a warmth travel under her skin. "They're similar to us," she thought to Pohevol.

Pohevol flew to Lily's side and tucked in his wings, "No, you are similar to them."

Ura looked to Zor, "I am sorry about how we welcomed you, but the winds have carried Dragons and Humans who would like to destroy our home." She motioned for the other Dragons to come forth. The Vine Dragons and children of Jha'mah walked into the clearing.

"When did they come?" Ius asked.

"Only one Sun ago," she motioned for some injured Dragons to step forward. "The Humans came on the backs of Dragons."

Ius began to speak only to have Caduceus silence him. "Now is the time to listen," he warned Ius.

A small group of Vine Dragons walked closer to Ura. Many were missing front legs, a few had empty sockets where eyes should have been, and three were missing wings.

Ura continued, "It has been a difficult time for our kin."

"Human children wreaked havoc upon your tribe?" Zor was incredulous.

"No," Ura corrected him. "Human men of age rode upon the Dragon's backs."

Ius could no longer hold back, "How did they control the Dragons? What spell could enslave a Dragon's heart?"

Ius and Zor snapped their heads toward Zun, and their disapproving eyes crawled over his tense Human skin. The invaders had come to Durga twelve Suns ago. In only eleven Suns they had altered their method of attack. They no longer enslaved Horses. Now they enslaved Dragons.

Ura spoke slowly and with absolute clarity, "They did not enslave the Dragons. The Dragons came under their own free will."

Zun, returning the Dragons' cold stares, cried out, "I told you! I told all of you! My visions are true! It is happening!" Frantically looking around the clearing, feeling the circle of Dragons pressing in upon him, Zun raced toward a Jha'mah child. "Listen to me! Listen to me!"

The child wrinkled his eyebrows, looking at Zun with confusion. He could not understand Zun's language.

Sophia flew toward Zun, "I will not translate your fear!"

"Tell them!" he screamed at her seven heads. "Tell them the truth! You know what I've seen!"

"The Jha'mah have only begun to tell their story," she hissed. "Be patient!"

Zun, fuming at Sophia's words, turned toward Lily, "Do you see now? It's all coming true!"

"This doesn't make any sense to me," Lily whispered. "I need to know more."

Sophia began translating again, "How do you know

the Dragons were not enslaved?"

Ura told the tale.

"Last Sun, during the Jez'mah feast, they came. Five Dragons, the size of your red Dragon with feathers or your blue one built like stone. On each back sat one man, with eyes the color of the Cerdwin-Askel Sea. These Dragons blew fire into the jungle and screamed hideous cries. When a group of us flew out of the canopy to meet them in the air, the destroyers attacked.

"The men raised long spears tipped with silver, and the Dragons beneath their thighs charged our kin. Blowing fire into their eyes, these destroyer Dragons tore at our kin's bodies while the men thrust spears into their hearts.

"Our kin screamed for recognition. They begged for an explanation. But the Dragons and their riders could not, or would not understand their words. Before we could reach the top of the canopy to help the injured, the destroyers flew away."

Ura paused and turned to the Dragons with missing legs, eyes, and wings. "We could not fly as fast as those five Dragons," she hung her head and stared at her small hands. "So we tended to the wounded."

She raised her head and regained her posture, "We have been preparing for another attack. We have joined with many tribes in Jha'mah to protect our home. The Snakes were the first to join us. The Jaguars are with us, and we have many Birds flying by our sides." Ura looked lovingly at the Jha'mah girl who first spoke, "Of course Kali and our children have always protected us."

Kali laced her fingers with Ura's, "And I will until my day of age."

Lily watched in wonder as Kali and the Dragon stood almost like mother and child.

The Sun lowered just below the canopy and shade rested upon the clearing. Pohevol flew to Zor and whispered in his ear. It was time to share their story.

Sophia asked everyone to sit down. Zun, still anxious and breathing heavily, backed away from the gathering. Lily walked over to him and whispered, "Don't draw attention to yourself. Come back and sit by me."

She pulled him back to the forming circle and forced him to sit by Sefani and Perjas.

With Sophia's heads hovering above the gathering of children and Dragons, Pohevol's story came rolling out. When Pohevol described the future devastation, the Jha'mah children nervously changed their positions and looked with questioning eyes at a neighboring Vine Dragon. Ura watched Zor and Ius. Her eyes clouded, and in their place she saw the destroyers.

Ius, feeling her eyes upon him, did his best to relax and calm his muscles. She fears me, he thought. How could Dragons fear Dragons? What was happening to their world?

Pohevol finished his story and looked to the Vine Dragons, "We need your help."

A male Vine Dragon with sleek armor spoke, "I am Jha'li, and I have seen over 200 Suns in this jungle. I have swung through the largest and oldest trees on Earth, and I have never seen a tree like this Cat describes."

"She's unique," Lily said. "If you meet us in Dreamtime, we can show you."

Caduceus glared at Lily. Pohevol thought to her, "Pace

yourself, let the Dragons communicate now."

Jha'li said, "You are quick to offer up Dreamtime. Our children understand it is to be used sparingly and for sacred spaces."

Kali came to Lily's defense, "I think we should meet them in Dreamtime." She nodded to Ura, "Of course when the time is appropriate."

"Before the destroyers came," Ura said, "I would never believe a tale like this. But now, anything is possible."

"Should we go to Lake Whydah?" an elder purple Vine Dragon questioned.

"Yes," Ura replied. "But, before we take that journey, we must visit the Cave of Hands."

The Vine Dragons chattered in agreement. The children of Jha'mah stood up, brushing leaf litter from their garments. The children's spears, bows, and arrows no longer looked menacing.

Caduceus asked, "What is the Cave of Hands?"

Ura took Kali's hand, "We will show you."

⊷ 25 ⊶

THE CAVE OF HANDS

The walk to the cave took only an hour. Following Ura and Kali, the gathering moved quickly through the jungle. Most of the Jha'mah children and Vine Dragons went back to their daily activities after the initial meeting in the Snakes' clearing. Only six Vine Dragons and three Jha'mah children, including Kali, led the way to the Cave of Hands.

Moving through the jungle, the Vine Dragons rarely used their wings. The lianas were just as fast, and with their grasping fingers, they could swing with little effort. As they swept through the trees, they cleared a path by using their wings to nip lianas and then tie back thick green boughs of jungle cover. The Dragons of Durga were too large to fly through the cleared pathway, but they could lope over the buttress roots with more dexterity and freedom. The air smelled of pineapple and fig.

Sophia followed first so she could translate. Pohevol

flew beside her, ducking under lianas and alighting on branches. Mortoof, still shaken from his encounter with the Snake, found comfort nestled inside Ius's shoulder armor. Whenever he peeked from the blue Dragon, he saw a hanging vine that looked just like a Snake and shuddered. He decided to be his normal adventurous self while inside the cave.

Zun and Lily walked together. "Can't you see? My visions are telling the truth," Zun whispered to Lily.

"Even if they are, these destroyers attacked other Dragons, peaceful Dragons."

"It doesn't matter, they'll kill Humans too."

"How do you know?" Lily turned her head to look directly at him, "They didn't kill any of the Jha'mah."

"They killed my parents."

Lily did not respond. All of this confused her. How could Dragons hurt other Dragons? How could Dragons allow adult Humans to ride on their backs? If Zun's visions were correct, what exactly was happening in this land of volcanoes, from which the destroyers came? A flash of her Dreamtime in Saja's cave came to her. She saw Zor in the fire and the cold, gray mountains. Would she travel to this dangerous land? Was this a part of Pohevol's plan?

In the canopy Monkeys swung from vine to vine and multicolored Parrots sang in erratic patterns. The Sun was setting fast, so the Vine Dragons lit candles that attached to their backs.

"Under the canopy, we have very little light even during the day," Kali said. "Our Dragons help us see through the darkness."

Sefani walked through the foliage and felt the floating candles moving before her. She felt warm and comfortable in this land, although she continued to feel Jha'mah eyes darting over her hair and empty eyes, "Is it my hair, my eyes, or both?" she asked the boy who was walking one Dragon's length behind her.

The boy stumbled and looked scared for a quick moment. Then he caught up with Sefani and whispered in her ear, "You speak Jha'mah?"

"When I was listening to your tongue, something came back to me, a memory I think. I spoke with Sophia, and she shared some of her secrets with me." Her voice produced the same rapid speech with clicks.

"But you are so different from us," the boy said. "And you look just like them."

"I'm from Durga," she stated with emphasis. "I've been told my yellow hair is strange, but it's just hair. Does it really matter?"

The boy reached out for her hand, "My name is Mar'du. I've seen thirteen Suns."

"I'm Sefani. I've seen eleven."

As they continued to move through the jungle, Mar'du stole glances at Sefani. He finally gathered the courage to ask, "What is wrong with your eyes? Did you have an accident?"

"I was born this way," she replied.

"Then you are Kino? You were given to the Moon?"

Sefani stopped walking and stood still. "Kino?"

"You are not originally from Durga, are you?" he persisted.

"I was born in Durga," Sefani reached for Perjas, who

began to growl.

Mar'du lowered his voice, "I am sorry. I mean no disrespect. Let me explain."

Sefani spoke to Perjas, and Mar'du watched as the girl's mouth moved like the Dog's snout and lips.

Amazed, Mar'du asked, "You can speak with this Dog?"

"Since birth," her voice had a distinct edge.

"Please. Listen to my story," Mar'du began walking and Sefani followed the sound of his footsteps moving over the roots and leaves.

"A long time ago in Jha'mah, a few babies were born with no color. Their skin and hair were pale, almost translucent white. Some could not see. A few could not use their legs. They were called Kino. They cried more than the other babies and could not be consoled. Their mother's milk did not help. They were unhappy.

"The Dragons took these babies in their lairs and surrounded them with egg jewels. They told our ancestors that the power from the stones would bring color to the babies' skin and warm their souls. But the babies did not change. They continued to cry, even inside the circle of gems.

"And so our ancestors decided the babies were unhappy living with the Jha'mah. They believed the Spirit of the Air wanted the children. They were not meant for Earth. The Dragons did not agree, but they did not want to interfere with Human decisions. Our ancestors took the children to the edge of Jha'mah and left them."

"Left them?" Sefani stopped abruptly, "How could they do this to babies?"

"Wait," Mar'du continued. "There is more."

Sefani began walking again, moving faster.

Mar'du walked quickly to keep up with her, "The legend says a young woman named Oba could not abandon the children to the savanna. She stole away that night to retrieve the Kino babies. She ran through Jha'mah praying to the Earth that the babies were still there and safe. When she came upon the baobab baskets, under the light of a full Moon, she saw a remarkable vision. A circle of Moon Dragons fluttered around the babies. Their Kino skin glowed under the Moonlight, and the Dragons lifted the babies and cradled them in their thin legs.

"And then, the legend says, Oba reached her arms up to the Dragons and begged for the babies. In a brilliant flash of light, the Moon Dragons and the Kino babies disappeared. Our ancestors believed the babies were taken to the Moon."

Sefani thought for a moment. Then she said, "The Moon Dragons of Durga have shared with us no story like this. Perhaps this happened in Jha'mah, but I couldn't be Kino. I've never visited the Moon."

She pressed Mar'du further, "Do your people still banish babies who are born different from you?"

"They were not banished," Mar'du corrected her. "They were given to the Spirit of the Air." He lifted a hanging liana for Sefani to duck under. "After Oba saw the Moon Dragons disappear with the Kino babies, she told the elders of Jha'mah to keep all Kino babies born to the tribe."

"How many Kino now live in Jha'mah?"

"We have not seen a Kino birth in over 500 Suns,"

Mar'du replied.

Sefani lifted her nose and smelled charcoal and chalk in the air, "Are we close to the cave?"

Mar'du looked ahead and saw a large hill of stone emerging from the lianas and trees. "Yes, it is near us now. How could you tell?"

"I can smell the paint."

"How did you know there was paint in this cave?"

Sefani turned to Mar'du and paused. She reached down to touch Perjas, "I don't know."

The Dragons and children stopped in front of the cave. The mouth opened just beyond a small pool. The light of the Dragon candles flickered and danced in the shimmer of dark water. To enter the narrow cleft each waded through the warm pool. Zor and Ius had to force their large bodies through the stone opening. Sophia was too big to enter, so she moved back and allowed others to go. With her body filling the entire pool, she slid one head into the cave.

Ura pointed to the high cave walls, "These markings are at least 50,000 Suns old."

The Jha'mah watched as the Dragons and children of Durga walked around staring at the paintings. Everywhere there were hands, hundreds of hands, painted upon the walls. Layered in colors of black, brown, red, and white were Human and Vine Dragon handprints. They looked identical except the Human hands were smaller, those of children, and the Vine Dragon prints had claw marks three inches from the tips of the fingerprints.

Zun crouched near the edge of a wall and sat immobile. He looked around at the others and lowered his head to his chest. Bridget and Tomal walked around, lightly touching their fingers to the endless march of hands, frozen in time. Lily stood an inch from one wall and peered at these ancient hands. The paint was fading, but the message was clear. Children and Dragons had been friends for a very long time.

Sefani asked Mar'du to describe the paintings to her. As he was detailing the colors, the shapes, and the sizes of the handprints, Bridget saw that Sophia was not translating. She left the wall and walked over to Sefani, "You understand what he's saying?"

Sefani reached out for Bridget's hand, "I don't know how, but yes, I can understand."

Sophia moved her head to Bridget, "No one has questioned her ability to speak with Dogs and Wolves. She listens well. She was made for speech."

Pohevol walked around the cave, sniffing the walls. He rubbed his mouth against the warm stone and brushed his tail against the painted surfaces. He walked to Ura and said, "You have a story to tell us."

The viridian Dragon opened her black eyes to Pohevol, "Yes, Visitor, I have a story."

Jha'li, the male Vine Dragon, motioned for everyone to sit. The Dragons from Durga looked around at the cramped space and imagined trying to make the cave accommodate their bodies in repose.

"There is no room for us to sit," Caduceus grumbled. "Proceed."

Anippe, raising one eyebrow at the ornery Dragon, added, "Caduceus means we would be happy to remain standing."

The Vine Dragons sat and the children moved to find room around them. Mar'du sat near Sefani, and Pohevol moved to stand between Zor and Ius.

Ura began, "We do not understand why the Humans left. How could the desire for never-ending light pull one away from his home?" She traced her claws against the walls covered with handprints. "Why would they leave their families, their lives in Jha'mah?"

Ius watched as her sharp claws moved over the painted hands. It was as if she were speaking to these Dragons and children from long ago.

"Thousands of Suns ago, a large group of adult Humans left us. We call them the deserters," Ura continued. "We have only one remaining Dragon, Zar'un, who remembers his mother telling him about their leaving. She told him the story and made him recall every detail. He has committed the narrative to his memory, and he tells the tale every Solstice under the full Moon."

Zor asked, "You say these deserters craved never-ending light? What do you mean?"

"As you can see, the jungle floor is dark. We Dragons can fly above the canopy if we desire the Sun's rays upon our backs. Humans must climb up the long and twisting lianas or travel a full day to enter an unbroken expanse of light. Most Jha'mah Humans are content basking in the rivers, near the falls, or in the clearings spread throughout the jungle. These brief moments of dry Sun heat the skin and dazzle the eyes. The Humans do not stay for long, as they intuitively seek the jungle's moist heat and shade. Most do not desire the dry heat of the savanna, or the constant watch for Cheetah and Lion."

Zun lifted his head from his chest when Ura mentioned this. He glanced at Pohevol and then asked, "Why would you fear Lions?"

Jha'li answered, "Because on the savanna, the Lion will kill anything to protect her cubs, even Humans."

Lily's puncture marks began to tingle. Pohevol thought, "Take a breath Lily. I am no Lion, and I have no cubs to defend."

Lily thought, "You're as big as one, and you might have cubs one day."

Pohevol released a soft meow.

Zor and Ius looked down at the Forest Cat. Lily clamped her lips shut. Pohevol never meowed. It made him sound like a wistful kitten.

Zor whispered, "Are you feeling well?"

"Listen to the story," Pohevol muttered.

Ura continued, "The deserters craved light. They said the Sun's light was like Spakelv, the ability to speak with Dragons and see things clearly without clouds clogging the mind. As children, their minds were lucid and everything was bright and clear, but when they went through the change and they could no longer speak with Dragons, a fog settled over their minds. They wanted Spakelv to continue as adults, but the elder Dragons denied their request. They said the Midsummer communing should suffice. The deserters disagreed. They wanted more. So they said they would find Spakelv in the sky, in the light of the Sun. They would burn the clouds away.

"Before they left they argued with those who stayed. They asked how the others could be satisfied with foraging in the jungle until the end of time, how they could wait for just one day each Sun to commune with the Dragons. So they told their families they were leaving. They would travel North to live in the land of immutable Sun, of burnished Spakelv in the sky."

Mortoof squeaked, "Why is this a problem? They were adventurous! This might be strange in your tribe, but many creatures seek out new paths!"

Ura smiled at the little Rat, "Perhaps we are not accustomed to differences like you. But we do not call them deserters only for leaving the jungle."

She asked Kali to finish telling the story. The dark brown child with plaited hair stood up.

"They came back into the jungle every two or three Moons," she continued the story. "They would take water from the rivers and fill their baskets and satchels with fruit and nuts. Our ancestors would welcome them home, but the deserters refused to speak. They would only take their fill and then leave again, as if they had never come.

"And when the children of Jha'mah went to visit the savanna to see where the deserters had gone, they would yell and scream for the children to step away and not touch their land. They called the Earth their territory."

"They said the Earth was theirs?" Anippe asked.

"Yes," Kali replied. "With plentiful Sunlight, they established rows and rows of vegetables and tubers by natural water holes and strung rope and spears to keep others away."

"A garden," Tomal said.

Kali looked at Tomal and paused. She thrust out her arm and pointed to the ground of the cave, "They pointed and said the Earth was made different by their hands, therefore it was their land. They said they created life out of the dirt and water."

Guldrun and Lin both murmured, "Mud."

Bridget asked, "Why would they come back to the jungle for water if they lived by water holes?"

"These holes dry up during certain times of the Sun. Elephants, Zebra, and Hyena migrate with the changing seasons—they follow the water—but the deserters did not want to leave their vegetables, what this boy just called gardens."

Jha'li added, "The jungle had plentiful water throughout an entire Sun, so they sent their strongest men back to take the water needed to keep their food growing."

Ius asked, "Did they reproduce? Did they make children?"

Kali turned to Ura and motioned for her to speak.

"Yes," the Dragon said, her voice was scratchy in her throat. "And when the children were strong enough, they came back to the jungle, in search of Dragons. Their parents warned them, shunned them, punished them, even embarrassed them, but they kept making the journey to commune. They remembered it in their blood. They knew to return."

Zun asked, "Until?"

Ura raised her eyes to the crouched boy at the edge of the cave, "Until they moved further away. Zar'un remembers it well, and he has shared this story with every generation of children that is born in the jungle.

"The children of the deserters came screaming into the jungle, 'They are moving us! They are taking us East, to the land of the Sun's birth! What can we do?' The

Dragons embraced the children and brought them to this cave. They showed them the hands. They brought fresh ochre, limestone, and their mixture of charred wood and ash. They made new prints upon the old," she pointed to the section of wall behind Zun. He moved away and looked at the handprints, clearly darker and newer than the others.

"They told the children to remember the colors, to remember the Dreams, and to have faith and hope in the memory. And then they said goodbye."

"But there would be Dragons in the East," Bridget said. "Wouldn't the children bond with these new Dragons?"

Ura walked over to Bridget and touched her hair, "My dear child, we were the first Dragons to accept Human children into our hearts. Not all Dragons share Dreamtime with children."

"Think of the Ice Dragons, Bridget," Tomal said. "They don't commune with children."

"The name that you chose—deserters," Ius added. "It is because they deserted Jha'mah, and they…"

"Migrated East, to the desert," Jha'li completed Ius's sentence.

"They left the jungles of Jha'mah to live in the driest, hottest, most inhospitable place on Earth," Ura said. She pointed one claw to the reddest ochre handprint on the wall, "The desert Sands of Ochre."

✥ 26 ✥

DREAMING IN JHA'MAH

Once everyone was outside the cave, Lily walked up to Caduceus. He was standing alone by a tall tree, rubbing his silver spikes against the smooth bark. The Vine Dragon candles made his scales shimmer purple and green. She touched his back, "Caduceus, I can't go to the desert."

"Really?" Caduceus glowered. "Why?" He turned around and adjusted the Snakes, now coiled around his front legs.

"I can't explain," she asked his green eyes for understanding. "But I know I should remain in Jha'mah."

"We have heard a strange story. A story that will be probed further in Dreamtime, but I will not allow you to leave our group."

"But..." Lily started.

"Do not test my patience, Human child. Everyone is tired, especially you. We need sleep."

As the group walked back to the clearing by the river, to eat and sleep, Lily searched for any sign of time in the jungle. She could not see through the tops of the trees. The lianas were black against the dark green leaves. She missed the Moon, which soon would be only a sliver in the sky, a shed Cat's claw, floating in the night.

The children noticed a change in the sound of the jungle. There were no Bird calls. An occasional Owl would puncture through the moist darkness, but there were no Parrot, Weaver, or Eagle cries. The Vervet Monkeys were silent, and the chatter from the Vine Dragons ceased. This must be nighttime, they surmised. As their eyes recognized the transition from cave to jungle, they could tell this darkness was different. It spread into all crevices of branch and root.

Sophia was ahead, translating between Bridget, Tomal, and two Vine Dragons. Kali held back, waiting for Lily to fall in step with her. She took Lily's hand and traced the sign of the Shift on her palm.

Lily smiled and repeated the action on Kali's palm, and then raised her eyebrows asking the girl if she, too, could Shift.

Kali shook her head, no, and brought her hands to her chest and crossed them across her heart. She bowed quickly towards Lily and kissed her own fingertips before placing them upon Lily's heart.

Lily, warmed by Kali's gesture, started to call for Sophia.

"I can translate," Sefani's voice came from behind the

two girls.

Lily stopped and turned around to find Sefani and Perjas walking with Mar'du.

Mar'du nodded his head and pointed to Lily and Kali and made a gesture to his mouth.

Sefani began speaking to Kali in the tongue of Jha'mah. Just as Bridget had stood in wonder in the Cave of Hands, Lily was agape. So many impossible things had occurred on this journey, she decided to simply accept Sefani's talent with no explanation.

With Sefani translating, Lily and Kali began talking.

Kali asked, "How long have you practiced Shifting?"

"At the age of four Suns I began my practice."

"Are there any other Humans of Durga who can do this?"

"No," Lily replied. "Can any Jha'mah Humans Shift?"

"No," Kali looked sad, "but there are some Dragons who can, and an elder Bonobo named Teleki." She then paused. "I wish I could. Please tell me what it is like."

The two girls, with Sefani's aid, walked through the night-drenched jungle talking about their lives. Sefani and Mar'du added their thoughts at times, and in the short distance of one hour, they were bonded.

"I feel like I have a sister," Lily smiled at Kali when they neared the river clearing. As she desired to see, the Moon was waiting for her in the break of trees. Lily turned to Mar'du and bowed, "And a brother."

"We look forward to meeting you in Dreamtime tonight," Kali kissed Lily on the cheek.

Mar'du nodded, "We are blessed to know you both."

As the Jha'mah children walked away, Lily felt a tingle

move up her spine. "Wait!" she called out to Kali in Jha'mah tongue. Sefani smiled at Lily, "You're remembering too?"

"Only a little," she said, feeling her mouth and tongue play with the clicking sounds. "Go ahead and sleep. Let me try this on my own."

Sefani and Perjas went to the Dragons to help prepare for sleep.

Kali walked back to Lily and held out her hands, smiling at Lily's newly formed words.

Slowly Lily said, "You, me, tonight, river, meet?"

Kali nodded her head and whispered, "I can understand you!"

"Meet?" Lily repeated.

"Yes, after Dreamtime I will meet you there," Kali pointed to the path where Zun and Tomal had walked for water.

"After Dreamtime," Lily said in Jha'mah.

"Yes," Kali pointed again. "There," she said in Lily's tongue.

☙ ❧

Lily walked over to Zun, who was preparing his bed away from the Dragons. He chose the edge of the clearing near the path to the river.

"Always finding the farthest spot from Dragons," Lily said standing behind him.

Zun turned around and quipped, "How can you trust them after the Jha'mah stories? I have proof now, can't you see? Dragons are dangerous. The Humans didn't force them to attack, they did it on their own."

"Just because Ura says they weren't forced, doesn't mean the Humans didn't perform some kind of evil magic on the Dragons."

"Come on, Lily," Zun pushed. "How could any Human trick a Dragon? You worship them. You, Bridget, and Tomal would defend their abilities to the end. You really believe mere men could deceive, capture, and tame a Dragon?"

Lily had to admit, it seemed preposterous. But what else could explain Dragons trying to kill other Dragons?

"I don't care what it looks like, there has to be another explanation," she persisted.

"Every step of this journey is proving my visions to be true," he countered.

Lily grabbed his arm, "And what does that give you?"

"Faith in myself."

"You don't already have that?" she asked softly.

"No," Zun pulled his arm away and lowered himself into his blanket. He laced his hands behind his head and stared at the small sliver of Moon.

Lily knelt beside him, "Visions of fire and Dragons killing Humans gives you faith in yourself? I don't understand, Zun."

He sat up and took her hand, "I don't have anyone in the world. Dragons allowed all that was truly mine to be taken away—my birthright, my home, my memories, my truth. All I have are these visions. If they are false, what is left?"

She felt his warm fingers around her hand, "Your friends."

"You are my only friend."

"Then me," she said. "I'm left."

Zun looked at her face in the soft beams of Moonlight. The image of her moving down the hill in Durga, agile as a Deer, came back to him. He saw her Shifting above the great chessboard in Iceloch. He saw her Shift into the red Dragon, and then dropped her hand, "Sometimes, I think my visions are more real than you."

Lily knitted her eyebrows and stammered, "What?"

"I'm tired." He turned away from her and faced the river, "I want to sleep."

"No," she said, "I'm tired of you hiding away from me and everyone else. Talk to me."

Without moving, without looking at her, he whispered, "How did you become a Dragon?"

"Zun," she grabbed his shoulder. "Turn around and look at me."

He slowly adjusted his body to turn and face her.

"It was a trick. I Shifted into the largest Lizard I could remember, and then Saja helped me to create an illusion. I wasn't a real Dragon."

"Sometimes your power scares me," a ripple passed over his skin. He propped himself up on one elbow. "It's incredible most of the time, and sometimes I even wish I could Shift. But when you became a Dragon…"

She stopped him, "I wasn't a Dragon."

"When your face disappeared, and a Dragon appeared, red and powerful with fangs and claws," he paused. "I just felt like you were gone. I can't get over that."

"Zun, if we're going to survive this journey," she squeezed his shoulder, "and if we're going to remain friends, you're going to have to accept me. All of me."

He sat up fully, "I want to," he whispered. "Believe me I do." He hesitantly raised his fingers to touch her cheek. He was about to pull them away when he heard a booming voice calling out her name.

"Lily!" Zor called again, "It is time."

Lily placed her hand over his fingers and closed her eyes, "Zun, have faith in me and in the Dragons." She opened her eyes, "Have hope. We're all connected." She let go of his fingers, stood up, and walked away. Zun looked down at his empty hand and could feel her warmth still on his skin.

The red Dragon lowered his head to Lily, "The twins will remain as watchers tonight."

"Zun won't leave," she replied. "He's exhausted."

After the Dragons' second meal, everyone curled together in a large sleeping circle. Caduceus would continue to lead, and Lily would do her best to find Saja. As the Dragon incense floated through the air, the children noticed how the humidity made the smoke linger like a bank of fog. Instead of floating over their bodies in airy wisps, it settled like a heavy blanket.

∽ ∾

Sleep captured their minds and bodies, and suddenly they heard a distant cascade of water. The land was a throbbing green, just like the real jungle, but everyone flew in this space, and everyone understood each other without translation.

Caduceus motioned to follow him toward the sound

of water. They approached the torrent of white and blue spray falling between two hills draped in foliage. Blue wings attached to their backs, the children of Jha'mah flew to the waterfall and hovered above the roaring water.

Kali spotted Lily, Saja's hazy serpentine form floating by her side.

"Who is she?" Kali asked with obvious admiration.

"Her name is Saja," Lily replied. "She's a Spirit Dragon."

"She is beautiful," Kali floated around Saja, "I have never seen a Spirit Dragon before."

Lily grabbed Kali's hand, and they flew around the waters together, "You have blue wings here?"

"Yes, we honor our ancestors by having wings," Kali answered.

"Then, it's true!" Lily almost shouted. "Humans used to have wings."

"Of course, silly," Kali playfully bumped Lily in the hip.

"Why did we lose them?"

"We don't know." She whispered so no one would hear them, "Mar'du says the Dragons know why, but that they won't tell us."

"Why would they keep it secret?"

"He says they don't want to hurt our feelings," Kali saw a flash of silver to the right of the falls. "Follow me!"

The girls dove toward the flashing sparkle nestled in lush ferns collecting mist from the water.

"Do you see it?" Kali yelled to Lily over the roar of water.

The noise from the fall was deafening, but Lily

managed to hear Kali. Nodding to her friend, she looked closely into the cropping of green ferns to locate the silver object. Cradled on a shelf, collecting water droplets and flecked with brown spores, was a miniature silver Elephant. At first she thought it was a statue or figurine, but then it moved. It raised its trunk and bayed at Lily! Its gleaming tusks poked the foliage, then it turned to collect water from the falls with its long nose. Turning toward Lily, the tiny Elephant sprayed her.

Laughing, Lily exclaimed, "It's wonderful! Is it a male or female?"

Kali floated next to her, "His name is Haemon, and he exists in Realtime too."

"No!" Lily turned back to Haemon, "He's real?"

"Yes. He often appears near a smaller waterfall right by the river where you are now sleeping."

"Can we go there tonight?"

Kali looked for the rest of the Dreamers, "It's dangerous. We shouldn't visit him without the Vine Dragons."

"Oh please, Kali," Lily begged. "I can Shift into an Owl or Albatross and carry you just as we are flying now, except it'll be real!"

Kali stared at her new friend, glistening in the spray of the falls, "You could carry me?"

"Yes!" Lily said without hesitation. "I can Shift and become as strong as Zor!"

Kali laughed, "All right, but we will have to be quiet."

Excited, the two girls flew back to meet the others.

Ura was flying between Pohevol and Zor. Caduceus had led them to the Great Tree in Durga, and both the

Dragons and children of Jha'mah were impressed with his story and her roots.

"This tree takes one through time," she pondered. "We have a deep rift in the land, an abyss in the Earth that acts as a portal to other parts of the world. I wonder if they are connected in some way?"

Pohevol asked, "This rift is in Realtime?"

"Yes, it is on the Eastern edge of Jha'mah. Jaguars guard it against accidental falls, for we have lost many friends to its depths."

"How do you know it is a portal?" Caduceus queried.

"A Dragon fell in once, and two days later he flew back exhausted. He said he had exited the rift on the Northern shores of the Cerdwin-Askel Sea."

"Why did it take him so long to fly back?" Zor asked.

"He was debilitated. He said the experience weakened his heart and made his bones ache and throb. He never wanted to do it again."

Caduceus lowered his eyes at Ura, "Have any others used this portal, to prove he was not imagining the entire trip?"

"Yes," she said, lowering her own eyes in response. "Despite the disappearance of many friends, a few animals have chosen to enter the rift, including a Stork, a Jackal, a Chameleon, and the last to volunteer, a Pangolin named Oku."

"And," he pressed her.

"And, they all returned."

"Can you travel to a desired location?" he asked quickly.

"Only one has done this," she paused. "Oku."

Caduceus looked to Sophia and Anippe with a glimmer in his eye, "I would like to see the rift, and I would like to meet this Pangolin."

"I can easily take you to the rift now, but you may meet Oku only in Realtime."

"Then," he cleared his throat, "I will follow your lead."

The children from Durga couldn't believe it. Caduceus was deferring to another's lead? Ura was an admirable Dragon.

Ura held her hands up to the sky, and suddenly, the scene shifted.

They were hovering above a vast swath of trees at the edge of the jungle. Just inside the seam where green canopy meets brown savanna, a crater, the size of two Tree Dragons, lay. Every few minutes, steam blasted from the chasm. Surrounding the pit were granite walls striated gray and brown. In little fissures green foliage seeped out, glistening in the wet steam. When the steam dissipated, the children and Dragons looked down into the void.

Zor called out to Saja, "Can you use your horn to light the crater?"

Saja slithered through the moist air and lowered her lightning horn to the deep cavity underneath her body. In a flash, her horn sent a brilliant white light deep into the hole. They searched and searched for an end. No end came in view.

"I will fly into it," Ius offered.

Ura stopped him, "You should not, even though we are in Dreamtime, you could disappear."

Zor held onto Ius's leg, "She is right my friend. I do

not feel comfortable testing this portal just yet."

Forgetting about Saja's light, Caduceus flew over the chasm. He winced, "You can turn that off now."

Saja smiled and lowered her light to a faint luminescence, "Is this better?" she winked at Lily.

"Much," he grumbled. Turning to Ura, he persisted, "Perhaps this is a portal, similar to our Great Tree. We have no proof that your portal is what you say it is, but we will believe you nonetheless. Will you believe our story? Will you help us?"

"Yes," Ura replied.

It was that simple. Bridget and Tomal looked at each other as if they had not heard her correctly. Ius and Zor furrowed the scales above their eyes. Mar'du gripped Sefani's hand and smiled.

Caduceus looked at Ura out of the side of his eye, "You agree so quickly?"

"Your Visitor's future does not come as a surprise to us. We have seen what is possible of men. We need no more convincing. We are doing many things to protect Dragons. A few Dragons who might sacrifice their lives for the survival of the tribe is nothing new to us." She found Jha'li and reached out to him. He flew to her, and they floated above the chasm with Caduceus.

"We have been preparing in other ways," Jha'li added.

Ura looked into Caduceus's eyes, "If you care to come to a Dragon's Circle, we will tell you more."

Caduceus whipped his head to view the children, "We are leaving Dreamtime now. You will need deep sleep for tomorrow. We will wake with the first warmth of dawn."

⸎ 27 ⸎

HAEMON AND THE FALLS

When Lily awoke, the Moon was below the tree canopy. She would need a candle to navigate her way to the river. She carefully extracted herself from her blankets and began to tiptoe away from the circle of sleepers. A rush of fear swept over her when she remembered Zor's adept hearing. I must Shift into something silent, she thought. She set the candle down and focused on one animal with excellent night vision and silent feet. She thought of his green eyes and dark fur. His focus. His confidence.

The Shift was immaculate. Lily, a Forest Cat, silently padded through the sleeping children and Dragons. Her fur was velvet black. She was smaller than Pohevol, and without wings, but she still looked like a replica of his regal body. Lily moved around the sleeping Pohevol, mindful not to wake him. Just as her tail cleared his body, he shifted in his sleep. She froze. He continued to doze, but his eyes were parted slightly. She waited a few minutes before testing his vision.

Sometimes Cats slept with their eyes half-open. One only could tell if they were asleep by testing them. She discreetly moved in front of his eyes, watching for recognition. He did not move. He's still asleep, she thought. Good!

She loped through the remaining sleepers and found herself at the edge of the path. She sniffed Zun who was curled into a tight ball with worry lines etched across his brow. Lily felt an instinctual desire to rub her body against his, or to lick his face, but she fought against it. Turning to the path, she began walking to the river. Her four legs carried her long back in a low sway. Her Cat eyes saw through the hanging foliage as if Saja's horn were lighting the way. She felt at home in this Feline body. She was strong, fearless, and fully aware of her surroundings.

As she neared the river, she sensed a small mammal rustling in the leaf litter. Her stomach rumbled, and she began to stalk the sound. Her head twitched at each miniscule change in pitch and tone. The creature knew she was pursuing it. It became silent and motionless. Trying to evade me, she thought. I'll catch you. She released a low growl and pricked her ears for a response. Then she caught herself. What am I doing? I don't want to eat an animal!

Afraid of what she might do next as a Cat, she lifted her head to the sky, closed her eyes, and Shifted back into Human form. Now on two legs, she made her way to the river. Focusing on the moment ahead and meeting

Haemon the silver Elephant, she did not hear a curious boy with tangled black hair behind her, following her slowly on the path. And this boy did not hear an observant green Spider closely following him.

When Lily reached the river, she looked down the shore for Kali. The darkness of the water merged with the night, so she had to strain to see any movement. Void of Bird sounds, an occasional wind made the leaves rustle and bend. Although it was the middle of the night, the air was still warm and moist. She moved along the edge of the river until she heard a distinct rush of falling water. She moved closer to the sound and saw a precipitous shelf of stone with glistening water falling over the tip.

Moving down another path, using a burning candle to light her way, Kali walked toward Lily. The flickering light showed her expectant face.

Kali motioned with her hands, "I am here."

"Want, see, Shift?" Lily asked in Jha'mah.

"Yes," Kali said in Durgan.

Lily focused on the Giant Owl of Durga. Larger than the Owls of Jha'mah, these raptors could hunt Deer and Puma with precision. Kali watched Lily Shift by candlelight. Her mouth fell open as she saw Lily's skin erupt into feathers and her face evolve into piercing Owl eyes.

"Can you still understand me," Kali asked.

"Yes," Lily's Owl face nodded.

Kali spoke slowly in Jha'mah, "We must fly over the falls and drop a few feet below. Haemon will be in the rock wall to our left."

Lily cocked her head. All she understood was fly, falls,

and wall.

"Where?" she asked.

Worry lines appeared on Kali's brow, "Do you understand me?"

Lily, impatient to see Haemon, replied, "Yes," in Jha'mah, and then flew above Kali. "Hold, feet!" she shouted down to her friend.

Lily grasped Kali's shoulders as lightly as she could, and Kali reached up and clutched Lily's thick, feathered legs.

They took off for the waterfall, Lily's night eyes seeing perfectly the rush of water and the slope of rock wall. Zun saw Lily's huge white body as a reflection in the river. Carrying Kali, she looked as if she just caught her prey. He followed the sound of her wings and came to a small opening in the trees by the rushing water. Looking down, he peered closely to see how far the water fell. He picked up a stone and threw it down into the falls. Judging by how far it traveled and the small splash at the end, he knew the falls were at least 100 feet.

Lily and Kali flew over the falls, and Lily used her wings to hover in one place. She then began her slow descent.

Kali quavered, "Lily, hurry, I think I am slipping!"

Lily couldn't understand the last word.

As she searched to find Haemon, Kali protested, "Go back to the top, your talons cannot hold me!"

Lily looked down at her struggling friend and saw fear in Kali's eyes. Before she could respond, she felt Kali's shoulders slipping. Instinctually, almost feeling as if the girl were her prey, Lily flew toward the rocky cliff, looking for a cleft to stash her bounty. But before she could find a shelf big enough for Kali, the girl fell from her grip.

Kali screamed as she dropped in the darkness. Lily panicked as terror ripped through her bloodstream. She flew away from the wall to search for Kali, hoping to grab her friend. In her frenzy, she thought only of her mother and Kali, which was a dreadful mistake. She Shifted back into Human form. Zun, horrified at the sight, saw Lily the Owl become Lily the Human in midair.

"Lily!" he screamed.

Kali focused on finding something to grab as her body tumbled through darkness. She felt branches jutting out from the rocky cliff and thrust her arms out to grab at them. She found one branch but couldn't grasp it. She crashed through many others as she continued to fall. Finally a cropping of thick boughs was large enough to support her weight. She landed roughly in the cradle of branches and lay exhausted with long scratches and tender bruises on her arms and legs.

Now Lily was falling too. Turning around, certain she was no longer a Bird—and confirming this by feeling her arms and legs—she looked down at the river below. She was far away from the rocky cliff where Kali fell. She would not survive this fall as a Human. She had to Shift again. Now.

A small animal, she thought. A mammal would be easier…a mammal with wings. A Bat! Quickly, just as the dark water moved to encase her body, she Shifted. As fast as a thought, she Shifted into a brown Bat.

Squeaking and flying with her wingtips just brushing the water, Lily escaped the fall into the roaring river and flew up the wet, stony precipice beside the waterfall. She had to find Kali.

Lily's eyesight was horrible now, so she had to focus on her hearing. She heard Zun screaming her name. Why is he here? she thought. Then she heard Kali talking to someone in a calm voice. Lily's heart skipped a beat. Kali was safe—she had survived the fall!

Following the sound of her voice, Lily the Bat flew toward Kali. When she approached the huge girl, tangled in a clump of branches and rock, she noticed a flash of silver. Before she could adjust her movement, she felt a powerful blow to her head and suddenly she was on her back, trapped under the silver trunk of Haemon.

Zun, unaware that Lily had Shifted into a Bat, took off his shoes and began climbing down the rocky cliff. He continued to scream her name. He heard Kali responding, but he couldn't understand what she was saying. The rocks were wet and slick, so he moved cautiously, his toes feeling for holds that would secure his weight. He kept looking down, searching for Lily's body, but could see nothing but the slick face of rock with dark foliage jutting out.

Whenever he came to a clump of green, he allowed the strong branches to hold his body while he rested. Then he continued down the falls, looking to his right at times to see the small cascade of dusky water. He slowly climbed down the wet ledge, hoping he could find Kali and Lily.

Haemon held Lily against the wet stone. She was trapped under his silver, Elephant foot.

"Why would you come alone in the night—clearly a dangerous decision—when you could easily visit under the Sun with the aid of Dragons?" his small voice queried.

Kali, who was tenderly touching her different bruises and scratches, looked to the small Elephant as he spoke in the tongue of Durga, "You speak her language?"

He answered her in Jha'mah, "I speak many tongues."

"Please release me," said Lily, breathing rapid and shallow breaths. "I am sorry. Please let me go."

Haemon did not remove his foot. His trunk played with Lily's Bat fur and wings, "I like you small, and if I lift my foot, you will try to Shift again. Like this, you cannot."

Lily focused all of her energy on a Shift, but realized something was blocking her focus. Was it the weight of his foot? Was it his silver skin? She could not control her focus on any one animal. She arched her head to find Kali. Tucked into the branches, looking jostled but in one piece, rested her friend.

In her most careful Jha'mah, Lily said, "I am sorry." She repeated it with more emphasis, "Kali, I am so sorry."

Kali allowed a slow smile to form, "I know."

"Why would you risk the life of another to come here?" Haemon questioned Lily.

"I wanted to do something alone with Kali, away from the others."

"Why?"

"I felt controlled by everyone else. I wanted some…" she paused and looked up at the Elephant's black eyes surrounded by smooth silver skin, "…freedom."

"And so, because of this desire for freedom, the lives of others are not important to you?"

"I was certain I could carry her," Lily stammered.

"You were wrong. You dropped her," his black eyes pierced her own.

Kali, sensing Haemon's growing admonishment, interjected, "I couldn't hold on to her legs. It was my fault too."

"Yes, you agreed to come." Haemon now used Kali's language, "You should have refused."

Both girls were silent.

Then the silver Elephant began speaking in a soothing voice that revealed both Durgan and Jha'mah words simultaneously. Above, Zun heard it as a lifting song. It traveled out of Haemon's throat like quicksilver, like liquid mercury. The girls were enraptured.

"I travel to this spot and enjoy preening in the wet spray. Sometimes I stay for one day, sometimes for full Moon. Many come to me looking for adventure, wanting to understand why I am here, and how I can be. They say, 'You are the only of your kind,' and ask 'How do you exist?' and they talk and talk and talk. Rarely do they listen. And that is the problem."

Haemon continued, "I remain at my pleasure and exist because I am. Because you have not seen others similar to me, does not mean they do not exist. I have never seen a brown Bat like you, yet I will not assume you are the only of your kind."

He lifted his trunk and bellowed a small trumpeting to the night sky. "Once a Human climbed down this wet rock and asked if he could have me," the Elephant chuckled. "Have me?" I asked him. "He persisted, saying I was his silver idol. He promised he would treat me with care and give me everything an Elephant could ever desire. He said he would free me from the waterfall's shelf."

Haemon looked at the two girls, his eyes flashing back

and forth, "When he slipped, I used my trunk to keep him from crashing below. I asked him if he would like me to set him free. Of course he declined my offer."

He used his trunk to collect some falling water, and then sprayed it over his head and back, "Sometimes you are already free, and sometimes it is wise to be controlled by others." He then locked eyes with Lily, "To focus on the self can save a life, but it can also destroy a tribe. The trick is to know when to exercise restraint." Haemon leaned back and gathered both girls in his vision, "You two made poor decisions tonight. The adventure was not in flying to observe me, but in learning when to say no. When to say no to others and to your own budding sense of self."

Haemon lifted his foot off Lily and proceeded to climb into the wet branches surrounding his shelf. He used his trunk as a kind of arm. He looked back at Lily, "Be careful if you decide to Shift, child. Sometimes it is best to wait and be saved."

Two Dragon's lengths away, Adrianne was climbing a tree, using her eight eyes to chart a path back to the sleeping Dragons. When she saw Zun climb down the cliff, she knew her small body could no longer help him. Scampering back over the path would not be fast enough. She looked up into the canopy and saw the hanging lianas, like thick webs.

Adrianne knew what she could do.

She reached the proper height, and then used two legs

to grasp a liana. With a quick jump, she used the vine to swing through the thick trees. She saw the next vine hanging, used her many eyes to chart it, and then made a seamless transfer in the air. The first liana swung back to its original place. Swinging from vine to vine, Adrianne moved like a flying green orb through the canopy. She rode the lianas like Spiders' webs, using four legs for gripping and switching, and four for balance and steering.

When she approached the clearing, she began a series of clicking and aimed her normal spinnerets at Sophia. She shot a web over the sleeping circle and watched as it landed on the giant Dragon's back. She then used the travel line to slide down from the canopy to the brown and green Dragon. Adrianne landed on Sophia's back and quickly walked to one head.

"Lily and Zun are in danger," she whispered. "Wake up!"

Sophia's one head shot straight up and spoke to the other sleeping Dragons, "Lily and Zun are in danger!" Her other six heads remained asleep.

Zor was the first to wake and assume an alert, fighting stance. Next, Caduceus whipped his head up from sleep and roared, "Who disturbs my rest?"

Again, Sophia translated, "Adrianne says Lily and Zun have gone over a cliff and are dangling from rocks beside a waterfall!"

Caduceus immediately Shifted into a Jungle Owl and took off without speaking to the others. "Ius and Anippe," Zor ordered, "come with me." He looked at the rest of the group, many of whom were still curled in sleep, "Sophia, stay with Guldrun and Lin and inform the children when they wake."

Sefani sat up, rubbing her eyes and listening carefully. Tomal and Bridget continued to sleep, unaware of the activity. Guldrun and Lin murmured in their sleep, groggily moving in and out of peaceful slumber.

The Durgan Dragons took off into the air above the clearing and followed the dark ribbon of water to the falls. They could see Caduceus already dropping below the falls and used him as their primary target.

Flying through the wet night, Zor muttered to Anippe, "I knew it was a mistake to bring this boy."

"We have no idea what happened."

"I can assure you, it was his fault."

They flew over the falls and saw Caduceus back in his Dragon form. He was cradling Lily in his front legs.

"Ius," he called out, "a Jha'mah child is stuck in these branches. Zun is whimpering on that rock wall. Zor, you and Anippe can fight over who would like the pleasure of saving him."

Caduceus flew back to the clearing with Lily. Zor nodded to Anippe and flew around the waterfall searching and listening for any other Human sounds. Ius carefully extracted Kali from her safe nest of boughs, and Anippe plucked Zun from his wet hold.

The children were silent as they flew back to the clearing in the tight grip of Dragons' claws. When they were lowered to the ground, Kali ran to Sophia and spoke in rapid Jha'mah, "This is my fault. Don't be angry. I should have never agreed."

"Agreed with whom?" Caduceus walked over to Kali and peered down into her face.

"Me," said Lily. She shook her head, as a real Jungle Owl flew low over the clearing. "I know you'll find me stupid and foolish, but I wanted to see something special in the waterfall rocks."

"Alone? In the middle of the night?" Caduceus roared. "In a foreign land?" his tail thrashed about, sending leaf litter flying.

All of the children were awake now, sitting up with sleepy eyes, watching the Dragon with the Alligator face lambaste Lily.

"Each Sun I ask myself why," Caduceus continued to grumble, "why I must work with a Human." He began pacing around the other Dragons. "Every time I think I understand you, when you begin to show me your talent and your potential," he snapped his head at her, "you do something foolish!"

Pohevol flew to Lily and interrupted Caduceus's tirade, "She is a child, Caduceus." Pohevol rubbed against Lily's body and licked her hand, "And the young make mistakes." He turned to face the ornery Dragon, "You were a Dragling once, remember?"

"Harrumph!" the green and purple Dragon pushed his way into a thick clump of trees. He turned back and glowered at Pohevol, "I am going to sleep in here, away from you all!" He then glared at Lily, "And I do not want to be disturbed!"

Lily looked away from his condemning eyes. "He hates me," she whispered.

"No, he needs to sleep," Pohevol thought.

Lily turned her face to her Cat companion and smiled. He always knew what to think.

"We all need to go back to sleep," Anippe's soothing voice called out.

"Yes," agreed Zor, "the Sun will rise soon."

Kali and Lily walked over to Sophia so there would be no misunderstanding when they spoke to one another.

"I can't tell you how sorry I am," Lily took Kali's hands into her own, careful not to brush against the scratches and bruises.

"Please," Kali replied, "Haemon was right, I could have refused. Besides," she looked up at Sophia and smiled meekly, "it was kind of fun."

Sophia translated while shaking one head.

Gingerly, the two girls hugged, and Kali disappeared into the jungle.

Zun ran over to Lily and grabbed her, "Don't you ever do that again!"

"I'm sorry," she was surprised at his burst of emotion.

"You could have died!"

Lily scowled, "I thought I was strong enough."

"You always think that," Zun chastised her. "You always think you're ready to do anything!"

The two stared at each other in the darkness. Fern fronds shifted in a gentle breeze, and a Vervet Monkey called out to a distant neighbor.

"I'll be more careful next time," Lily whispered.

"No, not only that," Zun countered. "You'll also ask your friends for help."

She thought about her previous Shifts into the Owl and Bat. She thought about Haemon's words and Kali's body as it fell into the night air. She thought about Caduceus rescuing her, and how she Shifted into her

Human form in the safety of his Dragon embrace. She found Zun's dark eyes and nodded, "I'll try to remember."

28

LAKE WHYDAH

A soft light crept through the clearing and the warm jungle began to rise in temperature. Dragon bellies began to rumble and Guldrun shot up with a start. Looking toward his brother, he sniffed the air. His scales were a dull orange and his furry earflaps were hanging low. His teeth did not protrude like normal. In fact, his face looked so sullen, one could not tell if he had any gleaming teeth at all. His gaze lingered over his still sleeping brother. Guldrun sighed.

Lin hastily sat up, "What is it brother?"

"I feel horrible."

Lin blushed bright purple and moved closer to his brother, "Why?"

"I blew smoke at you."

"But," Lin admitted, "I was being bad. You had to stop me."

"I don't care," Guldrun sulked. "It was wrong."

Lin moved closer so his wing could wrap around his brother, "I forgive you."

"No you don't."

"Yes," Lin smiled. "I do."

"You don't," countered Guldrun.

"Guldrun, I do."

"I don't believe you."

Lin looked around the clearing. The rising Sun revealed sleeping orchids, and Birds began twittering in the dark green leaves of the canopy.

Lin said, "I can prove it to you."

"How?"

"Let's find some mud."

Guldrun's ears stuck up straight, "We're supposed to go to the Dragon Circle this morning."

"I know, but if you go with me to find some mud, we can play together."

Guldrun looked at his muscular brother. Unlike his dull orange scales, Lin gleamed bright purple. Maybe he does forgive me, Guldrun thought. He sniffed the air again, "I think I smell a patch over there," he pointed his snout to the South.

"We'll only be gone for a few minutes," Lin prodded.

"You don't hate me?"

"Come with me," Lin implored his brother.

Guldrun stood up and helped Lin to stand. With a feisty look, Guldrun's lips curled back to reveal his boulder teeth. A dull scale began to peel, and a new bright orange scale lay underneath. Lin reached up to pull off the old scale, "See, brother, everything is going to be all right."

With a tremendous push, they both left the jungle

floor and dashed into the sky. Twisting their bodies and arching in the new light, they flapped their wings and turned South.

Zor woke up and stretched. He looked at Ius, who was sleeping on his back. Zor tapped Ius's chest, "Wake up."

Ius refused to move.

"First light, sleepywings," Zor chuckled. He then tapped Ius on the stomach, "Hungry?"

Ius opened his eyes and stared at the light blue sky, "Sleepywings?" He pulled his body from the ground and grimaced, "Zor, I am not one of your Dragling admirers."

The red bearded Dragon sighed, "I miss the Draglings. Human children are so. . ."

"Wingless?" Ius offered.

"Yes," Zor admitted.

Mortoof scurried from beneath Ius and stretched. He flew up and hovered in front of Ius's face. "Sophia!" he screeched. "Sophia, are you awake?"

Sophia lifted one head, "Yes, little Rat?"

"Could you tell the great Ius that I will accomplish any task he asks of me today?" he darted in and out, smiling and batting his tiny eyelashes at Ius.

Sophia translated for Mortoof.

Zor caught Mortoof and held him up to the Sun, "You would be most helpful if you found Ius and me some coconuts and pineapple."

Mortoof quivered, "Those fruits are so big, I don't know." He stopped himself. Zor doesn't expect I can bring them back, he thought. It's a test. Yes, he's testing my strength!

"Zor," he puffed out his chest and said with grave confidence, "I will return with a first meal for you and Ius!"

He scampered to his satchel and rummaged for tools. Tying a few around his waist, he darted around the clearing, sniffing the ground and the air. He caught a trace scent of pineapple and smiled, "I shall return shortly!" He then dashed into the trees.

"Do you think he will return before nightfall?" Anippe asked, walking over to Ius and Zor.

"The more precise question is do you think he will need to be rescued," Ius moaned. "Zor, I wish you would leave my Rat alone."

"But he is so committed to your service," Zor said.

"I see nothing wrong with that."

Anippe ate some soil fruit, "He is a fine looking Rat."

"If you like subservient creatures," Zor added.

"Well, I cannot wait for him to return," Ius stood up and stretched his wings. "I need to eat now."

The Dragons moved through the jungle, picking sweet fruits and hearty nuts from the trees. When they returned, the children were just beginning to rise. After everyone had bathed, dressed, and eaten, the Dragons spoke to the children. Before Zor could open his mouth, Guldrun and Lin came crashing through the trees. Both were gleaming bright orange and purple beneath a thick coating of black mud.

"Don't fret," Lin spoke to Ius before the Dragon could utter a word, "we've already eaten, and we're ready for the meeting."

Guldrun added with a sigh of relief, "Everything really

is all right!"

Zor looked at Ius, "It seems everything is all right between these two brothers."

Ius admitted, "Sometimes mud is necessary to heal the scrapes and wounds caused by close family."

Lin said, "We're more than healed. We're bonded. Guldrun is the best brother in Durga!"

"Long live fraternity," Caduceus grumbled. "Can we move on?"

Anippe used her tail to pat Caduceus, "It is nice to see them getting along again, is it not?"

"Delightful," Caduceus rolled his eyes.

"So," Zor resumed, "we have been asked to participate in a Dragon Circle, which means children cannot attend."

Caduceus queried, "Is it possible," he paused. "Do you think," he looked at each of the children and then rested his eyes on Lily. "Is it at all conceivable the five of you can stay in this clearing without moving, while we meet with the Vine Dragons?"

Bridget and Tomal turned to Lily. Zun walked up and grabbed her hand, "Yes," Zun said to the Shifting Dragon. "It's possible."

"I'll prove to you, master, that I've learned my lesson," Lily bowed her head.

Sefani added, "We'll remain here. I promise."

"I will keep my faith in you," Caduceus replied.

Lily looked around the clearing for Pohevol, "Is Pohevol going with you, or will he stay with us?"

"He is already with the Vine Dragons," Caduceus narrowed his eyes at Lily. "The Hawks are with him as well. You will be on your own."

Sophia added, "They will have Adrianne," she nodded to the green Spider standing at her feet.

"I will remain with the children," Adrianne said.

"Thank you," Anippe said to the Spider.

Adrianne raised one leg to the golden brown River Dragon. The heat was already rising in the jungle, so the Spider stepped into the shade made by a Dragon's basket.

"Sophia will fly back as soon as the Circle is over," Zor said to the children. "And then we can prepare for our trip to the desert."

Caduceus bent down to Lily, so that his huge Dragon face was only inches from her nose. "We will all leave Jha'mah together, no matter what feelings might waver inside our hearts," he whispered so only she could hear.

"Yes, master," Lily replied, "I fully submit."

"Good," and then the Shifting Dragon walked away.

"Are we going?" Zor asked Caduceus.

"Follow me," the purple and green Dragon moved into the thick stand of trees.

∽ ∾

The Dragons of Durga moved carefully through the jungle. As they followed the directions of the chattering Vine Dragons, the heat became oppressive. Zor and Sophia had to take quick breaks by hanging upside down in the trees, and Anippe found small streams into which they could lower their steaming bodies. Ius and the egg brothers bathed in any swaths of mud they could find in order to cool their heated scales.

Caduceus was the only Dragon not affected by the sweltering heat. His mother's Snake blood moved through his veins and changed to meet the rising temperature. His two Snake companions licked the air with their black tongues and smelled the redolent orchids and sweet date palms that soaked up the heat. The only baking warmth that would be better than this would be torpid heat, but Caduceus had to keep moving, to meet the Dragon Circle.

As they moved deeper into the jungle, the Dragons saw a heavy mist seeping through the trees. Parrots screeched and flew out of the wet fog. Spider Monkeys swung on the lianas, moving through the low clouds. Caduceus pushed away a large cropping of vines and saw over fifty Vine Dragons swimming in a massive green swamp. Resting in the branches surrounding the water were Pohevol and the Hawks.

Anippe's heart fluttered when she saw the large body of water. It made her think of the Lazuli River back in Durga. Only once had she taken the vial of its water out of her satchel to drink small sips. This green water was not flowing, but it had a similar smell to the Lazuli.

She immediately dove into the water. As she swam around using her long tail to navigate, she realized it was deep enough for the Dragons of Durga to stand partially submerged.

"Come in," Ura called to the Dragons standing at the edge. "Follow your River Dragon into Lake Whydah."

Zor and Ius waded into the serene water, then the egg brothers, and finally Sophia and Caduceus. Anippe was right—all of the Dragons could easily stand on the bottom with their heads poking out of the water. For Sophia, the water only came to the top of her legs. She decided to kneel in the water, so that she too could experience the cool sensation.

"Thank you for coming," Jha'li spoke. "We are excited to meet with Dragons who remember the ancient amulets and Dreamtime with children. We cannot allow the destroyers to ruin an epoch of peace." He swam around Zor and Ius, "We believe you have secrets to share, and we are ready to listen."

Ius turned to Zor and felt his blood begin to warm.

"Listen to him," said Zor with a calm face. "Now is the time—feel these waters. There is safety here."

Anippe swam over to Ius, "Zor is right," she nudged him. "We are with friends, those who will not doubt, those who will understand."

Pohevol added from the trees, "It is time, Ius."

Ius looked to find Pohevol and saw bright holes of Sun in the spaces between the dark leaves of the canopy. He then saw movement that made the light blink, "What is that?" he burst out.

"The Whydah Bird," Ura said. "Watch it land."

Ius followed a dark flowing shape until he saw it alight on a liana hanging horizontally across the lower canopy. Its black plumage was darker than any feathers he had ever seen, and its tail was long and broken into two distinct sections. The tail feathers crossed in such a way that the Whydah Bird looked like it was sitting above a Dragon's pupil.

"This lake is where they nest," Jha'li remarked. "They are guardian Birds."

Ius watched the Bird look down upon him, "Sophia,"

he uttered, "ask the Bird if it is safe here."

Sophia lifted a head to the black Whydah and peered at the wise eyes and beak.

The Bird spoke to her in a haunting caw. Sophia returned with a similar voice.

"She says you already know the answer."

Ius stared at the Whydah Bird, and she spread her wide wings and beat them in the air, directly toward Ius. A faint green light began to emanate from her black wings, and then it disappeared. She tucked her wings away and preened some breast feathers.

"Very well, I will speak," Ius said to the Circle of Dragons. "Twelve Suns ago, when I was charged with flying the men you call destroyers back to their land, I saw a horrible event."

The Dragons of Jha'mah moved in closer, swimming around Ius, peering up at his large blue face.

"When I dumped those men on the ground, I heard a Dragon's roar in the distance. I heard vicious fighting and saw smoke rising from a valley. I could not believe Dragons would live in a place peopled with such gruesome invaders, so I flew to see what was wrong."

He looked to Zor, and the red Dragon nodded his head, "You are doing it, keep going."

"I saw two Dragons fighting. One was as large as me, a golden Dragon male. It was slashing and tearing at a light green female with light brown eyes."

Ura repeated, "A golden Dragon?"

"Yes," Ius continued, "he was covered in small scales of gold and had black eyes." He glanced at Zor and stuttered, "He had two small spiraled horns over his eyes."

He looked around at the Vine Dragons, "The green Dragon was roaring at the gold one in a language I could not understand. And then I saw the fire. The gold Dragon unleashed his fire against the green, and I saw her scales burst into flame."

Ius's voice became deeper and the water rippled with his unease, "I did not intervene. I cannot explain why my wings sat like stone against my back."

"Ius," Zor began, "the elders have warned us against interference."

"No!" the blue Dragon roared. His bellow made leaves fall into the lake, "I could have saved her!"

A chorus of Whydah Birds began cawing from the trees.

"They are saying you were wise, you did not fail," Sophia whispered.

"The golden Dragon flew away from her burning body," Ius continued. "He left her to die on the valley floor. He looked back at her once, and I saw his piercing black eyes. They were filled with hatred and pride. I could see that clearly. Hatred and pride."

The Dragons watched as Ius lifted his blue wings out of Lake Whydah to allow water droplets to fall, making a long and thin rain curtain. He lowered his wings back into the warm water.

"I could not believe my eyes. When the golden Dragon flew out of the valley, I went to her. I landed by her side and smothered the flames. But I was too late. She stared at me, with those eyes, those light brown eyes, and spoke six words over and over again. And then she died."

Ura asked, almost as if she were holding her breath,

"What did she say?"

Ius turned to Sophia and lowered his head, "I am sorry, Sophia. My shame kept me from telling you the complete story."

"What did she say?" Jha'li pressed.

"Tell Sophia," Zor said. "Now is the time."

"She said, 'Ahargon ahmen, Ochre Ahargon narhen sarend' over and over until she could no longer breathe."

"Sophia?" Pohevol flew down and landed on her exposed back. "What did the green Dragon say?"

Sophia's heads stretched out until all seven hovered above the Vine Dragons, the Dragons of Durga, the Hawks, the Whydah Birds, and even the silent Vervet Monkeys, peering down from the canopy, "She said 'There are now Dragons of Men, send for more Dragons of Ochre.'"

Ius threw his head back and released a roar that shook the Earth.

Ura swam to Ius and placed her hand on his front leg, "Why did you carry this for so long without sharing with those who love you?"

He lowered his head to meet her questioning eyes, "I did not want to know the meaning of her words. Her death, and my refusal to act, was more than enough."

Ius turned to Zor, his eyes flashing with pain, "I have told them everything. Now, leave me be!"

Before Zor could respond, Ius burst out of the water and landed on the shore. His thick claws dug into the soft soil as he charged through the jungle, breaking small trees and slashing thick lianas into a rain of detritus.

∽ 29 ∾

NIGHTSHADE

While the Dragons were away, the children ate a silent meal together. Adrianne hunted for fresh Insects and came back to the clearing looking like a denizen of the jungle. Her belly bulged, and she collapsed by the children to clean her legs and spinnerets.

"What do you think the Dragon Circle is about?" asked Bridget.

Tomal replied, "I think the Jha'mah Dragons are planning to fight."

"But they agreed to send some of their kind into hiding."

"Yes," Tomal agreed, "but they also said they were preparing in other ways."

Sefani said, "Perhaps they will send one of their Dragons to come with us to the Sands of Ochre."

Lily hesitated and then decided to share her fears with them, "I'm afraid to go to the desert."

Zun looked at her, "Why?"

"If the adults who left Jha'mah live there now, I can't imagine what 1,000 Suns separated from Dragons would do."

Bridget said, "But there were Dragons when they got to the desert. They could have reconnected then."

"I'm not sure if Sand Dragons would want to reconnect with Humans who abandoned Jha'mah," Tomal remarked.

Perjas adjusted his resting body, and Sefani began rubbing his furry neck, "I don't think the deserters would tell the Sand Dragons they were from Jha'mah."

"But they'd most certainly ask," Bridget said.

"Do you think they'd tell the truth?" Sefani turned to Bridget and looked at her almost as if she were truly staring at the girl with the long black braid.

The children thought about Sefani's words. The deserters could lie to Dragons. It would be an ignorant thing to do, for if a Dragon learned that she had been tricked or deceived, she would never forget. But it could be done. All children except Zun had experienced the lying lessons.

To a Durgan child, a lie first entered the world like invisible magic. Unaware that adults could not read minds, until the age of four or five Suns most children simply did not lie. They did not understand how to manipulate what was obviously true. Some adults had a hard time appreciating the harsh truths escaping the mouths of the very young, yet there was reassurance in this reliable honesty.

But there always came the moment, that incredulous

special moment, when a child realized he had a secret mind with thoughts and feelings known only to him. He could tell others he felt sad, when truly he was pleased. He could say he felt sick, when honestly nothing felt wrong inside. This was the birth of lying.

Unlike adult Humans who became too comfortable with the enticing power of manipulating truth, children would stumble and falter with their first attempts at lying. Dragons could sense this shift like the change of seasons. When it began, the lying lessons commenced—two weeks of successive Dreamtime with Dragons. The children learned they had full power over this mental magic, but if they used it on a Dragon, they would pay a heavy price. The children practiced lying with each other, sometimes they even lied to their parents, but they never lied to a Dragon.

Bridget said, "The deserters would be crazy if they lied about their origins."

"I think they would," Sefani countered. "I think they would try and destroy all connections with Jha'mah."

"But look at their dark skin and hair," Tomal persisted. "No one has such beautiful skin and hair as the Jha'mah. The Sand Dragons would know they were from the Motherland."

Lily said, "Maybe time changed them." She held out her light brown arm and all of the children except Sefani looked down at their own arms and touched their own hair. "The ancients say Jha'mah was our Motherland too," she paused, "and we changed."

"In only 1,000 Suns?" Bridget protested, "They couldn't change so fast."

"I think they could," Zun said.

Bridget turned to Zun and pondered the wiry boy with tangled hair, "You've been too quiet." She had to clip her tongue, as it was close to uttering 'cave boy'. Instead she asked, "Why do you think the deserters could change so quickly?"

"Because they were unhappy," he said. "They willed the change, they encouraged it, they figured out ways to make it happen."

Lily looked at Zun and felt her blood pulsing in her temples.

"I think," he looked at Bridget with no malice or anger in his heart, "when someone hates his life, who he is, and where he lives, I think he changes so much on the inside, it can change the way he looks on the outside."

"I agree with Zun," Sefani said quietly.

Bridget felt Zun's sincerity. He was not exactly warm with her, but he certainly wasn't cool. The words 'cave boy' exited her mind, and she never used them again.

"Maybe they did lie," Tomal whispered.

Bridget looked at him and shook her head, "If they did, they were absolute fools."

∽ ∂

The Sun moved higher into the sky, and the heat became almost unbearable. The children knew they needed the dark shade of the canopy. Walking around the edge of the clearing, they looked for a nearby place to explore.

"Adrianne," Bridget called out, "can we gather food

for the trip to the desert?"

Tomal reminded her, "Sophia isn't here."

Bridget brought her fingers to her lips, "I forgot. How are we supposed to talk with her?"

"The ancient way," Tomal smiled. He walked over to the green Horned Spider and touched his stomach, his mouth, and pointed to the jungle.

Adrianne used one leg to touch her abdomen, and then pointed to the trees.

"I'm pretty sure she says it's all right," Tomal said.

The children moved just along the border of the jungle and the clearing. They collected satchels of dates, palm nuts, wild ginger leaves, stalks of sugar cane, and figs. Tomal told them to collect as many edible nuts as possible, as nuts would survive the heat more than the other foods.

Zun and Lily walked together, searching for low-lying berries. As they climbed over buttress roots and stooped under thick lianas, the soft light of the Sun crept through the leaves and landed like warm mist on their skin.

They could see Sefani and Perjas just one Dragon's length away, collecting fallen palm nuts and talking in Dog tongue. Tomal and Bridget were laughing as they carried a satchel of figs back to the clearing.

Lily bent next to a plant with soft purple flowers. The leaves looked similar to Caduceus's pointed, Alligator head. The segmented veins on the underside of the leaves looked just like Dragon scales. Near the flowers were clusters of hanging green berries, like tiny olives.

"Look, Zun, Dragon berries," she said plucking a few. "I thought Caduceus said these only grew in Durga."

Zun squatted on his knees and looked carefully at the

berries. He didn't see Lily place a few in her mouth.

"They aren't very sweet," she added.

"Lily," Zun stood up, still looking at a berry, "this isn't a Dragon berry." He turned to look at Lily and saw her face turn pale.

She immediately began coughing and gasping.

"Get it out!" he cried. "Spit it out!"

Lily's pupils dilated. She looked at Zun, and he was flooded in white light. She looked around and everything in the jungle became hazy. She heard the screeches of Birds and Zun's voice as if she were listening from underwater.

"Tomal!" Zun screamed, "Lily ate something poisonous!"

Lily reached out for Zun, "Help me," she panted, "help me."

Tomal and Bridget came charging through the trees, and Adrianne followed. Lily fell to the ground and sporadically shook as she panted into the dirt. Her eyelids became slack. Zun cradled her head with one arm while Tomal and Adrianne peered at the berries in Zun's other hand. Tomal knelt in front of the plant and stared at the yellow center that looked like a kernel of spring corn. After a few seconds he saw the miniscule pink dots on the inner purple petals and gasped, "It's nightshade."

Bridget cried, "No!"

Zun demanded, "What does it do?"

"If she doesn't get to Durga within a day. . ." Tomal froze.

Lily opened her eyes, "I'll die."

Adrianne sniffed the berries and raced back to the

clearing.

"What is she doing?" Bridget shouted. "Why isn't she spinning her web?"

Tomal began thinking out loud, "All right, wait…" he looked around and then held out his fingers as if to count them. "Nightshade, shade of night, covers you in shroud—fight shade, and nightshade, with water roaring loud…"

"She's going to the waterfall!" Tomal yelled. "Lily needs fresh rushing water to stay alive!"

"Can you Shift?" Zun lifted Lily's shoulders.

Lily heard his words, as if he were miles away, "I can try."

"Become the Raven," he begged. "Go to the waterfall and drink from the falls!"

Lily felt her blood thinning. Would the Shift make the poison worse? She couldn't think properly, but she knew she wanted to live. Tomal could be wrong. A boy of only ten Suns could be very wrong.

She allowed her blood to change, and as the Raven's black plumage settled over her skin, she knew her blood was infected with the poison. It felt meager, insufficient to sustain her large body. But as her Human form disappeared, she felt stronger and more powerful in the smaller body of a Bird.

"Fly!" Zun cried out, "and then meet us back at the clearing!"

Lily pumped her wings and dodged trees and lianas to make her way through the edge of the jungle. When she came to the clearing, she shot up into the sky and pumped her wings with force, determined to find the dark ribbon of water. She flew faster until she heard the falls moving over the steep cliff.

She flew over the falls and hovered on the left side, near Haemon's shelf. He was nowhere to be seen, but his shelf was still matted with soft grasses, and it was dry. She landed mindfully, making sure to grasp the grasses and rock with the full extent of her black talons. I will not slip this time, she thought, remembering the Alys River outside of Saja's cave.

She leaned her humped black beak to the water and cracked it open. The waterfall bathed her beak with cool water, and she gulped as much as her Raven body could hold. She felt her blood thickening, and the haziness dissipated. She felt almost normal. Lily continued to drink until her stomach felt as if it would burst.

Then, without thinking of anything else, she flew back to the clearing. As she flew and her wings beat under the light of the Sun, she felt the poison working its way back into her blood. She saw the children and Adrianne waiting for her in the clearing. She landed awkwardly with a hop step and stumble.

"Lily," Tomal said, "Adrianne needs you to Shift back into your Human form."

"I feel stronger as a Raven," Lily objected, cocking her head to an angle.

The Spider pointed to Tomal emphatically.

"Lily, she needs you to be Human now," Zun held out his arm.

Lily flew to Zun's outstretched arm and made quick sidesteps to his shoulder. She peered into his black eyes and felt safe.

"Please Lily," Zun whispered. "Trust us."

She cocked her head again and nodded. Trying to remember her mother's face, she focused on becoming Human again. But this Shift was hard, for while Zun had begged her to be Human again, she truly did not want it. The image of her mother and the Raven became mixed and her body suffered in the confusion. Zun warily placed her on the ground and watched as the Shift faltered.

"You can do this," his voice had an edge of doubt.

She concentrated on the sound of Zun's voice, and thought of him and her mother. Her Human body began to form and in a flash of pain, Lily felt the poison come roaring through her bloodstream as her Human body exploded through Raven's feathers.

"No!" she screamed. "It's killing me!" Lily writhed on the ground, twisting and pulling at her skin. She got on her hands and knees and tried to retch.

"No!" Tomal yelled, "Don't let her throw up the water! She needs to keep it inside!"

Bridget, Tomal, and Zun threw themselves on her and pushed Lily to her back. Lily fought, trying to Shift back into the Raven, but Sefani interfered, shouting, "Caduceus, Zor, Guldrun, Lin, Ius, Saja, Anippe, Labrys!"

Confused with the onslaught of Dragon names, Lily couldn't focus on the Raven. While the children struggled to keep her on her back, Adrianne navigated Lily's bucking stomach and chest. She stretched her healing web across Lily's heart. She then climbed up to Lily's face and pointed a leg to her eyes.

Tomal shouted, "Close your eyes Lily! Trust Adrianne!"

Lily's eyes were rolling into the back of her head, and once again, all of the children's voices seemed distant and far away.

Zun crawled over and placed his face inches from her own, "Close your eyes Lily," his voice was firm and resolute. "Close them."

Feeling her strength leaving, like a tree suffering a drought, Lily closed her eyes. As soon as they shut, Adrianne shot a fresh web from her horned spinnerets. The silky white threads created a blindfold over Lily's eyes, and she suddenly stopped thrashing. Her body became limp.

"What happened?" Zun asked.

Tomal answered, "She put Lily into a sleeping trance. It's good."

Sefani breathed deeply, "I know this trance, Zun." She reached for Perjas, "She used this on Perjas when he was covered in stinging nettle. He couldn't stop ripping his fur out, so she used this to calm him."

The children sat on their knees in a circle around Lily. They were all breathing heavily from their struggle. Zun stood up, "I'll go find the Dragons. We've got to get her back to Durga!"

Tomal grabbed his arm, "Zun, it will take at least three days to travel to Durga. She won't last that long."

"Maybe they have the remedy in Jha'mah!" Bridget burst out. "Every poison has an antidote nearby, right?"

"Not nightshade," Tomal's head sunk, "to survive one must be in the land of one's birth." He bit his bottom lip and looked up, "Nightshade can be slowed, but with the setting of the Sun unless Lily is in her homeland and with a

Dragon egg soon to hatch, she will not survive."

"The rift," Sefani whispered.

Zun turned to her, "What did you say?"

"The rift," she repeated, "Ura said a Pangolin could make the rift take him where he wanted to go. Maybe Lily could use the rift to take her to Durga."

"What rift?" Zun demanded.

Bridget answered, "Last night in Dreamtime, the Jha'mah Dragons showed us a deep abyss that acts as a portal. Animals jump in and they come out in a different part of the world. The Vine Dragon, Ura, said there is a Pangolin who can direct the rift to take him certain places."

Zun started for the trees.

"Where are you going?" Tomal called after him.

"To the Dragons of Jha'mah," Zun yelled back. "Lily and I are jumping in that rift."

30

THE PANGOLIN AND THE RIFT

This time Zor did not follow Ius. After Ius shared the secret that brought him shame, Zor knew he would need time alone to literally blow off steam. The red Dragon turned back to the Dragons floating in Lake Whydah, "In Dreamtime you said you were preparing in other ways. What are you doing?"

Jha'li swam over, "There are some of us who want to fight. If the destroyers come back, we will be prepared. I have been studying the ancient fighting positions and," he hesitated, "I have been withstanding fire."

Anippe swam closer to hear better, "What did you just say?"

"Because it sounds like you said you've been standing in fire," added Guldrun.

"Yes," Jha'li concurred, "that too." He raised a wing

and blew fire directly at it. The orange stream slid across his scales, but did not burn them. Jha'li invited Zor to try his fire.

Zor opened his mouth and blew a larger ribbon. Jha'li stopped his own flame and whipped his other wing around to feel the brunt of Zor's power. The fire moved around his wing as water glides over the fin of a Fish.

"How long can you do this?" Caduceus asked.

"I can withstand a full hour."

Caduceus did some mental calculations, "You will need to last much longer before you are ready to meet these destroyers again."

"I will double my effort," Jha'li offered.

Ura added, "We will ask more Dragons to train with Jha'li."

Zor stood up and climbed out of Lake Whydah, "Everything will help."

Suddenly there was a tremendous crashing through the trees. Ius, his stone body bending trees and crushing buttress roots, burst into the lake, "Lily has eaten nightshade!"

As Ius explained how he had seen Zun racing through the trees and lianas, screaming for the Dragons, Pohevol immediately leapt from his perch high in a tree and flew in twists and turns through the foliage to the clearing. Caduceus flew out of the water and Shifted into a Peregrine Falcon. He followed Pohevol into the jungle.

Just as Anippe was about to fly, Ura grabbed her leg, "She will need a Dragon's egg from her land of birth."

"I understand," Anippe said. "That is why I must prepare to fly her home."

"You will never make it in time," sadness spread across the Dragon's face.

"I see no other way," Anippe pushed Ura's hand away. "Please, I must go now!"

"Wait," Ura exclaimed, "there is another possibility."

Zor met her eyes, "The rift."

"Yes," the dark green Dragon nodded. "We must take you to Oku now."

Zor turned to Anippe. He knew she was ready to fly, to prove speed could save a child's life. But he also knew they had flown from Durga for three full days and two nights before viewing the shores of Jha'mah. Even if Anippe flew twice as fast without stopping, she could not get Lily to Durga before the Sun went down.

"Anippe," he whispered, "warm your wings and fly to the shores of the Cerdwin-Askel Sea. Go as fast as you can, and then turn around and come back. Time yourself. We will see how fast you truly can fly," he paused. "For if the rift does not work, you will be our only hope." He turned to Ius, "You and I will go with Ura and Jha'li to speak to the Pangolin." He found Sophia, "Sophia, come with me as well." He looked to Guldrun and Lin, "Follow Pohevol and Caduceus to Lily and the children, tell them Lily will not die."

Anippe tore through the jungle, searching above her for a clear path to the sky. Ius, Zor, and Sophia followed Ura and Jha'li back into the thick maze of lianas and trees.

"I should tell you this," Ius began as they raced through the dark green leaves and vines, "Zun wants to jump into the rift with Lily." He pulled lianas out of his way and stomped over thick mats of leaf litter, "Maybe we should let him go with her."

"Ura," Zor called out, "can two animals go into the rift at the same time?"

Sophia arched one head near Zor and perched another over Ura and Jha'li.

"No," she called back, "Two of our Dragons tried this, many Suns ago."

"The steam spit out their dry bones," said Jha'li.

"Steam?" Sophia asked.

"The rift releases a geyser of steam every few seconds. One must time the jump for when there is no steam," Ura said.

Zor turned to Ius, "Go back and find Zun. Tell him she must go alone. Tell Caduceus as well. This will be hard on them both." He then locked eyes with the blue Dragon, "Bring Lily to the rift. And friend," Zor lowered his voice, "fly fast."

Ius returned his friend's stark gaze, turned around, and looked at the crushed foliage they had just moved through. He looked up at the dark canopy and saw tendrils of light floating in from above, "Sophia, ask Ura if it is possible to break through to sky from beneath the canopy."

Sophia replied, "She says the trees will forgive you, if your body can survive the lianas."

Ius nodded his large blue head, "Where should I meet you?"

Ura replied, "Fly over the canopy toward the Sun moving West. You will see the brown edge of the savanna and two sharp boulders shaped like a Crane's bill. The rift is there. We will bring Oku."

Hearing her final words, Ius charged through the

jungle, bent on finding Zun. He needed only to follow his previous path. As if a mountain boulder from Durga had found its way into Jha'mah, Ius flew over the trail of flattened roots and limp lianas. Bright red flowers pulled back as if hiding from the trail, and colorful Birds swooped low, frolicking in the cleared flight path.

He saw Zun running back to the clearing, his hair flowing wild and drops of sweat beading around his face. The blue Dragon flew in front of the boy, turned around, and came to a full stop directly in front of Zun. Leaf litter blew around him as his claws gripped the Earth. Zun kept running, as if he were going to charge right over the Dragon.

"Halt, boy!" Ius bellowed. "I am going to lift you, do not fight me!"

"Where are the others?" Zun yelled up at the stony face.

"Racing to the rift," Ius snarled. "I must take you back to Lily. Then I will fly Lily to the rift."

"I'm going with her!"

"I do not have time for this!" Ius reached out and grabbed Zun with his front claws. In response, Zun arched and contorted himself, trying to escape the Dragon's clutch.

Ius bent his back legs and pushed off in a tremendous leap. Feeling the air become increasingly hot, he fought through gnarled boughs and curving lianas. Zun struggled, but kept close to Ius's chest as sharp branches brushed past him.

As Ius cut through leaves, small pools of water tipped onto his scales and over Zun's face. They both glistened as the Dragon pumped his wings around the labyrinth of greenery. He focused on the brightest point of light peeking through the top of the canopy. Zun looked up and saw Ius's determined gaze. He, too, saw the growing circle of light and held his breath as the Dragon carried him closer to the sky.

The point of light grew nearer and nearer, and finally, they burst through the circle of brilliance. Instantly the thick humidity evaporated from Ius's scales and Zun's face. The blue Dragon turned in the air, searching for his location. He marked the Sun and the distant mountains, sniffed for water and the sound of waterfall, and then knew where to fly.

Remembering Zor's words, Ius spoke to the boy trapped in his claws, "Control your fear, boy. She will not die."

⊰ ⊱

Zor, Sophia, Ura, and Jha'li approached the edge of the jungle. They could see the thinning of trees and a golden brown light resting just beyond the curtain of green.

"Oku lives in the roots of a baobab tree just North of the rift," said Ura. "Let me approach him first."

Ura reached for a vine and swung through the remainder of jungle faster than light. She switched vines quickly, and Zor realized this was her preferred form of flying. She landed near the baobab tree and darted around its base, peering in at the deep crevices running along the roots. Ura saw Oku clutching a low branch, almost touching the ground.

Hearing her movement, he instinctively let go of the branch and dropped to the ground. His horny scales clenched as he curled into a tight ball and released a powerful stench. His quick momentum propelled him against the baobab.

"Oku, it is me," Ura cooed.

The Pangolin remained still. After a few moments, he slowly relaxed and allowed his body to unfurl. Unlike most mammals, Oku was covered in armor. His thick olive green scales looked more artichoke than Dragon, but in the Sunlight, his strong claws and long, muscular tail made him appear more Dragon than vegetable. Unlike the Dragon tribe, Pangolins were warm-blooded, bore live young, and fed their babies warm milk from furry bellies. Some animals whispered Pangolins curled into armor balls to hide these sensitive stomachs, others said they simply preferred survival through physical defense and smell offense.

Oku had a small, elongated head shaped like a thin triangle and thick forelegs like miniature tree trunks. He peered up at Ura, "It's the middle of the day. I should be sleeping."

Ura looked around the baobab tree, "Why were you out of your hole, then?"

He sighed, "I couldn't sleep."

Ura nodded her head in understanding, "Oku, some Dragons from a distant land are here. They would like to ask you questions about the rift."

He commenced curling back into his armored sphere.

"Wait," said Ura with urgency, "they are kind. They

are not related to the others."

"What do they want to know about the rift?" he asked, relaxing his muscles and allowing one eye to peek from behind a scale.

Jha'li, Zor, and Sophia stepped out of the trees and allowed full Sunlight to illuminate their bodies. Oku looked toward the Dragons, and froze when he saw Sophia's seven heads. If he had been covered with hair, it would have stood on end. Instead he snapped back into his tight ball and began rolling backwards. His tail shot out to give a push every few seconds.

Sophia moved quickly to the Pangolin and lowered a head to the scurrying armor ball, "We mean you no harm."

The ball kept rolling.

Sophia persisted, "You obviously are closely related to our tribe, as your scales are magnificent."

Oku's tail jutted out and gave another push. The ball continued to roll away.

Zor strode over and lifted his red, clawed foot. With care he brought it down on the Pangolin.

Unable to move, Oku poked his head out and looked up at the huge, feathered Dragon face, "Ura says you're kind," Oku trembled. "She doesn't lie."

"I have no intention of proving her otherwise," said Zor.

Oku released himself, stood up on all four legs, and fully extended his long tail. His thin claws curled into the sandy dirt, and he arched his head to stretch his small neck.

With an earnest voice, Zor spoke to the Pangolin, "Oku, we are traveling with a Human child who is gravely ill. She has eaten nightshade and must return to her homeland before the Sun retreats for the night. Can you tell us how to use the rift to bring her home?"

The Pangolin looked up at the Dragon with a nonplussed, perplexed expression, "A Human has never jumped in the rift!"

"There is always a first time," Zor refuted.

"The others exit in random places," Oku arched the scales where his eyebrows would have been and wrinkled his snout. "I'm the only one who can choose my exit point."

"Why?" Sophia implored. "What is the secret?"

He stood up on his back legs, fidgeted with the claws on his front legs, and looked at Ura and Jha'li, "We aren't sure! You told them we aren't sure haven't you?"

Jha'li knelt by the armored Pangolin, "The child is very ill, Oku."

Oku curled his tail around Jha'li's leg, "We think it might be the layering of my scales. Each time I jump in, I curl into my ball, and make my scales as tight and strong as stone." He turned to Ura, "The heat surrounds me and at the moment when I feel I'll burst into flames, I imagine exactly where I want to be," he paused. "And then I'm there."

"Then, that is what Lily will have to do," Zor said.

"A Human couldn't survive!" Oku shouted up at the red Dragon. "An animal must have scales, she must have armor!"

Zor smiled down at the Pangolin, "She will."

Oku squeezed his eyes to small lines and twitched his nose, "I don't understand. This doesn't make sense."

To Sophia Zor said, "We must go to the rift now." He looked down at the Pangolin and arched one eyebrow, "Our Lily is a special kind of Human, but she will need your help. Come master Pangolin." Zor bowed to the small armored creature.

Sophia, following Zor's direction, prostrated herself by lowering all seven heads to the bewildered Oku, "Yes, please come with us."

∽ ∼

Back in the clearing Lily lay on the ground. Sefani sat cradling Lily's head in her hands, as a soft drone escaped her mouth. Sweat ran down Lily's forehead and Perjas licked the salty rivulets. Adrianne ran back and forth over the girl's weak body applying new web over her eyes and heart. Tomal and Bridget sat on either side of Lily, each holding one of her limp hands.

Pohevol was the first to come soaring over the clearing. Bridget looked up when his shadow crossed Lily's face. Close behind was a Peregrine Falcon with piercing green eyes. Before Bridget recognized the similarity, Caduceus Shifted back into his Dragon body and landed on the ground.

Pohevol did not land. He flew in circles around Lily, directing his thoughts to her inert form below, "Do not fight Adrianne's sleep. Let it take you someplace safe." He watched her eyes flutter under the closed lids. "Do not waste your energy," he begged her. "Conserve your strength."

Caduceus growled at Tomal and Bridget to move out

of his way, "Tomal, go to Anippe's satchel. Bring me gorse petals! And bring Labrys's jewels!"

"Pink or yellow gorse?" Tomal jumped to his feet.

"Both!" the Dragon demanded.

Tomal ran to Anippe's basket while Caduceus called to the trees surrounding the clearing. His two Serpents slithered out of the lianas and dropped to the floor. Caduceus spoke to them as they glided to Lily. One slid where Sefani's hands were, and upon feeling the cool skin, she pulled her thin fingers away. The other encircled her coils around Lily's ankles, shins, and thighs. Adrianne nodded to Caduceus and pulled away Lily's heart web.

The Snake now cradling Lily's head moved his head to just above Lily's mouth. The pointed face slowly parted the girl's lips and peered inside. The Snake turned to Caduceus and hissed in his ear.

"We are losing time!" Caduceus roared. "Where are Ius and Zor?"

Pohevol landed and with care moved toward Lily's horizontal torso. She did not look like she was sleeping. She looked dead. Her skin looked empty and gray, and her closed eyes sank into their sockets. A rush of fear spread through Pohevol's veins and made his wings shudder. He unfolded and extended them above her sallow and anemic face. A purr began in the depths of his throat and emanated from his entire body. Pohevol closed his eyes and brought his forehead to hers. He continued to purr.

Just as Tomal came racing back with the gorse and jewels, Ius and Zun came gliding into the clearing. The egg brothers were just behind Ius. Caduceus grabbed the bag from Tomal and placed malachite around Lily's head and bloodstone near her torso. He set two diamonds near her temples and three stones of obsidian near her waist. Finally he placed tiny sapphires in a circle around her whole body.

He then whipped the flowers from Tomal's hands and crushed them with his claws. He scooped a small amount on the tip of one claw, asked Pohevol to lift his wings, and delicately placed the yellow and pink mixture into Lily's parted mouth.

Lily's head moved, and she swallowed. Adrianne shot to her face and removed the web from her eyes. Lily's lids fluttered and slightly opened.

"We must take her to the rift," said Ius. "And she must go in alone."

"Now then!" Caduceus hissed. "There is little time!"

Lily moaned and turned her head. Through her parted eyelids she found the Dragons and children staring down at her. She saw Pohevol's face and tears pooled in her eyes, "What's happening," she thought to her dear friend.

"You are very sick. You ate nightshade. You must travel back to Durga through the rift in Jha'mah if you are to survive."

Lily let her eyes close as she vaguely remembered kneeling by the green berries. An image of the waterfall entered her mind. "A Raven. I must Shift into a Raven," she thought.

Pohevol cried out, "Caduceus, can she Shift?"

"No!" the purple and green Dragon commanded, "Lily Fearn, listen to me." He brought his pointed snout just inches from her face, "Do not Shift now. You must concentrate on quelling the poison in your blood. I will tell you when to Shift!"

Lily forced her eyes to open again, and she focused on her teacher's voice. She stared into his green eyes and then fell unconscious.

"The poison is attacking her brain. We must go," Caduceus picked Lily up and surged into the air. The many jewels and stones fell in a rainbow of sparkles.

"Fly as Anippe would fly!" Ius cried out from the ground. "Fly!"

Zun, still trapped in Ius's claws, pleaded with the Dragon, "Take me to the rift, Ius. If I can't jump inside with her, at least let me be there when she goes in."

Ius nodded his agreement and took off in the direction of Caduceus and Lily, now a tiny blot in the sky.

Just as Guldrun and Lin were about to lift Tomal, Bridget, Sefani, and Perjas into the sky, Mortoof came scrambling back into the clearing.

"I have the fruits!" he screeched in Rat tongue.

No one could understand what he was saying, so as Guldrun swooped over the puzzled Rat, with Sefani clutched in one leg and Perjas in another, Perjas reached down and snatched up the Rat in his thick jowls.

"Where are we going? Isn't Ius hungry? Where is Ius?" Mortoof screamed, struggling in the Dog's mouth and hastily looking around at all of the flying Dragons and children. "Great Malooks! What's happening?"

None of the creatures could understand him, so he muttered, "This is most unexpected, indeed."

༜ ༜

It was all Ius could do to catch up and fly alongside Caduceus. The great Dragon carried Lily as if she were his prized possession. The Snakes were still coiled around her, and she lay inert and limp in his grip.

"Fly toward the Sun!" Ius called out against the wind. "You will see two sharp rocks along the edge of the jungle. The rift is there!"

Caduceus's green eyes focused on the Sun, as if its burning rays could not blind him. He lowered his gaze and saw the pointed rocks far in the distance. Now he flew even faster. His wings looked as if they would break from his body, but he kept beating them faster and harder, leaving Ius and Zun in his wind wake.

The Dragons followed Caduceus, and saw Zor, Sophia, Jha'li and a small armored ball on the edge of the rift. Every few seconds, their forms were shrouded in a spray of mist as steam burst forth. Then the frothy water would settle, and the red Dragon and seven-headed Dragon would appear again. Ura and Jha'li stood behind them, and behind the Vine Dragons stood some children of Jha'mah.

When Caduceus landed, Kali ran up and touched Lily's hanging leg, "What happened?" she whispered. Worry lines spread across her forehead as she pulled back her braids to see Lily better.

Sophia answered, "She ate nightshade berries."

The children of Jha'mah opened their mouths and eyes wide. One child sucked in a breath and said, "This is not her home...she will surely die."

"No," said Sophia, "this is not her home, but she is going to be home soon."

"The rift," Kali brought her hands together to her mouth.

The other Dragons landed and set the children of Durga down on the brown soil. All around the rift stood immense baobab trees and Termite mounds that were pockmarked and covered with rough edges. A mist from the settling geyser left droplets of water glistening on the smooth, bare branches and tall, dusty mounds.

Oku poked his head out and looked at all of the new creatures. He focused on the skin of the Durgan children, a much lighter brown than the deep cacao brown of the Jha'mah tribe, and quickly turned to Ura, fear filling his tiny black eyes. She held up her hand and extended her claws, "These Humans are not like the others who came. These can be trusted."

He scanned the many Dragons and found Lily, limp in Caduceus's claws, "This must be the one." He waddled over in an awkward, guarded manner and stretched his neck to nervously sniff at her body. A Snake arched her back and spit at the Pangolin below. He hastily curled into a ball and rolled away from Caduceus and Lily.

Zor snapped, "Caduceus, this creature must speak to Lily, help him!"

Caduceus lowered Lily to the ground and told the Snakes to move away from her. He turned to Ius, "Set him down," and to Zun he snarled, "Come here and sit by her side." The Shifting Dragon looked into the air, "Pohevol, come to her other side." The boy and the Cat followed Caduceus's directions.

"Where is Anippe?" Caduceus spat.

"She will be here soon," Zor reassured Caduceus. "If

this does not work, she will fly Lily home."

Caduceus turned to Oku, who started to poke his head out of his armor, "How will we know if she has arrived in Durga?"

"You won't."

He roared, "This is unacceptable! What do you mean, 'we won't'?"

Zun stood up, "She can't go in there if we don't even know where she'll come out!"

Caduceus looked at the boy and nodded at him for the first time in both of their lives, "I agree. I will go with her."

"You can't," Oku countered. "Unless you both want to die."

"What is the secret, then?" Caduceus said with clenched teeth, losing his patience.

"I'll talk to her. I'll tell her everything I know," Oku turned to Ura and Jha'li and implored them with his eyes. "If she can survive the heat, she'll come out where she needs to be."

"Talk," he ordered the Pangolin, "tell her now."

Sophia slid two heads over to Lily and the armored creature.

Caduceus demanded, "Tomal, give me more gorse."

The boy, holding pink and yellow flowers outstretched in his hands, stumbled to the angry Dragon.

Caduceus crushed more petals into a fine powder. The Dragons and children sweltered in the heat, as they watched Caduceus prepare the elixir for Lily.

Zor asked, "How long will she remain conscious after taking the gorse?"

"Only a few minutes," Caduceus grumbled. "This nightshade is potent."

"Listen, Caduceus," Zor leaned over the Shifting Dragon as he worked on the petals, "Lily must successfully Shift into a Pangolin. It is the only way she will survive this rift. You must help her make the Shift."

Caduceus turned his head toward Zor, and then he lowered his eyes to the tiny armored creature. "Shift into that?" his voice dripped with condescension.

"Yes," said Sophia, "a Pangolin. He is a mammal. That should make it easier, correct?"

Begrudgingly, Caduceus nodded and placed the crushed gorse into Lily's mouth. She spattered and shook her head back and forth. "Take it," the Dragon growled, "swallow it now!"

Lily opened her eyes, saw Caduceus's green eyes glowing at her, and cried out.

Pohevol rubbed his face against her body. "Swallow," he thought. "It is good for you."

Zun squeezed her hand, "We're here with you, Lily. I'm here with you."

She turned to the sound of Zun's voice and felt his hand around hers. She felt Pohevol's fur against her cheek. Unable to think anything in response to the Forest Cat, she swallowed the gorse powder.

Caduceus used a claw to turn her face to his, "Open your eyes Lily Fearn." The Dragon narrowed his eyes to two points of extreme focus. When he saw Lily's pupils meet his own, he said, "This Shift is the most important Shift of your young life. It will save you. You must become the creature who sits beside you now. Look at him, Lily.

He is a Pangolin. He is covered in Dragon scales, yet he is mammal, like you. You must listen to him first. Before you go into this rift," he paused, "and you must go into this rift, you must Shift into his exact shape, size, form, and color."

Lily's eyes began to water again. The Shifting Dragon seemed so far away, "Caduceus," she whispered.

"Lily Fearn!" he roared. "Stay with me!"

Her pupils contracted and focused on his Alligator mouth, "I'm here," she breathed out, "my master."

Caduceus continued in short, pronounced bursts of speech, "I will Shift into a Pangolin. I will show you. Focus on me. I will perform the Shift multiple times. Follow my lead. Watch every turn. Follow me. You can do this."

He turned to Oku, "Now, Pangolin, talk."

Oku crawled over to Lily and spoke rapidly. Sophia translated into Lily's ear.

"This Dragon says you are a magician, a Shifter. Perhaps you can do this."

"Do not waste time!" Caduceus roared. "Tell her now!"

Trembling, the Pangolin released a deluge of instructions, "You must wait until the roar of the geyser stops. After you hear three popping sounds, you must roll in. Rolling is critical. You must not jump. You must hear the three sounds first. Do not go before. When you're falling, tuck your tail in tight to your undercarriage. You'll fall for what seems like an eternity, but it will end, I promise you." He leaned closer to her eyes, "This is the most important part, for I know you must leave the portal in Durga. It will be broiling in the rift. Your scales will sizzle, and you'll think you're burning," he bumped her nose with his own. "But you won't be. You must think of Durga only. You must see Durga in your mind. Make Durga fill your thoughts. Believe you can exit the portal in Durga, and you will."

"Why," Lily could barely form the words as she tried to focus on the Pangolin, "do I want to go to Durga?"

Zun grabbed her face, "Lily, listen to me! You're going to die if you don't make it to Durga! You ate nightshade! You must go home!"

Fear flooded Lily's eyes. She remembered.

"Think of Saja's cave," Caduceus placed a claw on Lily's heart. A tear from his eye dropped and landed on his claw, and he knew immediately what he must do. "I did not know until now, child," he clutched the claw and ripped it off his foot. A Dragon roar shook the savanna, and following his great bellow, a gush of steam spouted from the rift.

"Caduceus," Lily murmured. "Why…" she could not continue but could only stare at the blood dripping from where his claw had been.

Caduceus placed the long, sharp claw in her empty hand, took her other hand from Zun's grasp, and closed all of her fingers around the rigid claw, "You are the Dragling I will never have, Lily Fearn. Saja has the medicine that will fight the nightshade. Her egg will save you. You are my living egg. Now go and find Saja's egg. Go to Saja. Focus on becoming the Pangolin and try with all of your purpose, all of your soul to enter Saja's cave. You have three necklaces around your neck, little one. This trinity will protect you. My claw is in your hands. You can do this, Lily Fearn." He stopped and took a deep breath, "No, you will do this."

Lily's eyes fluttered.

"Now!" the green and purple Dragon thundered. "Lily Fearn, look at me and this creature beside me, Shift now!"

Caduceus Shifted in and out of Pangolin form. Oku stood motionless on the ground, afraid to move, afraid even to curl into a ball. From exhausted eyes, Lily watched the armored creature, and she watched the Shifting Dragon. She saw the furry belly on Caduceus as he Shifted in multiple ways. She saw the artichoke armor, the capped nose on the pointed head, the olive green scales, the curled claws, and the thick back legs. She saw all sides of the creature she had to become. All angles were revealed in pronounced flashes of light. She felt her blood thinning and knew she was slipping closer to death.

"Fight!" Pohevol's thoughts came in a rush of clarity. "Follow Caduceus! You have your Name! You have your Necklace! You carry Caduceus's claw! Shift, Lily, Shift!"

In a blinding light Lily began a weak Shift. Her body blurred, a faint ghost of a Pangolin form appeared, but then evaporated. Her eyes were heavy as they stared at Caduceus, locked on his changing form. She pushed her focus, tempered her control, and forced his evolving forms to take hold of her heart. After a long moment Lily's body let go, and she emerged looking exactly like Oku. She was an olive green, armored Pangolin.

Oku, who did not see Caduceus's Shifting behind him, became even more frozen, if at all possible. This pale, near-death Human was now a Pangolin.

Lily crawled her way to the rift and used her triangular

head to peer inside. A blast of steam came belching up, and she awkwardly pulled away. She heard a popping noise, and then another. No more sounds came from the rift. She heard one more popping sound and then silence.

She turned back to Oku. She looked at Zun and Pohevol and the children of Jha'mah. She saw all of the Dragons she loved. She saw Bridget, Tomal, and Sefani.

"Now!" Oku and Sophia screamed at the same, exact time.

Lily curled into a tight, armored ball and rolled into the abyss.

31

THE ABSENCE OF NOTHING

Falling. At first the heat felt like a slight tickle on her Pangolin scales. Then it was a blanket wrapping around her. Now it was a bath of fire. Lily dared not remove her Pangolin head from its protected position. She continued to fall with no pressure, no resistance, and no hint of an end. Just as her scales felt as if they would melt into liquid, Lily remembered her purpose.

Saja's cave, she thought. Saja's cave. She imagined the golden egg nesting in a bed of fur and feathers. She saw the diamonds and moonstone, the sapphires and platinum. She remembered Saja's serpentine body, her proud lightning horn, and then with a painful crack, her Pangolin body fell against hard rock. She tried to release her armor, but since she was so tightly compacted, her scales remained in a rigid ball.

Weak and exhausted, Lily lay still on the hard surface. The poison from the Nightshade crawled throughout her body, learning the new Pangolin shape. Lily heard movement, a soft whipping sound. She wanted to Shift, so she could exit this hard, armored ball, but she was too tired. All she could do was murmur, "Saja."

Suddenly she felt her body being lifted. Was she falling again? It felt like she was rising. Perhaps the rift was spitting her out. Lily whimpered. She had failed. She would die in Jha'mah. Or perhaps she was already dead. She remembered stories of the transition, how the body felt light as if it were floating into the air.

I must relax, she thought. I must accept death in my own body. She focused on her mother's face. She saw the gentle smile, the radiant eyes, and the soft, smooth, light brown skin. The Shift came gracefully. As the Pangolin body released its clenched ball, tail dropping, legs and claws loose and free, head arched back in a languid fall, Lily's Human form appeared, her skin blending the separate Pangolin scales into one smooth surface.

She smelled incense and saw a soft flickering behind her closed eyelids. She felt her body floating on a cool and curving surface.

"Why are you here, Lily?" the voice came from far away.

Lily tried to open her eyes, but couldn't, "Night. . . shade." The word came in two distinct parts.

The cool surface became warm. Lily felt her body being tossed and turned. She cried out for it to stop. This effort removed the last bit of energy she had.

"Lily!" the voice ordered, "Lily, open your eyes!"

Lily left her body. Floating above the scene, she clearly saw where she was. Below her, as if she were watching a play from the sky, she saw Saja's curved body cradling her splayed and lifeless form. She saw the golden egg resting in the nest, candles burning a hundred flames around the cave, and bowls of incense filling the room with a dry mist. Saja flew around the cave, speaking to the lifeless body, trying to move Lily's arms and legs, frantically trying to bring her back from the dead.

Lily's spirit drifted around the cave, lost in this theater. She felt a deep connection with her body, lying in Saja's thick coils, but she also was drawn to this new sensation. Unlike Dreamtime, she was moving with no present body. She knew if she wanted to, she could travel thousands, even millions of miles with a single thought. But she was drawn to this place, this moment, this drama occurring now, below her.

Instantly she knew, this scene was happening in a thousand other ways on thousands of other planets, in an infinite number of Universes. It overwhelmed her. The truth of her existence and her life made her pause, floating above this scene, mesmerized with the passionate movement below. While this moment was not unique to the many, it was precious to the few.

Saja wanted her body to live. The Spirit Dragon wanted Lily's blood and flesh, muscle and bone to live. Lily now understood the most miraculous truth: Everything and everyone would live for eternity in some way—not in the way most living entities experienced—but in a way, some way. She felt this truth like a force of energy, as if a powerful wash of lightning passed throughout her body.

Everything remained after death. Nothingness did not exist. After death, Lily might change shape, like when she Shifted in life. She might leave this planet and mingle with the stars. She might settle into the soil and sleep for a million Suns, but she would still be. She would still remain in a way, in some way. Nothingness was an illusion. There was always something, even in the spaces in between.

Lily's spirit watched as the Dragon placed her limp body near the pale egg. She removed all of Lily's clothes and moved the egg's jewels so that Lily's body could embrace the egg. Next, she newly arranged the sparkling stones and gems around Lily and the egg. Then she blew steam around the two inert forms. After a few moments, the egg moved. It was only a small rumble, but Lily was certain. The egg moved.

Without warning, Lily felt herself being pulled back to her lifeless body below. It was warm and inviting. While she enjoyed floating above, in the pulsating space of everything connected and knowing, she felt pangs of love. She wanted to speak to Saja, to feel the egg's touch, to hear the candles flicker, and to smell the incense wafting in the cave. Lily wanted more of this life. She now understood what death could be, but she still wanted more life on Earth. Beautiful, heart-wrenching, glorious, painful life on Earth. It called her back, so she allowed life to take her in, to capture her, and to claim her as its own.

Saja, too, saw the egg move. She continued to call out to Lily, "Open your eyes! Lily, hear me! Come back to me!"

Lily felt a pulsing vibration moving across her skin.

The veins inside her head pounded, as if tiny Mud Dragons were using her skull as their drum. She heard Saja's voice, warbled and disjointed, but she knew it was Saja. Wetness formed in the corners of her eyes. Lily could not open her eyelids, but she knew from the fragrant smell of incense and the soft fur and feathers she was home in Durga.

"Saja," said Lily in a weak, grasping voice.

The Dragon moved closer to Lily's face, "Talk to me."

"I ate nightshade in Jha'mah," the words tumbled out.

"Yes," the Dragon said, "my egg will help you, but listen carefully." Saja wrapped her body around the entire nest. Both Lily and the egg were encircled by her serpentine coils. She said, "This is a dance. The Dragling inside can save your life, but you must not take too much from her. Let her give to you willingly. Do not pull from her. You will feel stronger, as she will give you strength to fight the poison. But do not ask for more. If you do, you could hurt her beyond healing."

Saja continued, "If you both survive this moment, you will be forever linked, almost like egg sisters, but if you are demanding," the Dragon pushed her horn against Lily's cheek, "if you take from this small Dragling what she is not willing to give, I will shun you. I will sequester my Dragling away from you and never see you again."

Saja demanded once more, "Open your eyes."

Lily searched for the growing tendrils of strength to force her eyes open. Her eyelids gradually parted, as tears pooled above her lashes. "I would never hurt your Dragling," her pupils finally focused upon the violet and gold Spirit Dragon encircling her. "I will do everything exactly as you say." The tears fell down her face.

Saja rubbed her horn along Lily's wet cheek, "You are still Lily," she whispered. "The spirit world protected you. You must sleep now, and let my Dragling find you."

"Shall I enter Dreamtime?"

"No, you are too weak. Just sleep," Saja's voice sank deeper into the shadows as Lily closed her eyes. Lily listened to the voice as it repeated, "Sleep my child, sleep."

∽ ∾

In Jha'mah night fell over the trees and the Dragons of Durga sat inside the clearing by the river. They had said goodbye to the Vine Dragons and the children of Jha'mah. Ura and Jha'li promised four Vine Dragons would hide in a coned volcano in the middle of Cowrie Rise, a chain of rugged mountains. It was at the Southern edge of the jungle, far from any Human activity, so the isolated Dragons could leave their hiding space at times to gather food and receive messages.

Everyone was eager to enter Dreamtime, to see if they could find Lily. Anippe, with glistening scales and heaving breaths, returned minutes after Lily rolled into the rift. She had flown to the sea and back in less than an hour. Exhausted, she was the first to think of Dreaming.

Pohevol sat by the edge of the river. He stared at his reflection fluttering in the water, staring back at him. He stretched his wings and then tucked them away. He stretched them and tucked them. He continued to do this without passion and without focus.

After a time, Caduceus walked over and stood beside

the black and white Forest Cat, "Anippe's mind is clear. I could not think of meeting Saja in Dreamtime while at the rift. We will have our answer there." He picked up a broken tree bough lying by the slow moving water and broke it in two.

"We all had trouble thinking," Pohevol scratched at the dirt.

"I believe she made it."

"Will Saja understand her Pangolin shape? What if Lily cannot speak?"

Caduceus searched for another branch to break, "Saja will know. She will sense that it is Lily inside the Pangolin."

Pohevol yawned and Caduceus nodded, "It is time."

They went back to the clearing and saw Zun preparing his blankets inside the circle of children and Dragons.

"What is the meaning of this?" Caduceus hissed.

"I'm going to sleep with you," Zun said without looking up. "I'm going to Dream with you all tonight."

Caduceus looked blankly at the boy and then the other children.

Bridget dropped her covering and stared at Zun.

Tomal walked over and helped Zun smooth his blanket, "What's wrong with Zun Dreaming with us?" he asked, running his hands along the soft material. "He can do it if he has a willing Dragon."

Caduceus demanded bluntly, "Why now?"

Ius spoke before Zun could answer, "He wants to find Lily."

Zun rose from his blankets and walked over to the green and purple Dragon. He looked up at the shimmering scales that changed color with his every breath, "I'm willing to trust you." Zun stared at the red clot where Caduceus's claw had been, "If you can trust me."

Caduceus looked down at his missing claw and remained silent. After a few moments, he turned to Zor, Anippe, and Ius, "If he is to enter Dreamtime, he had better do it with me."

The egg brothers raised their eyefolds at each other and smiled.

Sophia reminded everyone that tonight's Dreaming was for one purpose only—to find Lily and Saja, "If she cannot be found, do not linger in Dreamtime. I will pull you back if need be, and it will not be pleasant."

"Did you hear what she said, boy?" Caduceus grumbled.

"Yes," Zun pulled his cover over him, even in the heat of the evening.

"I will guide you," the Dragon yawned. "But if you do not listen to me, I will have Sophia rip you awake faster than the hiss of a Snake."

"I understand," replied Zun.

"Good. Now go to sleep."

The children found tight crevices in the circle of Dragon bodies. Capes were drawn over scales and skin, and bodies stretched and turned, trying to find comfortable positions. Once everyone settled, it was quiet in the jungle clearing. A few Owls passed by, their wings making the air whisper. A Tree Frog chirruped in the dark leaves. Stars watched as the sleepers released the day's tension. Faces relaxed and wings drooped. Mouths parted slightly, and the Dreaming began.

❧ ❦

A formidable force swept the Dreamers into separate tubes of rainbow light. Some Vine Dragons flew by in their own tubes and waved as they went flashing by. As they traveled down and up the long funnels, new children appeared as each one entered Dreamtime.

Zun was the last to emerge, and his face softened in his bright tube. Ius looked at the boy and found his amulet glowing a deep red. He pointed to Zun's neck and nodded. Zun looked down, amazed to see the pulsing light.

"Welcome to Dreamtime," Zor swooped by Zun in his own brilliant funnel.

At the end of the tubes, the Dreamers were deposited onto a white cloud floating above Durga. The children crawled to the end of the billowy vapor and looked down at the verdant trees and towering mountains. Standing like the promise of time was Mount Calyps. Sophia's heads lowered to gaze upon her favorite place. Her many eyes glistened as she saw the clouds hovering above the steep crags. Pohevol flew above them in slow, circular passes.

"I will take us to the Alys River," Caduceus said.

He dove off the cloud and everyone, but one, followed him. The children rolled and soared, making sure to keep the green and purple Dragon in sight, but Zun remained stuck on the cloud. Caduceus looked back and suddenly appeared on the cloud again. Zun blinked hard and looked down at the flying Dragon leading the line of Dreamers, and the standing Dragon next to him. They were one in the same.

"How?" Zun began to ask.

"Dreamtime, boy," Caduceus cut him off. "If you could only accept your fate, you would know even more."

Zun fingered his amulet, "Why does it glow here?"

"You will understand when we are in the Sands of Ochre."

Zun watched the children flying through the sky following Caduceus's other self, "They can fly without fear here."

"As can you, if you would like."

"I'm afraid," Zun hung is head. "I want to find Lily and Saja, but I'm afraid."

"A kernel of wisdom is dormant inside you," the Dragon mused, "but it is still there." Caduceus lowered his head to meet the boy's dejected gaze. He reassured Zun, "You will not fall in Dreamtime, and you will not die. Jump and float, boy. It is easy."

The Dragon disappeared, and Zun saw Tomal flying back to the cloud.

"Zun," Tomal grabbed his hand, "come with me."

"I can't," he faltered. "I thought I could do this, but it's too much. Dragon magic is everywhere," he tried to clutch the cloud, but his hands grasped nothing tangible. "I can't breathe," he looked at Tomal with fear in his eyes.

"Yes, you can," Tomal squeezed Zun's hand. "For Lily, you can."

Zun's eyes squinted, as he looked at the line of Dragons below and in the distance. Pohevol and children were becoming more faint. He turned to Tomal and nodded his head, "Don't let go."

"I won't," Tomal smiled.

The two boys stepped off the cloud and drifted down slowly.

"See," Tomal turned to Zun, "it isn't like falling in Realtime. It feels like floating. Do what I do."

Zun shifted his position and became horizontal like Tomal.

"All you have to do to go faster, is think about it," Tomal turned his body so that his face was lower than his feet. "I'm going to let go of you. Trust me," he said as he dropped Zun's hand. Tomal flew five Dragon's lengths in an instant.

Zun thought about catching Tomal, and immediately he soared through the air and was beside his friend again. Tomal smiled, "I told you so." They continued doing this, Tomal moving farther, and Zun following, until the boys approached the others, hovering above the sparkling Alys.

Caduceus spoke into the cave, "Saja, are you here?"

Saja's spirit body appeared as mist outside of the cave. "I have been waiting for you," she flew to her Dragon kin and slithered through and around them many times. She used her lightning horn to touch their faces, legs, and wings.

"Is she here?" Zun's voice caught in his throat.

"Yes," Saja turned to look at the boy.

"Is she alive?" asked Pohevol.

Saja lifted her head and blinked at the Forest Cat, "Yes."

Caduceus looked at his missing claw, Zor and Ius released their breath, and Zun turned his face to the sky and closed his eyes. Anippe hugged the egg brothers. Sophia wrapped her wings around the children.

"I must know," Saja entreated the Dragons, "I last saw you in Jha'mah. Where are you now?"

Zor answered, "We are still in Jha'mah. We are traveling to the desert tomorrow morning."

"You have been successful then?"

Caduceus flew to her side, "Everyone has agreed to our request, save the Sand Dragons."

"Then Lily should remain in Durga once she has fully recovered," Saja said.

"Yes," Caduceus replied, "she is too weak to return to us. We shall proceed without her."

Zun looked at Saja and then at the missing claw of Caduceus, "Can we see her?"

"No," she said. "My egg is transferring power to her, so Lily must not enter Dreamtime. If you come too close to her, she will be attracted to your energy. You must remain here."

Zun furrowed his brows and turned to Caduceus, "Let me stay in Durga with Lily. I don't want to continue without her."

"You forget, boy," Caduceus Shifted into a Vine Dragon, "we are still in Jha'mah. We are many days away from Durga."

Zun let his eyes travel over Caduceus's new shape. He then looked at the Alys River below his own floating body. He remembered this was all a Dream. This was Dreamtime. He was truly sleeping in a jungle thousands of miles away from Durga.

"We will return to Durga soon," Zor reminded the group. He turned to Ius, "Our journey will end in the Sands of Ochre."

"I will tell the others," Saja swooped back in front of her cave, her spirit body flickering in and out of focus.

Caduceus held up his leg with the missing claw, "Did Lily arrive with anything?"

Saja used her horn to point at the cliff outside the cave's entrance. Gleaming like a polished white horn, Caduceus's claw lay on the rock.

"When she Shifted into her Human form, this fell from her grasp. It confused my Dragling, so I had to remove it."

Caduceus flew to peer closely at his detached claw, "When she has healed, give it back to her. Tell her to keep it with her at all times. Have her make a belt, if necessary."

"I will," Saja promised.

Zun flew awkwardly to Saja, "And tell her," he stopped and looked back at the hovering group of children and Dragons. "Tell her, I have hope."

Saja nodded her head, and her misty body disappeared.

Caduceus turned to the children and Dragons, "Leave this world now, sleep undisturbed till morning. We leave for the sand at first light."

"How do I leave?" Zun asked the Shifting Dragon.

"Follow the children," he pointed to Tomal, Bridget, and Sefani, "I brought you here, but they will take you back."

Zun watched as Sefani flew toward a black line in the horizon, "This is where we're sleeping," she called back to Zun.

He followed, focusing on her golden hair and the dark stripe. As the line came closer, he felt his body growing heavy. And then, before he could ask the others what he was seeing, he awoke in the jungle clearing. The light of the waning Moon rested upon his blanket, and the trees swayed in the breeze.

32

THE SANDS OF OCHRE

In the early glow of morning, Parrots trilled and Monkeys chattered as warm mist settled in the canopy. Dawn rose gently over the jungle. Silently, the Dragons and children ate their morning meal. Zun opened Lily's pack and looked inside. He found Pohevol's whisker and the tapestry Lily's mother had painted. He stared at her closed journal, and then looked up to find Caduceus. The green and purple Dragon was sitting far away from the others, talking quietly with his Snake companions.

"When do we leave?" Zun asked the Dragons.

Zor looked up and sniffed the air. He turned his face so he could hear the breeze better, "Rain is coming. We should go soon."

Ius nudged Mortoof, now sleeping next to the Dragon's claw file, "Eager to find your answers in Ochre?" he asked Zun.

The boy shook his head, "No, I'm eager to return

home."

Mortoof mumbled in his sleep and reached out to nuzzle against one of Ius's claws. He pressed his snout alongside the black talon and puckered his lips as if to kiss it.

Ius nudged the Rat again, "Wake up, Mortoof. It is time."

The Rat opened his eyes and spied the others looking down upon him. He scrambled to his feet and searched for a piece of paper and charcoal. Finding a scrap and nub, he wrote: I am ready! My destiny awaits in the Sands of Ochre!

He dropped the paper to the ground and scurried off to the tree edge to scrounge for fresh nuts and berries. Everyone else finished securing the food and packing items in the baskets. Anippe went for a quick swim in the river, and the Mud brothers were given leave to bathe in fresh mud.

"The Sun will be unforgiving," Guldrun reminded Ius.

"Yes," Lin added, "and mud is an excellent scale protector."

Ius gazed upon his blue armor and up at the rising fingers of light. The Sun would be intense on the desert journey. He did feel the call of mud, "I will join you," he said, "for a few minutes."

Zor, putting away his items, said to his friend, "Take only one minute. I do not want to fly through lightning. I hear a buzzing in the air."

"We will not be long," Ius raised his wings, and the Mud Dragons flew along the edge of the river.

Zun walked over to Sefani who held a beautiful bow

made of baobab wood and a quiver of arrows tipped with Whydah feathers.

"Mar'du gave these to me," she said, sensing his question.

"They think we're crazy," Tomal said, looking up from his satchel.

"Who does?" Zun asked.

Bridget walked over and touched the bow, "The children of Jha'mah." She reached for the handle of her knife. "But we're prepared."

"You think a knife and a quiver of arrows will help us in the desert?" Zun raised one eyebrow.

Bridget ran her fingers along the blade, "They believe the deserters have lost the skill to fashion arrows. They say without Whydah feathers, arrows can fly only one Dragon's length. Mar'du gave each of us a set." She rummaged through her basket and pulled out another bow and quiver, "Here."

Zun took the bow and looked at the carvings etched into the side. He saw tiny handprints, reminiscent of the Cave of Hands. He saw the rift and a Pangolin at the edge. The final carving showed the children of Jha'mah and Durga standing side by side, holding hands.

"They're beautiful," he said. "We gave them nothing in return?"

"No, of course not," Tomal answered. "Bridget gave them capes, and Zor let me share soil fruit."

Zun turned to look at the red Dragon. Pohevol was now perched on Zor's shoulder, speaking in his ear. Zun noticed how the Cat's fur lacked its normal luster. His eyes were a dull green.

Sefani walked over to Zun, "You're not the only one who suffers from her absence."

Zun nodded, "You always seem to know."

Caduceus flew over with his Snakes securely wrapped around his neck, "Let us depart. It should take three days to fly to Ochre."

Zor looked over the Dragons and children, "We are missing Anippe and the Mud tribe."

Anippe walked into the clearing, her golden brown scales wet from the river water and her Horse head dripping, "I am ready."

"Mud brothers!" Caduceus bellowed, "Come, now!"

They heard a loud sucking noise in the near distance. Guldrun and Lin came through the foliage with no visible spot of orange or purple. They were covered in sticky mud, and only their eyes could be discerned from this new reddish black skin.

Ius walked behind them, but there was only a light coating of mud along the surface of his scales, "They are ready," he grumbled.

The children climbed into the baskets, and Zun, after lowering himself in his, carefully placed Lily's pack in one corner. He turned to see Tomal and Bridget organizing their things in the basket next to him. Adrianne climbed up the side and dropped in next to Tomal. Zun looked behind their basket to Zor. The red Dragon was helping Sefani scale his back. She used his long, red claws as small stepping rungs, and then settled into her comfortable space atop his plumed neck feathers.

Pohevol moved to sit behind Sefani, "May I ride today?" the Cat asked Zor.

"You may rest for as long as you need."

Pohevol tucked his wings close to his back and closed his eyes.

Zor arched his head back to see the Feline, "Your vigor will return, and she will heal."

Pohevol opened his eyes to see Perjas come running through the clearing. He saw the link between the Dog and the child sitting in front of him. As the two locked senses, through smell and sound, Pohevol felt a great emptiness inside. Lily was thousands of miles away. He had not had the ability to protect her.

Sefani turned around and felt for Pohevol's paw, "Sometimes we have to make our own mistakes. It makes us stronger."

Perjas barked and Sefani nodded to the white Dog. The Dog charged Zun's basket and made a perfect leap inside. Zun pet the Dog's head, and Perjas licked his fingers.

"We fly East!" Caduceus thundered.

The Dragons of Durga rose one at a time into the morning light. The mist was rising, yet it still collected around the Dragons' wings. As they turned to fly toward the rising Sun, the children had to shield their eyes from the glare. In a steady line, the Dragons flew East, their baskets and satchels clutched securely in their claws.

As the jungle passed below, Zun lost his focus in the dark green canopy. He kept seeing the rift in his mind, and Lily's weak body Shifting into the Pangolin. When he saw her body roll into the gaping hole, he remembered how his heart felt compressed and tight. Now, riding in the Dragon's basket, his heart felt bruised.

They flew for three full days only stopping for quick respites and meals. Everyone seemed intent on completing the journey. With both Labrys and Lily gone, the group felt incomplete, as if two major organs or appendages were missing.

The scenery changed incrementally. At first the thick trees became sparse and savanna grasses dominated the landscape. Then cliff shelves arose in the brown dirt next to enormous baobabs without any leaves. These giants looked dead except for the egg-shaped fruits dangling from their boughs. Many of these trees stood alone in huge swaths of deserted land. Their only companions were large gatherings of flat stones, piled around the trees like the remnants of dry riverbeds.

As they moved farther away from Jha'mah, the hills became lower and the great desert appeared. The brown sand covered the Earth for hundreds of miles. Every so often Zor would tell them to look down at the tumbo trees. Like a collapsed Octopus, the tumbo did not look like a tree at all. Standing only five feet tall, the trunk remained underground, sending a long taproot below the desert floor. Its crown of curling, flat leaves spread across the sand like unruly hair. The tumbo was an ancient tree that could live for over two thousand Suns. It had broad, ribbed leaves and reddish, coned flowers.

On the third day of flying, the sand changed color. Instead of a creamy brown, similar to the arms of the Durgan children, it turned a golden orange, almost red. Geometric patterns appeared in the sand and large groups of Camels moved slowly over the rolling land. New hillsides appeared, covered in pink and white thorny broom, blue lupine, and yellow marigold. Honey Buzzards and black and white spotted Pelicans flew over the tumbo trees. Warblers and Goldcrests nested in the short bushes that sprouted near ancient river washes. The prickly cactus stood tall collecting any slight moisture from the desert air.

They saw herds of Gazelle and Roe Deer walking along the distant hills and after a few minutes, the tiny Sand Grouse began calling to them. The Dragons slowed their pace and started looking for Dragon and Human settlements.

"We are here," Caduceus said. "Sophia, we need you."

The seven-headed Dragon flew to the front to lead the group with Caduceus. As they flew over the desert, her many heads stretched looking for Dragon movement.

After a few more minutes of flying, they came to a huge mountain of sand growing out of the reddish floor.

"A dune!" exclaimed Zor.

The children looked down upon the majestic sight. They had heard stories of these immense ridges of sand. They were ripe for rolling and play. The dune was as tall as a small mountain, but soft and comprised only of red sand. Just as their group moved over the dune, marveling at the vision below, a loud wind began to crawl over the landscape. As the wind increased, small particles of sand rose in billowing clouds. It grew so suddenly, the Dragons were caught off guard.

"Sandstorm!" Caduceus shouted.

"What should we do?" Anippe whipped around, riding the wind like a water current.

Pohevol yelled, "Pull up, fly above the storm!"

But Guldrun began choking, and he faltered in the

wind, "I can't see!" The winds pulled him down, closer to the dune below.

Zor shouted, "Children keep low in the baskets, cover your mouth, nose, and eyes!" To Guldrun he yelled, "Try to land! Bring them down! I will take Sefani above the storm, I cannot land!"

The winds howled over the red sand and brought wave upon wave into the sky. Sophia and Caduceus fought at the blinding tide, squeezing their eyes shut and spraying fire to clear paths. Each time their fire hit the sand, sheets of clear glass would form and the Dragons would burst through them, spraying sharp fragments in all directions. Sophia's many heads arched back and screamed as she avoided the onslaught.

The Hawks and Pohevol flew away from the Dragons and tried to push up through the storm. Squinting to block the miniscule particles, they did their best to focus on the Sun behind the whipping and biting shards.

The egg brothers dropped through the sandstorm like heavy anchors. Lin kept looking to find his brother, but could only see the basket below him, "Don't worry!" he bellowed. "This is just like dry flaky mud, no problem!" He coughed and spit out a mouthful of sand.

The Dragons pushed and turned through the dry whirlpools, and Zor, now safely above the storm with Pohevol and the Hawks, found himself wishing Labrys were there to help the others navigate the currents, so similar to those of the sea.

Inside the storm, the Dragons battled the devouring sand. Caduceus and Sophia could not escape the torrent, and without warning, the dune rose up and met their struggling forms. The Dragons crashed into the sand, one atop the other in a jumble of rolling and groaning. Guldrun and Lin did their best to minimize the impact of the baskets, but the sand enveloped the latticed wood like an incoming tide.

"Remain inside!" Caduceus roared as the sand poured over his head.

Ius shouted, "Tuck in your wings! Become round!"

The Dragons did their best to pull their wings in, but the dune was now moving, and sand cascaded down the mountain in a rush. Rolling and turning, the Dragons and baskets came down the dune in a tremendous sandslide. Wings splayed out, cries came in staccato bursts, and steam escaped from underneath the sand in small spurts, like Clam spouts at the shore. In what seemed like an endless slide, the Dragons and children of Durga rolled down the dune. When they finally came to a stop, they were trapped under a Dragon's length of warm, red sand.

As quickly as it had commenced, the sandstorm came to an abrupt stop. An eerie quiet settled over the newly shaped desert. The wind disappeared, and the Sun pushed down on the red sand like a heavy hand. The dune that previously stood as a mountain was now a small hill, ten Dragon's lengths to the right of its original home. Nothing existed atop the red face. There was only sand as far as the eye could see. Zor, Pohevol, and the Hawks flew over the landscape and searched for any sign of Dragon or basket. They saw nothing but sand.

Deep below the surface were the Dragons and children, buried under the new mound of sand. Each Dragon and basket was isolated, separated from the others.

Caduceus tried to lift his wings and legs but could not get the sand to budge. He dared not take a breath, lest his lungs fill with the tiny particles.

Ius pushed against the weight with all of his strength, but could not move. He roared under the sand, which filled his throat, but also sent a small ripple to the surface. As Ius began to cough—desperately trying to expel the sand—the ripple continued like a persistent heartbeat.

Doren's sharp Hawk eye caught the slight movement and dove for the sand. Zor, Pohevol, and Rowan followed the adroit Hawk. Sefani slid off Zor's back and landed on her hands and knees. They all used their claws, paws, hands, and talons to dig. Furiously and without stopping, they worked to free those trapped below.

A Dragon's length away Mortoof was coming to his senses. Secured safely in Zor's basket, amidst soft capes and a clutch of figs, he knew the storm had stopped. He felt it in his bones. He also knew this was his true moment of glory. This was his destiny. He could save everyone trapped under the sand!

Like an underground Hummingbird, Mortoof flew into action. He burrowed his way out of the basket and into the wall of sand. With his tiny feet and pointed nose, he dug his way through the red granules, creating elaborate tunnels of air. Release the Dragons first, he thought. The children must have air trapped in their baskets, but the Dragons will not. Dragons first!

He plowed through the sand like an underwater Snake. His little body found Sophia first. She was pushing against the sand, making slow progress, so he merely traced her movements to their logical end until he reached the skin of the sand's surface. Once he tasted fresh air, he whipped his small head around and located Zor. He squeaked and caught the red Dragon's attention. Zor flew over, and watched with concern as Mortoof pointed repeatedly at the hole.

Zor nodded his head and commenced digging in this small hole while Mortoof dove into the sand to find another Dragon. Zor clawed up huge mounds, tossing them behind his body as a Dog would. He finally reached Sophia and pulled her out of the sand grave. Gasping for air, she looked around at the calm sky. She was perplexed to find no storm and no onslaught of grit in her multiple eyes.

As Mortoof and the others continued their efforts to rescue the trapped Dragons, Perjas began digging his way out of the basket he was sharing with Zun. When Zun tried to follow him, he turned around and barked twice. Uncertain what the Dog was saying, Zun continued to crawl after Perjas. The Dog whipped his head around again and growled at Zun. He must want me to stay, Zun thought as he fixated on the Dog's gleaming white teeth. He looked at all of the sand pouring in behind Perjas, and thought perhaps it was safer in the basket. At least there was an air pocket trapped where he was.

Perjas dug upwards until he broke through the top. He barked for Sefani and she called back to him.

"Zun is under Perjas!" she cried to Zor with urgency.

Zor flew over and started digging a new hole. With Perjas, Mortoof, and two Dragons digging, the rescue efforts multiplied. Pohevol and the Hawks circled the sand, calling out to Zor and Sophia whenever Mortoof or

Perjas found a new survivor. When Caduceus's Snakes appeared, Sophia dove into their sand holes, digging faster than ever. She stopped when she recognized a huge purple and green Snake slithering with angry eyes, "Caduceus!"

Shifting back into his Dragon body, he blew a torrent of sand out of his nostrils, shook his head back and forth, and coughed, "Where are the others?"

"We have found almost everyone," Sophia reassured him.

In a matter of minutes, they released the others. Spitting sand out of mouths and rubbing granules from watery eyes, the children and Dragons came out of the red depths of Earth.

Once everyone was safe, they collapsed on the sand and looked around at each other. They were exhausted and weak from the struggle. Mortoof was the only creature to continue his scampering.

"I never knew sand could be so heavy," Guldrun mumbled.

Ius replied, "There are many things you have yet to learn."

Lin smirked at his brother, but stopped when Ius glared at him.

Sophia watched as Mortoof raced over the sand and climbed in and out of the baskets, "What are you doing, little Rat?"

"Where is Adrianne?" he poked his snout out from Tomal and Bridget's basket.

Anippe approached the basket and looked inside, "Perhaps she fell out?"

"No," Bridget said, "she was here when Mortoof

found us."

The children looked in all of the baskets and Mortoof frantically ran around, searching for the green Spider. Sophia called out to Adrianne in Spider tongue.

"I am here," a small voice came from below.

Sophia's seven heads lowered and looked closely at the desert floor. She could see nothing except mounds and mounds of reddish brown sand, "Where? I cannot see you."

"I am raising two legs," said Adrianne, "look over here."

Sophia turned toward the voice, but could still see no Spider, "She says she is near me, but I cannot see her."

Caduceus walked over to Sophia and peered over the ground. And then, without any warning, Adrianne jumped on his face. The purple and green Dragon reared back and shook his head violently. Adrianne, no longer green but instead the color of the Sands of Ochre, held on expertly. When he finally stopped shaking, she climbed up his snout and sat atop his head. Faint clicking noises came from her furry body.

Sophia said, "She says she is sorry to inconvenience you, but she could not resist."

Caduceus looked at Sophia, and then tried to turn his eyes upward to find the new reddish brown Spider sitting on his head. He grumbled, "So you now have Chameleon properties?"

"I am just as intrigued as you," she crawled down his neck, heard the Snakes hiss at her, and quickly moved back up. "I did not know until now."

Caduceus lowered his head to the ground, "Thank

you—but would you kindly remove yourself from my head?"

Tomal ran over to Caduceus, holding out his arm, "Adrianne, you're beautiful!" The Spider carefully walked down the Dragon's snout to climb up the boy's arm.

Bridget asked, "Why haven't you changed color before?"

"I do not know," she raised one leg and then another, observing the new color. "But I hope I will not stay this way—I prefer green."

Mortoof, relieved to have found the final traveling companion, fluttered in the air around the Dragons and children, "All is not lost!" he squeaked. "No need to thank me," he coughed and cleared his throat. "No need at all. I am glad I could be of necessary service."

Caduceus grabbed Mortoof out of the air, "You were indeed of great help."

Ius walked over and bowed in front of the Shifting Dragon and Rat, "We are indebted to you."

Mortoof shuddered and blushed, "I," he stammered, "I don't know what to say."

Caduceus released the Rat, and he fell to the ground. Ius shot out a wing, just before Mortoof gained his wing balance in the air. "Say nothing, little one," Ius brought his wing up, "only remain my flying companion."

"Forever on your back," said Mortoof in his most reverent squeak.

At that moment, a thunderous boom was heard in the distance. The Dragons jumped to all fours and extended their wings and tails. All horns became straight and pointed. The children looked in every direction, searching for the origin of the sound. They heard another boom and then another. Whatever it was, it was moving toward them. The Dragons looked at the new dune of sand and watched as the top shuddered with every deep rumble. Caduceus flew into the air and rose above the dune. What he saw made him slowly lower himself back to the ground.

"Sophia," he said, staring at the space just above the dune. "We are about to need your help."

Everyone turned to face the direction Caduceus was looking. They saw something hazy in the distance, like a ripple in the sky. Then they saw a huge black egg moving slowly toward them, hovering high in the sky. Around the egg a shape began to appear. It was a brownish green, a deep olive color. And then they realized what it was. Moving toward them was the largest Dragon they had ever seen. The colossal black egg was one eye.

It moved deliberately, each step a pounding blast of thunder. It felt as if the Earth were quaking. The Dragon walked on four legs, stood as tall as a small mountain, and had hundreds of individual scales, each as wide as Ius's entire chest.

Sophia began a series of rapid voices, each trying a different Dragon tongue. She stretched her necks up as far as they could reach saying, "We come in peace!" over and over.

When the Dragon came to a stop, the children sucked in their breaths. Zun had to crane his neck back as far as it would go to see the Dragon's face. Tomal stared at one leg of the olive green creature and gasped as he realized the foot and claws were large enough to encase an entire Durgan hut. Bridget watched as the Dragon's mouth opened and a tongue smelled the air. The tongue was as big as Anippe's body.

Sophia continued to speak, and the Dragon turned its head slowly, bending spiral ear horns to meet her many voices. It lowered its head to move closer to her extended necks, and the children saw a ridge of rounded spiny bumps marching down the Dragon's spine. It peered at the children and Dragons below and then, hearing something familiar in Sophia's words, burst out in language. Sophia quickly began translating.

"I am Zarapho, the Sand Guardian of Ochre," the Dragon said. "What and whom do you seek?"

"We are from Durga," Zor moved to the front of his group. "We seek an audience with the Sand Dragons of Ochre."

"Why?"

Pohevol flew to land on Zor's back, "We have an urgent message."

The Dragon cocked his head to one side, "You have wings?"

Caduceus moved forward, "Many from Durga possess wings." He lowered his head and bowed to the giant Dragon, "Can you take us to your elders?"

"If you desire an audience with the leader of the Sand Dragons, you will not want to see any elder Dragon."

The Dragons of Durga turned to look at each other. Anippe spoke next, "Whom shall we meet?"

"Why the Dragon king, of course," Zarapho blinked twice.

"They have a king?" Tomal whispered.

Zarapho found Tomal and brought his head closer to

the miniscule Human boy, "What an interesting boy. You have never seen a Dragon king before?"

"No, we have no kings or queens in Durga," Tomal replied.

"Fascinating," Zarapho drummed his claws through the sand. "In the desert we have found decisions are best coming from one leader, so we have chosen Nivan to be our current king."

Anippe asked, "Have you no queen?"

"Yes, but she chooses to wear the title only," Zarapho's huge black eyes lingered over the small brown River Dragon. "Tiamat spends her days occupied with other activities. She does not enjoy the royal duties." He looked at the small gathering of Dragons and children around him, "Follow me, I will take you to Nivan."

Zarapho turned and began his slow walk East, from which he had come. The Dragons and children emptied the baskets of sand and made sure all provisions were tucked safely inside. The children then climbed back into the baskets, and the Durgan Dragons took off to fly alongside Zarapho.

As they traversed across the desert, the enormous Dragon turned to Zor, who was flying to the left of his face, "Why do you carry only children? Where are your adult Humans?"

Zor looked quizzically at Zarapho, "Adults? Why, we do not commune with them after they come of age."

"And they do not serve you?"

"Serve us?" Ius asked.

"After their childhood," Zarapho queried, "they do not become your servants?"

Ius turned to Zor and winced. Sophia looked back at Zun, flying in Lin's basket.

Zor said, "We have no servants in Durga. We respect the sovereignty of all tribes."

"So do we," Zarapho's nostrils flared. "The adult Humans choose to serve us in exchange for our Spakelv, our wisdom."

Anippe flew to Zor and whispered in his ear, "The rumors are true—they commune with adult Humans."

Caduceus, who was flying to the right of Zarapho, turned to the giant head, "We have no such agreement in Durga."

"Perhaps you will when you return home."

As they continued their trek across the desert, Zor flew away from the group and spoke to Sefani in private.

"You heard all that was said?"

"I did," she replied.

"This will only reinforce Zun's fear," the red Dragon focused on a rising tower, gleaming in the distance.

"It'll be strange to us all."

"Lily is no longer here to temper his emotions," Zor turned his head back so Sefani could hear him clearly. "We will need your influence."

"I understand," she clutched his neck feathers, "I'll speak with him before we land."

"Thank you," Zor banked right and found Lin flying behind Zarapho. Zun had convinced him to take this rear position. Zor lowered himself so Sefani was parallel to the basket.

Perjas jumped up and placed his two front paws on the edge of the basket. He barked and Sefani smiled. Zun looked at her incredulously, "What are you doing?"

"I want to ride with you."

"We should land then," he furrowed his brows. "This is too dangerous."

"No," Sefani said, "I can easily come over." She grabbed the side of Lin's basket while her legs remained straddled on Zor's back. Then with a perfect roll, she dove into the basket and landed comfortably at the bottom. Perjas began licking her face, and she nuzzled her forehead into his neck fur.

After the Dog and girl finished their greeting, she turned to Zun, "We need to talk."

"About what?" he lowered himself to sit by her.

"About the relationship between Humans and Dragons in Ochre," Sefani's blue eyes moved around, focusing on nothing perceivable. She grabbed his hand and held it over her heart, "If Lily were here, you would listen to her. You would truly hear her."

Zun's hand stiffened in her grasp, "She's not here."

"You must listen to me. Promise me you will hear me," Sefani's voice lowered, and a strange light appeared in her eyes. "Promise me you won't jump to any conclusions."

Zun felt compelled to agree, "I promise."

Sefani leaned closer to Zun and whispered, "Don't break this promise, Zun. It will break Lily's heart." And then she began pouring words into his ear. As she spoke, his eyes grew wide and the color drained from his skin.

❧ 33 ☙

THE DRAGON PALACE

The desert temperature began to rise, so the children and Dragons stopped to drink water. The air became heavy with heat, and sweat beaded along the children's faces. As the Dragons' scales began to loosen and expand, the Mud brothers' protective coating came off in a flaky dust. Any stray wind picked up the top layer of sand and sent small whorls along the desert floor. Nothing moved beneath the flying Dragons and their walking companion, Zarapho, except this gentle swirl of sand.

Zor turned to the huge Dragon, "Is another sandstorm approaching?"

"You were caught in that tiny shower earlier?" the Dragon laughed.

Ius flexed his claws, "Unlike you, we are not large enough to withstand its force."

Anippe shot Ius a condemning stare, "Would that we were."

Zarapho nodded to the tower ahead, "Do not worry, you will be safe at the palace before long."

Bridget pointed to the golden spires, "Look!"

Looming ahead was an immense palace of layered gold. It stood taller than three Mount Calyps's, one standing on top of the other. Multiple spires rose into the sky, but in the middle stood an immense dome with the tallest spiraled tower reaching toward the Sun. Carved into the tower was a representation of a thick Serpent, coiling to the top and painted a deep red. Massive turrets appeared in layered successions, some were crenellated while others were smooth and rounded. Most striking were the layered scales of gold that covered the entire manor. Like Zarapho's massive scales, these plates gleamed like the skin of a giant Dragon of gold.

They saw Dragons the size of Zor, all colored the same olive green as Zarapho, flying around the palace. As they came nearer, they saw Humans, adult Humans, walking outside and near the nestled crevices inside the vast compound.

At the left and right of the palace ran two slow rivers of blue, each flanked by various leafy trees. The two rivers curved behind the palace and flowed North until they joined at the right of another large structure. Swaying palm gardens encircled this domed edifice, also plated in gold. Surrounding both the palace and domed structure was a bustling village.

Zarapho outstretched his wings, which made everyone fly near his face, lest they be struck by his immense span, "The Dragon Palace sits to the right, and to the left is the Temple of Secrets. The two rivers that meet near the temple are the Ana'ava and the Ma'mara." He tucked his wings upon his back, "I will take you to the palace."

As they approached the gates, tall enough for Zarapho to enter without lowering his head, two Sand Dragons flew up and motioned for the Dragons of Durga to land.

"They are palace guards," Zarapho said. "I will speak to them."

As they lowered their baskets to the ground, a rapid conversation between the three Sand Dragons commenced. The two smaller Dragons looked identical to Zarapho, except in size. Although they were easily the size of Zor or Ius, they were small compared to Zarapho, the giant Sand Dragon. Ius could not stop staring at the guards.

Zarapho lowered his head to the Dragons below, "They would like to inspect the baskets."

Caduceus gestured for the children to climb out. As they did, the children looked around at the village in silent awe. They saw fully-grown Humans, adult Humans, Humans obviously of age, walking with and talking to Dragons! Many were whispering to Dragons, carrying packages for them, or scurrying along tall scaffoldings to pamper and preen Dragons who happened to be standing still.

Zun described the scene to Sefani, "You're right," he said. "The adults are acting like servants, like slaves."

"And your promise?" Sefani reminded him.

Zun crossed his arms, "For Lily, I'll honor my promise."

Tomal and Bridget gaped at the adults so candidly Anippe had to nudge them, "We are being summoned inside."

"Come," Zarapho beckoned. "Your baskets are benign, except for some miniature bows and arrows," he smirked at the children. "Come and enter the Dragon Palace of Ochre. Meet the Dragon king!"

Ius leaned into Zor's ear, "These guards—they look just like her."

"The female who was killed?" Zor asked.

"Yes," Ius swallowed, "her."

"Deep breaths," the red Dragon pointed one claw to the gates, "deep breaths."

The guards unlocked the gates and pushed the golden doors open. Zarapho entered first, taking careful steps along a cleared pathway of pebbled stone. The path ran through a large and fragrant courtyard filled with lemon trees and hundreds of red rose bushes that stood in immaculate rows. Hummingbirds flittered about, buzzing near the Dragons' ears. The Sun glinted off the golden walls enclosing the courtyard.

As they followed Zarapho, Zun felt his breath catch. Here he was, in the middle of a golden Dragon palace and about to meet a Dragon king. While his friends were clearly excited about the second set of golden gates looming ahead, he was numb. He promised Sefani he would control his negative emotions. He promised he would not scream out, leave the group, or share his visions. Now that the second gates were moving closer, he wanted to turn and run. As the Sun beat down on his exposed arms and tangled hair, he felt his heart pounding inside his chest. "For Lily," he whispered to himself, "I'll stay for Lily."

Zarapho walked to the gates and placed his claws into an elaborate silver lock. Tomal peered up at the lock, looming at least 200 feet above his head. Something about its design made him wonder. Where had he seen that pattern before? As Zarapho turned the lock, it came to him. Zor's book! The red Dragon had a similar lock attached to a book tucked away in his basket.

Tomal turned to look at Zor. The red Dragon was studying the lock as well. Out of the corner of his eye, Tomal caught Zor's tail brushing up against Ius's. What do they know about this lock? thought Tomal. Why are they the same design?

"Dragons of Durga," Zarapho pronounced, "I now present you to Nivan, King of the Dragons of Ochre."

Zarapho pushed the doors open and revealed an aromatic chamber of clove and cinnamon. The chamber was domed, with thousands of pieces of colored glass emitting a soft light. On a raised platform, also plated in dull gold, sat an immense slab of carved black obsidian, shaped in a thick arch. Lying on the long arch, four legs splayed over the curves like a Leopard reclining over a tree bough, was the Dragon king. He was half the size of Zarapho, but larger than the palace guards. He was the same olive green with thick scales and spiny neck bumps. His head rested at the edge of the arch, and his eyes were partly closed. Soft tendrils of smoke puffed from his nostrils.

The Dragons and children of Durga halted, for what they viewed next was a sight never to be forgotten. Surrounding the Dragon king was an intricate scaffold of interlaced gold and obsidian. It rose on both of his sides, and one part slid underneath the arch, where one could view the king's massive belly. Kneeling on the scaffold were Human servants. Eight servants flanked the king's sides, rubbing olive and coconut oils onto his thick scales of armor. Two servants filed his front claws. Two massaged his spiraled ear horns, and one lay on the lower scaffold fanning the king's belly. Behind the king, two Humans were washing delicately the underside of his tail.

Zarapho called out to the king, "Nivan, we have travelers from afar."

Zor turned to find Pohevol, who recognizing his cue, flew to alight upon the red Dragon's shoulder.

The king opened one eye, peered at the Dragons and children of Durga, and then closed it again. He said nothing in response.

"Great king," Zarapho continued with the slightest touch of impatience, "they say they have urgent news to share."

Without opening his eyes, the king questioned, "Is it about the games?"

"I have not questioned them, Nivan. I thought you would enjoy the honor."

The king opened his eyes and shook his huge body. The servants immediately stopped their ministrations and rested their hands in their laps. They turned to look at the Durgans. Blank expressions sat upon their faces.

Without raising his head or sitting up, the Dragon king spoke, "Let me guess. You've come to compete in the games and you'd like me to accept your exquisite athletes, many of whom will no doubt impress and amaze the likes of me."

Zor began to speak.

"Wait!" the king stretched out his left front leg and looked to the servant kneeling by his foot, "You down there, keep sharpening my claws!"

The servant hastily continued his job of running a heavy golden file along the king's sharp talons. He had to stand and stretch to file where the king's claw met his foot.

Zor winked at Ius and wiggled his red claws. The blue Mud Dragon glared in return.

"Now," the king sighed, "you were saying?"

"We have not come to enter any tournament," said Pohevol. "We have come to warn you about the future." The expression on one of the female servants who had been rubbing oil on the king's back changed. Her eyes looked scared, and her tanned skin grew pale. Zun, who had been watching these impassive Human adults, noticed her change.

"Warn me about the future?" the king mused.

"And the entire tribe of Sand Dragons," Caduceus stepped forward. "We would like to share with you our visions and our story."

The king blew more smoke from his nostrils, "You haven't come to compete in the games?"

Lin bowed to the king, "Your lordship, great king of Ochre, highest one, mighty and absolute, we would love to compete!"

Guldrun kicked his brother's right leg and grumbled, "What are you saying?"

"I think what he means," Anippe entered the conversation, "is that we would love to participate in any Sand Dragon ritual that would bring you pleasure." She turned to Caduceus and nodded her head, "But, we have a serious and most disturbing message that might cancel or postpone your important games."

"What?" roared the king. "Zarapho, what's the meaning of this?"

"Nivan," the giant Dragon blew steam from his nostrils, "perhaps you should invite these Dragons and children to share their story."

"If their news will hurt our games, I don't want to hear it!"

Tomal and Bridget were speechless. They couldn't believe this Dragon king. Not only was he supine and practically immobile on his reclining throne of obsidian, but he also was incredibly dense. How could a ruler not listen to an important message from Dragons?

A slow smile spread across Sefani's face, "King Nivan," she began sweetly, "If we promise to compete in your games, all of us, would you allow us to tell you a very short story about our homeland?"

The king followed the direction of this small voice moving only his eyes. When he found her seated upon Zor, he turned his entire head toward her and stretched his eyeflaps wide, "You dislike standing?"

Sefani heard an opening in his question. "Most of the time?" she responded with hesitation.

"You fly then?"

"Rarely."

"I like you," the king huffed. "I agree to this child's terms. She'll make an excellent servant when she comes of age." A slight smile escaped his resting lips. "I'll hear your story if you compete in our games."

Lin could barely contain his delight, while Caduceus dropped his head to his chest.

Anippe, now standing between Ius and Zor, whispered to them both, "This could be fun."

"When do the games start?" Zor asked.

"In three days," Nivan yawned, and Zun saw the tremendous mouth of teeth. Three sets of white arrow tips filled his upper and lower jaws. Over 100 teeth resided in Nivan's exhausted jowls.

"Then you will hear our story now?" Caduceus pressed.

"Who will tell it?" the king asked.

Pohevol extended his wings and bowed to the king, "I will tell our story."

"A winged Cat?" King Nivan looked up at Zarapho, "I want him to compete in the SandLuge!"

Zarapho craned his head to whisper in the king's ear.

"There's no need to go and get her," he snapped at the larger Dragon. "Cat," he said turning back to Pohevol, "I'll listen to your story now." He paused, "And, you may compete in any game of your choosing." After glaring at Zarapho, he turned back to Pohevol, "But I'd suggest that you try the SandLuge."

Bridget whispered into Tomal's ear, "I'd like to see a meeting between Nivan and Dett!"

Tomal put a hand to his mouth to keep from laughing. He quickly nodded his head, "That would be perfect."

"Thank you, King Nivan," said Pohevol. "And so my story begins."

As Pohevol spoke and Sophia translated, the king motioned for his servants to begin massaging him again.

Zun watched carefully as the pale woman rubbed olive oil over and under the individual scales. Sometimes her hand would disappear completely, only to reappear on the other side of the scale. When Pohevol mentioned that some Dragons were going into hiding, her hand froze. She looked down at Pohevol and then to Sophia who was speaking for him. When Pohevol finished his tale, all of the Durgan Dragons and children bowed to the king.

Caduceus spoke, "We hope you will consider our request with deep contemplation. All of the Dragon tribes have agreed to our terms. Your tribe is the only one to remain."

"All of them?" asked the king. "Even the Ice Dragons?"

"Even them."

"Fascinating," the king lifted his head and coughed. Long plumes of smoke escaped his throat. A small ball of fire popped out, and Zarapho used his foot to extinguish it.

"Sorry," the king muttered, lowering his head back to the hard shelf of obsidian.

Zarapho gave the king a stern look.

"I said I was sorry!" the king suddenly looked even more tired. "I must rest. I need to be alone. Zarapho, take our guests to the travelers' chambers."

"Are you certain?" asked Zarapho. "You do not want to consult with any others?"

"No!" the petulant king raised his tail, and a servant fell off the scaffolding.

"Nivan!" Zarapho scolded.

"Is he…" the Dragon king lifted his head again and

looked behind him, "...all right?"

"Yes, your greatness," the woman whom Zun was watching said. "He's fine."

"Good," the king dropped his head again. "I'm quite certain I don't want to share this with any others at this time. I'm tired and want rest."

Zarapho nodded to the king and looked down upon the Dragons and children, "Please follow me."

As they left the golden chamber, Bridget snickered into Tomal's ear, "He needs to rest? He hasn't done anything but be pampered!"

"It must be hard work," Tomal said with a serious face.

"Exhausting!" Bridget wiped pretend sweat from her brow.

Anippe used her tail to lightly thump the heads of the two laughing children, "Be quiet, you two."

They stopped giggling and apologized. Pohevol flew to Caduceus, "What can you discern from this?"

Caduceus shifted the weight of his Snakes to the other side of his neck, "I did not know our distant kin practiced this kind of decadence. You know as I do that we are opposed to kings and queens."

"Except in Dragon chess," Pohevol said.

"That is a game."

"Like the games we are to play in three days?"

"I have heard of these tournaments from Saja," Caduceus replied. "I believe besides the SandLuge, there is the DragonBall race and a RiddleQuest."

Pohevol and Caduceus stopped talking when Zarapho stood in front of a long walkway between two long and narrow pools of water. Willows stood along the edge of the left pool, their green feathery boughs lightly touching the surface. To the right, spread out at equal intervals, were smaller pathways that arched above the other pool and led to brilliant golden doors with dark red handles. There were at least twenty such doors following the length of the pool. Standing alert at the right side of each door was a Human servant.

Sophia asked, "How can this palace sustain so much green foliage? Willows in the desert?"

"Yes," Zarapho replied. "Many wonder how we maintain such resplendent palm gardens, roses, and willows while the dry sand encircles the village beyond."

"I assume you use aqueducts and water conduits," offered Caduceus.

"You are correct."

Anippe wrinkled her brow, "But you are changing the natural course of rivers. You are altering Earth's veins."

Zarapho nodded, "Not all of us agree with the decisions of the past 1,000 Suns, but we have seen no horrific effects."

"Yet," Caduceus added.

"True. Hopefully our queen will reclaim some of her power. Till then, we must follow the direction of our king."

"You mentioned earlier that your queen was busy doing other activities," Anippe said. "What could be more important than deciding how to live in balance with nature?"

Zarapho seemed to ignore her question and instead pointed down the walkway, "These are your chambers.

Our servants have brought your baskets and satchels inside the palace. Your baskets remain in the courtyard to your right, and your satchels will be brought to you once you have picked your rooms. We assume you will all welcome a moment of relaxation." As he could not continue down the walkway, he allowed his tail to linger along the edge of the left pool. "Please inform your servant if you are in need of anything."

As he walked away, Sefani noticed how his steps did not thunder as they did in the sand. She wondered how the palace could withstand so much weight without groaning.

As the Dragons and children chose their sleeping chambers, Zun remained by the left pool, watching Zarapho. Sefani turned her head to Zun, "Aren't you coming?"

"In a minute," he said. When he could no longer see Zarapho, he looked at the roots of the willow trees. Perjas barked, and Sefani walked over one arched pathway and into a chamber.

When all of the doors had closed, Zun heard a woman's voice call to him, "Would you like to sleep in this room?" She spoke in the tongue of Durga.

He turned to the servant and saw the same woman who had been massaging the king, the same woman who had blinked twice and turned pale.

He walked over and held out his hand, "My name is Zun. How do you know our language?"

She held her fingers up to her lips, "Shh. Come inside."

Zun followed her into the chamber. It was large enough to accommodate three Sand Dragons the king's size. There were many gold Dragon candles flickering in carved niches. A large bed sat in the middle, draped with luxurious golden blankets and pillows. The walls were bare, save the glowing candles.

The woman turned to Zun, "You and your friends must go to the queen at once."

"Why?" Zun knit his eyebrows. He then added, "Please, answer me—how do you know our tongue?"

The woman shuddered, "There's no time for explanations. The queen has predicted what your Visitor has shared. She must know you are here. She must meet with you, now!"

"Why are you whispering? Do others know how to speak Durgan?"

"Yes, and I don't want others to hear me. No outsiders are to enter the Temple of Secrets, but you must go." She grabbed his shoulders, "You and the Visitor must meet with our queen."

⁖ 34 ⁖

THE TEMPLE OF SECRETS

Zun stood outside Zor's chamber door and held his hand up to knock. Something kept his fist frozen in its position. Just knock, he told himself. His fist remained still. The woman standing next to him wrinkled her brow and held up her hand.

"No," Zun stopped her, "I can do it."

Before Zun could lower his hand, the door swung open. "What do you want?" Zor stood groggily at the opening. Quick to sense Zor's displeasure with the intrusion, the servant dropped her head submissively.

"Zor," Zun began, "this woman says we must meet with the queen. She says it's urgent."

Zor looked down upon the woman, "Who are you?"

"My name is Haida," her head remained in a reverent prostration. "May we please come inside your chamber?"

she whispered.

"You speak our tongue," he mused. "Come inside," Zor moved to the left to allow their entrance. Once inside he asked, "Why must we see the queen? Zarapho says she is uninterested in these matters." Zun wondered why Zor did not question her ability to communicate without translation.

Haida lifted only her eyes, afraid to speak directly to this Dragon from a distant land.

"Please raise your head," Zor said, "from where I come we do not employ servants. You are not considered inferior to me."

Haida raised her head and curtsied, "Thank you, sir." She continued in a hesitant voice, "Our queen is the keeper of secrets, and she's predicted a future similar to your Visitor's story. She would be most desirous of a meeting with you."

"Cannot this wait until evening? My companions and I are tired. We are in need of rest."

"Now is the most opportune time," she lowered herself to one knee. "Most of the Dragon guards are napping too. It will be easier to go unnoticed now."

Zor looked quizzically at the woman, "Go unnoticed? We are not allowed to visit your queen?"

"No," the woman stood, "outsiders aren't allowed in the Temple of Secrets."

"Then arrange for your queen to meet us here."

"She doesn't leave the temple."

Zor's spiraled horns lay flat against his neck, "You are asking us to defy your land's rules and sneak into the temple?"

"I don't know what else to do," she hung her head again.

Zor drummed his claws against the floor. He looked at Zun and flicked his long tail back and forth across the room, "What do you think we should do, boy?"

"I think we should see the queen."

"I do not want to wake the others," replied Zor. "We will go, just the three of us."

"Thank you, sir," Haida bowed, "thank you."

"There is no need to use such formalities with me. Now, let us see," he looked around the chamber for his satchel. "Do Sand Dragons wear cloaks in the desert?"

"Yes," she answered, "often when the Sun is at its hottest."

"And do your people believe today's temperature is hot?"

"Yes," she smiled, "today is indeed very hot."

"Good," Zor rummaged through his satchel and pulled out many cloaks. "Please pick one that matches the color of a Sand Dragon cloak."

Haida walked over to the pile of Dragon cloaks and ran her fingers along the smooth fabrics, "These are lovely."

"Thank you," Zor cleared his throat, "but please pick one to hide me."

She chose a white cloak with golden tassels, "This one is most like our Dragon capes."

"Excellent. Now, should we change the boy's attire?"

She looked at Zun, "He's almost of the age to be a servant. You could pretend he is your servant-in-training."

Zun felt his face grow hot, and Zor chuckled, "My

servant-in-training. Do you think you can accomplish this deception?"

Zun nodded, "It will only be for an hour or two, right?"

"Yes," Haida said. "Tiamat's guards will not sleep all afternoon."

Zor whipped his head to the servant, and his voice reverberated throughout the chamber, "What is her name?"

Haida blanched at his tone of voice, "Our queen, sir, is named Tiamat."

"I have changed my mind. We must wake Caduceus."

Zun looked up at the red Dragon, "He'll be furious if you wake him."

Zor grabbed a second white cloak, "He will be more than furious if I do not. Come, we must meet this queen immediately!"

The three walked out of Zor's chamber and quietly found the sleeping Shifting Dragon. At first his face looked as if he would relish breaking all of their bones one by one, but when Zor told him of Tiamat, he face flushed a warm and bright purple. He quickly followed Zor's instructions.

As they moved through the outdoor courtyards, Zun noticed how quiet the entire palace was. Many Dragons were sleeping in chambers with open windows as servants fanned them with immense palm fronds. The afternoon Sun glared off of the palace walls.

Once they approached a large clearing, Zor grabbed Haida and Zun, "I will carry you now, stay tucked inside my cloak and do not move."

Zor and Caduceus took off into the sky, careful to fly with their cloaks riding just atop their wings. They looked like white Birds hovering above the golden palace walls. When they saw the Ana'ava and Ma'mara Rivers stretching North of the palace, they banked and landed by the placid water. Servants strolled alongside the banks and tended to the palm gardens.

When Zor released Haida and Zun, Haida moved to assume a deferential position to the right of the Dragon. Watching Zun walk in his straight-backed, proud gait to the left of Caduceus, she eagerly showed him how to hold his head, back, and arms in a subservient way, "Like this," she modeled the humble pace and posture.

Pulling their white cloaks tightly around them, Zor and Caduceus walked to the entrance of the temple doing their best to be confident and purposeful. Within, their spirits were filled with concern, as Tiamat was inside this structure. Two Sand Dragons ambled by and nodded toward the group. They spoke a few words, and Caduceus grunted in response. One Sand Dragon whipped his head back at the cloaked Shifter, so Haida immediately bowed to him and uttered a few words in their shared tongue. The Sand Dragon huffed and blew thick smoke. Haida bowed again and watched intently as he moved farther down the path.

"That was close," she whispered.

When they stood in front of the temple's entrance, Zun was amazed to see no elaborate doors like those of the palace, "Why is the entrance not guarded with gates? I thought you said no outsiders were allowed?"

"The temple only has Dragon guards, and now they

are asleep," she said. "Quickly, we must go in."

Caduceus looked at the temple's gleaming walls. Like a giant golden Tortoise flanked by trees of palm, the temple sat patiently, as if waiting for his entrance. The golden scales rippled under the waves of heat and Birds flew low over the temple, landing on the structure only to push off again. Caduceus placed his foot with the missing claw upon the golden wall, "Lily should be here," he said.

Zun looked up at the green and purple Dragon and felt his heart shift ever so slightly. Zor placed a wing upon his friend's back, "Walk carefully, Caduceus."

The four moved under the gold archway and saw a round pool of clear water in the center of the temple. A bench made of pink and white marble surrounded it, and a simple sandstone altar stood directly behind the pool. On the altar rested a small green and gold Snake, curled into a tight ball. As Caduceus walked slowly towards the Serpent, never removing his eyes from its gleaming coils, Zun and Zor looked around the temple, noticing many gold doors with simple red handles. Beside each door in a tiny niche, sat a burning Dragon candle.

Haida walked to the pool and sat on the marble bench. She dipped her fingers into the water and brought a few drops to her lips, "Come and taste." She motioned for the others to come. Zun walked over and dipped his own fingers. The water was cool and sweet.

Only the soft flickering of the Dragon candles moved in the temple. No Sand Dragons were present, and no Human servants. The only creature to be seen was the Snake coiled on the altar.

Caduceus stopped before the altar and bowed low to

the Snake. He lowered his body close to the floor and then raised his front legs above his head. Rising from underneath the white cloak, he fashioned his claws into the sign of the Shift. "Tiamat," he whispered.

Suddenly, like the change in wind, the Snake on the altar Shifted, and in its place a tiny golden Dragon appeared.

"Caduceus," the golden Dragon said with a musical voice, "remove your cape and let me look upon you."

Caduceus stood, pushed away the white cloak, and revealed himself in full. Tiamat flew down from the altar and slowly moved around him. As she circled him, examining his form, she Shifted numerous times. She remained the same golden Dragon, but she grew a bit larger with every Shift. When she stopped Shifting, she was the same size as Caduceus.

Draped in tiny scales of gold, Tiamat had two sets of wings and two spiraled horns just behind her shining black eyes. She looked very much like the other Sand Dragons, except for her scales. Instead of olive scales of armor, her scales gleamed like fragile raiment, pouring over her smooth muscles and powerful body.

"Why are you here," she stopped her slow circle around Caduceus. "I know how you hate cities swarming with Humans."

Zun stood up from the pool, and Zor grabbed his shoulder, "No," he whispered, "let them talk."

"She knows our Durgan tongue too!" Zun exclaimed.

"You'll find answers to many questions soon," Haida whispered in his other ear.

Caduceus looked into Tiamat's deep eyes, "I did not

know you were still alive."

Tiamat stretched her wings and smiled, "2,500 Suns and still quicker than many." She Shifted seamlessly into a Leopard, a Flamingo, a Mouse, and then back into the gold Dragon.

Caduceus bowed again, "Always a master Shifter, Tiamat. I am honored to witness your skills again." He raised his eyes to her, "My mother adored you."

"As I did her," Tiamat's eyes shimmered, "as all sisters should." When he stood again on all four legs, the golden Dragon encircled him in her wings.

Zun turned to Zor, "The Dragon Queen of Ochre is Caduceus's aunt?"

Zor looked down at the boy, "The temple has revealed one secret. I am sure there will be more."

Tiamat lifted her wings and stepped away from Caduceus, "I must have my answer. Why are you here, my sister's son?"

Caduceus looked to Haida, "This woman has brought us to you. She says you will want to hear our story."

"They have a Visitor who has seen a future much like your secret books," said Haida. "I knew you would want to meet with them."

"And who is this boy?" Tiamat asked.

"He is a seer," Zor suddenly said. "He has visions that our elder seers have seen for many Suns."

This was the first time Zor had used the name seer in front of Zun, and it was the only time a Dragon had acknowledged his visions as anything but absurd. The boy opened his mouth to speak, but Zor gave him a look that kept it closed.

"What future has your Visitor seen?" Turning back to Caduceus, the Dragon queen ran her tail along the edge of the marble shelf. Zun watched as it lingered near his side.

With no hesitation, Caduceus answered her, "An Earth with no Dragons."

"And what of this child seer?"

"He has seen Dragons killing Humans."

Tiamat turned to Zun, and her black eyes turned to stone, "Come here, child."

Zun walked to the queen as if in a trance. Her eyes pulled him closer to her body, as her scales rippled in the candlelight. She extended her wings and peered down upon his trembling form, "Give your mind to me, child. Let me see what you see."

Zun saw visions appear upon her scales. Like a rock thrown against water, the visions appeared on her surface and then moved across her in steady circles. He closed his eyes and saw the walls of his cave in Durga. He saw the circle of Dragons standing around the fearful man. He saw their angry eyes and fire streaming from their mouths. He saw the jagged mountain and lava erupting. He saw the dead woman and the Dragon's claw piercing her heart.

Tiamat closed her wings around Zun, as a white light emanated from her black eyes. Zor's eyes filled with terror as the golden Dragon seemed to be taking Zun's energy. He called out, but Caduceus bade him be quiet, "She is not hurting him," he hissed. "This is not Ius's power. Be patient."

In a flash the white light disappeared, and Tiamat spread her wings. Zun opened his eyes and felt a weight lifted from his heart, "What did you do?"

"I honored your vision," she replied.

Zun turned his head as if to hear her more clearly, "You mean you believe me?"

"What you have seen is a possible truth," she touched his cheek with a gold front claw, "but there are those of us who would like to nurture other possibilities."

Zun turned to Zor, "Which Dragons in Durga have seen my visions?"

"We do not share everything with your tribe," Zor replied. "There are some things that will remain ours alone."

Tiamat moved to a door and pulled on a red handle, "Please follow me."

The Dragons, Zun, and Haida followed her into a small circular chamber filled with books. Books filled the rounded, stone walls, books sat on carved shelves extending from the walls, and books stood in various piles on the floor. In the middle of the chamber stood a tall and rectangular slab of black obsidian.

Tiamat walked along the wall of books and ran a claw along their spines. She stopped and reached for a green book. As she pulled it out, Zun saw a silver lock fastened to the outside. The queen placed the book on the obsidian column and inserted her claws. With one swift motion, the lock clicked and she opened the book. She backed away to allow the Dragons a view.

Caduceus and Zor leaned over the book and read silently. As they read, Zun asked, "What does it say?"

Tiamat answered, "It is our history of those who were banished."

Zun turned to her, "Banished? From where?"

"From Ochre."

As Zor and Caduceus turned the pages, Tiamat told Zun and Haida to sit. "As they read for themselves, I will tell you a story. Haida has heard it many times before, and it never does harm to hear this tale again and again. In fact, the more one hears this history, the more it benefits our struggle."

The queen lowered herself to the floor and swept her tail around her body. She stared directly into Zun's eyes as she told the story, "It began around 4,000 Suns ago, when the Humans first arrived. They saw Sand Dragons sleeping under the Sun and Dragon eggs throbbing in pools of heat, jewels, and rare stones. These Humans waited and watched, entranced with this sight.

"The Sand Dragons had heard about this tribe—your tribe—the Humans. They knew our kin in Jha'mah honored ancient Dragon words by sharing Dreamtime with the Human children of Jha'mah. These Humans looked similar to the Jha'mah Humans, so the Sand Dragons welcomed their children and opened their wings to the youth of this tribe. The Humans were hesitant at first—their eyes anxious and suspicious—but they looked up to the shining Sun in the sky and agreed.

"Many Suns passed, and the Human children eventually learned our tongue. These children grew up under the wings of Sand Dragons, and all was peaceful and well. Until the stealing began. Egg jewels went missing. Precious gems and stones vanished from the sleeping eggs. The Humans told their children to warn the Dragons about leaving eggs so open and vulnerable in the sand. They said the Dragons should build great chambers to hide and protect the eggs and jewels."

Zor turned away from the book and looked at Tiamat. His spiraled horns twitched, "You do not lay your eggs in the sand anymore?"

"No," she lowered her eyes and sighed, "Sand Draglings now grow inside dark, shaded rooms." She looked back at Zun and continued her story, "The Humans said the thievery would stop if Dragons sheltered the eggs in secure palaces of gold. That is how the Dragon Palace was first constructed. But even as the palace grew into the sky, the thievery continued. Dragon mothers had to spend their days guarding the eggs and gems. Dragon fathers became agitated and nervous. Finally, the Dragons found the culprits.

"Tucked in a cave, miles away from the heart of Ochre, was a cache full of egg jewels. To capture the thieves, many Dragons hid in the hills and dunes surrounding the cave. They waited for days until they saw the creatures returning with their capes and stolen treasure. Over twenty grown Human males came to the cave, laughing about their exploits.

"The Dragons captured the thieves and brought them to the palace. Dragon elders communed for over a Moon, trying to decide what to do with the men. Many children supported their fathers, asking the elders to forgive and not punish. They said the men were lost without Dragon instruction. They said if only they could receive Spakelv—our ability to share wisdom and communicate with Human children after the onset of age—they would change and be better.

"This went against the stories of the Dragon elders of

Jha'mah," Tiamat pointed to another row of books, high along the curved wall. "The elders knew it should not be done. But the children were passionate, and they made a promise in which many of the Dragons became interested. They said in exchange for Spakelv, in exchange for communing with Dragons for a lifetime, the adult Humans would cook and clean for the Sand Dragons, they would massage and tend to their every wish and desire. They said the eggs and jewels would be safe because the Humans would now have Spakelv to guide their way. They would no longer turn to jewels to find wisdom."

Zun thought of the Siir and how they had promised similar things to him.

"The Dragons argued for weeks," Tiamat continued. "It was during this time that the question about whether to have a king and queen arose. The usual council of elders was tedious and long. Younger Dragons wanted to try the Humans' new agreement. The thought of sharing their lives with adult Humans intrigued them. The time with children went too fast, like the flick of a tail. If they could spend 70 or 80 Suns with a Human, they could have a relationship with him or her, like a pet. They also enjoyed the idea of having servants, for the days are long and hot in the desert, and sometimes a Dragon can become lethargic and filled with torpor in the stifling heat.

"And of course, they wanted to protect the eggs. Our tribe was not used to protecting eggs so vigilantly. Against the occasional sandstorm or Scintha Bird yes, but they were noticing that having to constantly act as a guard affected the growing Draglings. Many hatched with defensive personalities," Tiamat paused and looked toward

Caduceus. "They were suspicious upon first hatching, even of other Dragons. This had to change, and so the agreement was made. The Sand Dragons would share Spakelv with adult Humans in exchange for accepted servitude and the end of thievery."

Zun was incredulous, "I'm confused. They didn't banish the thieves?"

Caduceus snorted, "The Dragon elders should not have listened to children. They should have banished the twenty from the start."

"Many believed this," said Tiamat, "but that did not happen. So a different possibility occurred." She turned back to Zun, "For many Suns time passed and the eggs were safe. Some Dragons noticed a change in the Draglings born in shade, but the jewels seemed to keep them strong, and they no longer were as defensive as the ones hatched from over-protective mothers. The Humans enjoyed serving in exchange for Spakelv. Everything was calm and peaceful."

"Until," said Zun, "someone broke a promise."

"Yes, my child. Until some servants began stealing jewels again. No longer having to protect constantly and feeling safe in the palace of gold, the Dragon mothers left their eggs unguarded for long stretches of time. And the thievery began again. This time there was no discussion. The traps were laid, the Humans were caught, and the Dragons of Ochre banished these men from the desert.

"They knew no Dragons existed in the rocky steppes of the North, so they chose this land for exile. They allowed the families of the dishonorable men to choose whether or not they wanted to stay or leave. Most families chose to leave with the men. With heavy hearts, the parents of the thieves apologized to the Dragons. They asked the Dragons to forgive their sons one day, if not that day. Many Humans cried bitter tears.

"Unlike their penitent families, the thieves screamed horrible curses as they were flown North. They promised to enact their revenge one day in the future. They spit at the Humans who chose to remain in Ochre. They called them ignorant and without vision, as they said the egg jewels uncovered secrets Spakelv never revealed. When the banished ones—around 500 in total—disappeared in the Northern mist, the Dragons of Ochre believed the pain to be over."

"It wasn't?" Zun asked.

"No," Caduceus snarled. "It seems that was just the beginning."

Tiamat closed her eyes and continued, "One of the over-protective mothers had a Dragling named Maldur. He hatched before the palace was finished to a mother who was filled with fear. Because of her anxiety, Maldur did not fully connect with his jewels during his egg growing time. When the Dragon Palace was finished, as a young Dragling he was constantly spying on the egg chambers, watching and coveting the jewels. When his mother laid a new egg, he spent hours glaring at it only leaving when she banished him from the room. He would steal back in late at night and pilfer jewels, like snatching milk from a nursing mammal.

"His mother reprimanded him on numerous occasions, and he spent many Suns sequestered with Dragon elders who tried to sway him against his errant ways. He would not listen. He was suspicious of everyone, even his own mother." She turned to Caduceus, "When she became queen, he demanded to know why he could not Shift. She explained it was her fault, that her fear had blocked the transfer of her powers. She begged him to accept who he was and said he was whole and powerful, even without the Shifting skill."

Tiamat opened her eyes and her scales began to tremble, "He was inconsolable. He raged against her and said he could no longer tolerate life in the desert. He said he would find a new land where he was not beneath his mother, where he would not feel her regret and remorse. And so he left. Looking to the North, he flew away from the Sands of Ochre."

Caduceus's nostrils flared as he growled, "And so my cousin went North to where the banished Humans settled."

"He flew back to me once," she added, "to inform me that a new age was approaching. He described a cold land filled with burial mounds dedicated to him. He said he was a god in this land, a magical being who was worshipped, and that he did not need to be trapped inside an egg to feel the power of jewels. He said he lived in this mountainous land filled with a strong group of Humans who brought him offerings of gems and precious stones every Sun. He called the land Kurga and said one day I would know of its incredible power."

All of the color rushed from Zun's face, "What was this land called?"

"Kurga," she repeated. Her words cut into his heart, "Of the Kurgan people."

"But," Zun quickly turned to Zor and then Caduceus, "we're nothing like . . ."

"No," Tiamat stopped him. "My son said 1,000 Suns ago a group of Kurgans broke away. They disagreed with the jewel hoarders, and they never felt comfortable worshiping him. They chafed against many new practices of the Kurgans, so they left. Over 200 people followed the Sun down and out of the mountains. He said they walked West until they settled in a forest populated with many diverse tribes, including Dragons. He said one day they would receive a visit from their powerful cousins, one day soon."

Pain filling his eyes, Zun asked Caduceus, "Did you know this story?"

The Dragon shook his pointed snout, "I knew nothing of this."

"Zor?" Zun searched Zor's feathered face.

"I am only 250 Suns. The elders have said nothing of this to me."

"Perhaps these Humans wiped their history clean, as their ancestors did thousands of Suns ago," said Tiamat. "Our elders said the first Humans to walk into the sand denied any connection to Jha'mah. Maybe those who left Kurga also denied their kin."

"But what of our name?" Zun asked.

Caduceus responded slowly and deliberately, "I do know the answer to this. My mother told me the following tale many times during my early days of Shifting. She told me Durga was not always named such. She said many names had been used to describe the ever-Shifting forest. She said so many different tribes gave it so many different names, we had to take turns, Shifting the name as I was learning how to Shift my body. She said the forest now wore a name honoring the Human tribe, and they had chosen Durga. She said the urg was for strength and power, and the D was for Dragons."

Tiamat's black pupils narrowed upon her nephew, and her scales turned a pale almost white gold. She pulled her neck and head up and back like the bend of a defensive Cobra, "Maldur told me Kurga meant the same thing, only the K was to kill."

Turning the deepest shade of red, Zor asked the queen, "Tiamat, twelve Suns ago we flew a group of Horse-riding men, men the Jha'mah call destroyers, back to this land you call Kurga. My friend saw a Dragon kill another Dragon. What does your son look like?"

"He is like me, golden with black eyes."

Zor slowly nodded his head, "And is he the only Dragon to have left Ochre to join these Kurgans?"

"No," her white gold scales rippled. "A few Suns ago some disgruntled Dragons—only 100 Suns old—flew North, swearing to go where they would have true power."

"Could these Dragons . . ." Caduceus moved closer to Tiamat, "could your son kill other Dragons?"

"That is what the pool tells me," she whispered. "The pool says they will kill anyone who stands in their way."

Zun dropped his head to his chest, "The Humans who left Jha'mah, searching for light, they started this. All of this can be traced to them." He then looked up, tears filling his eyes, "My own cousins killed my parents! My clan did this—my people! They killed their own!"

Tiamat lowered her head, now turning back to its

original warm and golden hue, "Horrible things happen when fear, hate, and the desire for power find a home in our hearts. This is why I renounced my power as queen. With love and patience and the desire to share, we can right the wrongs. We can alter the future with the flick of a tail or the turn of an eye."

"How?" Zun begged, exasperation filling his voice.

"We will send two Sand Dragons into hiding before the new Moon. We will band together, plan the next move, and hold fast to hope."

Zun thought of Lily, his parents, and the lonely nights painting in his cave. He carefully reached out to the Dragon queen and placed his hand upon her claws, "Show me."

⊷ 35 ⊶

EGG SISTERS

After three days nestled by Saja's egg, Lily awoke with a start. She sat up and looked around the cave trying to bring focus back to her eyes. Although there were two Dragon candles burning, she could not see the Spirit Dragon anywhere. Turning back to the Dragon egg, Lily ran her hands along its smooth surface.

"Thank you," she whispered.

The egg jostled slightly.

"Will you hatch soon?"

Again the egg moved. Lily stretched and heard a rumble come from her stomach. She called out for Saja, but there was no answer. Without moving the egg, Lily climbed out of the nest and searched for her clothes. After finding extra coverings to brace herself against the chill, she looked for food.

On a stone shelf near Saja's sleeping alcove, Lily found two loaves of bread and a pot of warm tea. Like a famished Dragon, Lily ate without stopping. When she finished, she looked back at the egg in its protective nest. She saw a deep imprint where her body had lain. She went back to the nest and fluffed the reeds, feathers, and fur to erase all signs of her presence.

Satisfied with her efforts, she walked slowly around the cave and looked for any hints regarding Saja. As she moved around, strange visions appeared in her mind. Feeling dizzy, Lily dropped to her knees. The memories of Jha'mah came back in a nauseating rush. She saw the waterfall and Haemon, the berries that almost killed her, the Pangolin in his ball of armor, and finally the eyes of Caduceus as he gave her his claw.

In a panic she looked down at her hands and realized his claw was gone. She jumped up and looked for it, swaying and tripping over herself as she searched the cave. It was nowhere to be found. I lost it, she thought. I must have dropped it in the rift.

A deep sobbing began in her throat. The nausea returned, and she felt a wash of exhaustion overpower her limbs. She knew this felt different than before and instinctively understood she should not return to the egg. Turning slowly around the cave, she found Saja's sleeping space and cautiously made her way to it. Once there, she climbed into the coverings and blankets.

Sleep came quickly. Unlike any entrance into Dreamtime, Lily found herself falling through a long, gloomy cavity and then hitting a hard bottom. She could not see any light, and the air was thick and warm. She could hear strange voices above her, similar to the Durgan tongue, but with a slight accent. She was certain this was not Dreamtime. Something was wrong.

Suddenly, light flooded the void, and she saw standing in front of her a muscular gold Dragon with black eyes. His scales flexed and fell with his steady breathing. He began pacing, pawing at the ground, and flashing his teeth at her. Lily shuddered even in the heat. He screamed at her and blew fire just above her head. When the fire dissipated in the air, Zor appeared, his red body rippling in the pool of light. He started walking toward Lily but was unable to see the other Dragon. The gold Dragon smirked as he followed Zor, the way a predator plays with blind prey. Zor took a few steps, and the Dragon followed without sound. Zor turned quickly, and the mimicking Dragon disappeared.

Without warning, unleashing horror throughout Lily's heart, the gold Dragon appeared just as Zor turned back to her. This menacing Dragon released fury upon the unaware red Dragon. Claws, teeth, and fire engulfed Zor. In one terrifying instant, the gold Dragon killed Zor. Lily screamed and screamed until her vision blurred, and then she woke up. She was back in Saja's cave.

Shaking and covered with sweat, Lily slowly sat up and looked around. Her dizziness and nausea were gone. Her skin prickled with intent and will. She knew she must find Saja. The egg was still resting heavy and strong in its nest, and the two candles were burning. Lily checked the wax and noticed little had melted. She knew Dreamtime could not have come so quickly, especially without a Dragon nearby. She needed Saja's help.

Lily felt her way through the long hallway, making her way to the cave's entrance. As she neared it, she realized the door was already open. "Saja must be near," she whispered. The Dragon would never leave the cave door open if she were gone for long.

"I am here, child."

Lily saw the Spirit Dragon resting in a hazy coil along the gray rocks at the edge of the cave. The waning Moon was a sliver of a Dragon claw floating in the black night. Saja stared into the waterfall that fell in front of her cave's door. Spray fell in a light mist upon her violet and golden scales. In front of Saja lay Caduceus's claw.

Lily gasped, "I thought I'd lost it!"

"No," said Saja without emotion, "when you Shifted, it fell from your hand."

"How long have I been here?"

"Just over three days."

"Do the others know I made it?"

The Dragon turned to Lily, "Yes, they know."

"What's wrong?" Lily's voice wavered. "I can tell you're not well."

Saja pointed to the claw of Caduceus, "I already know what you are going to ask of me. And I know what my answer must be."

Lily dropped to her knees, "Saja, we must go there."

"I do not know where you went, but it was not Dreamtime."

"You saw what I saw?" Lily placed her hand on Saja's smooth scales.

"I felt it," a shiver ran across her long, serpentine body, "I felt Zor's pain."

"Then you will take me?"

"I will take both of you," the Dragon looked back into

the cascading water.

Lily became silent for a long moment as the full weight of her request settled upon her. After a time she whispered, "Your egg, she'll hatch soon."

"Yes, I cannot leave her."

Lily stared into the water as well. When she recognized a small Moonbow form—an arch of various colors made by the light of the Moon—she slowly crawled into Saja's thick coils. The Spirit Dragon stiffened at first. But when she turned away from the waterfall and looked into Lily's eyes, she relaxed her coils. Lily leaned forward to grasp Caduceus's claw, "If she hatches on this trip, we'll protect her. Nothing will harm her. I promise you."

Saja said nothing.

"You'll see, Saja," Lily turned around and hugged the Dragon's strong neck. "This Dragling of yours is powerful. I did exactly as you said. I didn't take more than she wanted to give. But Saja, she wouldn't let me take more. She won't need our protection, because she already knows how to protect herself!"

"I have never carried a Dragon's basket before."

"If Guldrun and Lin can do it . . ." Lily began.

"I know," Saja interrupted. "I will use one of Labrys's."

"Perfect! They are covered in jewels!"

Saja looked back into the falling water, "You are still weak. You need more rest by her side."

"I'll do whatever you say."

"Listen carefully," the Spirit Dragon uncoiled and floated to the right of the waterfall so she could look directly at Lily without bending her neck. The faint

Moonlight made her wet body glisten, "Caduceus insisted that you fashion a belt to hold his claw. You will make this sturdy belt before we leave, but you must not wear the claw near my egg. I will make a Dragon belt to carry it during the flight, but when we land and you are safely away from my Dragling, you must carry the claw in your own belt."

"Why would his claw hurt your egg?"

"The essence of another Dragon Shifter would be most confusing to my egg. She must be flooded with my Dragon spirit only. Caduceus is a powerful Dragon. Deep magic resides in his flesh and bone," Saja brought her head close to Lily's. She peered into Lily's brown eyes, "Do you know what he has given you?"

Lily looked down at the Dragon claw that fit so perfectly in her lap. She knew she must be honest, "I know that it was a sacrifice, but no, I don't really understand."

"Lily, Caduceus shed a part of his spirit world. He is saying you are his adopted child, his Dragling outside of tribe," Saja paused and pulled her head back. "He is giving you Dragon magic," her lightning horn began to glow, and then she uttered words that would forever change Lily's life, "as long as you are in possession of his claw, you can Shift into a Dragon. No illusions, no masks. A true Shift."

Lily whispered, "I can become a Dragon?"

"Yes," Saja lowered her head and smiled at Lily, "a Dragon."

∽ ∾

Thousands of miles to the South and East, in the red Sands of Ochre, a small group of Dragons and children sat listening to a story. They had just eaten a delicious meal hosted by Nivan, the Dragon king, and now they were ready to sleep for the evening. But one Dragon insisted they listen to a story first.

Tucked away in the largest chamber, with Dragons encircling the children, they listened. A black, winged Cat sat near a burnished red Dragon. A reddish brown Spider curled near the legs of one child, a white Dog near another. A brown and white striped Rat lay snoozing in the open claws of a blue Dragon. Perched on large stands of wood, three Hawks peered down at the group. Caduceus told everyone from Durga Queen Tiamat's story. When he finished, stillness echoed in the room.

Finally, Ius said, "Maldur."

"My cousin," Caduceus nodded.

"Kurgans," Sefani said, "they're our kin."

Bridget stood up and stormed around the chamber, motioning with her arms, "Kin we abandoned. Kin we left. They're no longer kin to me!"

Tomal wrapped his arms around himself and began rocking back and forth, "I don't trust this story. I don't believe it."

Sophia moved one head to be closer to the boy, "Your ancestors chose a different path. For that you should be proud. Bridget is right, the Durgans walked away."

Sefani felt for Zun's hand and squeezed it, "What do you believe?"

Zun looked around at the children and Dragons, "My whole life I have hated Dragons." He turned to Zor and

Ius, "I thought you were responsible for the death of my parents." He looked down at Sefani's hand holding his, "I no longer think that way. I believe Tiamat. I think the Kurgans are to blame. Our ancestors recognized their ways were wrong and left to start anew. Our tribe is no longer Kurgan." He stopped and looked up at everyone in the room, "We're Durgan."

Pohevol spoke, "But now what will we do?"

Zor turned to the winged Cat, "Exactly as we have planned. We ask two Sand Dragons to go into hiding."

Bridget asked, "Is that all?"

Anippe shot a glance at Ius. The blue Dragon growled, "No, that is not all. We will fly to Kurga and stop Maldur. We will do what I did not have the courage to do twelve Suns ago."

Zor said, "Do you know what you are saying?"

Sophia added, "Our elders have warned us not to interfere."

Anippe burst out, "Our elders come from a land and time of peace. They do not know of these young Dragons who are bent on hurting others. These Dragons may be from the sand, but they are still our family and our tribe. We have every right to involve ourselves!" She looked to Caduceus, "What do you say?"

The Shifting Dragon looked down at his missing claw, "This story pains me. It shames me to have kin who are violent and selfish." He turned to Zor and Ius, "It will not be enough to simply hide and wait. My cousin is sick. He must be stopped."

Bridget whooped in relief, her Ochret shining brightly. Sophia hushed her. "This will be no great adventure, girl," the seven-headed Dragon hissed. "We are deciding to do battle against Dragons."

Bridget wrinkled her brow and lowered herself to the floor, "I just want to help right the wrongs," she muttered. "I just want to help your tribe."

Sophia touched the child's black hair, "I understand your loyalty. But do not allow the temptation for battle to overwhelm your young heart. War is always the last decision. We will try to stop Maldur and his followers from killing Dragons, but we must tame our hearts from hurting them."

Confused, Tomal looked up, "How can you stop them without hurting them?"

Bridget added, "Banishment wasn't enough to stop them."

"That will be our challenge," Zor said. "Hopefully the Temple of Secrets will be our guide," he turned his head to the side and glanced at Caduceus.

Lin spoke for the first time, "Does this mean…"

His brother finished his thought, "That we aren't going to participate in the games?"

Caduceus looked to the egg brothers and shook his head, "No. We promised the king we would complete. I will not diminish the bond of our words."

The brothers let out sighs of relief and hugged each other. Guldrun whispered to Lin, "I heard the palace has a room full of red mud!"

"No!" Lin whispered back. "Are you certain?"

Anippe nudged the two, "Quiet!"

Zor opened the chamber door and stepped into the courtyard. He came back inside, "It is late. We should rest."

When the Dragons and children went back to their chambers, they noticed the servants were no longer standing outside the doors. The courtyard was silent except for a gentle breeze beneath the Moonlight. The stars blinked and clouds crept across the night sky. Zun looked up and down the walkway for any sign of Haida but could not see her. Before going into his room, he walked over to Ius who was trying to open his door, "I forgot to say something on the day you flew me to Lily."

Ius turned around and flared his nostrils, "And what is that?"

"Thank you," Zun turned and walked to his chamber.

Ius stood under the glowing stars and watched the boy close his door. Zor walked up and stood by the blue Dragon, "He has changed."

Ius nodded, "If only Lily were here to see."

∽ ∾

Lily sat in Saja's cave working by Dragon candlelight. Using a recent Snake shedding, she designed a belt to be worn low around her hips. Caduceus's claw was too large for a regular belt position around the waist. Measuring as long as her arm, the claw would have to sit low in order to protect her underarm.

She stitched a sturdy sheath with extra padding at the end, and had it run alongside her leg until it came just above her knee. Once cradled inside, around eight inches of claw remained exposed. When the belt was finished, Lily was ready to fly.

Saja returned with Labrys's basket and maneuvered it inside the cave. It was laced with diverse jewels and precious stones. The Spirit Dragon had already lined the basket with extra feathers and fur she had found throughout the forest. When she set the basket down, Lily walked over and peered inside. There would be just enough room for the two.

"What time is it?" she asked Saja.

"Only a few hours before Sunrise."

"When shall we leave?"

"As soon as the egg is safely inside," Saja said. "I will need you to lift some jewels as I transfer her to the basket. You must make sure the jewels are in constant contact with her shell."

Lily started to move toward the egg but felt the smallest tug in her heart. She looked down at the claw and remembered. She backed away from the egg and undid the belt, "Did you finish making your flying belt?"

"Yes, it is done." Saja watched as Lily placed the belt far away from her egg, "Is she speaking to you?"

Lily looked at the egg and listened. She heard a tiny rustling in her ears, almost as if a Cricket were trapped inside, a soft clicking, "I don't know what she's doing, but I knew she didn't want to be near the claw."

"It has happened sooner than I expected," Saja's eyes glistened. "You are now egg sisters."

"What does that mean?"

"The two of you will answer that question, it is not for me to say." Saja coiled herself around the egg and motioned for Lily to move forward, "On my word, lift the bloodstone and the platinum. Keep them firmly pressed to the egg. One, two, three, now!"

Saja lifted the egg from its nest, and Lily lifted the two stones. She made sure the gems would not falter. As Saja transferred the egg and slowly lowered it into the basket, Lily saw the egg shiver. A ripple of light ran under the shell's pale white surface and in the blink of an eye, Lily saw the outline of the Dragling inside. She was coiled in the exact shape of her mother's body. Her head pointed up, and her lightning horn pressed against the right edge of shell.

Lily slid the gems up the egg, as Saja let the egg slide deeper into the basket. Lily had to navigate the basket to make sure she didn't break contact. Once nestled inside, Saja used her horn to take the bloodstone from Lily. She then lowered it along the shell until it found its new home. Next, she lowered the platinum. She turned to Lily, "Now we need to surround her with the others."

Saja and Lily collected all the jewels and placed them around the egg. When Lily expressed doubt, Saja directed her where to place one. Once they had finished, Lily looked inside, "Will there be room for me?"

"It will be tight, but I reserved a spot on this side for you." She pointed to the front of the basket where a small crevice was lined with gray Rabbit fur.

"Where did you find this much fur?" Lily was amazed. "It would take a full Sun to save this much shedding!"

"I have my ways," Saja winked at Lily.

Lily reached inside and felt the fur. No matter how cramped the basket might be, with this comfortable shedding she would ride in comfort, "Shall I climb inside?"

Saja looked around at her cave and sighed, "Yes. But

first, attach your belt and claw to my own belt," she pointed to where her large belt lay, "and then slide it around my body."

Lily found the belt and picked it up. Despite its large size, it was deceptively light. She tied her belt and claw around the bigger belt, and slid them both around Saja's tail.

"Pull it snug around my lower abdomen," the Spirit Dragon instructed.

Lily looked at the long Dragon, "Where? I can't even find your belly!"

Saja arched her body into a curve and pointed with her horn, "Right there."

Lily pulled the belt until it would no longer budge, "How's that?"

"Perfect. Now climb inside."

Lily went back to the basket and carefully climbed over the edge. As she lowered herself inside, she caressed the egg and felt it move again. Saja blew out the two candles and lit her horn. In the glowing white cave, Saja slid her head under the basket's handle and glided until the basket was just behind her neck flaps. Gently, she lifted it from the ground. The basket swayed at first, then slowed to a steady rocking as the Dragon flew through the long hallway. When she approached the door, she whispered the words of exit. The door opened into the cool night. Outside the cave, Saja turned around to check the claw belt. It was secure and a safe distance from her egg.

The Dragon uttered words to close the door and turned to view the stars, "We can visit your parents before we fly to the desert. Would you like to see them?"

Lily looked into the thick woods. She had yet to think of her parents since her recovery in Saja's cave. "No," she said simply, "we must go to the Sands of Ochre. There's little time."

"As you wish," replied Saja, and she lifted her body and the basket into the night sky. As Lily's body became accustomed to the steady rocking of the basket, she rested her head against the shell. She looked up at the stars slowly moving by and breathed deeply. The cool night air refreshed her. Another long ride in a Dragon's basket, she thought. This time without Zun. She thought of his black eyes staring down at her when she was poisoned, how focused they were.

"We're doing the right thing, aren't we?" she whispered into shell.

"Yes," came a tiny voice from within the shell, "take me to Ochre."

Lily opened her mouth and eyes wide, "You can speak now!"

"I can do many things," the Dragling whispered, "my mother would not agree to fly us there if it were not the right choice." The Dragling moved inside the egg, and her tiny horn began to glow beneath the shell's surface, "Do not worry. I was meant to hatch in the sand."

⋖ 36 ⋗

THE GAMES

For the next three days most everyone prepared for the king's games. While Caduceus, Zor, and Ius had clandestine meetings with Tiamat in the Temple of Secrets, the children, Pohevol, Mortoof, and other Dragons practiced different skills.

Zarapho informed them of the events to occur on the first day. The StoneLaunch interested Zun and Tomal, and the WindFray excited Anippe, Sefani, and Perjas. King Nivan invited Mortoof to enter a sand-digging contest after hearing of his daring rescue. Pohevol, intrigued by the king's previous insistence, was thinking of entering the SandLuge, and Adrianne said she would go along for the ride. Sophia and Bridget thought they would try the RiddleQuest. The contest that had Guldrun and Lin peeling their scales in excitement was the DragonBall race.

The king requested they practice their forms in front of him. He enjoyed watching others perform daring feats from the comfort of his throne. But Tiamat warned them not to mention Maldur's name in front of Nivan. Under the new rules of Ochre, the Dragon queen could name her king. When Maldur left, she had chosen her youngest son to inhabit the throne. Even with this honor, Nivan always felt second best. He was not golden like his brother, and he could not Shift like his mother. Tiamat explained how Maldur had lowered a heavy sadness over the Sand Dragon tribe, but Nivan never truly understood how his brother could do this. To remove the pain, Nivan found reassurance and comfort in feasting. He allowed his burgeoning Dragon appetite to consume him, and feeling insecure on this throne, he rarely left the obsidian slab.

As Nivan's body grew, so did the throne. When his belly became too large, the servants removed a section to allow the girth to hang. His brother's memory haunted him and consumed much of his thought. Recognizing Maldur's influential history, he forbade all servants from uttering the name, lest other young Dragons and Humans fall under his memory spell. Every time he remembered his brother, he enjoined the servants to bring him another platter of sweetened dates.

Nivan missed having an older brother and felt a deep shame for lying on a throne that was meant for another. No matter how often Tiamat visited Nivan, hoping to comfort him, it seemed food was his only solace. To protect him from further pain, the queen agreed with the prohibition of speaking her first son's name. To honor the Dragon queen and king, no one mentioned Maldur.

The Dragons and children of Durga were careful to act as if nothing was occurring in the Temple of Secrets. In fact Sefani and Tomal often asked the king if they could go inside and meet the queen. He would belch puffs of smoke and growl his refusal. Haida, at the king's side massaging the enormous scales, acted as if she knew nothing at all.

One day the king invited them to practice in the outdoor throne room. Located behind the palace along the banks of the Ana'ava, there was an identical slab of obsidian and golden scaffolding. A rolling lawn of trimmed bright green grass stretched before the throne. Hundreds of contestants practiced in front of the king over and on the lawn.

The children marveled at the various tribes who came to compete in the Sands of Ochre. Dragons flew by at mind-throbbing speeds, Lizards practiced mind puzzles, and Humans threw stones as far as the eye could track. Colorful DragonBalls thundered over the lawn as long sticks pushed and turned the smooth and shiny orbs. Pohevol and Mortoof were the only missing ones, as they had to practice digging and sliding in the tall dunes far from the palace.

The night before the games started, King Nivan held a feast for all competitors. The crescent Moon waned nearer to new, and the stars shone bright. The sand lay undisturbed from any storm and a peace settled over the participants. The king's guests entered the dining hall under an elaborate trestle of braided gold and intertwined red roses. As they emerged from the archway, servants standing high upon balconies sprinkled cucumber essence and rose water over their heads.

The guests were led to oval tables of various heights. Some were clearly for Dragons, while multiple tribes could share the ones that stood not so high. Once everyone found an appropriate seat, servants brought out steaming food heaped onto gold plates and baskets of herbed flat bread. Cauldrons of aromatic stews and soups lined the feasting hall, and platters filled with pomegranates, apricots, sour cherries, and dates dotted the many tables. Dragon wine poured from gold decanters, and servants offered to wipe the mouths of any Dragon who dribbled food or drink. Soft music wafted from behind woven tapestries, no doubt played by servants who were not charged with delivering the feast.

The Dragons of Durga ate with curious attention, politely refusing the raised napkins offered by servants and subtly turning their heads to watch the Sand Dragons partake in the nutritious spectacle. The children, at a table near the Dragons, ate as if famished. Absent from the tables were Pohevol, Adrianne, Perjas, and the Hawks. Sand Dragons—similar to the Dragons of Durga—served no flesh at their feasts, so the carnivorous tribes took to the desert night hoping to find an unlucky Rabbit, Sand Fly, or Grouse traversing under the stars.

The king, lying on yet another throne in the center of the hall, had a servant raise his goblet high into the air. The children of Durga watched as small Sand Draglings moved about the hall asking if the various tribes needed translation services. When an olive green Dragon approached the Dragons of Durga, Sophia said she would welcome a break from her duties. The little Dragling bowed and stood at their table.

When all tables were ready, the king bellowed, "Welcome to the Sands of Ochre!"

The guests pounded tables and cheered in response.

"Tomorrow the games will begin," he continued, "and I'm sure many of you would like to bring Dragon gold home with you!"

Again, the tables cheered and a loud pounding shook the dining hall.

"Remember to play hard but fair. We wouldn't like to disqualify any competitors, as we had to do last Sun," he raised his eyefolds and smirked.

Murmuring was heard at the tables as the guests remembered the previous games and the embarrassing actions committed by the Hyena tribe. Many faces searched the hall for the offending players. No Hyenas were present this Sun.

"Enjoy the rest of the feast, and please accept the queen's and my well wishes," Nivan nodded to his servant, who brought the goblet to the king's mouth, "to the games!" Nivan threw back his head and allowed the drink to be poured down his throat.

"To the games!" the tribes cried out in their various tongues. Goblets raised, liquids gushed, and servants worked to wipe moist mouths.

When bellies became full and King Nivan began to fall asleep, the guests knew it was time to leave. The Dragons and children of Durga moved as one procession through the hall and down the different walkways back to their courtyard of chambers. They said goodnight and agreed they would not enter Dreamtime this night, as tomorrow they would need full rest to compete in the games. After everyone had gone to bed, Zor, Caduceus, and Ius slipped out under cloaks of white. Again they were to meet Tiamat in the Temple of Secrets.

༄ ༅

The Moon grew brighter in the star-filled sky, as the cloaked Dragons made their way to Tiamat's Temple. Again, no guards stood at the entrance, and she was waiting in her Snake form.

She Shifted into her Dragon body and led them to a new chamber this time. Inside there were no books. Instead the smooth walls displayed tiny sketches, miniature symbols carved into and painted on the sandstone. Tiamat pointed to a sketch of a Dragon on a throne, "This is one possibility that went astray."

"Our elders tell us we have not had kings or queens for over 30,000 Suns," Caduceus said. "How could yours allow this to happen?"

"A moment of crisis," she said, "a moment of weakness."

Ius asked, "How will your Dragons respond if you suggest an elimination of this practice?"

Tiamat pointed to another carving. This one showed a Dragon Circle, "We all have memories of this," she paused. "But it would mean that we are equals, and that would challenge the servitude of Humans. If we admit equality amongst ourselves with no king or queen, the Humans might desire their emancipation."

Zor interjected, "And what is wrong with that?"

"I would welcome this change, but others would not."

Caduceus spoke, his voice calm and controlled, "We cannot change the future without addressing all lines that swerved off the balanced path. I will not challenge Maldur unless the Sand Dragons admit to their errors and change their ways."

"You saw the feast tonight," Zor said. "It would be hard for any Dragon to give up that kind of attention."

Caduceus pondered Zor's statement. He nodded his head, "Yes, but when you accept a queen and king, you make room for goddesses and gods, and then you are no longer Earth's living magic. Instead of finding answers inside yourself and your tribe, you turn elsewhere, missing the essence of what makes us alive." He looked around at the carvings and paintings that filled the walls, "No, we must remind the Sand Dragons that equality must reign. Separation along imaginary distinctions will only cause anger and resentment. If we are to have peace, if we are to stop Maldur, we must embody our beliefs. There is no room for hypocrisy or lies."

Tiamat's golden armor rippled, "Then you are ready. Follow me."

She led them out of the chamber of symbols and into another room. This room was bathed in a red light from hundreds of Dragon candles. It was bare except for a gold chest sitting in the middle. Fastened to the chest was the same type of lock found on the palace doors and Zor's book.

"We have been waiting for you," Tiamat said gently.

"We?" Ius asked.

"Those of us who want to go back to the beginning, to start over, to begin anew."

Zor went to the lock and touched his red claws to its metal. Tiamat watched as he drew his leg away, "You have seen this before?"

"My mother gave me a book with a similar lock. She told me to never leave Durga without it. I have never been able to solve its puzzle."

"No Dragon can," she said. "Come closer."

The three Dragons watched as Tiamat Shifted into a Hummingbird. Kneeling even closer to peer at the metal lock, they saw her tiny beak hover just outside the opening. Her black tongue, as thin as a Mouse whisker, darted in and out of the lock. After a full minute, the lock clicked open and Tiamat Shifted back into a Dragon.

"I want the three of you to open it," she said.

Ius looked at Zor, and Caduceus looked at both of them. They each placed a set of claws along the edge of the rim and waited.

Tiamat stepped back, away from the kneeling Dragons, "Do it now."

The Dragon males lifted the lid, and with a rush of light and sound, they were pulled inside the golden chest. Staring at the now empty chest, Tiamat stood alone in the room.

The morning Sun rose along the horizon, sending soft light stretching across the sand. Bass horns called the competitors to rise out of bed, and soon a loud bustling filled the Dragon Palace and surrounding village. Sand Dragons flew and servants ran to help prepare for the first day of games. In one hour, everyone was ready for the games to begin.

Bridget and Sophia remained silent, refusing to speak to anyone lest they lose their mental concentration. Zun and Tomal stretched their arms, and Guldrun and Lin practiced using their tails to hold the DragonBall stick. Anippe flew towards the Sun and back three times, and Sefani ran up and down the slick stone walkways, using her fingertips along the wall as a guide. Mortoof, Pohevol, and Adrianne had already left, as they were more than ready to compete in the sand.

As they parted ways for the various contests, Zun looked around the courtyard, "Has anyone seen Zor or Ius?"

Anippe went to their chamber doors and peered inside, "They are not in their rooms."

Sefani asked, "Is Caduceus here?"

"No," Tomal said, "he's missing too."

Bridget offered, "Maybe they went with Pohevol to the dunes?"

"Maybe," Zun said. "Or they could be at the temple. The first to finish a contest should go looking for them."

"Our race will finish first," Anippe said, stretching her wings, "I will fly around afterwards and find them."

Everyone agreed and fell in the countless lines exiting the palace. Servants held large signs with distinct drawings marking routes to various games. When they exited the palace gates, the air swarmed with Dragons. Even in the early morning, the desert temperature began to rise. Zun looked up, searching for Zor's bright red body. He saw one red Dragon, but it was a thin River Dragon, half the size of Zor. There flew no Dragons of blue or purple and green.

King Nivan, who was transported from game to game on a throne with runners, was decorated with a white and gold cape. His servants erected great mirrors to direct the Sunlight to his face and his eyes sparkled in the glare. He whipped his tail about in pleasure if the games were especially close. He groaned if a Sand Dragon lost.

As the day grew hotter, the games took on an air of urgency. Contestants exerted more energy, and the audiences fanned themselves with palm fronds. Sand Dragons flew from contest to contest sharing the scores from other games.

The DragonBall race occurred in an arena with a freshly cut lawn. The race was reserved only for Dragons, and the object was to hit the many colored balls into large circles at the ends the field. They could use any body appendage to move the sticks, but no Dragon could touch directly a ball or another Dragon. As flying was prohibited, the skill resided in the pass and aim. Blocking was useful but dangerous. Sometimes sticks would clash and balls would fly into the air. The Dragons on the field had to avoid falling balls to escape disqualification. If the balls landed without touching a Dragon, the race continued. If a Dragon felt a ball tap even one edge of a scale, the Dragon had to exit the field. The game would continue only when the tail left the lawn. Guldrun and Lin played on the same team and placed fourth overall.

At the Western edge of the village, the RiddleQuest commenced. Encircled in a tremendous ring of fire, the competitors had to gather puzzles from complex hiding places and follow directions to attain even more puzzles. Some had to wade through ponds of silver water, while others had to fly and retrieve golden keys dangling over deep sand pits. They had to accomplish all of these tasks without crossing the line of fire. If one wing or leg moved across the actual fire or above the imaginary line that rose high into the sky, the competitor would be eliminated. Sophia came in third, and Bridget surprised the seven-headed Dragon by placing eighth. For a Human, her efforts were exemplary.

As Anippe had predicted, the WindFray was over in a matter of minutes. It was a simple race of speed. Who could fly the fastest in the air? Who could run the fastest on two, four, or six legs? Who could swim the fastest in the Ma'mara River? Who could roll, hop, or slither the fastest? Anippe won the flying race, Perjas placed eleventh in running on four legs, and Sefani came in sixth for running on two.

In the red dunes, multiple digging contests tested strength, speed, and accuracy. Mortoof took third place in accuracy, which he thought was most unpredictable. Next to the digging dunes stood the SandLuge track. This competition required four competitors to ride in golden sleds upon tracks cut into the sand. Dragon fire hardened the sand tracks into tubes of glass, twisting and turning in fast spirals and dangerous banks. Unlike other games, SandLuge competitors were randomly chosen to ride together. Not only did they have to be skilled in riding and guiding the sled, but they also had to work together as a team, even beyond language. Pohevol was paired with a Mountain Lion, a Crocodile, and a Striped Ostrich. On dangerous turns, he and the Ostrich splayed their wings to balance the careening sled. Adrianne rode on the prow of the sled, and her furry legs became smooth under the force of the wind. Pohevol's team took fifth place.

The last game of the first day was the StoneLaunch. The audience, popping toasted almonds and hazelnuts into their mouths, walked to a long strip of smoothed sand. As the Sun lowered, the competitors' bodies were bathed in soft light. They stood at one end, stretching their arms, legs, tails, and wings far back and then releasing stones with loud grunts. The audience stood on either sides of the strip, enthralled with mere practice throws.

Sophia, Sefani, Perjas, and Bridget came to the final game to watch Tomal and Zun whip their arms in precision throws. Pohevol, Adrianne, Mortoof, and the Hawks landed by them. Anippe flew in brandishing her first place medallion.

The River Dragon looked down to Pohevol, "I could not find them anywhere."

The Cat looked at the position of the Sun. He then turned to the temple and focused on its gleaming plates of gold, "They must be with the queen, again."

Anippe grumbled, "Why must she stay inside that temple? I would like to meet this Tiamat."

Sefani reached for Anippe's scales, "Don't worry," she said. "I'm sure we'll all meet her soon."

Just then a horn blew, and a tall Crane threw the first stone with his wing. The Sand Dragons had distributed small seeing glasses to the audience, so numerous golden tubes turned in the same direction, following the rapid progression of the stone.

Deep in the distance, a Dragon flew out to the sand and marked the stone's landing by placing an oiled ring around the stone. She then blew a stream of fire upon the ring.

The next competitor, a large Sand Snake, used the underside of her head to throw another stone. It went farther than the first. The contest continued, each landing marked by a new circle of fire. When it was Tomal's turn, his stone landed between the two stones of the Crane and the Sand Snake. Bridget's eyes sparkled as she cheered.

Zun was next to throw. As he stepped back, feeling the light stone in the palm of his hand, he swung his arm in circles and imagined the rock soaring through air. He looked far into the distance, staring at the last circle of fire. So far away, it looked like a lone Dragon candle, flickering in the Sunset. As he leaned back to ready himself for the throw, something caught his eye.

Far in the orange sea of Sun spilling across the horizon, he saw a ripple. At first it looked like a ribbon, a dark hair ribbon caught in the Sun's wake. But as it moved closer, he saw it was a Dragon, a Spirit Dragon. The lightning horn glowed powerfully, like a star had descended from the sky.

Zun lowered his arm and focused keenly at the approaching Dragon. Underneath the serpentine body moving steadily toward the glossy red strip of sand was a glimmering Dragon basket. Zun saw the sparkles flashing in the setting Sun, and then he knew. It was Labrys's, and Saja was the Spirit Dragon carrying the basket laced with gems. His mouth slowly parting, Zun looked to the shapes inside the basket. He saw the tip of Saja's pale egg, and he saw the brown hair. Hair whipping around her face, her brown eyes even darker in the shadow of the Dragon's body, Lily stood perched at the edge of the basket.

Zun pulled his arm back and focused on the Dragon carrying Lily straight to him. With a tremendous cry, he released the stone. It soared through the air as if it had wings of its own. Saja and Lily watched as the stone sailed toward them, like a small gray Bird. And then, with the slightest dip, the stone arched and fell right below them, landing a Dragon's length in front of the last burning ring of fire. The audience erupted in applause, and Lily watched as the boy who threw the stone came running toward her. He had tangled curly black hair, black eyes, and an Ochret glowing bright red around his neck.

ॐ 37 ॐ

A SHIFT OF HEART

When Anippe realized Saja was flying towards them, she took to the air. The setting Sun glowed around the Spirit Dragon's body and covered the tip of her egg in a warm light. Lily looked at the red sand dunes below and whispered to the egg, "We're here. We're in the Sands of Ochre."

As she approached Saja and Lily, Anippe's face revealed worry lines, "What is wrong? Why are you here?"

"I must land quickly," Saja said, "I am tired of this body and have not rested in three days."

"We had to come," Lily said, "Zor is in danger!"

"What do you mean?" Anippe pulled her head back and lowered her snout to see Lily better.

"I had a strange experience, not Dreamtime, but similar. I saw a gold Dragon with black eyes," Lily gripped the edge of the basket. "I saw this Dragon kill Zor!"

Anippe flew alongside Lily and looked inside the

basket, "I am grateful you came to Ochre to tell us this, but I worry for Saja's egg."

Saja began her descent from the sky, focusing on an acceptable landing spot, "Lily is connected to her, and she has revealed she would like to be hatched in sand."

Anippe looked at the pale egg, surrounded by the jeweled basket. She saw it move and reared back, "She might be hatching now!"

Lily calmed the River Dragon, "She's been moving for a while now. Don't worry, she won't hatch until we place her in the sand."

The two Dragons flew lower and touched down on the burning hot sand. Saja lowered the basket first, and then slid out of the handle. Lily immediately climbed out of the basket and ran to Saja's abdomen to remove the claw belt.

Saja turned her head to Lily, "Now that you are away from her, you can wear your belt." The Spirit Dragon, released from her heavy load, allowed her body to change. It was not a Shift, as that was impossible while the Dragling was still inside her egg. It was more like a gentle leaving. Her body grew warm and bright, the violet and gold scales began to shimmer, and then she became hazy, almost like a desert mirage. In this spirit form, Saja could find rest from her weary flight.

Lily attached her belt low around her hips. The stitching was strong and the sheath held Caduceus's claw securely along her right leg.

Lily looked around at the vast landscape of reddish brown sand, "Where can we make a nest for her?" She saw a gleaming tower in the distance and a rounded structure plated with gold. Palm trees waved along the banks of two blue rivers. She turned to Anippe, "What are those buildings?"

Anippe followed Lily's gaze, "The Dragon Palace and the Temple of Secrets. But Saja," she turned to the tired Spirit Dragon, "Sand Dragons no longer make egg nests in the sand. They keep eggs inside the palace now."

Lily wrinkled her brow, "She must be in sand. That's how she wants to hatch."

As they looked around the desert, watching the crowds walk back to the palace and village, Lily saw Sophia and the others moving closer to the landing spot. Pohevol flew just above their heads, and Lily wondered why he had not met her in the sky like Anippe. Even though she had not been gone long, the group from Durga seemed foreign to her, distant after her journey into the rift.

Looking at the entire group, her eyes kept coming back to Zun's Ochret. Even with her black and white flying companion drifting towards her like the memory of safety and home, she was locked onto Zun's neck. She knew his hair was long and tangled. She knew his eyes were as black as night under the new Moon. She knew he had slight scars etched across his arms and legs. But the Ochret, the amulet, was different. It was glowing bright red.

When they were a Dragon's length away, Bridget broke into a sprint. Arms outstretched and black hair flowing freely, she ran to Lily shouting, "You're here! You're here!"

Abruptly drawn away from staring at Zun's neck, Lily focused on Bridget. The girls embraced and stepped back to look at each other. Bridget saw the new belt and claw attached to Lily's leg, "Caduceus's claw! Lily, do you remember him ripping it off? It was incredible—we couldn't believe it!"

Tomal ran up and hugged Lily next, "I knew you'd beat the nightshade! I just knew it!"

Lily squeezed his hand, her eyes brimming with gratitude. She turned to Sefani and Perjas, "I missed you all so much."

Then Zun walked up, his stride fixed and steady. He stopped in front of Lily, and she could see a glimmering gathering in the corners of his eyes. He reached out, took her hands into his, and dropped to his knees, "Don't ever leave again. Where you are is where I want to be."

Lily lowered herself to the sand, "Your amulet," she let go of his hands to touch the glowing stone. "You've changed."

"A lot happened after you left," Zun's black eyes revealed flecks of indigo in the fading Sunlight, "I learned of secrets that answered many of my questions, that removed my fears and doubts."

"You trust Dragons now?" she asked, her eyes stared at his glowing Ochret.

He raised one hand to the amulet and placed it over Lily's fingers, "Yes." He used his other hand to lift Lily's face. When her gaze met his, he said, "I trust a golden Dragon most of all."

Terror spread across Lily's abdomen like a disease. She jumped up and away from Zun and reached for Caduceus's claw. Whipping it out of its sheath, she backed away hissing, "Traitor, deceiver, murderer!" Slicing her head around frantically, she looked to Saja and her egg sister, then to Pohevol still hovering in the sky. Everything seemed to grow bright, and the setting Sun vanished from her vision, "He's lying!" she cried out to the others, "He's deceived the amulet!"

Zun scrambled to his feet, "Lily! Stop! What are you saying?" Reaching his arms out, he shouted, "I'm different! Trust me, I've changed!"

In a flash of confidence, she held out Caduceus's claw and pointed it directly at Zun. Trembling, she screamed, "You lie! I've seen this golden Dragon of yours! I know of his trickery and hidden stealth!" Her eyes filled with rage, "I know about whom you speak!"

Calling all of her courage and strength, she focused her intent and desire and began a Shift. Unlike other Shifts, her body enlarged slowly. She tripled in size and kept growing. Her torso extended and her arms and legs morphed. Her face extended and her teeth grew long and sharp. Her skin rippled and changed into red scales. Her body continued its metamorphosis as she continued to point the claw at Zun. Finally, she dropped into the Silent Space, and the Shift was complete. A red Dragon stood where Lily once was, and she was crouched on all four legs in an attack stance, flapping her wings in deafening beats and breathing fire at Zun.

Zun stumbled away from Lily, his eyes wide with fear. Lily was now the same red Dragon as when she helped Anippe win against the Ice Dragons. She had the same thick armor, the same spikes protruding from her back, and the same triangular spear at the end of her tail. Her face was serpentine, and her eyes were a brilliant yellow.

She screeched at Zun in Dragon tongue, "Where is Zor? What have you done with him?"

Zun cried out, "I don't understand what you're saying!"

"Stay by your egg, Saja!" Lily shrieked, "Don't believe a word he says!"

Saja changed back into her full body and flew to the basket. She coiled herself around the egg, "Come near my egg, and I will destroy you!" she hissed at Zun. Her lightning horn burned bright, and her violet and gold body began to pale.

Sophia walked carefully to Lily. Twelve of her eyes were fixed on Caduceus's claw, while two stared into Lily's Dragon eyes. "Lily," she spoke in a steady drone, "Zun has changed. He is a friend to Dragons now. Change back. We must talk."

"He's tricked you!" Lily screamed. "I've seen visions! I know about the golden Dragon!" She burst into the sky and flew in dramatic swoops through the air. Needing Pohevol, she flew near the Cat and thought, "Where is Zor? What has he done with Zor?"

Before Pohevol could answer, Lily flew around the desert, her keen eyes searching the sky and sand for another red Dragon. Finding none, she flew back to the group from Durga, "If you can't show me Zor, I'll destroy him! I'll kill this insipid boy!"

Sefani pulled out bow and arrows from the satchel tied behind her back. Quickly she fastened an arrow and pulled it taut. Listening for Lily's movement, she aimed into the sky, "Lily, he's no traitor!" Sefani called out. "He promised he wouldn't hurt Dragons. He's fulfilled his promise!"

Pohevol thought to Lily in his most focused voice, "You speak of a golden Dragon. Lily, there are two! Zun was speaking of Tiamat, a good Dragon queen!"

"I've seen a Dragon scaled in gold who kills Zor!"

Pohevol flew next to her red Dragon body, "I swear on the marks embedded in your neck, I swear on my Feline tribe safe in Durga, Zun is true! He is faithful! He is now a friend to Dragons!

Lily looked down upon the trembling boy standing in the sand. Her Dragon eye searched for recognition.

Zun grabbed the Ochret around his neck and pulled the necklace taut toward Lily, "I swear by the memory of my parents, by the blood in my veins," a tear ran down his cheek. "I swear by the love I have for you—all of you—in all of your many forms. Please Lily, please believe me. I no longer hate them. Dragons are my family. Stay a Dragon until the end of time, and I will never stop loving you." He dropped again to his knees, "I would sacrifice my life for you and the Dragons of Durga. You must believe me!"

As his plaintive words filled her Dragon body, Lily felt her heart turn. She looked to Saja who was slowly uncoiling herself from around her egg. She saw Sophia reaching her many heads into the sky, begging her to land. And then she saw three Dragons flying low, riding hot air currents directly toward her. Ius flew on the left, Caduceus on the right. Behind them shone the golden Dragon Palace and Temple of Secrets. In the middle flew Zor, his red scales resplendent in the setting Sun.

Caduceus's claw grew warm in Lily's own Dragon claws. She thrust it out toward her Shifting master, "Do you trust Zun!" she screeched.

Zor turned to Caduceus, "That Dragon is Lily?"

Caduceus shot toward her without answering his friend. He flew around her red body and a smile stretched across his Alligator face. He flapped his wings twice and hovered in front of her, "Do not fear that boy! He has shown fidelity to Dragons. Zun is one of us now."

Zor flew to the side of Caduceus and hovered, staring at the immense red Dragon, almost his twin.

Lily cried out, "You're alive!"

A playful twitter flashed across his feathered face, "You doubted my longevity?"

"Zor, I saw your death. In a vision I saw a golden Dragon kill you!"

Ius flew alongside Zor and said to Lily, "We know of this Dragon, but your vision will not be a possibility." He nodded to Zun, "And your friend, that boy down there, is helping us make sure."

Caduceus held out his foot with the missing claw, "Land red Dragon, my dear child. We have much to reveal."

Lily focused on her master's voice and eyes, and she knew he was honest and true. Her blood began to cool, and the fire in her throat grew thinner. She followed the Dragon males to the sand and landed by extending her thick red legs and claws. Once on the ground, she tucked her red wings behind her back and slowly walked over to Zun. Flaring her nostrils and snorting the last remnants of fire, she stopped in front of the still kneeling boy. "You have truly changed?" the words came out in her Human Durgan tongue.

"Just as you now have the power to Shift into a

Dragon, my heart has shifted." Zun stood up and walked to the red Dragon. She loomed above him, her fangs like swords and claws like sharpened iron.

"I now love Dragons," Zun said, "and I've always loved you." He brought his face to her Dragon foot that clutched Caduceus's claw. Like the brush of a Moth's wing, he kissed her scales and gripping claws.

With a flash of pressure and wind, Lily collapsed back into her Human form. Standing in front of him, she glistened with sweat and took in shallow breaths. Zun let his eyes fall to her fingers, still grasping the Dragon claw. He bent down to kiss her tense grip. Lily slowly let her fingers relax. He then kissed her forearm and her shoulder. Zun stopped and turned his head to look into her dark brown eyes. A look of wonder flashed across her face, and Zun's face brightened. He brought her face to his and kissed her on the lips.

As they embraced, Sefani lowered her bow. Bridget leaned close to her, "Could you have really released that arrow?"

"I don't know," Sefani replied, "but I was ready."

Caduceus, Zor, and Ius looked at the group from Durga. As they turned their heads, taking in the various members, Anippe noticed something strange about them, "Where have you been?" she asked abruptly.

Zor quipped, "Always observant."

Caduceus looked around at the near empty landscape. As the temperature had cooled, most guests were in the palace for the evening meal, "We must commune away from the palace." He pointed to a dune where the Sun had just set, "There, we will share everything."

Guldrun and Lin flew in just as Caduceus lowered his claw. Wet mud dripped from their scales. Lin gasped, "What did we miss? Did anyone win gold?"

Guldrun added, "We came in fourth! Can you believe it? We celebrated in the palace's mud room!"

"It was amazing!" cried Lin. "The balls were flying, and we didn't get touched once! And the mud room, Ius, you have to go there!"

Guldrun looked at the group and saw Lily standing by Zun. His eyes flashed toward his brother, "Lin! It's Lily, she's here!"

Lin looked at Lily and the others. He saw Saja coiled on the sand next to Labrys's basket, her egg tucked inside. "Saja!" he screamed, "What in Durga are you doing here?"

Ius calmed the brothers, "We are happy about the results of your competition, but we have more pressing matters to share. Follow Caduceus behind that dune."

"Oh," Guldrun pushed back some wayward scales, "yes, of course."

Lin cleaned mud away from his furry earflaps, "Right, we'll follow!"

As the Sun released its low arms of orange and red across the desert sand, the group from Durga walked toward the dune.

∽ ∾

Safe behind the dune, Saja and Lily worked to pull the egg from Labrys's basket. Lily gave Bridget her claw belt to examine, and Zun stood to the side, watching the egg slowly rise from its protective sheath.

Ius, Zor, and Mortoof dug a hole in which to place the egg, and Anippe searched through Labrys's satchel to find new gems to set around the pale oval. As they tended to the egg, Caduceus and Pohevol conversed a Dragon's length away from the group. At times the purple and green Dragon would pale, but then he would warm and flap his wings with fervor.

Once the egg was secure in the new nest, Caduceus and Pohevol walked back to the group, "Please form a circle around Saja's egg," he called out, "for this Dragling is part of our story."

Saja turned to Caduceus and flared her neck flap, "My Dragling?"

"She is powerful and crucial to our journey ahead."

The Dragons and children of Durga formed a large circle around the egg, and Pohevol and the Hawks landed on Dragon shoulders. Mortoof tucked himself into Ius's bulging wing muscles, and Adrianne curled herself next to Sefani and Perjas.

Caduceus began, "On Earth in this age, there are three portals that cross space and time. Our Great Tree in Durga is one, the rift in Jha'mah is another, and a gold chest safe in the Temple of Secrets is the third. While Pohevol is the only one to travel through our Great Tree, and a Pangolin is the only animal to navigate the rift," he nodded to Lily, "anyone can move through the gold chest."

Anippe leaned forward, "Where did you go?"

"The three of us," he said glancing at Zor and Ius, "went to Kurga, a mere two Suns in the future."

Lily's eyes flashed, "This is where the golden Dragon from my vision lives?"

"Yes," he answered. "But another golden Dragon, his mother, will help us defeat him."

Zun grabbed Lily's hand and squeezed, "She is the one whom I trust." To Caduceus he asked, "What happens in two Suns?"

Caduceus turned to Zor, "Would you like to say?"

"We have a choice," Zor said. "Pohevol has described his time travels as distinct points, one path, one vision. The rift takes a mind to one destination. This gold chest is different. Once inside, you see numerous columns of choice, with distinct and separate worlds at the end. You can visit each world with a thought or glance, but you cannot understand exactly how the world or time was made possible."

Ius added, "But you can collect clues, signs from these potential worlds."

"Yes," Caduceus said, "there are many clues that exist in these futures. We must be collectors, to map the future of peace and balance."

Saja raised her head, "You say my Dragling is crucial to this journey?"

"She is present in multiple columns," Zor said. "She is a powerful Shifter, and she is always linked to Lily."

Lily, who was sitting next to Saja, leaned her head into the Dragon's body. Saja stared at her egg, which was resting in the center of the discussion. Every few moments, the egg shook.

Zor continued, "We have seen three columns that will create a peaceful future, columns where Dragons remain on Earth and Pohevol's future is no longer a possibility."

"But," said Ius, "we have also viewed three different

columns that lead to the future of death and despair."

"How do we secure one of the peaceful futures?" Zun asked.

Caduceus leaned back and stared at Saja's egg, "By righting the wrongs. This egg hatching in the sand—the way Sand Dragons were meant to be born—surrounded by love and warmth is the first step."

As if the words spoke directly to the Dragling, the egg began to shake and tremble vigorously. After a few seconds small fissures appeared on the shell. Saja lifted herself from the ground and began flying circles around her egg, cooing to it in a language the Dragons did not understand.

Saja found Lily's face in the circle below her, "You may now wear the belt as freely and as often as you desire."

Zun turned to Lily, "Don't ever remove it." His eyes reflected the sparkling jewels that glowed in the setting Sun.

Lily stood up and retrieved the hidden belt. She fastened it around her hips and touched the hard claw. Once the belt was secure, she felt whole again, complete. As she walked back to the circle, she saw the most beautiful sight, arresting her movement. The egg split into two jagged halves, and another Spirit Dragon almost identical to Saja burst out of the shell.

The Dragling was violet and gold, with a serpentine body and a small curved lightning horn. She had neck flaps and small, feathered ears, but unlike her mother, she had brown eyes instead of violet. Dark brown eyes that looked exactly like Lily's.

Saja and her Dragling flew around each other in a swirl of loops and quick ascents and dives. They spoke to each other in the strange language, and then Saja nodded in Lily's direction. The Dragling flew to Lily and dove into the sand. Lily watched as the Dragling pushed through the sand, making several tunnels. When she surfaced, she flew above Lily and said in a tiny voice, "The sand speaks to me, sister. Do you hear its language too?"

Lily shook her head and blushed, "You'll have to teach me."

"There is time," the Dragling turned to Caduceus and winked, "time for all of us to learn."

Sophia spoke to the newly hatched Dragling, "Tell us your name, little one. There are many who would like to know."

The Spirit Dragling turned to her mother, who spoke a few hushed words, "I am Baliea, of Saja and Balen."

Sophia raised all of her heads to the sky. The first stars began to appear just as she released the name in various tongues, "Baliea of Saja and Balen, welcome to Earth!" Her voice thundered across the desert twilight.

"And now," Caduceus said, "this is what we must do. Sophia will fly back to Durga. In two of the possible futures we must prevent, Sophia and Zor are killed. Zor has decided to fight this future in a most creative way, but we have agreed Sophia must hide in Durga."

"How will you understand these Kurgans?" Sophia protested.

Zun said, "We're related, remember? That's why Haida and Tiamat can speak Durgan."

"But you might need. . ."

Caduceus stopped Sophia, "You are too precious to our tribe. You must go home, tell the elders our story, and protect yourself deep in the belly of Mount Calyps."

Sophia thought of tulis berries and sweet mountain air, "I will go home."

Zor turned to Guldrun and Lin, "You will accompany Sophia and make sure she arrives safely."

Lin was about to protest, when Guldrun jumped up on all four legs and gripped the sand with his claws, "We accept this charge!"

Lin turned to Guldrun and whispered, "They're getting rid of us!"

"No, they aren't," Guldrun said. "They need guards, like the great Sand Dragon guards of the palace! We will be the protectors of Sophia!"

Lin looked to Ius, and the blue Dragon raised the scales above his eyes and nodded. "Certainly!" Lin shouted. "We shall escort you home, Sophia!"

"Tell all tribes in Durga of Tiamat's story, and prepare the Dragons for hiding," ordered Caduceus. "Tell them we are working to right the wrong, and we have a new hope that Pohevol's future will not come to pass."

Bridget stood, "What did you see of us in these future lines?"

The green and purple Dragon looked down upon the young child with black hair and shining eyes. Tomal stood up next to her and grabbed her hand, "Yes, Caduceus," he said. "What of us?"

"In the three lines we will fight to secure, the children of Durga live," the Shifting Dragon paused. "But in the other three, some of you live and some die."

"Who?" Sefani asked.

"Tiamat warned us not to say," Zor spoke before Caduceus could respond. "We would benefit from your presence in Kurga, but you must choose your own paths. While it will be difficult, we are prepared to change the future without the five of you."

"Without us?" asked Bridget.

Caduceus nodded, "Our new journey will be dangerous. We must fight. If we fail, some of you will not return to Durga."

Zun said, "There is no question for me. You know my intent."

Sefani reached down to touch Perjas, "Continue on or go home?" She dropped her head and remained silent for a moment. She spoke to the ground, "I don't know what I want."

"Well, I do," Bridget declared. "I have faith in the three lines of peace. I'm staying."

Tomal placed his hands on his hips, "I'm staying as well."

Zor turned to Sefani, "There is time. You do not have to decide tonight."

Caduceus stepped back and viewed the entire clan from Durga, "Listen closely my family. If we fail, our tribe will still be in hiding across the Earth. They will survive. They will never lose hope. The progeny of these Dragons will rumble from deep caverns below the ground and release their fire from the safe havens of volcanoes. They will swim below the seas and lie waiting in caves of ice. They will lurk in the shadows of the forests, in the great dunes of sand, in the dark of the new Moon, and in the edges of a rippling mirage."

"But," Zor finished for Caduceus, "failure is only one possibility. For Dett and Riema, for Labrys and Merdon, for Sophia, for all the Dragons who have agreed to hide, and for the future generations of peaceful tribes, we must stop the Kurgans."

Ius added, "We must stop the Dragons of Men."

Lily raised Caduceus's claw into the new night sky, "To the paths of peace!"

Zun raised his arm, "To the Dragons of Durga!"

In a chorus of tongues, each honoring their various tribes, the group shouted, "To the paths of peace! To the Dragons of Durga!"

Acknowledgments

This book would not be in its present form without the encouragement and support of significant muses. To Stephanie Bell, your faith in nature and animals continues to teach and inspire me. To my daughter, Saja Spearman Weaver, this book would not exist without you. Thank you for listening to and reading multiple drafts and for inhaling books as if they were air. To Jason Weaver—my mate and partner in walking through forests and urban landscapes, over sandy beaches, and under redwood canopies—thank you for helping me bring this book to life and for being my foundation, my rock. To my father, Theodore Spearman Jr., I will never stop listening to your advice—even beyond the veil—and I will do my best to continue your good work. Thank you for modeling a life of service and gratitude. To my mother, Marie Mullenneix Spearman, you were my first mentor, my first nature guide, and the first person to place a book in my hand. Thank you for introducing me to words and for modeling a life of unconditional love. Thank you for gently nudging me to share this book with others and for always believing in me.

SIMONE SPEARMAN has taught English in public high schools in Northern California for over 20 years. Named the 2011 State High School Educator of the Year by the California League of High Schools, she is committed to public education. She lives in Guerneville, California.

Made in the USA
Lexington, KY
24 September 2017